Books by Barbara Michaels

*Available from Harper

Patriot's Dream

ELIZABETH PETERS
WRITING AS
BARBARA
MICHAELS

HARPER

An Imprint of HarperCollinsPublishers

HARPER

An Imprint of HarperCollins*Publishers*
195 Broadway
New York, NY 10007

Copyright © 1976 by Barbara Michaels
ISBN: 978-0-06-082869-1
ISBN-10: 0-06-082869-2

First Harper paperback special printing: September 2007

HarperCollins® and Harper® are registered trademarks of Harper-Collins Publishers.

Printed in the United States of America

Visit Harper paperbacks on the World Wide Web at
www.harpercollins.com

10 9 8 7 6 5 4 3 2

TO SANDY
In whose gracious drawing room the idea
for *Patriot's Dream* first came to me

Prelude

I. Leah

THE MAN WHO BOUGHT HER CALLED HER LEAH. SHE HAD forgotten her real name long before. She had also forgotten the name of her tribe, if she ever knew it; but a modern anthropologist would have had no difficulty in classifying her. The brown skin, long, curly dark hair, thin lips and aquiline nose were typical of the Fulani people who lived in the inner regions of Senegal.

The voyage to America was Leah's second encounter with slave traders. She was six years old when she was stolen the first time, along with three other small children whose mothers had left them playing under a tree while they worked the fields. The slavers were Mandingoes. The great Mandingo empire, with its university city of Timbuktu, was in decline, but the Mandingoes were still powerful planters and traders. The trade included slaves, as one of many commodities, for the vast plantations required hundreds of field hands. The economy had a superficial resemblance to one that was developing on another continent far to the west.

Leah became a house servant and eventually bore her master two children. Both died. She was approximately sixteen when the next group of slavers entered her life. Her master fought bravely to protect his property, but in vain; the raiders were professionals, who earned an excellent living supplying human cargoes to the ships that came in increasing numbers to the West African coast.

The raiders acquired approximately fifty prisoners, including Leah. The march to the coast took five days. There the captives joined several hundred others who were crammed into the barracoons. Leah spent only one night there, since a ship was already at anchor out beyond the bar. It was an English ship, but it might as easily have been Dutch or Swedish, or even American, although the Yankee traders did not enter the Guinea trade in force until later, after slave trading had been legally abolished and the profits were correspondingly higher.

Early in the morning two hundred and fifty slaves were chained together and marched to the shore. The mounting roar of the surf sounded like the voice of a great angry beast to the captives, many of whom had never seen the ocean. They began to cry out in fear. Some tried to run away. Held by the chains that bound them together, the weaker were dragged by the stronger as the panic spread. The shouts and blows of the drivers soon restored order. Weeping and groaning, the prisoners went on. When they reached the top of a low sandy rise, they saw the ocean.

Of all her experiences, this sight impressed Leah most. She often described it to her children. Mountains of water broke on the desolate shore. The sound of the surf was like thunder, and the wind chilled her bare skin. Leah flung herself down, digging her nails into the sand; but rough hands dragged her up, removed her chains, and forced her out into the water. The foam swirled around her ankles as she was flung into one of the waiting canoes. The canoe crewmen were experienced sailors, who knew the tricks of the treacherous waves; at precisely the right moment the paddles were driven in, and amid triumphant shouts the small boats flew out and over the bar, toward the waiting slaver.

Two of the bigger, stronger men in Leah's boat managed

to jump overboard and drown themselves, but she made no attempt to escape. She was numb with terror. She knew what awaited her and the others. The whispered rumors had spread among the captives the night before. The ship came from a distant country called Jong sang doo, "the land where the slaves are sold." The men of Jong sang doo were savages who ate human flesh.

It was a bad trip. The fault was not the captain's; he took every precaution. Each day the male slaves were brought on deck to be "danced." The exercise was rather hard on wrists and ankles chafed raw by the chains, but it was considered helpful in preventing scurvy and the suicidal melancholy that took almost as many lives as disease. The women and children were allowed to roam free, except at night, when they were stowed like cordwood in the hold. Like the other women, Leah was allotted a space five feet ten inches long and sixteen inches wide. The men had a little more room— six feet by sixteen inches. Unfortunately, the ship ran into bad weather, and for two weeks the slaves had to be confined in their coffin-shaped spaces day and night. Dysentery and smallpox ran rampant.

It would not have made Leah feel any better to know that the mortality rate among the black cargo was slightly less than the one that prevailed among the white crews of the English ships in the Guinea trade. The slaves were worth money to the captain, but the sailors were not. Flogged, starved, crippled by scurvy and syphilis, they were so badly misused that the slaves, out of pity, sometimes gave starving seamen part of their own meager rations.

When the ship finally reached Virginia, only six crewmen were on their feet. A hundred of the original two hundred and fifty slaves were still alive. A sentimentalist might say that Leah was one of the unlucky ones. Not being a sentimentalist, Leah was glad to be alive, and glad to be out of the hold.

She was sold on the block at Jamestown to a tobacco planter named Johnson. The Fulani complexion and bone structure, refined by several weeks of inadequate rations, appealed to his tastes; and Mrs. Johnson, a long-nosed, sallow woman who had been a minor Byrd before her marriage, was no more surprised than anyone else when Leah's baby was several shades lighter than its mother, with the distinctive Johnson chin. The second child, a girl, resembled its father to an astonishing degree, but this did not prevent Johnson from selling it, when he found himself short of cash.

Leah lived to be almost sixty, and she lost count of the number of her grandchildren before she died. It is regrettable, but true, that she had not found life in the New World particularly unpleasant. It was not much different from the life she had known in Africa—serving a man and bearing his children. And in Virginia, her children lived.

II. Charles

Charles Wilde was named after a king. It had seemed like a good idea at the time. But the time was 1630; and in 1649 Charles the First of England lost his throne, and then his head, and Charles Wilde's father lost everything but his head. It must be admitted that he had very little to lose. In years to come, proud descendants of Cavalier families would explain the absence of family silver plate by saying that it had been melted down in the King's cause. The Wildes made the same claim, but in point of fact they had never had any plate, or any furniture to put it on. The manor house was a tumbledown ruin in 1630, and the tenants had long since left for greener pastures. The upheaval of civil war provided Charles's father with a good excuse to leave home and the embarrassing debts that had reduced the family to a state somewhat less prosperous than that of a hard-working craftsman.

Francis Wilde went first to the Continent with his son; and then, finding that area oversupplied with men whose only talents were drinking and gambling, he proceeded to his Majesty's colony of Virginia. Shocked by the execution of the King, the colonial legislature had proclaimed the dead monarch's son King Charles the Second, and Governor Berkeley gave fleeing Cavaliers support and comfort.

The Wildes took kindly to the new country, which was not surprising, since Berkeley and his friends were doing their best to reproduce the old system of a landed aristocracy. Being officially a "gentleman," Wilde obtained a land grant and settled down to the occupations of his station—drinking and gambling.

It would be pleasant to be able to report that Francis Wilde died in a manner befitting his station. His descendants cherished a legend that he was killed in a duel. In fact, he drowned in six inches of muddy water, having fallen face down in a stream while on his way home after a prolonged drinking bout with a friend.

In 1660, when the English restored Charles the Second to the throne, Charles Wilde was thirty years old. He had a wife who had brought him three hundred acres adjoining the property he had inherited from his father, and he had no inclination to return to England. He was doing very well.

Berkeley, a clever old aristocrat, had quietly bided his time during the rule of the Cromwellians. With the restoration of the monarchy he came out into the open. He and his adherents packed the council and deprived the lower legislative body, the House of Burgesses, of most of its power. The councillors voted themselves land and ample salaries. Charles was one of the council. By the time he died, in 1670, his estate had grown from five hundred to almost seven thousand acres.

His son, Nicholas, was not a chip off the old block. Charles hated the boy, whom he called "changeling" and "prig," among other things. A slender, fair-haired youth whose delicate features resembled those of his mother, Nicholas had taken to reading—which, as Charles was wont to point out, is a pernicious vice. Even so, it is hard to explain why Nicholas should have taken the course he did. His father was dead, so annoying the old man could not have been a motive.

The reasons for Bacon's Rebellion have been much debated. The men who followed Nathaniel Bacon in 1676 were people who had seen their hard-won western lands stolen by Berkeley and his crowd, frontiersmen whose desperate calls for help against Indian massacres had been ignored by the governor, safe at home in Jamestown. The rebellion might be regarded as a protest of "the people" against the aristocracy. Bacon himself was a "gentleman," but he was not one of Berkeley's pets, so perhaps his motives were not unselfish. At any rate, Nicholas had no reason to join him. But he did.

The rebellion was crushed. Berkeley, the suave, civilized aristocrat, hanged twenty of the rebels. He was scolded for this by Charles the Second, who remarked irritably, "That old fool has hanged more men in that naked country than I did for the murder of my father." This was true, but it was not much consolation to the men who had been hanged.

Nicholas was not hanged, nor were his estates confiscated, as were those of many of the rebels. The Assembly decided on his punishment: "that Nicholas Wilde, gentl, doe with a rope about his neck, on his knees, begg his life of the governour and councell, and in the like posture acknoledge his crimes of rebellion and treason in the country court, and that he be fined to the king's majestic fifty thousand pounds of merchantable tobacco and caske. . . ."

The experience was apparently an educational one for Nicholas. He became one of Berkeley's councillors, and not only paid off his fine, but prospered. His descendants spread over two hundred thousand acres of the Tidewater. At the time of another rebellion, a century later than Bacon's, the name of Wilde was as well known in Virginia as that of Byrd or Carter. Nicholas' heirs owned a house in Williamsburg and one of the most beautiful mansions in the Tidewater, which Nicholas, for reasons known only to himself, had named The Folly.

III. Johann

The "killing winter" of 1705 became proverbial in Germany. They say that the birds froze in the air and dropped to the ground with, presumably, a solid thud and a sparkle of ice particles. This may be exaggerated. However, it was an extremely cold winter. Thus nature finished what man had begun, and the family of Johann Müller, in the village of Bergstein, was reduced to Johann himself.

He was seventeen, or thereabouts, that day in December when he rose from his knees. He had been praying beside the body of his father, who had died of starvation and cold. Johann's mother had been killed five years earlier, when partisans of the Catholic duke rode through the Protestant village looking for sport and infidels, in that order. His brothers and sisters had perished in various ways which it would take too long to relate. The village was in an area devastated by religious wars. The hapless peasants seldom had a chance to state a preference for Pope or Luther before they were massacred by whatever party happened to be in town.

Johann's people were no strangers to persecution. Five generations back, one of his ancestors had died in the Münster massacre, for the crime of rejecting infant baptism. Others had lost their lives, not so much for their religious beliefs as for their slowness in changing them. The Peace of Augsburg, in 1555, had established the principle "like master, like man," which meant that the peasants had to follow the religious affiliations of their lords. But the local Electors changed religions four times in as many reigns, which made it a little difficult for their subjects to pick a safe church.

Not all the Müllers died nobly for their faith. There were plenty of ordinary nonreligious wars as well, all followed, predictably and monotonously, by famine, plague, and other conditions unfavorable to life—not to mention liberty and the pursuit of happiness, both of which concepts were as alien to a European peasant as psychotherapy. The only reason why an occasional Müller survived is that there were so many of them.

Prolonged suffering carries its own merciful anesthesia. When Johann rose stiffly to his feet that December day, his only conscious emotion was a dull wonder as to what he was going to do next.

A towheaded, blunt-featured boy, he was meant to be stockily built, but semistarvation had reduced him to a point where the heavy bones seemed to push against the flaccid skin of his face and arms. He was slightly dizzy from lack of food; his head spun as he stood up, and he caught at the rough wooden wall for support. A sharp splinter, slipping into his palm, roused him a little, and he stared down at his father's stiffening features. They were as white as the white strands in the long, unkempt beard that covered Herr Müller's chest—white as ice, already half frozen. The cold of death was no colder than the chill of the tireless house.

Johann reached out to close the staring eyes, and then drew his hand back. Turning, he walked out of the house. He took nothing with him. He did not even close the door.

Only the stern Protestant God he had once believed in knew how he made his way across half of Europe in winter, and on foot. He knew where he was going. Some of his neighbors had already left for America, after hearing the agents of Penn, the Quaker, describe its broad and fertile acres, free to anyone who would till them. Penn also promised freedom to worship God in one's own way. That seemed an impossible hope to Johann; at this point in his life, it was also irrelevant. As he stumbled through the winter forests, league after starving league, a single urge took shape in his mind. It was one of the few abstract ideas he had ever entertained. Perhaps that is why it was to become an obsession as time went on.

He had no money for the passage to America, but he did not expect that would be a problem, and he was correct. The ship's captain in Rotterdam was happy to sign him up in exchange for seven years of servitude.

There were four hundred passengers in the *Good Intent*. Water was so scarce that the rats licked the sweat from the faces of the sleeping passengers and gnawed holes in the top of the water barrels. By the end of the two months' voyage, the latter expedient no longer served: the water level was too low. But there was plenty of sweat.

When the boat docked in Pennsylvania there were two hundred and fifty passengers still alive, most of them redemptioners. A wealthy speculator bought the lot and marched them from town to town, selling off part of his produce at each place. Johann was bought for ten pounds—the going rate—by a Philadelphia merchant who had a large estate west of the city. It would be more accurate to say that his services were bought, for he had one conspicuous advantage over Leah: if he didn't die of overwork or disease, he could look forward to freedom one day. He did not view the situation in this optimistic light. He ran away twice. He was caught both times, and the second time his master, annoyed at his ingratitude, had him flogged. Johann did not run away again. It was not the two hundred lashes that changed his mind so much as the fact that the weeks of his absence were added to his term of servitude. He settled down and became an excellent worker. His master, finding that he had a certain skill in wood carving, had him trained as a carpenter.

Having served his time, Johann received his certificate and his freedom dues. Had he arrived a few years earlier, these would have included fifty acres of land. By 1700 land was getting scarce. Johann's prize for seven years of labor was two suits of clothing (one new), an ox, a grubbing hoe, and a weeding hoe. He set out to find some land on which to employ the last three items. The idea that had first come to him as he made his way toward Rotterdam had been intensified, by his years of servitude, into a sullen passion. Never again would he plow another man's land.

There were already German settlements in western Virginia, established in the Piedmont by Governor Spotswood as a form of frontier defense against the Indians. Johann spent some time with the settlers in Germanna, but found their rickety fort and two small cannon unreassuring. He was also disconcerted to discover that he and his fellow settlers were regarded as tenants by the governor, Spotswood having claimed some three hundred acres as his own property. Johann moved on, taking with him his ox and his two hoes, and his more recent acquisitions—a wagon, a horse, and a wife, the daughter of one of the Germanna families. That his wife was Lutheran, and a heretic, by the rigid standards of the Mennonite faith, did not concern Johann. He had stopped thinking much about God.

He found land farther south and remained there for several years. Why he left is uncertain. The death of his wife and two of his children may have had something to do with it, plus the fact that once again he learned that he had no legal title to the land he had cleared with such back-breaking labor. The aristocrats of the east, the Berkeleys and Fairfaxes, had been given huge grants in the western counties, and even the settlers who had bought their land from speculators were in danger of being evicted, or having to pay again.

Johann was forced to the conclusion that he had been using the wrong methods to attain his goal. He left his surviving child with neighbors and moved east. He turned up as a craftsman on a plantation along the James. The planters were building handsome homes in the style of the English manor houses, and Johann's skills as a wood-carver were in demand.

He was thirty-five at this time, and built like Hercules. The rough, unremitting labor that had killed so many immigrants had only hardened him; and his thatch of flaxen hair contrasted strikingly with the deep tan he had acquired from the Virginia sun. He was not vain about his personal appearance, but he could not help noticing the way his employer's wife looked at him, and the transparent excuses she invented for meeting and talking with him. When the master of the manor died, it seemed to Johann like a nod of approval from God. In fact, in his old age he returned to his former faith and became something of a bigot. He was not an analytical man, and it did not occur to him that there was irony in the fact that he had finally attained his dream of land and independence, not through virtue and hard work, but as the result of a quality he and his God frowned on—in other people.

IV. Anne

In 1642 the Virginia Assembly passed a law exempting debtors from prosecution by their creditors back in England. Anne Brown had not heard of this law, but she knew that Virginia was a long way from London, and that her father's creditors would have a hard time finding him there even if he were fool enough to retain the name he had been using for the past years. The name was not Brown.

Born into a virtuous family of farmers in the Border country between Scotland and England, Frederick was one of those children who confound the theories of heredity. Strikingly handsome, with long, slim hands and fine bones, he bore no resemblance to his square brothers and sisters. His mother suffered considerably from this fact as Frederick grew in beauty and length of limb—quite unjustly, for Frederick was in fact his father's son. He was simply a throwback to some long-forgotten collection of intrusive genes; but it is no wonder that his mother, rubbing her bruises, came to dislike him as thoroughly as his father did, and Frederick left home as soon as he was old enough to attract the attention of a lady passing through the village on her way to London.

His was a facile, if shallow, mind, and within a year he had learned to ape the manners of the class he aspired to join. When he left his first patroness, he changed his name. He always modestly disclaimed any connection with the noble Fairfaxes, but his hearers were left with the distinct impression that he had been cruelly cast off by that great clan. Unfortunately he lacked the ruthlessness that would have brought him even a moderate degree of success, and the beauty that won the lady's attention did not endear him to the husband of the lady, or to other husbands. His looks faded early. In a period of brief affluence he had married the pretty daughter of a merchant in Bristol. Her portion kept the couple going for a few years. Perhaps luckily for her, the young woman died in childbirth before the money was quite spent.

Frederick might have abandoned the child. He did not, for his kindness was as genuine as his inability to be of any real benefit to the people he loved. In later years he had cause to bless his charity, for his daughter kept him alive a good deal longer than he had any right to expect.

Anne inherited her father's looks, including eyes that were enough to make any woman's face beautiful. Deeply fringed with thick, dark lashes, they were a striking shade of pale, pure green, as hard and opaque as jade. She was fifteen the year she decided that emigration was the only hope for the Fairfaxes, but she looked several years older, with a figure that confirmed the promise of the jade-green eyes. The eyes and the figure had gotten Frederick out of a number of scrapes, and the long, slim legs had gotten Anne out of the consequences. She could squirm away from trouble like an eel.

She got her father out of Newgate, where he had spent considerable time, with the inadvertent help of a ferret-faced evil-minded old nobleman whose name she never knew. Misled by her innocent face and coppery curls, he had made her an invitation and sent his man away for the evening. Anne left him snoring on the floor of his opulent bedroom, with its ceiling of naked goddesses. She took with her the silver candlestick with which she had put him to sleep, and all his spare cash. She doubted that he would complain against her; it would be too humiliating to admit that he had been bested by a girl half his size; but she took no chances. She was adept at disguise, among other useful skills acquired in her brief but hectic career, and when she went out on the street thereafter, the curls were hidden under a kerchief and the generous curves muffled in a ragged servant's dress.

It took a week to arrange her father's release and get the two of them on board the *Deliverance*. The curls and the figure reappeared for this transaction. Certain difficulties arose as a result, but Anne was perfectly capable of dealing with them. She attached herself to the only lady of quality who was making the trip, the wife of a Virginia planter, and this gullible female, bewitched by the tear-filled eyes and pleading hands, was able to keep the captain away from her sweet little friend. Anne had no intention of selling her most marketable commodity so cheaply. She had heard that women were scarce in the colonies, and there was only one respectable career open to them.

The noble lady's patronage did not end when the ship docked. She persuaded her husband to buy the services of father and daughter, and since it was obviously impossible for such a fragile, well-spoken man to work in the tobacco fields, Frederick was installed as overseer. It was a task for which he was completely unsuited, but his master had no time to find that out. The plantations were located along the rivers, which provided the only practical means of transporting the tobacco crop, and mosquitoes breeding in the swampy ground fed hungrily on the bodies of men weakened by the long, difficult passage. Frederick died within a month, like four-fifths of the newly imported servants.

Anne was genuinely grieved at his death, but she had no time to mourn him. Her mistress had already learned to regret her generosity and to suspect the readiness with which her husband had agreed to acquire the useless pair. Being an unsubtle woman, she offered to cancel Anne's indentures and give her a nice little dowry, so that she could marry one of the men who had begun to cluster around. Anne had been correct in her assumption. Women were extremely scarce, and she could have had her pick of half a dozen small farmers. But her aspirations went higher, and her hopes were based on astute calculation. Her mistress was another of the unfortunates who died in that first year, before she could become "seasoned" to the climate. Shortly thereafter Anne married her former master. She was a good, if extravagant wife, and bore her husband twelve children. She also survived him.

There were rumors to the effect that she had poisoned him, but of course nothing could be proved. Her children were all fairly well behaved, by the standards of their time, but Anne's genes were still active, and they popped out among her later descendants in ways that were occasionally disconcerting. The old rumors of Anne's skill with poison were revived when one of her granddaughters suffered from a similar informal accusation. It was Mary's wealthy, vicious old husband whom she was accused of sending on to his reward—and nobody doubted what that would be, for if any man deserved to be poisoned, he did. Still, Mary's neighbors rather avoided her after that, and when she married one of her own employees the men nodded smugly and wondered how she could lower herself with a member of an inferior class. The women nodded, too; but they didn't wonder.

Men and women like these were the first families of Virginia. Most of the emigrants came from the servant class, almost a hundred thousand of them in the years before 1700. Black slaves constituted over forty percent of the colony's population by the time of the Revolution. "Gentlemen" like Charles Wilde were rare, and "gentle blood"—whatever that may be—was no asset to the growing nation. The founders of families had one quality in common: not dreams of freedom, or devotion to God, only a highly developed capacity for survival. The dreams came later.

Chapter
1

Summer 1976—Spring 1774

JAN WOKE WITH A START THAT LEFT EVERY MUSCLE IN HER body quivering. The room was dark and silent, as it is in the dead hours of early morning, but she was as wide awake as if she had slept for a full eight hours. Oh, no, she thought in disgust . . . not the damn insomnia, not here!

She had come to Williamsburg for a nice rest. "A nice rest" was her mother's phrase, and her mother's idea; but Jan knew what Ellen's real motives were. Not that there was any use in pointing them out. Ellen would have opened her big blue eyes even wider, and wept. She wept neatly and prettily, like the Southern belle she had always yearned to be. No one would have guessed that she had been born Betty Jo Billings, in Wichita, Kansas, and that her father had been a bricklayer. When she had married into the Wilde family of Virginia, she had taken on all the pretensions of their class.

Jan knew she shouldn't be thinking about her mother, not if she wanted to get back to sleep; but she could not help recalling the interminable arguments that had preceded her departure from New York. She had pointed out that Williamsburg was hardly the place for a rest, especially in the Bicentennial summer of 1976.

"The place will be absolutely crawling with tourists," she

had protested. "And if the old servant—what's her name?—
is in the hospital, I'll have to work myself to death. That's
why Aunt Camilla and Uncle Henry invited me, they want a
free maid for the summer. They never gave a damn about our
branch of the family."

Ellen's raised eyebrows indicated ladylike distaste for her
daughter's vulgarity. As usual, she answered the least important question first.

"Bess. Dear old Auntie Bess. She's been with the family since she was a tiny pickaninny. She would never have
deserted your great-aunt and uncle if she hadn't broken her
hip."

"It's a wonder she didn't break her neck," Jan said. "She
must be seventy—and a fool if she spent her life playing old
family servant for those two. At that, she isn't as old as Aunt
Camilla—and Uncle Henry must be eighty-five. They need
a full-time nurse, not me."

She expected Ellen to produce the arguments she had
used before—the ostensible reasons that concealed her real
motive. The lovely old family mansion was about to pass
out of the hands of the family, after two hundred and fifty
years; Jan really ought to see it before it became public property. Imagine, having to buy a ticket to see the home of one's
ancestors!

So Ellen had argued, on previous occasions. But she was
smarter than Jan realized. This time she simply raised her
delicate eyebrows and said softly, "But where else is there
for you to go?"

There was no other place. Only Ellen's stuffy little apartment, which was always crowded with Ellen's friends, flut-
tering in and out for bridge and tea and luncheon, chattering
in shrill voices like the flock of molting birds they resembled. During the school year, while she was teaching, Jan
was able to keep out of their way. In the sticky New York
summer, with her nerves in their stretched state. . . . Even
tourist-ridden Williamsburg and two decrepit relatives might
be an improvement.

Williamsburg had turned out to be less of a trial than she had expected. During the day it was certainly crowded. As the capital of Virginia during most of the Revolution, the town had a fascinating history. Washington, Jefferson, and Patrick Henry had dined at the Raleigh Tavern and debated independence in the red brick Capitol. Lafayette had lived there, with his commander in chief, before the decisive battle of Yorktown, only thirteen miles away. But the factor that made Williamsburg a tourist mecca was not so much its history as the fact that its historic past had been recreated with a thoroughness no other town or city in America could claim.

When John D. Rockefeller became interested in the town, in 1922, there were over eighty colonial buildings still standing. The original street plan had not changed since 1776. Even so the project had not been easy or cheap. Surviving buildings had been restored to their eighteenth-century appearance, and important structures which had disappeared, such as the Capitol and the Governor's Palace, had been rebuilt, brick by brick, after painstaking research.

The Wilde house was on the Duke of Gloucester Street, the main thoroughfare, and during the day the inhabitants couldn't walk out the front door without encountering a circle of staring visitors, guidebooks in hand. But by midnight the streets were virtually deserted, and from the first night Jan had been delivered from the sleeplessness that had cursed the winter and spring months in New York. She slept like a baby, deeply and without dreaming.

Until tonight.

She had fallen asleep quickly enough. Something must have awakened her—if she was awake. Squinting in an attempt to see through the smothering darkness, Jan realized that the room felt different. For one thing, the night was utterly still. The house was air-conditioned, so she kept her windows closed against the muggy Virginia heat, but even through closed panes one could usually hear the occasional sound of a passing car or the distant hum of traffic on

Route 60. Tonight there was nothing, except silence so intense her ears rang with it.

Though she could see nothing, she knew the contents of the room by now. The old four-poster bed, with its chintz tester and curtains; the Chippendale chest on the right wall, the fireplace on the left. Between the two windows, opposite the foot of the bed, was the portrait that had fascinated her from the first moment she laid eyes on it. The features took shape in her mind now, without conscious effort: the face of a man with a snub nose and high forehead, his mouse-brown hair drawn back and tied at the nape of his neck.

Jan shifted impatiently in the bed. She was wide awake, her mind too active for sleep. Reaching out, she groped in the dark and failed to find what she was seeking—the bedside table and lamp. She had moved the table back, before going to sleep, fearing that a flailing arm might shatter the delicate porcelain of the lamp. Cursing, she got out of bed. Why did inanimate objects have that nasty habit of moving around in the night so you couldn't find them?

She reached the door, after stubbing her toe on some object that should not have been where it was. There was usually a light in the hall, for the convenience of the two elderly people who inhabited the house; but tonight the hall was as dark as her own room. No—far off at the end, near the staircase, a feeble glow showed. There was also a murmur of voices.

Her bare feet silent on the floor, Jan walked along the corridor toward the head of the stairs. It had been midnight before she turned out her light; it must be far into the morning now. Perhaps she wasn't the only sufferer from insomnia. Old people often slept badly.

The staircase was one of the glories of the house, made of walnut and beautifully carved. Her hand on the newel post, Jan leaned forward and looked down.

The voices and the light came from the open door of the library, to the right of the entrance hall. What on earth was going on down there? The library was Aunt Camilla's pride, one of the handsomest rooms in the house, with the original oak paneling and a mantel of imported marble. With the assistance of the Williamsburg Foundation, Camilla had located much of the furniture that had originally stood in the house, and the library was her masterpiece. Uncle Henry was allowed to play chess there, but the room was never used for ordinary social gatherings.

Jan started down the stairs. She was more curious than alarmed; burglars wouldn't turn on lights and sit around chatting. And if one of the elderly pair had been taken ill, the other would have aroused her. Yet she could not think of a hypothesis that would explain the use of the library at such an hour.

If she had not been so preoccupied with these speculations, she might have noticed something that did not strike her until she stood in the open doorway. The flickering, unsteady light was not that of an electric bulb. It came from candles in a silver candelabrum that stood in the center of the circular library table. Three men were sitting at the table. Two of them were in profile to Jan; the third sat with his back to her. The room was pure eighteenth century, from the painted linoleum summer rug on the floor to the red wool moreen draperies and valances at the window. The clothing of the men was of the same era.

Jan was familiar with the costumes; she saw them every day, on the Foundation employees who guided visitors in the restored area. However, no employee had a suit as elegant as the one worn by the elderly man at her right. It was a dark green, plushy fabric, with gold buttons on the wide turned-back cuffs. Lace fell from below the cuffs, and more lace trimmed the ruffles under his chin. Either his hair was powdered or he was wearing a wig. It had been set in snowy curls, three neat horizontal sausage rolls over each ear. The rest was tied back, with the ends tucked into a black satin bag.

The man facing him, at Jan's left, was younger, no more than a boy, and extremely good-looking. His fair hair re-

flected the candlelight like yellow silk. The hair at the nape
of his neck, tied by a black ribbon, was a cluster of unruly
curls, and loosened tendrils coiled around his ears and tem-
ples. The duplicate of his garb might have been found on
any of the young men who worked as waiters or craftsmen
in the restored town: a high-necked, white shirt with billowing sleeves gathered into tight wristbands, and a sleeveless
mulberry tunic. Jan couldn't see the lower part of his body,
but she deduced the regulation knee breeches, white stockings, and buckled shoes.

The third man, whose back was toward Jan, had thick
brown hair that was pulling loose from the queue ribbon. His
long tunic-waistcoat was hung over the back of his chair, and
the sleeves of his blue shirt were rolled above the elbows.
She was unable to make out any other details, except for the
unusual breadth of his shoulders, which filled the gathered
back of his shirt.

If she had been in any other city in the world, Jan would
have known by this time that she was dreaming. She had
begun to suspect she might be; but the room and the costumes were not impossible to the waking world of twentieth-
century Williamsburg. The fact that she did not recognize
either of the faces visible to her was not conclusive; she had
not met all her aunt and uncle's friends. . . .

But common sense rebelled at the thought. Her aunt and
uncle would not be entertaining at three in the morning.

Her eyes had taken in these details in a flash of time, no
longer than the time her brain required to draw the obvious
conclusions. There had been silence among the three men.
Now the handsome fair-haired youth spoke.

"How much longer must we wait? In God's name, I could
fight a war in the time it takes your friends to plan one."

"Your language," the older man said reproachfully.

"Sorry, Father." The fair-haired boy shot a quick glance at
the man whose back was turned to Jan. Apparently he found
silent support in that quarter, for a smile curved the corners

of his mouth as he went on, "If this old Puritan does not object to my speech—"

"It is not the speech of a gentleman," said his father. "As for your question—which displays the same hasty temper as your language—an attribute you must learn to control . . ." He broke off, smiling, as the younger man grimaced. "But I will spare you the rest of the lecture. You have heard it often enough."

"I have," said the younger man emphatically.

"But have not profited from it." The third man spoke for the first time. From his voice it was apparent that he was as young as his bright-haired friend, despite his considerable size. "Now if Charles would only be guided by *my* example—"

Laughter from both his hearers cut him short. The older man's chuckle was quickly quelled, as if he feared to insult his guest, but the boy named Charles laughed so hard he slid sideways in his chair and only caught himself with a quick, hard hand on the table.

"Jonathan the hothead," he exclaimed, still laughing. "Jonathan the radical—who advocates full citizenship for atheists, Papists, and slaves—"

Jonathan straightened, his broad shoulders stiffening. When he broke into his friend's speech, his voice had lost its light humor.

"It is no joking matter, Charles."

"Indeed not," the older man said soberly. "You are both young. The young have radical opinions—and God knows, rebellion is in the very air. . . ."

"If you mean, Mr. Wilde, that my opinions are the result of ignorant youth, you are mistaken," said Jonathan.

The older man gave him a paternal pat on the shoulder.

"My dear boy, I don't mind your opinions. I only ask that you be more discreet in voicing them."

Jonathan did not reply, but the way he shifted his body suggested that only courtesy toward his elders kept him silent. Charles leaned back in his chair and contemplated his friend with amusement. He had striking eyes, of bright green, with thick dark lashes that contrasted with his fair hair.

"Your concern is unnecessary, Father. If you had seen him knock three hulking apprentices flat on their backs last month, you wouldn't worry about his ability to defend himself. For a pacifist, he has a very hard fist."

Jonathan groaned and hid his face in his hands. His friend went on remorselessly.

"Don't be such a hypocrite, Jon. Your principles of nonviolence are impractical; a man must defend himself. As for your opinions, they don't differ greatly from those of men like Mason and Wythe and Jefferson. Even Colonel Washington . . ."

He did not look at his father, but it was obvious that his speech was aimed in that direction, rather than at his gloomy friend. The older man frowned angrily.

"Colonel Washington dines with Governor Dunmore later this week. He is no radical."

"Precisely," Charles said eagerly. "He is no radical, but even he finds Britain's recent acts intolerable. If you would only—"

He stopped speaking as a soft knock came at the door across the room. After a pause the door swung open.

Jan knew that the door led into a rear hall that passed the dining room and serving pantry. The girl who stood hesitating in the doorway had apparently come from that part of the house. She carried a tray with a decanter and several glasses. The liquid in the decanter shone like a garnet in the subdued light.

She was very young, hardly more than a child, but the simple blue cotton dress and white apron did not conceal the fact that she was entering adolescence, and that she was going to be an extremely lovely woman. A frilled cap covered most of her hair; the waving locks that had escaped its confines were a glossy nut brown. Her skin had the smooth pallor of ivory, and her dark eyes were apprehensive.

"Ah, Leah," the older man said in a kindly voice. "So you are beginning your new duties. Mrs. Wilde has gone to bed, I take it? That's right, child, put the tray here on the table."

The girl obeyed, letting out a little sigh of relief when she had deposited the tray safely. Her eyes were demurely lowered as she moved away from the table. When she passed Jonathan, he spoke.

"Leah, I swear you have grown two inches in the last month. I hope your mother is better?"

There was a smile in his voice, and the girl responded, showing even white teeth and a charming dimple.

"Thank you, Mr. Jonathan, she is recovered. It was only an ague. And your grandmother, Sir—is she well?"

"As always," Jonathan said. "I think she sends for me whenever she becomes bored with life. I've missed a month of my studies as a result—and I missed all of you. But I fear our games are over, Leah; you are too old and dignified for tag nowadays."

Charles, who had watched the exchange with a smile, reached out and tweaked the apron bow. The girl squealed and clapped her hands to her skirts, and Mr. Wilde said quickly,

"Thank you, Leah. Go to bed now, we won't need you again."

The girl scampered out, her cheeks flaming.

"Charles," said Mr. Wilde.

"I know, Father, I know. But it seems only yesterday that she was a skinny little thing with pigtails and long legs, following us around like a puppy."

"Following you," Jonathan corrected. "And you teased her unmercifully, when you deigned to notice her at all."

"Mrs. Wilde is quite attached to her," the older man said. "She is extremely quick to learn; you observed how nicely she speaks. You must stop treating her like a child, Charles."

Charles, quite unrepentant, began to laugh.

"Jon, do you remember the time she climbed the apple tree because I dared her, and then couldn't—"

"Speaking of time," his father interrupted, "it is late. Surely you two should be at your books."

"But, Father," Charles protested. "You said we might stay and speak with Mr. Jefferson."

"You would do better to emulate his habits," was the austere reply. "When he was at the college, he studied fifteen hours a day."

"He must not have slept at all, then," Charles said with a grin. "For he certainly did other things besides study. As a member of the Flat Hat Club. . . . Besides, Father, times have changed. And so have Mr. Jefferson's interests."

"They have indeed. This latest scheme of his may well force Governor Dunmore to dissolve the Assembly."

"That would be nothing new. Do you suppose the burgesses will retaliate by canceling the ball they are giving for Lady Dunmore?"

"Certainly not," his father answered in a shocked voice. "I hope my colleagues do not lack the instincts of gentlemen."

Charles glanced at Jonathan again, his eyes twinkling, as if inviting him to share the joke his father did not see.

"Well, but what is this new scheme?" he asked. "Something in which Mr. Jefferson hopes to gain your support, I suppose."

The older man hesitated, and then shrugged slightly.

"There is no reason why you should not know; it will be public knowledge tomorrow. He and a few others mean to offer a resolution in the Assembly proclaiming a day of fasting and prayer in response to the closing of the port of Boston."

Charles's lips pursed in a silent whistle.

"The governor won't like that. Will you support the resolution, Father?"

"It will certainly do us no harm to pray," Mr. Wilde said dryly. "I have no objection to the resolution itself, but Henry seems to be mixed up in this affair, and I don't trust his motives."

"Mr. Henry's looks are against him," Charles said. "That long sallow wedge of a face. . . . I am not the first to be reminded of Cassius, I suppose. But they say he speaks like Demosthenes. You heard him, Father—the Stamp Act speech—"

"He speaks like an actor," the older man grumbled. "Oh, yes, I was impressed at the time. But he is too clever with words. Well, you may stay a little longer. But, Jonathan, I must ask that you refrain from questioning Mr. Jefferson as you did last time. For a boy of your age to quiz such a man in the manner of a lawyer examining a hostile witness is quite unbecoming. And the subject is—er—"

For once his facile tongue failed him. Courtesy kept Jonathan from replying, but the set of his shoulders expressed stubborn resistance. Charles, in an effort to relieve the atmosphere, added,

". . . unimportant. After all, Jon, we are concerned with greater matters, the issue is nothing less than—"

"Freedom?" Jonathan swung on his friend with an air of relief; he could speak to a contemporary with a warmth he was too well bred to use toward an older man. "Isn't that the issue, Charles? 'The colonists are by the law of nature free born, as indeed all men are, *white or black*'?"

"Whom are you quoting now?" Charles asked. "For a student of your mediocre attainments, you have quite a memory for inconvenient quotations."

"But Mr. Jefferson agrees," Jonathan said ingenuously. "He has already taken a stand on the issue. Four years ago he defended a mulatto who sought freedom, on the grounds that his great-grandmother had been a white woman—"

"And lost the case," Mr. Wilde said sharply. "He did his client no service. If he had restricted his argument to the legal issue, that the status of the mother determines the status of the child, instead of expressing radical sentiments—"

Jonathan forgot himself so far as to interrupt his elder. His voice shook with emotion.

"'Under the law of nature, all men are born free, and every man comes into the world with a right to his own person.' Sir, are these not the very sentiments our statesmen are voicing today, to justify our complaints against Great Britain? If men like Mr. Wythe and Mr. Mason believe men are equal in the eyes of God, how can they limit natural rights to white men?"

Charles had withdrawn from the discussion, his eyes downcast, his thick lashes casting shadows on his cheeks. Mr. Wilde, his own cheeks flushed, started to speak forcibly. Then he relaxed, with a patient smile.

"Well, my boy, you seem to have learned rhetoric at least these past two years. When you are a little older you will understand that these issues are not so simple."

"With your pardon, sir, age has nothing to do with the truth," Jonathan said in a stifled voice.

"Perhaps not." Mr. Wilde regarded the young man with an affectionate, tolerant smile. "But it has a great deal to do with one's perception of that many-shaped goddess. Jonathan, I speak for your own good. You'll find yourself in the stocks one day, being pelted with rotten vegetables, if you—"

Jonathan pushed his chair back and stood up.

"Excuse me, sir," he said in a choked voice. "You may criticize me—you have that right; you may denounce me, that is your privilege; but in heaven's name, do not make fun of me!"

Mr. Wilde shook his head with a rueful smile and started to speak; Charles called out, "Save your questions for Jefferson, Jon, he should be here soon."

Jonathan paid no attention. He strode toward the door.

His face, which Jan saw for the first time, was that of a very young man indeed. As she had guessed from his crumpled attire and from Leah's remarks, he had just arrived in town, and he had not shaved recently. The fuzz along his chin and upper lip shone soft as a kitten's fur in the candlelight. His flushed cheeks and outthrust jaw also betrayed his youth—too old to find relief in angry tears, too young not to feel ridicule acutely. But it was not his youth that paralyzed Jan, it was his face—the face of the man in the portrait that hung in her room.

As she stood frozen, clutching at the doorjamb, he walked straight through her.

Chapter

2

Summer 1976

IT WAS A BEAUTIFUL MORNING. SUNLIGHT FRESHENED the faded colors of the old carpet and made the polished surfaces of the furniture glow. Birds sang. Someone was pounding persistently at the bedroom door.

Jan opened her eyes. She rolled them toward the clock on the bedside table and sat up with a start. The pounding continued.

"Aunt Cam?" Jan called. "Is that you? Come on in."

She knew her great-aunt wouldn't come in. Camilla had not entered her bedroom in the morning since she discovered that Jan slept *au naturel,* as she expressed it. After that first awkward encounter Jan had started wearing a nightgown, but she had not seen fit to mention this concession to her aunt.

"I'm sorry to wake you, honey," Camilla said, from behind the closed door. "But it's eight o'clock. Are you feelin' all right?"

"Yes, fine. I overslept. I'm sorry, I'll be right down."

"Don't hurry, honey. Breakfast is all ready. I just wondered if you were feelin' well."

Jan fell back on the pillow with a groan. Breakfast was at eight sharp in the Wilde household, and it was a minor sin to be late—especially if you were the cook.

She hopped out of bed and reached for her clothes. No time to shower this morning, that would have to wait until after breakfast. The meal would probably consist of cold cereal and Camilla's awful, watery coffee. Well, it would serve her right to eat it, after oversleeping.

Like Williamsburg, her aunt and uncle had turned out to be less annoying than she had expected. They were both rather sweet—although Camilla's sweetness could be as cloying as a straight spoonful of sugar. Camilla was old, by anyone's terms. To Jan's twenty-three years she seemed as antique as Methuselah and as fragile as cobwebs. Jan meant to spare her old bones as much as she could. It was really too bad of her to oversleep. But that dream . . .

It was not surprising that she should dream about her colonial ancestors, who had lived in this very house. Camilla talked about them often enough. Jan had only paid casual attention, since she was not at all impressed with genealogy; but evidently her subconscious mind had absorbed a considerable amount of information. All that talk about Washington dining with the governor, and the burgesses' resolution to hold a day of mourning for Boston. . . . She had firmly refused to do any official sight-seeing in Williamsburg, and she had not studied American history for years. Her subconscious must be packed with facts. What a pity one couldn't tap that source at will.

The dream had been unusual in another way. The details were still fresh in her mind, as sharp and clear as if she had actually experienced the events. At the beginning, when she had seemed to walk along the hallway and down the stairs, she had not been aware that she was dreaming.

A frown creased Jan's forehead. Perhaps she really had walked, in her sleep. She had never been prone to somnambulism, but there was always a first time. . . . It was not a pleasant thought. No, surely she had dreamed the whole thing, from the moment of her apparent waking. As the dream proceeded she had been less and less aware of herself as she became interested in the three men. Not until the very end had she thought of herself as being present, an invisible spectator to the conversation.

Not only invisible. Impalpable. That had been a nightmarish, shocking moment, when the man named Jonathan had seemed to walk right through her.

Jan looked at the portrait. It was a bad portrait, in every sense of the word. How clever of her dreaming mind to invest those flat, wooden features with such a personality.

Jan was not one of the many people who admire American primitives. The picture fell into that category; it had probably been painted by a self-taught itinerant artist, one of the anonymous craftsmen who wandered the muddy roads of the colonies. It had nothing to recommend it except a finicky fidelity of detail. The cameo pin that fastened the man's cravat was rendered with miniature accuracy, and one could almost count the hairs on his head.

He was dressed more formally than he had been in her dream, in a sober blue coat and neat white neckcloth. The painter had exaggerated the breadth of his shoulders, so that his head looked too small. The wide dark eyes were out of perspective, almost like an Egyptian painting. The whole face was flat, without any suggestion of personality. And the painter had the nose all wrong; it was narrower, not so bumpy at the end.

Jan caught herself with a smile and a shake of the head. She could not know whether the painter had caught the shape of the unknown's nose or not. The dream figure of Jonathan was a figment of her imagination and probably bore little resemblance to the long-dead original of the painting. Still, it would be interesting to find out who the man in the portrait was. If his name turned out to be Jonathan. . . . But of course it wouldn't.

When she reached the kitchen her aunt and uncle were seated at the table. The pale-tan liquid in their cups confirmed Jan's worst suspicions, but she sat down and resignedly picked up her own cup.

The kitchen of the house built in 1754 had, of course, been

in a separate outbuilding. The heat from cooking and baking would have been unbearable during the summer, and there were plenty of slaves to trot the dishes back and forth. In the early 1900s, a kitchen wing had been added to the house, and Jan suspected it had not changed much in the ensuing sixty or seventy years, except for the substitution of a few modern appliances for the original range and icebox. A big, inconvenient room, it had cupboards and pantries instead of built-in cabinets, and the sink was badly worn. The Foundation, which was responsible for the maintenance of the historic old mansion, had no interest in the later excrescences. When the present inhabitants no longer occupied the house, the kitchen wing would probably be torn down in order to restore the house to its eighteenth-century appearance.

It was a pleasant room, though, with its wide windows opening onto a view of lawns and green trees. Camilla had explained that they ate breakfast there in order to spare their aging servant; but Camilla looked as out of place in the utilitarian surroundings as a Meissen shepherdess in a discount store.

She had once been tall, and she still carried herself as straight as arthritis and eighty-odd years would allow; but the delicate skin of her face had crumpled like tissue paper clenched in the relentless fist of Time, and her fine hair was as white as cotton. As she bent her head, reaching for the sugar bowl, Jan saw the pink scalp through the thinning strands that had been combed so carefully over her head. It looked pathetic and defenseless, like a baby's scalp, and when Jan looked at the neatly set table, with its incongruous silver and dainty white embroidered mats, she felt ashamed.

"Why didn't you wake me up?" she asked. "I must have forgotten to set my alarm—"

"Oh, no," her aunt interrupted. "I heard your alarm. I guess you didn't."

Jan's feeling of guilt disappeared in a surge of pure annoyance at Camilla's tone. It also occurred to her that she would have to launder the dainty little mats and napkins. Why couldn't Camilla use paper napkins and plastic mats?

"You must have been dead tired," said her uncle. "Not surprising, poor child, the way you've been workin'. Even the darkies used to have one day a week off."

He grinned at her and winked, with the eye that was on the side away from his wife. Jan smiled back, her evil humor forgotten. She liked Uncle Henry. She wished she had known him in his prime; the twinkle in his brown eyes must have fascinated a lot of women when he was young.

He was still a handsome man, with the good looks an elderly face acquired from a lifetime of kindness. His mane of white hair was thick and springy, and his grin showed strong white teeth which, as he had boasted to Jan in the first hour of their acquaintance, were all his own. His teeth seemed to be his major vanity, and eating his only vice. So far as Jan could see, Camilla's acidulous comments on his drinking were unjustified; as a result of her nagging he had a tendency to sneak drinks on the sly, but not to excess.

"Well, I've had my morning off," she said. "I'll cook something really fattening tomorrow."

Her uncle chuckled and her aunt's head came up. Then Camilla smiled faintly and shook her head.

"Gluttony is the vice of old age," she said.

"It's the only one left to us," said her husband, with another wink at Jan.

"Aunt Camilla," Jan said, "who is the man in the portrait in my room?"

Two faces turned toward her in surprise, and Jan felt herself blushing absurdly.

"Sorry, I didn't mean to change the subject so abruptly. But I've been wondering about him. It's an—interesting face."

"Do you find it so? I must have another look, for I confess you see something in it that I do not. But I am glad you are beginnin' to take an interest in the family portraits and traditions."

Jan decided to ignore the gentle reproach implicit in the speech.

"Then he is—was—a member of the family?" she persisted.

"We assume he is a connection of some sort, since his portrait has been in the house for as long as anyone can remember. But his precise identity . . ."

"The costume is mid-eighteenth century," Jan said. "With all your genealogical research you must know the names of the revolutionary Wildes."

Camilla's face brightened. This was her favorite hobby, and it delighted her to have a fresh audience. Jan had been conspicuously disinterested in the subject so far.

"Naturally," she said. "As I told you, our ancestor, Charles, was a captain in the war."

"Charles," Jan repeated. Hearing the name, the same name as that of the bright-haired boy who had talked of rebellion, sent a little chill through her. Then she remembered that Camilla had said, "As I told you." She must have heard the name and its history before last night, even if she hadn't paid attention.

"His father was James Wilde," Camilla went on, warming to the subject. "James and Charles have been family names for three hundred years, my dear. The revolutionary James Wilde was a friend of Patrick Henry and Jefferson and Washington. His wealth was not as great as that of the Byrds and the Carters; but he was second to none in honor and in his devotion to the Patriot cause. . . ."

She paused, frowning slightly as she saw Jan's expression. Jan hastily wiped off her smile. What was she doing, grinning in that nasty way, as if she were in possession of secret information? Her dream Wilde, who considered Patrick Henry an uncouth rabble-rouser, had no basis in reality.

"He was, of course, a burgess," her aunt continued. "He built this house when he realized he would be spending several months each year in Williamsburg attending the sessions of the legislature."

"But the man in the portrait," Jan said patiently. "Aren't there family records that tell who he is?"

"Alas, the greater part of the family papers were de-

stroyed when the Yankees burned the plantation house," Camilla said.

Jan shifted uneasily. She considered herself a Yankee—
and suspected that Camilla did, too. Whenever Camilla said
the word she fancied she could hear an unspoken "damn" in
front of it.

"Weren't any of the family papers kept here?" she asked.

"Very few. Fortunately some of the portraits were here.
You remember I showed you the one of Captain Charles
Wilde."

"I'm afraid I didn't study it very closely," Jan admitted.

Camilla pushed her chair back. "We'll have another look
at it now."

"For pity's sake, Camilla, let the child finish her breakfast," Uncle Henry protested.

"That's okay. I'm through. I'd love to see Charles again."
Jan smiled at her aunt, who looked pleased.

Camilla led the way into the parlor. Like all the other
major rooms, it had been beautifully restored by the Foundation. Its twin fireplaces and sage-green paneling looked
as new as they had when Captain Charles Wilde entertained
his friends there. The wide bow window, facing on the Duke
of Gloucester Street, was curtained for privacy, but the fine
white muslin, intricately pleated, let in ample light.

There were two portraits in the room, one over each mantel. Jan's eyes went to the one of the man in a powdered wig,
but her aunt took her firmly by the arm and led her to the
opposite side of the room.

"The founder of the family," said Camilla impressively.
"Sir Francis Wilde, Baronet, of Wildernesse, Essex."

And I, thought Jan, am Martha Washington.

The costume was all right—a plum velvet coat, broad-
brimmed, plumed hat, huge wig with black ringlets framing
a narrow aquiline face. The face was plausible, with its cynical, close-set black eyes and narrow clipped moustache. But
the state of preservation was far too good for the portrait to
be almost four hundred years old.

"It must be awfully valuable," Jan said craftily. "From that period. . . ."

Camilla hesitated for a moment, but truth won out.

"Tragically, the original was destroyed by the Yankees. It was fortunate that the Wilde of that day had this copy made for the Williamsburg house."

"Uh-huh," Jan said. But she had a strong suspicion that the portrait had originated in the nineteenth century, based on speculation—and on a portrait of King Charles the Second of England.

Then she was allowed to turn to the portrait at the other end of the room.

Never before had she been so forcibly struck by the cruelty of old age. Her great-aunt's withered beauty, her uncle's faded vigor—these were sad, yes. But this was almost blasphemous.

She knew her distress was illogical. The golden lad of her dream was pure fantasy. But the Charles Wilde of the portrait had once been young, if not so gloriously young as her dream Charles. Time had no right to turn youth into this. . . .

This great pompous patriarch. He had dignity, and the plump face held a good humor that reminded her a little of Uncle Henry. It was a good face, benevolent, kindly, perhaps a little sad. But it was old.

She must have spoken the word aloud. Camilla picked it up.

"He lived to be over seventy, a great age in those days. We are a long-lived family, honey. That should be a cheering thought."

Jan shivered. Cheering, my God! Better to go to dust, like Shakespeare's golden lads and lasses, than come to this.

She turned away. "I'll do the breakfast dishes, Aunt Cam. To make up for my sleeping late this morning."

She knew the offer would be refused. Camilla didn't really trust her with the precious Haviland. And, Jan thought with a new awareness of infirmity, perhaps the hot water was soothing to her arthritic fingers.

"No, honey, I'll do the dishes. Why don't you enjoy your day off—go sight-seeing—or maybe buy yourself a new dress. For the party."

"The party?"

"I expect you forgot," her aunt said, gently reproachful. "Our little social activities must seem pretty dull, after New York."

"I don't spend much time in the giddy social whirl of Manhattan," Jan said with a smile. "I'd like to go out for a walk, but I'll be back in plenty of time to clean house, so don't you start. Shall I pick up anything at the grocery store?"

"There are just a few items. . . ."

"Okay. Just let me shower and change. I won't be long."

When she came back downstairs, Camilla was waiting. She handed Jan a letter, along with the shopping list.

"I plumb forgot to give you this yesterday, honey. I do hope it isn't important."

Jan recognized the writing.

"No, it's not important," she said truthfully. "It's from Mother. I know what she—I mean, she never has much to say."

She thrust the letter into her shoulder bag. When she opened the front door she dislodged two women who were crouched on the porch, trying to peer in the curtained window.

Jan glared at them.

"This is a private home," she said icily. "If you can read, you'll see that information on the card—yes, that one, right where you were standing."

The broader of the two women glared back at her.

"You don't need to be so uppity," she said, in the mellifluous accents of the Deep South. "You-all live off tourists like us."

Her companion, less brash, tugged at her.

"Come on, now, Marge, the lady's right. Beg your pardon, miss. Come on, Marge!"

They scuttled away.

Her hand on the narrow iron railing, Jan watched them go. Shaded by gracious green boughs, the Duke of Gloucester Street stretched off to right and left. It was only a little past nine, but the street was already crowded. The exhibition buildings opened at nine sharp, and the wiser visitors got out as early as possible. There were lines in front of the most popular attractions.

Early as it was, the air was damply warm against Jan's bare arms. In limbo between the house and the town, not part of either, she leaned against the railing and looked out at the street.

The thoughts that passed through her mind were not particularly original; many of the more sensitive visitors to Williamsburg probably shared them. But they were new to Jan, who had determinedly resisted the historical nostalgia that was so much a part of the restored capital's charm.

Now she wondered how it would have looked two hundred years ago, to a girl who walked out of this same house onto this same street. In 1776 the house had been about twenty years old. The white paint of the window frames and shutters had already faded and been renewed. The brick of the handsome Georgian facade had mellowed in succeeding seasons of heat and cold.

Jan went down the stairs and headed west, walking quickly. It did not take her long to get to her destination, but perspiration was trickling down her neck by the time she reached the red brick building on Francis Street. It was going to be a hot day.

Her aunt had introduced her to the staff at the Research Library, in the fond hope that Jan would be moved to take advantage of its resources. This was the first time she had done so; but the girl at the desk remembered her, and waved her toward the shelves with a friendly smile.

It was not difficult to find the material she wanted; most was standard textbook history. She had forgotten much of it, though. It was English literature she taught to bored high school students, not American history.

When she came out of the air-conditioned building an hour later, the sun hit her like a blast furnace. Having no particular destination in mind, she turned toward the shady sidewalks of the Duke of Gloucester Street. A grotesquely twisted paper mulberry tree stood at the corner, like a Martian monster; Jan found a curved section of trunk that fit her back and leaned against it, thinking.

In the eighteenth century the Duke of Gloucester Street had been a morass of mud during the rainy seasons. But in summer, when the sun had dried the earth to pale-brown dust, it would not have looked much different than it did in 1976. The modern paving was neither black macadam nor glaring white concrete; a discreet buff, it looked rather like sunbaked earth, if you squinted a little.

An open carriage jingled past. The giggling tourists in it would have shocked eighteenth-century Virginians, they displayed so much bare skin; but the coachman, a bored old black man in knee breeches and white shirt, was not anachronistic. He wore a black tricorn. So did many of the tourists; it was a cheap, popular souvenir, on sale in every shop in town.

At the end of the street, half a mile away, the pinky-red brick walls around the restored Capitol shone in the sunlight. The green rows of trees lining the street converged on it like pointing arrows.

One of the most attractive things about the town was the blend of colors. White frame houses had trim of mustard gold and sage green; or that curious dark shade, not quite black and not quite charcoal gray. Yellow was a popular color; not daffodil yellow or gold, but a soft buff that soothed the eye. The red brick facades and the occasional barn-red house were bright splashes of color against trees and grass. The inn signs were reproductions of old paintings; their charm was not fully realized until the traveler moved out of the restored area to be assaulted by neon lights and garish signboards along the highway.

Jan had been surprised and impressed to learn how carefully the Foundation had matched colonial color schemes. Samples of paint had been found when the woodwork was scraped down to the original surface. There were even contracts between painters and Williamsburg homeowners specifying the colors to be used: straw, yellow ocher, chocolate, dark brick, Spanish brown.

The restoration had been meticulously carried out. Old drawings and descriptions, scraps of material found in cellar excavations, had permitted the Foundation to rebuild destroyed houses almost exactly. And, of course, many of the homes and shops of the eighteenth-century town had still been standing when all this work began. The lower end of the Duke of Gloucester Street, with its shops and taverns, must look today almost as it had looked in . . . 1774.

May 1774, to be exact. A hot, muggy night, not unusual in Virginia at that time of year. The kind of weather when a man and his friends might relax in the privacy of his home with coats off and shirt sleeves rolled up. The kind of weather that made wavy hair curl, out of control.

It was in late May 1774 that the House of Burgesses had passed a resolution proclaiming a day of mourning for Boston. British taxes had infuriated all the colonies, but only Massachusetts had taken direct action. The Boston Tea Party, in December 1773, evoked prompt British retaliation—the closing of the port to all trade after June 1, 1774, unless the city paid for the tea that had been dumped into the harbor. The Virginia resolution was an expression of sympathy for an oppressed sister colony, and a slap in the face of the Crown which could not be ignored. Governor Dunmore had indeed dissolved the Assembly. But the proprieties of life were observed; Washington had kept his appointment to dine with the governor, and the burgesses' ball for Lady Dunmore had taken place as planned.

That well-known radical, Patrick Henry, had been mixed up in the meeting that planned the resolution, but he was not the only one involved. Thomas Jefferson, the young delegate from Albemarle County, later admitted that he had "cooked up" the resolution with Henry and a few others. The meeting had taken place on the night of May 23.

All in all, it had been an astoundingly accurate dream—even to the day of the month.

Jan shifted restlessly, finding this train of thought disturbing. As she did so, she heard paper crackle, and her frown deepened into a scowl. She had forgotten her mother's letter.

She knew what it said. The same old demand, the demand that had sent her to Williamsburg in the first place, and that had been reiterated in the letters she had received since.

Jan peeled her damp back off the tree and turned away from the Capitol. She would have to get home soon, before Aunt Camilla drove herself into a stroke cleaning house, but she wasn't going to go back before she got a decent cup of coffee.

She went toward Merchants' Square, the modern, pseudo-colonial shopping area that was the only intrusion into the restored area. The whole block was closed to traffic and the shops were quaint and expensively chic. It was an attractive place; but this morning not even the shady trees and the cafe tables on the brick sidewalk looked cool. Jan was about to go in search of her coffee when a sign caught her eye. She passed over the name, it was irrelevant. The important thing was the title: "Lawyer."

Why not get it over with? There was no use saying she had checked, when she hadn't. Ellen could always get the truth out of her. She might as well do it now, since it had to be done. . . . Without breaking stride, Jan plunged into the doorway and climbed the stairs to the second floor.

Thank God, the place was air-conditioned. She paused to mop her streaming face and then opened the office door.

The receptionist was young and blond and Southern. Which was not surprising. Jan answered the soft inquiry and was told to take a seat. Mr. Whatever had a client in his office but would be free shortly.

"Client" didn't seem an appropriate word. From the

sounds that came through the closed door it sounded as if the lawyer had a mad bull in there. And he was mad too; the shouts were a duet, gradually rising in volume.

Jan glanced at the secretary. Leaning back in her chair, the girl continued to buff her nails. She was humming.

Then the office door burst open. A man backed out. He was young, black, and furious.

"You're a helluva lawyer," he shouted at the as-yet invisible occupant of the office. "What the hell kind of a lawyer are you, anyhow? A guy comes to you with a perfectly valid bitch—"

"Bitch, yes. Case, no." The shout that interrupted him was even louder. The frosted glass in the office door rattled. "I'm a lawyer, not a housemother. Go cry on somebody else's big broad shoulder."

The young black man grabbed the knob and slammed the door. He turned blazing eyes on Jan, who was interested, but not alarmed; she knew the rage was not directed at her.

"That son of a—"

"Go ahead, say it," Jan suggested. "Don't mind me."

The young man's shoulders relaxed.

"No, ma'am, not me," he said bitterly. "Us Southern gentlemen don't use bad language in front of ladies, hadn't you heard?"

"Why don't you find another lawyer?"

"Why? Well, I'll tell you why." The young man turned and propelled his voice straight at the closed door. "Because the son of a bitch is the only honest lawyer in town, that's why." Having gotten this off his chest, he smiled wryly at Jan. "He is, you know."

"Which? Honest, or a—"

"Both," said her informant briefly. "Damn him," he added, and walked out of the office.

The inner door opened before Jan could decide whether the comment constituted a recommendation or the reverse. It was too late to leave now. When she saw the man who was standing in the doorway she was sorry.

He was ugly. Not homely—ugly. His coarse dark hair stood up like a brush on his massive head. His features were equally massive—a bulging brow with eyebrow ridges like a Neanderthal hunter's, a scooped-out nose and prominent cheekbones. The only incongruous feature was his mouth, which ought to have been wide-lipped and sensuous, to match the rest of his face. It was long enough, but the tight-set lips were cruelly thin. And he had the biggest ears Jan had ever seen on a man.

For a few seconds he stood there, his bristly head brushing the lintel, his big knotted hands pressing hard on the wood frame. Then his black eyes focused on Jan.

"What do you want?" he demanded.

"Nothing," said Jan. She rose.

The secretary interposed a twittering sentence, and the lawyer's gaze sharpened.

"What did you want to see me about, Miss Wilde?"

"I've changed my mind," Jan said.

"I don't always scream at clients."

The secretary giggled. Her employer scowled at her. She giggled again.

"I'm about to go out for coffee," said the lawyer. "You can join me." And, as she hesitated, he said impatiently, "We can talk if you want to, or you can drink in complete silence and walk away. Suit yourself."

Jan went with him.

He deposited her at one of the glass-topped tables in front of the café and disappeared inside, returning before long with two mugs. He hadn't asked Jan whether she took cream or sugar. The coffee was black, and quite strong.

He was in and out so fast she didn't have much time to think about what she intended to do; but when he planted hairy forearms on the table and fixed her with an inquiring stare, she decided she might as well go through with it. He might not be the only honest lawyer in town; he might not be honest. But he was a lawyer, and that was the essential item her mother had been demanding.

Haltingly she explained the problem. She was usually glib enough—you had to be glib to hold the minimal attention of a classroom of squirming adolescents—but the steady black gaze was oddly disconcerting, and it seemed to Jan that the man's expression became increasingly inimical as she proceeded.

"I see," he said, when she had stuttered to a stop. "You want to know whether there is any way of breaking the agreement your great-aunt and uncle made with the Colonial Williamsburg Foundation, so that at their death the house will go to the next of kin instead of to the Foundation. I take it you aren't inquiring for them, but for yourself."

"Yes." Jan felt the blood rising to her cheeks. To mention her mother would sound like a cop-out—just the excuse a greedy hypocrite would produce to account for her interest.

"No way, baby."

"What?"

"No way." The man's black eyes shone maliciously. He was smiling, but it was not a pleasant smile. "The transaction was a sale. The Foundation bought the property and paid for it. One condition of the sale was that your relatives would be allowed to live in the house during their lifetimes. It's a common transaction, although the owners don't often hang on as long as the Wildes have."

"I know it's been done," Jan said. "I just wondered—"

"Stop wondering. You think John D. Rockefeller couldn't hire smart lawyers? There is no loophole in those sale contracts. You'd have to prove duress or undue influence or incapacity. Nobody's ever succeeded in doing that."

"Hasn't anybody ever tried?"

"I suppose they have. There are a lot of greedy people in this world."

Jan pushed her chair away from the table. Her companion shot out a long arm and jerked it back, so abruptly that the edge of the table contacted Jan's diaphragm with a painful crunch. The pain was welcome; it provided an excuse for the uncontrolled quiver of her chin.

As her companion studied her face, his expression changed.

"I didn't mean to hurt you," he growled. "For God's sake, don't cry here, my local reputation as a bully is bad enough already. Look, the Foundation isn't gypping people. Really. It's a good deal. More than generous. You should have seen the town when John D. took over. It was a mess. Corrugated iron roofs and rotting timbers, garish signs nailed onto eighteenth-century shutters. . . . The Wildes were broke like everybody else. They're still living on the money they got for the house; they didn't have to leave their home, and it is being maintained and restored in a style they could never have afforded. If you think they were taken advantage of—"

"Oh, no," Jan said. She had her voice, and her chin, under control now, and anger had dried her incipient tears. "Don't bother attributing noble motives to me. I don't have any. I'm greedy and mercenary. How much do I owe you?"

The man made no attempt to detain her as she stood up. He leaned back in his chair and allowed his lip to curl.

"I'll send you a bill."

"Not to the house. I wouldn't want my relatives to find out what I've been up to. Leave it with your secretary and I'll stop by one day when you aren't in."

He called something after her as she walked away, but she didn't turn.

II

Jan poured out some of her anger and embarrassment in a letter to her mother. After rereading it she tore it up and produced a milder version. After all, she thought drearily, as she flushed the scraps of the first letter down the toilet, why should I despise her when I don't have guts enough to refuse the dirty work? She went downstairs in a spirit of utter self-contempt and sought salvation, like Saint Teresa, in scrubbing floors.

By five the house was clean enough to satisfy even Camilla, and Jan had made several trays of canapés. A quick supper and a shower revived her, but she was not in a particularly gracious mood as they sat in the parlor awaiting their guests. The prospect of meeting her aunt and uncle's friends, whom she visualized as a collection of wobbly old ladies and gentlemen, did not excite her, and she listened with only half an ear as Camilla chatted, giving her a brief and boring biographical sketch of each. Uncle Henry was in the kitchen with Andrew, the hired bartender. Jan wished heartily that she were with them. She heard glasses tinkling and a burst of laughter only slightly muffled by distance.

Jan had not bought a new dress. She was wearing her best, but she feared the unbleached muslin and garish Indian embroidery were not Camilla's idea of suitable party wear. All at once the content of her aunt's speech penetrated, and her heavy silver earrings jangled as she turned her head to stare at Camilla.

"Richard Blake is a delightful young man," that lady was saying placidly. "You may prefer him to Dr. Jordan, although there is something so respectable about a physician. . . . Richard is quite a gifted musician. Are you fond of music? Proper music, I mean?"

"I like all kinds of music," Jan said. "Aunt Camilla, just what are you—"

But it was impossible to finish the sentence, not with Camilla's bland, smiling eyes fixed on hers. Nor was there any need to ask the question; Jan knew the answer. She didn't know whether to laugh or swear. Camilla's matchmaking techniques might be simply habit, or they might be serious—an attempt to find a suitable spouse for the last scion of the house of Wilde. Had this been one of the old lady's motives for suggesting the visit, along with a wish for free maid service?

In spite of her prejudice, Jan couldn't help liking Richard Blake. Slender and fair, with sleepy gray eyes that sparked

flatteringly at the sight of her, his manner had a gentleness
that strongly attracted Jan. And when, at Camilla's insistence,
he sat down at the antique spinet, Jan forgot everything but
admiration. He played with great skill. The cheerfully precise airs and madrigals suited the formal room. Occasionally
Richard sang a few words, quite unselfconsciously; he had
a mellow tenor voice. Then he played a lovely old air by
Thomas Champion; it was one of Jan's favorites. He saw
her start of pleased recognition, and his smile invited her to
join in.

Never weather-beaten sail more willing bent to shore,
Never tired Pilgrims limbs affected slumber more;
Than my wearied spir't now longs to fly out of my troubled
*   breast:*
Oh, come quickly, sweetest Lord, and take my soul to rest.

The audience applauded as the two ended in perfect har-
mony. Surprised at herself—for she did not ordinarily burst
into song in public—Jan turned away. As she did so, her eyes
met the eyes of the one man in the room who had not joined
the chorus of applause. She caught at her aunt's arm and
hissed. "Who is that man over there?"

Her aunt followed her gaze. Scarcely moving her lips, she
answered softly, "He's just a lawyer, name of Alan Miller.
No one who matters; a crony of your uncle's."

Since she was not accomplished in the genteel art of staring without appearing to stare, Jan's eye was caught by her
uncle, who was sitting next to the lawyer. He beckoned to
her. As she passed through the crowded room, Jan had time
to regain her self-possession. The lawyer was just as ugly
as she had thought him. He was arguing with Uncle Henry;
acrimony did not sweeten his features, and they needed all
the help they could get. He didn't look up as she stopped by
the table where they were sitting.

"You call yourself a liberal, Henry; you're just a jackass.
Can't you damn fools get this states' rights stupidity out of

your heads? You support every stinking scream for independence without stopping to ask—"

"Watch your language, you young peasant," said Henry. "There's a lady present."

The big head turned toward Jan. From under the heavy brows malicious black eyes viewed her without favor—and without any sign of recognition.

"There are no ladies left, Henry. Not in your terms. She can probably teach me a few words I don't know."

"I probably could," Jan said. "Wait till Uncle Henry isn't around."

Her uncle let out one of his peculiar piercing yelps of laughter.

"I knew you two would get along," he said, beaming, "Here's the man for you, Jan. Not like those wilted, prissy prigs your aunt drags out."

"Oh, for God's sake," said Alan Miller angrily. "You're drunk, you old reprobate. Don't worry, Miss Wilde, you are safe from me. I'm sure you are relieved to hear it. Now take care of your great-uncle before his wife finds out he's been tippling."

He rose and stalked away.

Jan looked at her uncle, who sat chuckling to himself. His eyes were slightly filmed over.

Jan removed the decanter that had been placed inconspicuously behind a row of books on the table.

"I suspect Dr. Jordan wouldn't approve," she remarked, cradling the decanter in her arms and eyeing her relative critically.

"He's always fussing," Henry grumbled. "They all fuss. Even your aunt. Fine woman, mind you. But she will fuss."

"I'll get you some coffee," Jan said. She cast an apprehensive glance toward her aunt and saw that the offensive Mr. Miller had Camilla backed into a corner. He was talking animatedly, and Camilla's social smile was slipping.

"She'll be occupied for a while," Jan said, wondering whether the lawyer had deliberately headed her aunt off.

Such thoughtfulness didn't seem to be in character for him. Yet he had not mentioned their earlier meeting. . . . "I'll get the coffee," she went on.

"It won't do a bit of good. Never does." Her uncle rolled one eye toward Jan and she began to laugh.

"How right you are. I guess you don't need it. You're cold sober, aren't you?"

"Alas, yes. You know," Henry said, "it's relaxing to let go now and then and say exactly what you think. I can't do it with anyone but Alan."

He looked mournful. Jan patted his shoulder.

"You can be honest with me," she said. "Anytime. Your friend is right, I'm not a lady."

"Aren't you?" Her uncle smiled at her. "I rather think you are, my dear."

III

After that disconcerting episode the party turned out to be a success for Jan, primarily because of Richard. He monopolized her without apology; toward the end of the evening he led her out into the garden.

The garden was one of the features of the property, which occupied an entire city block. As Jan looked out over the moon-silvered mathematics of maze and topiary trees, she had to admit that the display would have been far beyond the physical and financial resources of her two old kinfolk. She wondered how many gardeners it took to keep the flower beds weed-free and the herb garden a blend of fragrances.

Practical considerations left her mind when Richard put his arm around her and led her toward the maze. As they approached the narrow entrance Jan realized that the heady scent of that time-worn Southern romantic asset, the magnolia, was being overborne by another, less seductive smell. Something stung her neck.

His arm still around her, Richard hesitated at the entrance

to the maze. All at once he began to laugh. Jan looked up at him. Moonlight flattered him, turning his sleek hair to silver, erasing the faint lines on his face, and bringing out the well-designed bone structure around his eyes and jaw.

"What's so funny?" she asked.

"I forgot about the boxwood. And the mosquitoes. A Virginia garden in the summer moonlight sounds like the quintessence of romance, doesn't it? I don't think this is going to work, though."

"Is it the boxwood that smells like—like—"

"Cats," said Richard. "Many, many cats, all male. Let's try the arbor. Maybe if we run it will take the mosquitoes a few minutes to figure out where we've gone."

He took her hand and they ran along the path. Jan was breathless when he pulled her into the darkness of the arbor, and into his arms.

Uncle Henry's description of him had been inaccurate. There was nothing wilted about the knowing hands and nothing priggish about the warm experienced mouth that found hers so neatly, even in the dark. When he let her go she was quite willing to try again.

"No," he said, laughing softly. "That's enough for now. I must return you unruffled and unmussed to your very proper great-auntie; and if we do that once more, I won't be responsible for the consequences."

"You're not afraid of Aunt Camilla, are you?"

"Yes," said Richard promptly.

"Chicken."

"Honey, I've lived here all my life. I know her; she'll be out here in about thirty seconds calling—See? What did I tell you?"

The stretched-out oblong of yellow light from the open door reached halfway down the path. "Jan-ice," called a tremulous voice. "Honey?"

"Coming," Jan called back. Her voice was tremulous too, with laughter.

"Lunch tomorrow," Richard said, smoothing her hair back

from her face. "Twelve. Come to the shop, you might like to see what I do for a living."

He kissed her again before he escorted her dutifully back to the house.

The other guests were leaving. Jan bade them farewell like a good hostess, then helped Andrew clear away glasses and crumpled napkins and crumbs. Not until she was alone in her room did she allow her face to relax into a smug reminiscent smile.

Then her eyes fell on the portrait. She gasped and reached for something to cover herself, as even a liberated young woman will do when she finds a stranger's eyes upon her.

The impulse lasted only for a second. Jan relaxed, feeling like a fool. The painted face was as flat as the canvas under it. What fault of eyesight had made those eyes seem to sparkle with life and awareness?

She dreamed again that night. And this time there was no transition, no imitation of waking.

Chapter

3

Spring 1775

JONATHAN'S BODY HIT THE GROUND WITH A THUMP THAT sent dust billowing into the air. It whitened his disheveled brown hair and settled muddily onto the damp shirt that clung to his heaving chest. His opponent bent over him, eyes narrowed, brown face intent. The circle of watching faces were darker than his, ranging from shining blue-black to mahogany.

Jonathan let out a whoop of laughter.

"Well done, Martin. Try it again."

He scrambled to his feet, grinning, and dropped at once into a wrestler's crouch, knees bent, arms crooked and half extended. His opponent grinned too, but shook his curly black head. He was a young man of about Jonathan's age, but slighter and several inches shorter. The dirt on his coarse tan shirt indicated that he had already taken his share of falls.

"No, suh, I know when I been lucky. Next time you break my back for sure."

At first Jan didn't recognize the setting. Its general nature was clear enough; she had seen the reconstructed outbuildings and workers' quarters of the big Williamsburg town houses several times. This place was somewhat like the area behind the Wythe house, but it resembled that immaculate reconstruction the way a barnyard resembles a Grandma Moses painting of the same scene. The small structures surrounding the bare, dusty courtyard were wooden, and they needed a new coat of whitewash. Chicken droppings smeared the ground and the shirts of the wrestlers; weeds framed the less traveled portions of the yard, and the tools scattered around were muddy, rusty—used.

But the greatest difference was the smell. It was a blend of many odors, some pleasant—herbs drying in the sun, bayberry and smoked bacon—some not so pleasant, like the steamy pungency of harsh soap. Overriding all others was a strong smell of manure.

Then, over the top of a shielding hedge, Jan saw the familiar roofline of the Wilde house. In the eighteenth century the outbuildings had occupied the space where the modern garden stood.

Finally Martin yielded to Jonathan's laughing insistence, and the two began circling one another.

The spectators were the first to see the newcomer; it was amazing how they simply faded away, into the various buildings where they ought to have been working. Martin was the next to sense the change in the atmosphere. He straightened, as if at attention, and his dark face became expressionless.

Leaning on the white picket fence, Charles Wilde spoke.

"See to my horse, Martin. She's in the stable."

His voice was casual, but the implied rebuke sent the servant trotting away. Jonathan turned.

"How long have you been there?"

"Long enough to see you humiliated." Charles's lean face, bronzed by the sun, broadened into a smile. "Now it's my turn."

He was unbuttoning his waistcoat as he spoke; throwing it and his coat over the fence, he advanced on Jonathan. It took the latter less than thirty seconds to put him on his back. The dust cloud billowed up again, and Charles lay still, his eyes closed, his outflung arms limp.

Jonathan's flushed face turned pale. He dropped to his

knees, completing the ruin of his white stockings, and put his big brown hands on either side of his friend's still face.

"Charles! Oh, God, what have I—"

Charles's eyes opened and his arms snapped together like the jaws of a trap. The two close-pressed bodies rolled over and over, limbs weaving like a spider's legs. Charles was getting the best of it—probably because Jonathan was afraid to exert his full strength—when a horrified voice stopped the match.

"Boys! Boys, what are you doing? Stop it at once!"

The voice was a woman's; the speaker was a slender gray-haired lady. Her costume indicated her social status—a dove-gray silk gown with voluminous skirts over the customary farthingale. A wide white collar crossed over her breast and was tied behind the waist. She had a broad-brimmed straw hat over the ruffled cap women wore, even in the house, and she carried a basket over her arm. Her face was flushed with heat and indignation; but as the combatants untwined and scrambled sheepishly to their feet, the corners of her mouth quivered with amusement. She kept her countenance under control, however, and surveyed them with a sternness that made them shuffle their feet and look elsewhere.

"Charles, you ought to be ashamed, tussling like a schoolboy. Jonathan—I did not know you were here."

"Forgive me, ma'am." Jonathan brushed the hair out of his eyes and spoke between gasps. "I was on my way to pay my duty when—when—"

"When I came and distracted him," Charles interrupted smoothly. "Your pardon, Mother, for both of us. You always do pardon us, you know."

His grin was cocky and irresistible. His mother's face melted.

"Oh, get along with you," she said, trying unsuccessfully to sound stern. "And for pity's sake, sweeten yourselves. Jonathan, your room is ready, as always. I will see you at dinner. We have guests, you know."

She swept past them, toward a building from which Jan

could hear the clack and crash of a loom. Her basket contained skeins of yarn; apparently she was on her way to supervise the maids who were weaving.

The two young men gave each other guilty glances. Charles burst out laughing, and then sobered.

"All the same," he said, collecting his discarded garments as they started toward the house, "you must give over socializing with the servants, Jonathan. If anyone but myself had found you wrestling with Martin—"

"Wrestling or anything else," Jonathan said, "I wished to lend him some of my books, but your father—"

"He is the kindest master in Williamsburg. If he had not sent Martin to the Negro school he would not know how to read."

To the right and left of the graveled path, boxwood hedges framed flower beds riotous with late spring flowers—cabbage roses, violet-blue Canterbury bells, pinks of every shade from white to mauve, sapphire-blue cornflowers.

Jonathan stopped and turned to face his companion. He mopped his streaming forehead with the sleeve of his shirt, leaving a wide smear of mud across his face. His long hair, curling under at the ends, had streaks of gold on the crown where the sun had bleached it, and his black queue ribbon dangled over one shoulder.

"He sent Martin for two years, and took him out at eight, when he was old enough to work; and gave him to you." His eyes darkened. "Heavenly God, Charles, how can you *own* another man?"

"But we are friends," Charles protested. "We played together as children."

"That makes it worse."

Before the earnestness of his gaze the other man's eyes fell. Charles sighed and sat down on a nearby bench, hard enough to produce a small puff of dust from his breeches.

"When you are riding your hobbyhorse there is no use in trying to talk about anything else," he said resignedly. "You know my views on slavery—"

"You speak platitudes and do nothing."

"What can I do?" Charles spread his hands wide. "You know that in this colony an owner cannot even free a slave without special permission from the Assembly."

"Then work to alter the law." Jonathan's demeanor had changed. He was still growing, and not quite sure what to do with his hands and feet; but there was a new set to his shoulders and a quiet force in his voice.

"I shall, when I am in a position to do so. You know that is one of Mr. Jefferson's plans."

"You and Jefferson and the others are much alike," Jonathan interrupted. "Full of fine ideas that must wait for the coming of the millennium. I suppose you share his views on the inferiority of the Negro?"

"Now, Jon, have they ever produced a painter, a poet, a—"

Jonathan's voice drowned him out.

" 'Suppose that our ancestors and we had been exposed to constant servitude, in the more servile and inferior employments of life; while others, at ease, have plentifully heaped up the fruit of our labor, we had received barely enough to relieve nature; and, being wholly at the command of others, had generally been treated as a contemptible, ignorant part of mankind; should we, in that case, be less abject than they now are?' "

"You must spend half your time memorizing tracts," Charles said, after a moment. "Whose words are those?"

"John Woolman's. He published the pamphlet in 1754."

"A Quaker," Charles said.

"What other faith has lived up to the teaching of the Redeemer in helping the oppressed?"

"What of your own faith? Or have you turned Quaker?"

He was trying his best, but there was a thin edge of contempt in Charles's voice. Jonathan flushed, not with embarrassment but with suppressed anger.

"The religious freedom our ancestors sought in this land is still some distance away, isn't it? You Anglicans penalize other sects—"

"The Quakers are all Tories," Charles said stubbornly.

"They are pacifists," Jonathan corrected. "So are my people. The followers of Menno Simons share many beliefs with the Friends. A Mennonite signed the first protest against slavery made on these shores, almost a century ago."

"Is that where your ideas come from?" Charles looked down at his dusty shoes. "I didn't mean to offend you, Jon. We have never discussed these things, I don't know why . . ."

"We were too busy with other things. Such as wrestling." Jonathan's singularly charming smile warmed his face. He sat down beside Charles, shaking his head. "I don't know where my ideas come from, Charles, or even what they are. I have been so troubled and confused these last months—"

"I know," Charles said. "I too have felt as if my brain were bursting with new ideas. What of the ones we shared, Jon? Last year you could talk of nothing but natural rights."

"But, Charles, that is why the issue of slavery bothers me. Can't you see the monstrous inconsistency? How does it suit your glorious cause of liberty to keep your fellowman in bondage?"

"I am inclined to agree with Mr. Henry," Charles answered. "I consider the practice against the law of God and man—but find it excessively convenient." Jonathan jumped to his feet with an angry exclamation; and Charles, half laughing still, caught at his sleeve. "Wait, don't always take me so seriously! Only give us time, Jonathan. Events are occurring so quickly—why, we are seeing history made, and the climax is yet to come. You missed the excitement here last month."

"The affair of the powder?" His brief anger forgotten, Jonathan sat down beside Charles. "We heard of it, of course. But tell me what happened."

"You should have been here. It was exciting, like the old Indian raids—the whole town awakened in the dead of night by cries of alarm, drums beating. . . ." Charles's green eyes shone with the recollection. "It seems that late last year the crown forbade the exportation of powder and arms to the colonies—another of those stupid gestures that accomplishes nothing except to increase resentment. The *Gazette* printed the news in January; I didn't see it, but our clever governor did, and decided that the order applied to the powder that has been stored in the Magazine. Which is nonsense, of course; the powder was ours, kept against the danger of raids or insurrections. At any rate, Dunmore decided to steal the powder—it was nothing less than theft, and he acted like a thief, sending royal marines creeping into the Magazine in the wee small hours. They were seen and the alarm was given; unfortunately they made off with fifteen barrels before we could get our sleepy heads together. Father tried to send me home," Charles added, with a sly smile, "but I pretended not to hear him. I wouldn't have missed the scene. I truly believe the crowd would have marched on the palace, but the mayor and Mr. Nicholas talked them out of it."

Jonathan had listened with glowing eyes, his big hands clenched; but at the end of the story he shook his head.

"Violence is never a solution, Charles."

"You're a fine one to talk. Who came close to breaking my neck just now?"

"That's different," Jonathan said, shifting uneasily.

Charles laughed, but he sobered quickly.

"Sometimes violence is unavoidable, Jonathan. I don't see how we can win our goals without it now. There has been fighting in Massachusetts already."

"'Our brethren are already in the field; why stand we here idle?'"

"So you heard of Mr. Henry's speech in Richmond?"

"Yes; Mr. Dix was there, and took it down as he spoke. They are great words, stirring words; but . . ."

Charles turned to face him squarely.

"What bothers you, Jonathan? Is it your pacifism or loyalty to the crown that makes you shake your head?"

"It isn't so easy," Jonathan said evasively. "Your father was undecided, last time I spoke with him."

"You will find that he has come much closer to my point of view," Charles said with unconscious arrogance. "He will come around; no man of conscience could do otherwise."

"Mr. John Randolph, they say, is returning to England. Mr. Nicholas still hopes to retain our ties with the King—"

Charles gestured impatiently.

"The old men, perhaps. But for the young—Jonathan, this is an unparalleled opportunity. Out there"—he waved an eloquent arm—"there is a continent to tame. Virgin, unspoiled. . . . We can make this new world an earthly paradise, teeming with abundance; and, for the first time in history, we can form a government founded on reason and goodwill, where all men have the right to decide on what will promote their happiness."

"At any rate, we share that hope," Jonathan said, smiling. "Let's not quarrel, Charles. Whatever happens, we'll always be friends."

Charles took his outstretched hand and their fingers clasped. Then a voice called from the direction of the house, and with a slightly embarrassed laugh Charles leaped to his feet.

"We're late. Mother will skin me alive. Come along, Jon, and defend me from her wrath—and help me entertain Mary Beth. She and her father are dining, did I tell you? She's as dull as ever, poor girl; I shall need your support."

II

Unlike the library, the parlor of the twentieth-century house did not much resemble the room of two hundred years earlier. The twin fireplaces and painted paneling were the same, but the furniture was entirely different. The festooned window curtains of blue-and-ivory-striped silk moiré framed the wooden slats of the Venetian blinds which the colonists of the hot South had adopted with enthusiasm. The carpet was turkey work, in shades of black, scarlet, gold, and blue.

The room was similar to others in the town houses that had been restored and refurnished so that they could be shown to visitors; but there was one overriding difference—the quality of contemporaneity. There is an air of the museum about any place that is deliberately preserved. This room was lived in, and the antique pieces were not antiques to Mr. and Mrs. James Wilde, they were the latest fashion, carried across the ocean from England at considerable expense.

Charles entered as his mother was showing off her new curtains to the guests. The speed with which he had changed might have led an observer to suspect he had only changed the outer layers; but they were magnificent—a peach brocade coat and dark-brown knee breeches, with a long-skirted waistcoat embroidered with birds of paradise. The latter was probably the work of his mother's loving hands. The bright silks glowed crimson and gold, aquamarine and emerald. The buttons were hand-embroidered to match. The silver buckles on his square-toed shoes shone no more brightly than his fair head. Mrs. Wilde's face softened with pride as she turned to greet her handsome son. He kissed her outstretched hand and then took the hand of the girl who stood beside her.

She was plain. Not even her fine feathers could make a bird of paradise out of this little wren. Her hair was blond; it had been pulled and puffed into fat ringlets which were drooping with the heat. They framed a long thin face that had neither animation nor beauty of feature to recommend it. The girl was only about sixteen, and her figure had been slow to develop. The dress did the best it could—a pretty flowered chintz, white on pale green, the wide skirts showed off her tiny waist, and the exquisite lace around the heart-shaped neckline lent fullness to her flat bosom. She had pretty arms and hands, set off by the wide elbow ruffles of the gown. A string of magnificent matched pearls encircled her throat, and rings sparkled on her fingers.

Then a wave of pink washed her pale cheeks, and her blue eyes lit up. For a moment she looked almost pretty. Jonathan had come into the room.

His coat, of sober blue cloth, looked new, but there had been no time to have it pressed, and it was badly creased. His white neckcloth was crumpled too; Jonathan's impatience with matters of dress showed in the carelessness with which it had been knotted. He was among friends, though, and his brown face beamed with pleasure. Unaware of the deficiencies in his attire, he crossed the room with long, inelegant strides, to take Mrs. Wilde's outstretched hand. She made clucking noises with her tongue and reached up to straighten his tie.

Then Charles, who had been talking to Mary Beth's father, a portly red-faced man in a rich mulberry satin coat, swung around.

"Jonathan! Mr. Banister has brought the latest news. His royal governorship has absconded!"

"What?" Jonathan turned, twitching the cravat from Mrs. Wilde's fingers, and leaving it in a worse state than before.

Mr. Banister nodded, his chins quivering.

"Her ladyship and the children went with him; they crept out of the palace at about 2:00 A.M., and are now on board the *Fowey,* at Yorktown."

"No wonder the King's cause fares so badly in Virginia, with such an incompetent in command," Mr. Wilde said angrily. "What ails the man? One would think his life had been threatened."

"His position has not been precisely comfortable," said Mr. Banister dryly. "Don't forget that Henry was actually marching on Williamsburg with his fire-eating militiamen when Dunmore capitulated and agreed to pay for the powder. No, I think he had cause to fear for his safety. But as for Lady Dunmore and the children—"

"There is not a man in town who would so much as speak roughly to her ladyship," said Mrs. Wilde, who stood behind her husband. "Where will this madness end? Gentlemen, dinner is ready—if you can leave politics for a while. . . ."

Mr. Banister extended his plump mulberry arm; Mrs. Wilde took it and the pair led the way toward the dining room.

Politics were avoided during dinner. It was an interminable meal, including fish and chicken and ham and all the other fabled Southern delicacies. Conversation was stilted. It was obvious that the men were dying to get back to the engrossing topic of the governor's latest trick, but Mrs. Wilde's distaste for the subject had been made clear.

Only once during the second course did the talk skirt the forbidden topic. In a gallant effort to make conversation, Mr. Banister asked the Wildes about their plans.

"I suppose you will be returning to The Folly soon."

Mr. Wilde frowned. "As soon as the Assembly adjourns. When that will be, I don't know; this latest news throws everything into uncertainty. Heaven knows, I am anxious to go," he added, smiling at his wife. "The heat in town is insufferable in July, and you know, Banister, a plantation does not run efficiently when the master is away."

"You are the most efficient of masters," Banister said. "I believe The Folly is one of the best-run plantations in Virginia."

Mary Beth was seated beside Charles, who obviously found her company depressing. He had tried to engage her in conversation, but she replied in monosyllables, keeping her eyes fixed demurely on her plate, and finally Charles gave up. Now she cleared her throat.

"It is such a curious name," she murmured. "How did it come about, I wonder?"

Delighted by this sign of life from the girl, Charles turned a brilliant smile upon her.

"I don't believe old Nicholas ever said; did he, Father? He was my great-grandfather; or is it great-great— Well, never mind," he continued, smiling at his mother, who had started to speak. "He named the place, and heaven knows what he meant by it. But I agree, it is a foolish name. I have proposed a better, but Father won't hear of changing it."

"Ridiculous," said his mother, giving him a look in which there was little maternal fondness. "The name has the weight of tradition; and to change it for the one you propose—"

"What name is that?" Jonathan asked, since Mary Beth had relapsed back into her modest coma.

Charles hesitated. Jonathan's was the only sympathetic face he saw; Mr. Banister was watching him with amusement, and his parents with ill-concealed disapproval. Then he threw his shoulders back.

"Patriot's Dream."

"Bravo," Mr. Banister exclaimed. "A fine name for a Virginian's home. I'm with you, Charles."

Mrs. Wilde's lips pinched together, but neither she nor her husband spoke; to express their true opinions would have been to contradict a man who was obviously an honored guest. Conversation languished thereafter. It was a relief to all concerned when Mrs. Wilde finally rose and led Mary Beth out of the room.

The men sat down with a general air of loosening belts and unbuttoning waistcoats. Mr. Banister helped himself liberally to wine and leaned back in his chair.

"I apologize, Wilde, for distressing your good wife," he said, his plump, good-humored face showing genuine regret. "The ladies take these matters to heart, I fear."

"Mrs. Wilde has family connections in England, you know," her husband said gravely. "The course of events has distressed her deeply."

"It distresses all of us," Banister said. He did not appear greatly distressed, however; refilling his glass, he drank with relish. "Yet sooner or later, I fear, we must come to a fateful decision."

"Admittedly, the King's advisers have acted unwisely," Mr. Wilde said. "But God forbid that we should imitate their folly. A majority of the Congress is in favor of reaffirming our loyalty to his Majesty—"

"While they fire on his Majesty's troops at Concord and besiege his army in Boston?" Mr. Banister shook his head. "I fear George the Third will not appreciate the distinction, Wilde. I have heard a rumor that Colonel Washington will be appointed commander in chief of the Continental forces."

The two young men had remained discreetly silent while their elders spoke, but at this piece of information Charles could contain himself no longer.

"And you won't even let me drill with the militia! Father, if a man like Colonel Washington is—"

"This is neither the time nor the place for such a discussion, Charles," his father interrupted. Seeing that his friend was really angry, Banister tried to relieve the situation.

"Young men are always fiery," he said indulgently. "One of my clerks is off with Morgan, that backwoodsman who is forming a company of riflemen from the western counties."

"Charles wouldn't qualify for Morgan's troop," Jonathan said cheerfully. "Those lads can shoot the ace out of a playing card at sixty paces."

"It is no wonder the young men are fiery when their elders set them such an example," Mr. Wilde said, his cheeks still flushed with anger. "Patrick Henry, for one—"

"Yes, indeed, what do you think of our Mr. Henry?" Banister demanded. " 'On what meat has this our Caesar fed, that he has grown so great,' eh?"

He chortled, pleased, at having produced such an apt quotation, but his host looked grave.

"I do suspect his ambition. He has been outlawed, you know."

"By a governor who has abandoned his post," Banister said with a snort. "It was an empty threat in any case. Every county in Virginia promised to protect him from arrest."

"Did you hear his famous speech, sir, the one in Richmond?" Charles asked eagerly.

"No; but I heard it described. The entire meeting sat spellbound. You may shake your head, Wilde, but he is a master orator. Jefferson says he speaks as Homer writes."

"I have also heard it said that he throws himself into a sentence and trusts to Almighty God to get him out."

"His trust is justified then," Banister said, with a chuckle. "Indeed, it almost seems as if he had the gift of prophecy. He had not heard of Concord and Lexington when he spoke of fighting in the north—what was it he said . . ."

"'The next gale that sweeps from the north will bring to our ears the clash of resounding arms! Our brethren are already in the field! Why stand we here idle?'"

The others looked at Jonathan.

"Well done, my boy," Banister cried. "Go on. Do you know the rest?"

Jonathan shook his head.

"I get carried away by words," he said apologetically. "They are magnificent, but . . ."

"Magnificent, but seditious," Mr. Wilde said.

"Is it true what I hear about Henry's wife?" Mr. Banister inquired.

Charles looked disgusted at this descent from oratory to idle gossip, but his father was evidently relieved at the change of subject.

"Alas, she has lost her reason altogether, poor lady. It is said that she must be confined in a strait dress."

"Every man has his personal tragedies," Banister said sanctimoniously. "There are stories about that sister of Jefferson's—what was her name—"

"This is sad talk for such an occasion," Mr. Wilde said.

"Yes, yes, quite true. At any rate, there is nothing like that in the Banister family." He smiled knowingly at Charles. "Good, healthy stock. Nothing to concern you there."

For once, Charles was at a loss for words. He glanced helplessly at his father, and Mr. Wilde said,

"Shall we join the ladies, gentlemen?"

Mr. Banister drained his glass. The butler threw open the door and the party proceeded toward the parlor, from which the sound of a harpsichord could be heard. It was being played very badly.

The two boys, bringing up the rear, exchanged glances. Charles's face was full of derisive laughter, Jonathan's was reproachful. Charles replied with a jab at Jonathan's chin, which induced a grunt from the victim.

"Jonathan?" Mr. Wilde turned his head.

"Nothing, sir. I—uh—tripped."

"Clumsy fellow," Charles said, and stood back to bow his friend into the parlor.

As the only young lady present, Mary Beth was expected to display the genteel skills which were taught with the sole aim of catching a husband. She found the music as painful as did some of her listeners; her mouth was set and her eyes narrowed with concentration as she struggled through a Bach prelude.

"Bravo," Charles exclaimed, when she lifted her hands from the keys with a sigh of relief. "How you've improved, Mary Beth!"

"Charles, you're teasing me," Mary Beth mumbled. "But I don't blame you; I never do play well, and when someone—I mean, when there is a person present who plays better—"

"She means you, Jon," Charles said, as Mary Beth's voice died away. "I agree, Mary Beth. It isn't fair. He never practices, and when I look at those big clumsy fingers of his—"

He pretended to duck; and Jonathan, who had not raised a hand, said mildly, "You're quite right, Charles. I don't practice, and I have no intention of disgracing myself by attacking that defenseless spinet. In spite of Mary Beth's undeserved flattery."

"What about a duet, then?" Charles said, looking a little ashamed of himself. Teasing Mary Beth was like tormenting a rabbit; she was utterly helpless. "You two used to play well together. There's your old fiddle, gathering dust. . . ."

"Now, Charles, when has anything in this house gathered dust?" Mrs. Wilde asked indignantly, looking up from her embroidery.

"A figure of speech, Mother."

"A reproach to my idleness," Jonathan added, picking up the violin and running affectionate fingers over its polished surface.

"Very well, I'll try, if Mary Beth will play loudly and cover up my mistakes. You must all join in singing, as well."

So the afternoon ended in an impromptu concert, common in an era when people had to make their own entertainment. Charles, who had a fine lusty baritone, sang louder than anyone, helping to conceal Mary Beth's blunders. With her eyes fastened on Jonathan, she played worse than before. Her father, who obviously had no ear for music, radiated fond approval and joined in the singing with a bellowing bass. Mrs. Wilde neglected her embroidery as she watched her son with a doting smile. Charles's father smiled too; but his eyes were troubled.

Chapter
4

Summer 1976

WHEN JAN WOKE UP, THE CLOCK SAID SEVEN THIRTY. Instead of getting out of bed she lay still and pulled the sheet up to her chin. She stared fixedly at the gathered muslin of the canopy over her head; but she was intensely aware of the portrait. She could almost feel the gaze of the painted eyes.

She was afraid. The first dream had been disturbing enough in its vividness and coherence—more like a segment of real life than a product of the sleeping mind. But last night's experience made it almost impossible for her to regard what she had experienced as an ordinary dream. The same people grown a little older, just as they would have grown—for it was clear, even in her ignorance of historical detail, that approximately a year had passed between the events of the first dream and those of the second. Again, there was that disturbing consistency; so far as she knew, not a single detail of fact or furnishing was out of kilter.

Even more abnormal was her position in the dream. Although all her senses functioned as they would in life, she was invisible to the actors. It was like being a spectator at a play, where darkness and the self-contained world of the drama make the spectators anonymous, unseen, nonexistent to the players. And the dream had the vividness of a well-produced play—with one vital difference. Her characters were not performing for an audience.

Shivering—although the room was not cold—Jan tried to remember what little she'd heard about extrasensory perception. Her mother was fascinated by the subject, and by the related fields of psychic phenomena. Jan had never done more than skim such reading material, scornfully. Now she wished she had paid more attention. There had been several books on things like ancestral memory and reincarnation. Was she the reborn incarnation of one of the actors in the eighteenth-century drama?

She had enough humor left to smile faintly at the idea. Surely one would recognize one's former self with some degree of warmth or sympathy. None of the women interested her particularly—the bright-eyed servant child, the mousy young lady, or the motherly Mrs. Wilde. If she was drawn to anyone, it was to the bewildered and endearing Jonathan. She knew his state of mind so well; apparently adolescents in all ages since the world began suffered from the same confusion of ideals. Well, she had no sexist biases; why shouldn't she have been a man in some other life? The most important thing about a human being is his or her humanity, not the accidental structure of the body.

Feeling a little calmer, Jan lowered her gaze to meet the brown eyes of the portrait. The face was still and unmoving.

Camilla's footsteps went down the hall. Jan got out of bed and started to dress. Something had to be done. She was not going to let the experience throw her; but something had to be done about it. She was still frightened, and the fact that she felt a growing fascination with the shadowy actors frightened her even more.

Jan left early for her lunch date, explaining mendaciously that she wanted to do some sight-seeing first. She was in good odor with Camilla, who approved both of sight-seeing and of Richard Blake. She pressed money into Jan's hand, with the embarrassed smile of someone proffering a bribe, and whispered something about a new dress. From the way

Camilla eyed her scanty cotton dress, Jan realized that she would probably be doing her aunt a kindness to buy a new dress. Unfortunately she had a pretty good idea of the kind of outfit Camilla would want her to get.

She tucked the money into her purse and headed for Merchants' Square, but as soon as she was out of sight of the house she turned down a side street.

Not all the houses in the restored section were owned by the Foundation. Dr. Jordan lived in one of them, and it was clear, from the fresh yellow paint and the neatly trimmed boxwood, that he was doing well. Tall trees shaded the tiny pillared porch and cast a shadow across the dormer windows on the second floor. The shingles were of the type that gave Williamsburg houses part of their charm, rounded at the ends to prevent them from splintering. There was a screened-in porch at the side, and a fat yellow cat sunned itself on the brick steps. It didn't even open its eyes as Jan stepped over it on her way to the door.

She had learned long ago, from dealing with her mother, that an appearance of candor is the safest form of subterfuge. That was why she had decided to go openly to Dr. Jordan instead of trying to find a doctor her aunt and uncle didn't know. The fact that she had no appointment was not a problem. She was whisked into the inner office with flattering speed, and Dr. Jordan rose from behind his desk to greet her. He was a nice-looking young man with hornrimmed glasses and a droopy moustache, just a little too well tailored and too precise in his speech.

Jan had already selected a medical problem. It had to be one that Aunt Camilla would find mildly embarrassing, so that she would not expect Jan to discuss it with her; but it didn't embarrass Jan or Dr. Jordan. He nodded when she explained that her own doctor had examined her within the past year, and had given her a bottle of pills for painful menstruation. He seemed more relaxed on his native turf, and Jan found him much more pleasant than she had at the party. Apparently he shared her feelings, for he asked her to have dinner with him on Friday. As she was about to leave, she casually asked the question that would lead up to her real reason for being there.

"There's no danger in taking these with sleeping pills, is there?"

"What sort of sleeping pills are you taking?"

"Oh, I'm not taking them now," Jan said truthfully. "I was, in New York, for a while; you know how life is there, so hectic and nerve-racking. . . . I've been sleeping like a baby here. Actually," and she managed quite a convincing laugh, "I've been having the most delightful dreams. Have you ever heard—I mean, there is such a thing as recurring dreams, isn't there?"

"Oh, certainly," Jordan said. "I've never had them myself; but my brother used to claim that he had a sort of nightly serial going, in glorious technicolor." His smile made him look much younger. "He was twelve at the time and I was ten; I used to be quite jealous of him. I imagine he made up the more exciting episodes, though. I'll pick you up at seven on Friday; will that be all right?"

Jan didn't realize how relieved she was until she got outside and felt her knees go weak. She sat down on the front steps, beside the cat, and stared sightlessly at the brilliant display of marigolds along the walk.

It was a relief to know that her experience was not necessarily abnormal. But that was not the main cause for relief. What would nice, smiling Dr. Jordan have said if she had told him the whole truth?

For the danger was not so much in the dreams themselves as in her attitude toward them. If she had explained *that* to Dr. Jordan; if he had suggested tranquilizers and psychiatrists. . . . Maybe she would stop dreaming. Jan realized that that was what she had really been afraid of—not that she was crazy, but that she would never see her dream people again, never find out what was going to happen to them: how Jonathan would resolve his perplexities about freedom and slavery, nonviolence and the cause of liberty; whether Charles would fight for his dream, against his parents' wishes; whether he and Mary Beth would marry. But Mary Beth was in love with Jonathan, who was unaware of her blushes and sidelong glances. . . .

My God, Jan thought, it's like some stupid soap opera. But I care about these people. I really want to know. . . .

She got to her feet and marched down the walk. The cat opened its big golden eyes and watched her go.

II

The music-instrument maker's shop was one of the craft shops that were open to the public. Before she came, Jan had pictured Williamsburg as a town with houses and taverns, rebuilt as they had been in the eighteenth century. It was that, but it was much more. The craft program was a major project in itself. Cabinetmaking, silversmithing, and other skills were practiced as they had been in the eighteenth century, with authentic tools and methods. The makers of musical instruments fashioned violins, harpsichords, lutes, and other stringed instruments, and their products were in such demand that they were three years behind in filling orders.

The shop was on Nicholson Street, in a little hollow where a brook flowed under the foundations of the frame house. The girl who punched the visitors' tickets was dressed in a full, gathered skirt with a low-necked white blouse. She looked inquiringly at Jan. As soon as the latter mentioned her name the girl smiled.

"Oh, yes, Mr. Blake said you'd be coming. Go right on in."

The shop was surprisingly small. A row of benches separated the craftsmen and their tools and materials from the visitors. There were quite a number of the latter, dressed in shorts, carrying cameras, and towing bored children; but the group was silent and attentively interested when Jan slipped in. One of the young men behind the barricade was in the middle of a lecture.

"This is a mandolin. We make it on a frame—" He held up a mold which had the same round-bellied shape as the instrument he held in his other hand. "The wood is cut in strips and bent to fit over the frame. The wood? Cedar and ash; that's why the alternating colors, red and yellow. The glue . . ."

Richard was perched on a bench, his fair head bent over the violin he was sanding with delicate strokes of his fingers. He wore the costume of colonial Williamsburg craftsmen— knee breeches, white stockings, buckled shoes, and the shirt Jan had already had occasion to admire on Charles and Jonathan. Its full sleeves were tucked up, baring Richard's arms to the elbows.

At first he didn't see her, he was so absorbed in his work. The sandpaper, curved around his finger, moved with tiny strokes over the mottled surface of the wood. It didn't have the shining red-brown gloss Jan had seen on other violins, but was a pale tan streaked with brown. One of the tourists asked the question that was forming in Jan's mind, and Richard looked up. His eyes narrowed in a smile as he saw her; he answered the question.

"I've just given this instrument its first coat of varnish. It sinks into the wood, that's why it has this mottled appearance. I'll give it another fifteen or twenty coats before I'm through. Yes, that's why it takes so long to make a violin, the varnish has to harden and be sanded down before the next coat is applied. Most of the wood we use comes from Europe. It has to be air dried, and that takes several years. Oven-dried or kiln-dried wood doesn't have the same resonance."

His assistant, who sported a magnificent black beard, took over the lecture, and Richard hung the violin carefully on a hook, by means of a leather strap attached to the curved neck. He stepped over the bench and took Jan's arm. Several of the tourists turned to watch as he led her out.

As the door closed behind them, Jan said, "I'm impressed. Do you really make those lovely things?"

"I'm learning. It's a fascinating trade, Jan. Luckily the

boss prefers people who are trained in music rather than in woodworking, or I wouldn't qualify."

"I can understand that," Jan said. "The important thing is the sound, isn't it? Not the appearance."

"Exactly." Richard smiled at her. "To get the proper sound out of a violin—well, it's something you have to learn by experience. Each instrument is just a little different from every other. But don't let me get started, I can go on for hours. I hope you don't mind walking. I don't use the car unless the weather is bad; but it's several blocks, maybe half a mile. . . ."

"Good heavens, do I look that fragile?"

"You look tired," Richard said, his eyes searching her face. "Are you sleeping all right?"

"Yes, of course. Where are we going?"

"My house. I hope you don't mind; I had planned to take a little extra time, but we're shorthanded today, and the local eating places are so crowded—"

"Stop apologizing for everything. It sounds fine to me."

He laughed and squeezed her arm; his fingers were warm and firm. They had left the historic area. The sidewalks were cement instead of brick, but old trees cast a grateful shade, and the houses, with their neatly trimmed shrubbery, had the same restful charm as the public part of town. A few of their fellow pedestrians were tourists, lost, or more energetic than the rest; but most were townspeople, and Richard greeted many of them. His knee breeches and buckled shoes attracted no attention; indeed, Jan thought, they were more suited to the locale than her own modern dress.

"I ought to be wearing sprigged dimity and a farthingale," she said. "I'm out of place."

"You'd be wading through your own sweat," Richard said inelegantly. "If the Foundation hadn't air-conditioned the exhibition buildings they'd have a hard time hiring hostesses."

"Is that why they did it?"

"No, they realized that controlled temperature and humidity keep the antiques in better condition. This climate is awfully hard on wood, especially—alternating periods of heat and cold, considerable humidity. Not that the Foundation isn't a good employer. This is one of the extra inducements."

The hand he placed on the white wooden gate was proprietary, as was the fond glance he gave the house. But he did not open the gate at once, and Jan gave the house the attention he obviously expected.

It was a diminutive, miniature house, like a reduced version of the buildings on the Duke of Gloucester Street; and it had the same simple elegance of structure. There were two gables in the sloping roof, matched by narrow shuttered windows below, one on either side of the door. The house had no porch or outside entry, only a short flight of steps that were of brick, like the walk that passed between low hedges of boxwood. Shutters and trim were painted sage green, which contrasted handsomely with the gleaming white paint.

"It's darling," Jan said sincerely.

"Bachelor quarters," Richard said casually; but his eyes lingered on the white walls like those of a lover admiring his mistress's curves. "It was built about 1740. The Foundation lets senior employees rent places like this."

He opened the gate. The old-fashioned device of a heavy iron ball suspended on a chain between gate and post pulled it closed after them.

The inside of the house was as charming and immaculate as the outside, and it was Richard's favorite hobby to furnish it with the antiques it deserved.

"I'm an antique buff," he explained, his fingers absently caressing the curved top of a carved black cherry side chair. "It's getting harder and harder to find bargains, but that increases the triumph when you do find something good."

The house had only four rooms, plus a bathroom and tiny modern kitchen; the basement contained Richard's workshop and the heating and air-conditioning equipment. The kitchen was so small only one person could work there, so Jan sat on a chair near the door, sipping the chilled wine Richard had poured, and chatted while he cooked. He was as neat-handed and quick with domestic details as with his work; it was not long before the simple meal was on the table. Enjoying the crisp salad and the subtle seasoning of the puffy hot omelet, and listening to Richard's enthusiastic descriptions of his antiques, Jan knew that some men would probably consider Richard effete. She had the best of reasons to know that there was nothing effeminate about his basic drives. His body was as hard and effective as an athlete's, and the lean brown hands that gesticulated so gracefully were callused and scarred by the tools of his trade.

"And this," Jan said, glancing around the cool, quiet room, "is how you plan to spend your life."

"Yes. It's the only real ivory tower left, Jan. I've got friends in the education business, and from what I hear that is a real jungle."

"You hear right."

"You teach, don't you?"

"I did." Jan spread butter on her roll and watched it melt. "I may be looking for an ivory tower myself."

"Then you don't despise me for copping out? Some people do."

"I hate that phrase," Jan said angrily. "That, and all the other slick, stupid slang. I've heard too much of it, mouthed by empty-headed brats with no sense of decency or responsibility . . ."

She had sense enough to stop before her voice became strident; and for a little while she concentrated on the food, while Richard watched her with quiet gray eyes, his head tipped to one side.

"That bad, eh?" he said, after a while. "If you don't want to talk about it—"

"It wasn't that bad, and of course I can talk about it. I feel melodramatic and silly complaining. My gripes seem so trivial compared to other people's problems. But I started out with such ideals. Going into a public school I knew I'd have trouble, even in the suburbs. I expected violence, drugs, indifference. . . . And I got them. Worse than I expected, because no amount of talk can really prepare you for a world that is outside your experience. The worst was the indifference. They don't care. They despised me and everything I stood for, every idea, every touch of beauty and kindness. I stood it for two years. Then *I* copped out. I found one of those expensive private girls' schools. Took a cut in salary, but I thought it was worth it. Oh, boy."

She liked the way he listened, his face grave, his eyes never leaving her face, responsive to every change in her voice. Now he said,

"I suspect the same kind of thing went on a century ago, Jan, even in the ladylike finishing schools. You're bound to have problems when you pen up a bunch of burgeoning adolescents, of the same sex, in—"

"Oh, that wasn't it. They aren't that isolated these days. There were three pregnancies the year I taught there—all quietly handled, as money and social pull can handle them. It wasn't that, or the drugs, or the alcohol. . . . Those handsome kids, beautifully tended, like fine horses, with every advantage money can buy, rotting their poor little brains and harming their bodies. . . . No. It was the same old indifference. Words like 'honor' and 'wisdom' made them snicker. At least they snickered behind their hands, instead of laughing in my face the way they did in the public schools. I think I'll take a job as a veterinarian's assistant, and help the dogs and cats conquer the world."

She ended with a laugh, enjoying the catharsis of complaining, but Richard's face remained serious.

"You're pretty cynical for one so young."

"And how do you feel about life?"

"The same. Different experiences, leading to the same conclusion. There's some excuse for this kind of life, you know. The monasteries of the Middle Ages had the same rationale. When the world goes mad, a sane man can only hope to keep a small island of learning safe."

"Right on," Jan said fervently. Then she laughed. "See?

I'm contaminated. Can't break the habit. Richard, thank you, you are sweet to listen to me. I haven't talked this way to anybody else."

"That is probably the finest compliment you could pay me," Richard said. He glanced at the clock, and added in a lighter voice, "And, damn it, I don't have time to press my advantage. Got to get back."

By the time they reached the shop Richard had explained that Saturday was one of his days off, and had offered to show her Jamestown, complete with picnic. They bickered amiably about who was to supply the food, and finally agreed to share the job. There was a gaggle of hot, perspiring tourists waiting patiently in line when they reached the shop, so he didn't take her hand, but his expression, as he stood looking down at her, made Jan feel as if she had felt a warm touch.

"Thank you for lunch," she said. "That was a marvelous omelet."

"It's the only thing I can cook," Richard admitted. "You may get very tired of omelets, Jan."

But for all the feeling implied by that gracefully turned comment, there was an eager swing to his step as he started along the path. He obviously loved his work. Jan didn't mind that, nor was she put out by the way the heads of the women tourists turned to follow the movement of his tall, erect body. Yet as she turned away, toward Nicholson Street, her thoughts were not of the man who had just left her. She was wondering whether the shop had been there in Jonathan's day, and if he had ever visited it.

III

Jan took a nap that afternoon—something she never did unless she was sick or very short on sleep. It didn't work. There were no dreams, except for whirling, confused fragments of faces and sound. She woke groggy and cross, as people do who are not used to a daily nap.

Then she heard Camilla tiptoeing past her door, and swore with a wealth of inventive imagination that owed very little to the limited vocabularies of her former pupils. Recently she and her aunt had fallen into an idiotic little game, where each tried to anticipate the other in performing the household chores. Camilla should not have been doing any heavy work: she had an unnerving habit of going blue around the mouth whenever she did too much. Jan had every intention of taking over the responsibility, and Camilla's performance aggravated her to death.

"But I'm too well brought up to say so," she mumbled to herself, studying her heavy-eyed reflection without approval as she ran a comb through her flattened curls.

When she entered the kitchen, silent on sneakered feet, her aunt was investigating the lower shelves of the refrigerator.

"Isn't it a little early to start dinner?" Jan asked.

Camilla straightened.

"Yes, I expect it is. I keep forgettin' I have a nice young helper, whose joints don't creak when she moves. Oh, honey, did I tell you we're havin' a guest for dinner?"

"I planned on chicken; there should be plenty. Who is it?"

Her aunt's fine-boned face remained calm, but distaste edged her voice.

"That lawyer. He's such a crony of your uncle's; comes to play chess with him 'most every week, and Henry insists we should feed him. 'Course that's only right; and he doesn't accept every time; but . . ."

"I don't like him either," Jan said cheerfully. "But it is nice of him to spend so much time with Uncle Henry."

"Oh, honey, I don't dislike him. It's just that he's so—well, he's such an awkward, loud person. Not quite our kind. . . . As for being nice to Henry, well, I wouldn't want to disparage anyone's motives; I'm sure he means well. . . ."

"You think he's after something?"

"Well, you never know about a person like that," her aunt

said darkly. "And naturally he doesn't get invited by many of the old families. . . ."

Her voice died away. Jan raised her eyebrows but decided not to pursue the subject. She was not really interested in the uncouth Mr. Miller.

It really was too early to start dinner; she had no intention of wearing herself out with a fancy meal in order to impress this guest. She decided to read for a while, after extracting Camilla's solemn promise that she wouldn't start cooking; but as she left the room it occurred to her that her aunt was rather stressing the "why don't you rest a bit" routine these days. She stopped in the hall to examine herself in the mirror, and decided she didn't look consumptive. A little shadowy around the eyes, perhaps—but that was the result of sleeping in the daytime; she ought to know better than to do that.

A glance out the window told her that Uncle Henry was "gardening"—a euphemism for his post-nap snooze in the shade of the cedar of Lebanon, a unique giant of its species. His trowel and gloves lay beside him on the bench, and his hands were folded comfortably over his stomach.

Jan grinned and turned from the window in the library to the shelves of books. She had not investigated them in any detail; the collection was not inviting, with its fine leather bindings and its air of having been assembled for show rather than entertainment. Now she searched with a new interest, for entertainment was not her aim, and was rewarded by finding an entire shelf of volumes on American history.

Her impression had been correct. A year had passed between the events of the two dreams. The second one had taken place in 1775.

In March of that year Patrick Henry had made his second great speech—the "give me liberty or give me death" speech, in Richmond. The affair of the powder magazine had occurred on April 21, and Henry had played hero again, marching on Williamsburg with several companies of militia. The governor had agreed to pay for the stolen powder and Henry had disbanded his little army—reluctantly, no doubt. Yes, the dates were definite; again Jan was able to pinpoint the very day of the dream, for Governor Dunmore and his family had escaped from Williamsburg on June 8, 1775. Once more that unnerving precision of detail. . . .

Engrossed, she read on. It wouldn't hurt to get a little ahead in the story. Camilla had to call her when it was time to start supper.

IV

The meal was not a social success. Camilla, her sweet voice icy, contributed very little to the conversation, and Uncle Henry bolted his food as if eager to escape to the masculine privacy of the chessboard. Jan realized that Alan Miller was quite well aware of his hostess's feelings, and found them a source of considerable entertainment. If she had not disliked the man so much she would have laughed at his delicate baiting—the exaggerated deference that was worse than a hearty slap on the back, the pointed references to old families, decadence, the D.A.R., Yankees. He touched on almost every subject that makes a Southern lady writhe, but he did it in such a way that no one would have taken exception to his actual words.

After the first searching glance he spoke very seldom to Jan, but as the meal progressed she saw that his eyes had a tendency to wander in her direction when he thought she wasn't looking at him. She had greeted him pleasantly—Camilla's contempt had aroused all her sympathy for the underdog—but after listening to him for a while she decided he could perfectly well take care of himself. She offered to serve coffee in the library, so that the men could get to their game, and Camilla gave her a glance of approval and appreciation.

The tormentor turned his attention to her.

"Why, ma'am, I wouldn't think of troubling you that way.

In fact, you must let me help with the dishes. I've a delicate hand with fine china, though you wouldn't think it."

And he held up his broad-knuckled fists, his black eyes gleaming at Jan.

"Now you must just let us girls do that woman's work," she replied, simpering at him. He grinned, enjoying her caricature, and she went on, "By the way, I find your accent perfectly fascinating. I can't quite identify it, though. Is it Texas, perhaps, or Kentucky?"

Disconcertingly, her adversary let out a shout of laughter.

"Early Gary Cooper, with a top layer of *Gone With the Wind.* Not very good, is it?"

"That depends on what you're aiming at," Jan said, rising. "Now you boys just go right on into the library and start your game. Goodness, I don't know how you do it; my l'il old brain would just bust if I tried to play such a complicated game."

This produced another whoop of mirth from Alan, and Uncle Henry, who had been glancing uneasily from one to the other, smiled too, reassured by the laughter.

"It took me over an hour to checkmate her the other night," he said. "She's just joking you, Alan."

"I thought she might be," said Alan, his wide mouth stretched to its limit.

In the sanctuary of the kitchen Jan thought for a moment that her aunt was going to hurl a delicate Wedgwood plate onto the floor.

"Goodness, that man wears me out," she said, her nostrils flaring. "He was worse than usual tonight. If I weren't a lady . . ."

"Maybe it's me," Jan said, with a certain guilty knowledge. "Aunt Cam, you go watch TV or something. I'll do this. Really, I'd like to. He makes me mad too, and I need to work to get rid of my aggravation."

Her aunt was not hard to persuade. This was one of her favorite nights for television, and since she had a tendency to drop off to sleep during the program, the reruns were often new to her. She wandered away, muttering in her soft voice, and Jan prepared the coffee tray.

She did not linger in the library. Both men seemed absorbed in the game and did not speak except to thank her. By the time she had finished washing the dishes and cleaning the kitchen and dining room, Camilla had gone peacefully to sleep under the soporific influence of *The Waltons.* Jan woke her and sent her upstairs, and then sat down to pursue her research.

Earlier, she had found a book with an old map of the town. Now she opened it and began to compare it with a modern map showing the buildings in the restored area. The old map had been made in 1782, and although the structures then existing were carefully indicated, none of them was identified, and it was difficult to decide which of them still survived. She was deeply engrossed, her head bent over the papers, when a movement behind her made her jump. Alan was leaning over the back of her chair, his dark, saturnine face heavily shadowed and his white teeth gleaming.

"Do you have to sneak up on people like that?" she demanded. "Where's Uncle Henry?"

Alan pulled out a chair and sat down.

"I did not sneak. You were absorbed in your reading. As for Henry, he's gone to bed. I usually let myself out. He trusts me with the silver and the bric-a-brac, odd as that may seem."

"I hope he beat you," Jan said.

"He did. This was his night."

"Oh, you take turns, do you?"

"He wins most of the time," Alan said equably. "But I can't let him beat me all the time or he'd get suspicious. I see you've joined the antiquarians. Up to your neck in the past, are you?"

Jan looked at him suspiciously and then realized that the remark was only a reference to her maps. She was getting paranoid. He couldn't possibly know about her secret absorption.

"It's quite fascinating," she said primly. "I hadn't realized how unique this place is."

"Oh, it's not unique. Unfortunately."

"I take it you don't approve of what the Foundation has done."

"Stop trying to sound like an old-maid schoolteacher," he said rudely. "You can't knock the Foundation's methods—not if you admire meticulous, picky scholarship. The question is not how they are doing it but whether it is worth doing. I don't believe in preserving an embalmed corpse, like Lenin in Red Square."

Jan couldn't help smiling. "It has been suggested, I believe, that that display is a wax effigy."

"That does not destroy the validity of my analogy," said her companion, imitating her prim voice.

"You're being unfair. Civilization consists of preserving things—the ideas, the art and culture of past ages."

"Like all beautiful theories, that has its limitations. We can't keep everything; there wouldn't be room for new ideas or new buildings. Antiquarianism can become an obsession that stifles creativity."

"You really enjoy arguing, don't you?" Jan said. "Just arguing, you don't care what it's about."

"Clever girl," Alan said approvingly. "What do you want to argue about?"

"I don't want to argue. Uh—can I get you something? Coffee?"

"No, thanks. Why don't you say what you mean, for once, instead of being polite?"

"Okay," Jan said, startled into honesty. "Okay, I will. I don't want to argue, or talk. I want to look at my maps. Why don't you leave?"

"Good, good. A few more lessons and you'll be as unpopular as I am. You have a natural aptitude for rudeness. I am sticking around because I want to say something."

"Say it," Jan snapped.

"It isn't easy," Alan complained. "I'm not in the habit of

retracting anything I say. But it did occur to me that perhaps I might have been unjust the other day, and that I owed you an inquiry, at the least."

"What made you question your omniscience?"

"Watching you, this evening. You got mad when I was baiting the old lady, didn't you?"

"It was cruel and unnecessary."

"Oh, no." Alan shook his unkempt black head. "She loves it. She couldn't stand it if I were nice and polite. Those characteristics are reserved for Southern gentlemen, and I, my dear, am neither. The kindest thing you can do for a hidebound old conservative like Camilla is to conform to their prejudices. They get all shook up if you act out of character."

"Well," said Jan sarcastically, "that's the most pompous, long-winded explanation of malice I've ever heard. So what difference does it make to you whether or not I resent your behavior toward my aunt?"

"I made an assumption about your motives on the basis of a single meeting," Alan said. "I saw, tonight, that your feelings toward your aunt and uncle contradict purely mercenary motives. So maybe I owe you an apology. I'm not sure yet that I do; but I'm willing to entertain the possibility."

"If you think I'm going to resolve your doubts you're mistaken." A horrid suspicion flashed into Jan's mind. "Damn!" she exclaimed. "Has Uncle Henry been gossiping? About my—private family matters?"

"Irrelevant, immaterial, and none of your business," her companion replied calmly.

"If that isn't my business I don't know what—"

"The subject is closed. What are you doing for amusement these days?"

Jan gaped. "Are you asking me for a date or something?"

"Or something. I know you're being rushed by the acceptable types, but if you get bored with soft music and antiques and spoon bread, I'm available for some livelier activity."

"Such as?"

"Oh, beer and chili dogs, the racetrack, roller coasters,

American-made films with no artistic merit whatsoever. You need some exercise," he added, eyeing her critically. "Do you like to swim? Play baseball?"

Jan had been wavering between amusement and outrage. The last question, gravely asked, tipped the scales and she began to laugh.

"Think you're smart, don't you? I happen to have been the star second baseperson of the Woodrow Wilson eighth-grade team."

"Saturday, then." He started to rise.

"Wait just a minute. Who am I going to be playing with?"

"Bunch of kids I know," Alan said. "It's just sandlot stuff, but it's good exercise."

"No! I can't Saturday, I have a date. . . ." Ordinarily Jan would have stopped at that; it was the truth, and it was a perfectly valid excuse. With disbelief she heard her own voice continue, "Besides, I don't want to socialize with a bunch of smart-aleck school kids. I've spent all year with them and it's not my idea of fun."

"Hmmm." His hand on the back of the chair, Alan stood looking down at her. She had expected rudeness or disagreement, but his expression was blandly enigmatic. "Okay, if that's the way you feel about it. What about Sunday? We'll do something equally vulgar."

"Oh, all right," Jan said crossly.

He could move quickly and quietly when he wanted to. She heard the front door close before she could formulate the next question; so she said it anyway.

"What do you mean, I need exercise?"

Looking back on the conversation, she knew how a hypnotist's subject feels after he has been awakened by a snap of the fingers. Why had she consented to spend time with a man she thoroughly disliked?

It was with considerable surprise that she realized she no longer disliked him—not as much as before, at any rate. He was a peculiar character, but she could see what Uncle

Henry had meant when he spoke of being able to relax with
Alan. There was something restful about being able to say
precisely what you felt, without fear of angering—or worse,
hurting—the other person.

Then her eyes went back to her map and she leaned forward, tracing with eager fingers the contours of a structure
that had crumbled into ash in a conflagration two centuries
before. She was still thinking about the eighteenth century,
not about Alan Miller, when she went up to bed.

Chapter
5

May 1776

CHARLES WAS COMING DOWN THE STAIRS WHEN JONA-than burst in the front door, his face flushed and his clothes looking, as usual, as if they had been put on in the dark by a one-armed man.

"Charles! The Convention is voting on the resolution. Hurry, man, they'll be announcing the results soon, down at the Capitol—"

Charles stopped in midstride, his eyes widening; but since the preceding episode he had added an inch to his height and an air of comical sophistication to his manner. Two hundred years later, his age group would refer to this quality as "cool."

"Just wait until I get my coat," he said, drawling.

"Coat! What d' ye need a coat for? They are about to read—"

"Jonathan," Charles interrupted, holding out his arms for the blue satin coat being held for him by a ubiquitous servant, "my dear boy, you really must not allow yourself to be carried away thus. No gentleman appears on the street without proper attire. . . ." Then he broke out laughing and shook his head at Jonathan, who was staring at him with his mouth ajar. "You're hopeless, Jon. Couldn't you at least button your waistcoat? And smooth your hair and tie your neckcloth, and—where is your coat?"

"I left it somewhere," Jonathan said vaguely. "Hurry, Charles."

The front door opened and the two young men stepped out onto the Duke of Gloucester Street—Williamsburg—1776.

It was early summer. Lilac and apple blossoms had bloomed and faded, but there were still pink-and-white stars on the dogwood trees, and clumps of azaleas formed masses of flame red and vivid pink. The new bright-green leaves hung motionless in the warm air. A haze of white dust hung over the road, which was filled with traffic. Gentlemen on prancing horses, draft horses pulling wagons and carts loaded with a bewildering variety of goods, from firewood to furniture; cows, ambling stupidly down the road and getting in the way of the chariots and carriages, whose drivers shouted furiously and with little effect; human pedestrians of both sexes, both races, and all sizes—each added to the dust and the noise.

For what was to be her penultimate moment of self-awareness, Jan thanked the impulse that had prompted her to spend time researching the appearance of the eighteenth-century town. Excitement gripped her as she recognized one structure after another. It was like the reconstruction, and yet different in many small ways.

The most noticeable difference was the view toward the west, where the three red brick buildings of the College of William and Mary could be seen, without the intervening obstacle of the modern shopping center. The Capitol, at the other end, was partially obscured by summer foliage. All in all, it was not too unlike the street she knew. But the living creatures who walked that street. . . .

A dignified black upper servant, his grizzled head erect, carrying a letter; a group of gentlemen, dazzling in emerald satin, gold brocade, and brown nankeen, their white wigs bobbing as they argued; three small urchins teasing a dog too lazy to move out of their path; a lady in a broad-brimmed straw hat tied under her chin with green velvet ribbons that matched her swaying skirts. . . .

And the animals. Chickens, swinging ragged tail feathers along the grass verge and scuttling, squawking, from under running feet; cats reclining on fence rails and watching the antics of the humans with cynical eyes; dogs running; hogs wallowing happily in the dust. . . . It was a scene of great color and animation—and smell, a rich blend of stenches the modern world has forgotten, even in the throes of a garbage strike. The smell of garbage was ripely redolent, but mixed with it were aromas of manure, open privies, and unwashed, overheated humans.

Word had spread, and half the population of Williamsburg seemed to be running toward the Capitol. There, in the sticky heat of May, members of the Fifth Virginia Convention were debating on the instructions they must send their delegates to the Continental Congress in Philadelphia. Patrick Henry, as usual, was in the thick of the extremist camp. The moderates, like Robert Carter Nicholas, still hoped to preserve the bonds with the mother country.

Jan knew all about this event. To the historians of Williamsburg, May 15 overshadowed the Fourth of July as the beginning of American independence. After all, the actions in Philadelphia that culminated in Jefferson's most famous literary work were the result of the decision taken in Williamsburg in May. Virginia was the first of the colonies to come out unequivocally for separation, the first to refer to the brawling colonies as united in purpose. Even though Jan knew what was going to happen in the red brick building at the end of the Duke of Gloucester Street, she was caught up in the excitement.

The Capitol surprised her; it was not the building tourists see, for the Foundation had chosen to rebuild the first Capitol, which had burned down in 1747. This later structure was like it in plan, a modified H-shape, but the distinctive rounded end walls of the first building had not been retained in the second. The red brick structure, with its gray-glazed headers, had a simple dignity. One feature was the same. As in modern colonial Williamsburg, the flag that flew on the staff over the octagonal cupola, with its four-faced clock, was the flag of England. The red, white, and blue stripes hung limp in the sultry spring air.

The brick-paved yard in front of the building was crowded with people. Unable to penetrate beyond the fringes of the crowd, Charles prodded one of the spectators and demanded, "What is going on? Have they voted?"

The man he had poked, a tall, very thin fellow in a shabby green waistcoat, turned around. At the sight of Charles his face lit up with a smile of singular charm.

"Wilde! Still pushing and shoving, I see. They are voting on the Pendleton resolution. It's the one Mr. Henry favors, he just spoke for it. Thunder and lightning, as always. . . ."

"Hello, Tucker," Charles said. "I didn't realize you were still in town."

"My dear boy!" St. George Tucker drew himself up to his full height and tried to look stately, but his grin destroyed the effect. "I've been admitted to practice before the General Court. I have a feeling it won't be for long, though; if matters go as we hope, today, I may find myself pursuing a more strenuous profession than law. I'm glad I was here to see this."

"It's a great day," Charles agreed. "But it will take forever for a hundred or more delegates to vote. Damn, this sun is broiling me. Come, Jon, let's try to get closer."

Jon grinned at Tucker, who nodded affably at him, and the two younger men pushed forward.

The crowd parted, with frank comments on their manners and morals; and one man, thrust unceremoniously aside, turned to deliver a particularly vulgar epithet. He saw Charles and Jonathan at the same moment they saw him. Charles muttered something rude and made as if to turn, but it was impossible; they were all pressed together by the surging movements of the crowd.

"Cousins!" the newcomer cried. "What a pleasure to see you here!"

"Hello, Henry," Jonathan said.

"Walforth." Charles's acknowledgment was barely civil.

Walforth appeared to be approximately the same age as the men he had addressed as "cousins." A verbal description would have made him seem to be much more like Charles in appearance than was actually the case. Almost six feet tall, lean and fair-haired, with regular features, he had gray eyes instead of green; but that was the smallest of the differences between the two. It was not so much a physical difference as one of demeanor; Walforth's eyes were habitually narrowed, and his smile looked like a sneer.

"I suppose it isn't surprising to find you here," Walforth said. "You are as hot for madness as the rest of these empty-headed fools."

"Better lower your voice," Charles said curtly. "These fools are in no mood for treasonable utterances, today of all days."

"Treason!" Walforth threw back his head and laughed. "I beg, Cousin, that you will oblige me with a definition of that word. I have a strange recollection of once hearing an oath of loyalty spoken by those same gentlemen who are now planning to break it. 'To our sovereign lord, King George the Third, by the grace of God—'"

He did not trouble to lower his voice, and one or two heads turned toward him.

"Be quiet, Henry," Jonathan said. "You needn't show off; we know how brave you are."

"Oh, let him talk," Charles said disgustedly. "Someone will knock him down presently, and I for one will be delighted to see it."

"No, no," Jonathan said earnestly. "Don't you see, Charles, if he is attacked I will have to defend him, since I don't believe in violence; and I might hurt someone."

Charles began to laugh, and Walforth flushed angrily.

"You've always hated me," he said, between his teeth. "The two of you together, two against one—"

"Stop hissing like a stage villain," Charles said, still chuckling.

"You see, Henry," Jonathan explained, "you were a very unpleasant child. A sneak, a bully—always picking on some-one smaller, girls especially. That's why we didn't like you. But it's not too late for you to change your ways; if you would only—"

Charles exploded again. Walforth, who had no defense against honest goodwill, let out an inarticulate snarl of fury and retreated, leaving crushed toes and aching ribs in his wake.

"Now what did I say?" Jonathan demanded in an ag-grieved voice. "I was only trying to help him."

Charles didn't answer. Having dismissed Walforth as the petty nuisance he was, he stood on tiptoe, straining to see what was happening. There was an eddy in the front section of the crowd; voices rose in unintelligible shouts, and the spectators on the fringes shifted impatiently. "What are they saying? What is it?"

Then the word came, tossed from mouth to mouth, through the crowd.

"Independence! It's unanimous!"

Charles, smiling broadly, exchanged glances with his companion; and Jonathan, reading his mind, said, "Unani-mous. Were you afraid your father would vote 'nay'?"

"It would be embarrassing to be the son of the only man who refused to follow the will of the people," Charles an-swered. He caught his companion's arm. "Look, Jonathan. Look!"

High above the heads of the crowd, over the cupola, the brave, bright flag was coming down. The crowd fell silent; and as the new flag rose and the wind flung its folds wide, a roar went up from the throats of the spectators.

The drama was so superb, and their collective mood so exalted, that few of the spectators noted a minor irony; for the red and white stripes representing the thirteen colonies were broken, in the upper left corner, by a miniature copy of the Union Jack which had just been ignominiously lowered.

"We need a new flag," Jonathan remarked, narrowing his eyes against the sun as he stared up.

"That's the Continental flag," Charles said. "Rather amusing, when you think that it was first flown by rebels besieging royal troops in Boston. Even then they hadn't faced the inevitability of independence. . . . Jon! It's actually happened. I can't believe it. Let's get away—go somewhere where we can talk. There is something I want to tell you."

The crowd was thinning, some returning home, others heading for the taverns to celebrate. Charles was about to turn away when Jonathan tugged at his arm.

"Here comes your father, Charles."

"Damnation," Charles muttered. "I suppose he will try to persuade me. . . . Hello, Father. My felicitations. This is a great day."

"I hope so," was the grave response. "I hope it is not the beginning of a tragedy . . . Where are you boys off to now?"

"The Raleigh, I suppose," Charles said; and, as his father frowned, he added, "After all, sir, we are no longer boys, though you may call us that."

Mr. Wilde was immaculately dressed; neither the heat of debate nor the warmth of the crowded chamber had wilted his snowy neckcloth or put one hair of his powdered wig out of place.

"Will you join us, sir?" Jonathan asked.

Mr. Wilde's stern face softened as he replied.

"Thank you, Jonathan, but I must go back. Someone must carry a copy of the resolution to Philadelphia; our delegates have been awaiting instructions too long as it is. The fireworks are over, but now the real work begins."

Father and son were of a height now. Their eyes met and locked, like the clasped hands of wrestlers striving for a fall. Mr. Wilde was the first to look away.

"I must go back," he repeated. "I expected to find you

here; I came to ask you to—not to do anything rash until we have had time to discuss it."

"We have discussed it, Father, many times. You promised me I might go this summer."

"Yes, but. . . . You will wait till I come home this evening?"

Charles shrugged angrily. "I certainly won't pack up and leave this minute."

Mr. Wilde turned away. The younger man watched his spare, erect figure until it disappeared.

"So you mean to enlist," Jonathan said.

Charles took his arm. They started walking.

"You know I've wanted to ever since Colonel Washington was made commander in chief. In God's name, Jonathan, that was almost a year ago. Father wouldn't let me join Morgan, or the second Virginia regiment, when they took Norfolk away from Dunmore—"

"Morgan and many of his men were captured in that disastrous loss at Quebec," Jonathan said gravely. "And Norfolk was retaken after all."

"Ah," Charles said. "That's because I wasn't there."

Jonathan grinned reluctantly.

"What will you do?" he asked. "Go north to join Colonel Washington, or south, to reinforce General Lee? What a pity you can't be in two places at once; we'd win in a month."

"Not with Lee," Charles said, acknowledging the sarcasm with a playful blow at Jonathan's head, which the latter ducked absentmindedly. "He was here for a month, you know. You missed such a lot, being gone all winter."

"I'm fortunate to have returned in time for this. But I had to go, Charles. We really thought Grandmother was dying this time, and you know what a termagant she is. No one can make her take her medicine or stay in bed except me."

"She'll live forever," Charles said cynically. "She's too mean to die, and she exploits you mercilessly. Now don't look at me with that gentle reproach, I'm not Henry Walforth."

"Tell me about General Lee," Jonathan said.

Charles laughed.

"Jon, he had the entire town by the ears. He looks no more like a general than I do—long and lank and indescribably dirty—and that pack of mangy hounds that follows everywhere he goes doesn't add to his dignity. His mouth is as foul as his person. You know what the Indians call him? Boiling Water. As always, they have a gift for the *mot juste*. He boiled and bubbled and spluttered—criticized everything and everybody in town. You should have heard my father. 'Frightful man; but what can one expect from the bastard of a British duke!' Of course he didn't say 'bastard,'" Charles added. "My mother was there, so he said, 'the er-um of a duke.' Our parents' generation is so hypocritical, Jon. I mean, the man is a bastard, in every sense of the word. Why not say so?"

"But you couldn't say 'bastard' in front of your mother," Jonathan said seriously.

Charles looked a little nonplussed.

"I suppose not. . . . Anyway, Charles Lee is supposed to be a good leader—British training and all that—but he doesn't appeal to me. No, I'll go to Washington. There's a man who looks like a general; six two in his stocking feet, and stately as a duke."

"He wasn't always so stately," Jonathan said with a grin. "You should hear Uncle Herman's tales about going to war with him."

"I can't keep your relatives straight," Charles said. "What sort of uncle is he?"

"Lutheran, of course; the Mennonites won't fight, remember?"

"Oh, yes. He's the one who was with Washington and General Braddock at Fort Duquesne. It seems like ancient history, doesn't it? Twenty years ago . . ."

"Well, it was before we were born. But I've heard Uncle Herman's stories often. He used to hold me spellbound when I was a child. At that age, you know, one is fascinated by fighting and such nonsense."

Charles's lips twitched at Jonathan's pompous tone, which was belied by the eager light in his eyes as he went on.

"If the British haven't learned any more flexible fighting methods since then, Charles, you ought to lick them in a week. They weren't used to enemies who hid behind trees and refused to march in a nice neat line, to be shot at. Even after the ambush began, Braddock tried to keep his men in parade-ground formation, in spite of Washington's protests. Then Braddock was hit, and Washington got him away in a cart. Almost all the other officers were killed. Washington had two horses shot out from under him, and his hat was shot off, and his coat riddled—but he was untouched. Uncle Herman said it made him think of the old stories his father used to tell about the *Hexen,* the witches back in Germany, and how they could put a spell on a man to protect him against bullets."

"Nobody believes in witches," Charles said. "But guardian angels. . . . Perhaps God meant to save him for this need."

"Then stick close to him," Jonathan advised gruffly. "Perhaps you can share the angels' shield."

"That smacks of heresy," Charles said, smiling. "But it's good advice. I only wish you—"

He broke off, his pride not allowing him to finish the appeal. But Jonathan understood it, and his eyes darkened as if with pain.

"It will be the first time we haven't stood back to back in a fight, Charles. But those other battles were with fists. I cannot bear arms. Not even for you."

They began walking again, Charles kicking at the dusty weeds as they went. It was his only expression of discontent, however. Smiling ruefully, he said, "I wish you were a Lutheran, like your Uncle Herman—and your neighbor, Mühlenberg. We heard of that sermon of his in Winchester."

"I was there," Jonathan said; and as Charles turned to look at him with surprised interest, he added mildly, "I am not such a bigot as to attend only my own services. I went with the Hellmuth cousins, who are Lutheran; the family is

as divided in sentiment as I am myself. . . . It was certainly
a stirring experience. The Lutheran congregations are fiery
Patriots, almost to a man, so the tinder was there, and Pastor
Mühlenberg's sermon applied the spark. He is a fine-looking
man, and he looked imposing in the pulpit in his flowing
black robes. He took his text from Ecclesiastes: 'To every
thing there is a season, and a time to every purpose under
heaven . . . a time of war and a time of peace. . . .' Then he
went on, 'In the language of Holy Writ there was a time for
all things—a time to pray and a time to preach—but those
times have passed away. There is a time to fight, and the
time to fight is here!' And with that he tore off his robe and
stood, high above the congregation, in the blue and buff of
a colonel's uniform. I almost enlisted myself, on the spot,"
Jonathan admitted, with a sheepish grin. "The congregation
sang 'A Mighty Fortress Is Our God,' then the men kissed
their wives and marched out to enlist—nearly two hundred
of them."

"With men like that we can't lose," Charles said. "Well,
Jon, if you can't fight, you can drink to victory. Here we—"

But Jonathan had stopped and was staring fixedly.

A small crowd had gathered in front of the Raleigh Tavern, with its signpost that bore the painted face of the first
colonizer of Virginia. It was an apathetic crowd; the sight
it watched was a common occurrence. Jonathan must have
seen it a dozen times before, and Charles's puzzled face
showed his surprise at this unusual reaction.

"They are Mr. Wharton's slaves," he said. "The estate
is being settled; the sale was announced in the *Gazette* last
week. . . . What is it, Jon?"

The scene lacked the drama and the air of tragedy com-
monly associated with such transactions. There were no
half-naked girls, shrinking from the leers of the purchasers;
nor were chains and whips anywhere in evidence. The slaves
numbered no more than half a dozen, two of them children.
They were all neatly, if plainly, dressed, and one of them
was talking cheerfully with a man in the crowd. The others

leaned at ease against the wooden railing to which horses were normally tied. The children played in the dust at the women's feet. One of them slapped the other; a wail of infant fury arose, and its mother upended the complainer and gave it a sharp smack on the bottom.

Charles took his friend's arm and shook it.

"Come on, Jon, what's wrong with you? You aren't thinking of buying—"

The look his friend gave him silenced him. Walking quickly, Jonathan pushed through the crowd and went through the gate into the courtyard of the tavern. The public bar was at the front, but it was frequented by the rowdier elements—although none of Mr. Southall's patrons could really be called rowdy. The Raleigh was one of the best taverns in town, and its clients were expected to behave themselves, drunk or sober.

Charles followed Jonathan to the back entrance that led directly into the public dining room.

It was already full of men, drinking and laughing and arguing at the top of their lungs. Charles managed to attract the attention of a hurrying waiter; the two young men, served with ale, pushed into a corner, where they stood in a relatively quiet spot. The tables, of course, were all occupied.

Charles shoved the sweating pewter tankard into his friend's hand and waited until he had taken a long swallow.

"That's better," he said, looking relieved. "Were you ill? I vow, you were quite pale for a moment."

"I must be mad, or moonstruck," Jonathan said bitterly. He tugged at his crumpled neckcloth, as if the white folds choked him. "Am I the only one to be moved by such contrasts?"

"Oh." Charles stared fixedly at his mug. "I see. That again."

"Yes, that again. How suits it with the glorious cause of liberty to keep your fellowmen in bondage? Our townsmen cheer themselves hoarse for freedom, and walk twenty paces down the street to watch men and women being sold like cattle. If that is your cause—"

Glancing apprehensively around the room, Charles covered his friend's mouth with a hard brown hand.

"In God's name, Jon, not so loud! Spirits are high today; and it's too hot for a suit of tar and feathers."

Jonathan wrenched his head away.

"—then I begin to think it cannot be my cause," he finished defiantly.

"Jon, please don't—"

"Lord Dunmore has offered freedom to any slave who will fight for the British—"

Again Charles's hand flashed out to cut off the words. This time he was not smiling. His eyes narrowed to green slits. Jonathan made no move to free himself. When Charles's hand dropped, the marks of his fingers stood out whitely on Jonathan's flushed cheeks.

"Let's go," Charles said curtly. "You're behaving like a fool, but I don't want to see you mobbed."

Jonathan followed him out. His face was set stubbornly. The auction was still in progress; Jonathan glanced at the crowd, his mouth tightening, and then lengthened his stride to catch up with Charles.

"You and your thoughtless tongue," Charles said, after they had walked a while in silence. "Will you never learn? Dunmore's proclamation outraged the colony; even the burning of Norfolk did not create such a storm of anger. If anyone thought you. . . . Jon. You weren't serious, were you?"

His lower lip protruding, Jonathan plodded on without answering.

"You can't mean it," Charles insisted. "I would respect your decision, if you supported the King; I would respect your honesty, at least if not your good sense. But to arm our slaves—why, man, that would start an insurrection—murder, looting—"

"A man who has a gun is no longer a slave," Jonathan muttered. He stopped walking, so suddenly that a respectable middle-aged lady carrying a basket ran into him and went staggering back. Charles caught the woman's arm and steadied her; she went on, with a smile for him, to which he responded with automatic charm, and a muttered reproach for Jonathan, who paid no attention.

"Charles," Jonathan said, "forgive me for speaking with such heat. At such a time—when you may be leaving any day. . . . I do have a cursed tongue and I don't seem to be getting any better at controlling it. But I hate slippery talk and implied half-truths. If I can't speak honestly with you, my best friend. . . ."

Charles's tight mouth relaxed.

"You old fool," he said affectionately. "All I want you to do is keep quiet in front of other people, who may not understand your peculiar notions as I do. Promise you'll keep yourself out of trouble while I'm gone."

"I'll miss you," Jonathan said simply. "And I'll worry, Charles."

"I'll be careful. Believe me, I take an even keener interest in my skin than you do. But you didn't promise, Jon."

"I won't fight," Jonathan said. "For either side. My sympathies are with you, you know that, but I can't. . . . I'll tell you what, though. If you decide to go north, to Washington, I may travel partway with you."

"Where and why?" Charles asked, still suspicious.

"Philadelphia. I have relatives there, you know. Grandmother has letters and parcels she wants carried there; one of the cousins is getting married next month, and there is some female fuss over a gewgaw or bit of lace."

"You have more cousins than anyone I know," Charles said, his good humor completely restored. "That would be splendid, Jon." His smile faded. "If I can only convince Father—and Mother, she's the real stumbling block. She'll never reconcile herself to what she considers disloyalty to the King. You must promise to support me. She dotes on you; tell her you're joining the army as my personal bodyguard."

He was still laughing at the idea when a carriage went by, and Jonathan jabbed him in the ribs.

"Make your bow, you boor. There's Mary Beth and her father."

"Try to look as if you were late for an appointment," Charles muttered. "Then they won't stop."

He swept his arm wide in an exaggerated bow. Mary Beth, simpering under a lacy parasol, waved, and Mr. Banister called a cheerful greeting, but the carriage did not stop, and Charles let out a breath of relief as they resumed walking.

"On her way to the milliner's, I suppose. She needs more than a new hat or a tippet to make her presentable."

"That's not a nice way to talk of your intended," Jonathan said, grinning.

The grin vanished when Charles said maliciously,

"She may be intended for me, but you're the one she simpers at, my lad. Don't tell me you haven't noticed."

"What a horrible thing to say," Jonathan gasped. "I never—she doesn't—"

"Oh, but she does. I'm something of an authority in these matters, you know."

"I do know. You're a heartless flirt, Charles. That little Burwell girl—"

"Women," said Charles, with an affected sigh. He flicked dust off his lace-trimmed cuff. "Oh, I shall marry the poor little creature; she won't like it any better than I do, but it must be done. But"—and he brightened visibly—"I can put it off for a few years. Thank God for wars! If they do nothing else, they keep the women away from us."

Chapter
6

Summer 1976

UNFORTUNATELY THE NEXT DAY WAS FRIDAY, WHEN Camilla insisted that the house should receive its weekly cleaning. Jan dusted and polished and swept with automatic efficiency, but her mind was not on the job. After lunch, when her aunt and uncle retired to their room to nap, she fled to her own room and closed the door with a long sigh of release.

During the morning she had carried upstairs all the books she could find in the library that pertained to her problem. Now she removed the bric-a-brac on the desk top and sat down with paper and pen before her.

She had told Camilla she was going to write a book. A ridiculous story but Camilla had accepted it delightedly. At least it would provide an explanation for a good many things that might otherwise be difficult—her increasing absentmindedness, for one thing. Everyone knew writers were impractical creatures who talked to themselves a lot.

Her hands shook with excitement as she took up the pen. Her first project was to write down everything she could remember about the dreams. Then she would see how much filling in was necessary.

When she read over the pages an hour later she was surprised at how much she could remember, and surprised, too, at the relative coherence of the narrative. Even if Camilla snooped among her papers she would find nothing to disprove the story Jan had told her; the page read like those of a novel. Nor was it difficult to fill in the gaps, although a number of minor points remained unsolved.

The first incident had taken place in 1774—May 23, to be exact. Apparently, Mr. Wilde was a burgess, who owned a town house in Williamsburg as well as the plantation called The Folly. Of the two boys who had shared his vigil that night, one was his son, Charles. . . . Her ancestor. Jan remembered the portrait in the library, with its pompous, kindly face, and a cold breeze of common sense shook the fabric of her fantasy. Could that splendid youth ever become the solid citizen of the portrait?

She dismissed this objection with an impatient shake of her head. Not only could such a thing happen, but it always did; it was the inevitable result of old age. The young, handsome revolutionary had become a complacent, fat old conservative.

It was the other boy who fascinated Jan, and she was frustrated to find how little she really knew about him. Like his friend Charles, he had been about sixteen in 1774. She had spent enough time with adolescents to be able to identify their ages without much error, although Jonathan was certainly a well-grown specimen, in his or any other era. But who was he?

Evidently both boys were students at the College of William and Mary in 1774. Jefferson's alma mater, eighty years old even then, it had an excellent reputation, and men sent their sons there from all over the colonies, rather than have them risk the long trip to England. The Wilde house in Williamsburg was kept open for the use of the heir while he was attending school. Otherwise the family would have spent its time in the country, on the estate, except for the periods when Mr. Wilde was attending the Assembly.

She had suspected from the first that Jonathan must be related to the Wildes somehow. Southern hospitality was proverbial and, in those early days when the population was sparse and the difficulty of travel enormous, it was something of a necessity. Yet the warmth with which the Wildes regarded Jonathan, and his constant comings and goings, suggested a relationship closer than friendship. Jan had deduced, however, that Jonathan's last name was not Wilde. The Wildes were conventional WASPs of their era, and in that era church and state were not separated. All officeholders had to belong to the Anglican church. Jonathan's unusual and, at that period, unorthodox religious beliefs must have come to him from his father's family. Women had no more control over their children's faith than they did over any other important question.

The Mennonites had been dissenters from the first; their founder was one of the enthusiasts spawned by the intellectual ferment of the Reformation. Luther had sowed the dragon's teeth when he nailed his theses onto the door at Wittenberg. Dozens of small dissenting sects had sprung up. The sons of the dragon turned on one another as soon as they could stand, persecuting each other as vigorously as they were persecuted by the established church. The Mennonites had emigrated quite early, many of them settling in Pennsylvania, since their faith had a great deal in common with that of the Quakers. Like the Quakers, who were still insisting on loyalty to the King as late as January of 1776, the Mennonites were pacifists and refused to bear arms for either side.

Some of the Pennsylvania Germans had left the colony in the early eighteenth century, following the western trails down into Virginia. Jonathan's ancestors might have been of that group. Presumably his absences from Williamsburg were spent at his family home in the west. Clearly, though, his affections and loyalties lay with the Wildes.

The most interesting facet of Jonathan's personality, of course, was his preoccupation with slavery. Jan had not realized how strong the abolitionist sentiment was before the Revolution. The Quakers were among the first to see the monstrous inconsistency Jonathan had mentioned, and Pennsylvania passed a limited emancipation law in 1780.

But Jonathan didn't know about that. In 1776 he was a typical adolescent, struggling to understand and assimilate the new ideas of a time of turmoil.

Jan gnawed on the end of her pen—an unsanitary habit her mother had often derided. So far she had seen her characters three times—once a year. The second episode had taken place in 1775, a year after the first. The boys had developed just as one would have expected them to—a little taller, more adult, but still responding with youthful enthusiasm to the talk of independence. Probably they were still attending classes at the College in 1775. Although Jonathan was more intellectually curious than his friend, neither seemed to be a compulsive student.

The 1775 episode had given more information about the family. The boy Martin, with whom Jonathan had wrestled, was a family slave—a house servant, who had grown up with Charles. They had played together as children. . . . Jan had located a reference to the school Jonathan had mentioned; it had been founded in 1760 by an English philanthropic group that had started several other Negro schools in the colonies. Indeed, Mr. Wilde would be considered a kindly master if he bothered to send a slave child to such a school.

That wasn't all Jan had learned from the 1775 episode. Mary Beth had made her first appearance, and Jan's theories about the girl had been confirmed in the latest dream. She was Charles's intended, a young lady of good family and apparently her rich father's only child. Obviously Charles was far from enthusiastic about the match, and only the fact that he had no strong preference for another girl kept him from rebelling. Mary Beth didn't look as if she had enough gumption to object to anything her father chose to do with her. Of course girls had no rights in those days. Marriages were still arranged by families, but the old customs were breaking down; occasionally, a man might choose his own bride, so long as the lady was of the proper social class.

Then, last night, the most recent chapter in the story.
The boys were no longer boys; eighteen or nineteen, each
was ready to assume a man's role, and Charles was about
to go to war. Anyhow, Jan thought, I don't have to worry
about Charles's getting killed. He lived to be seventy. I wonder how long Jonathan has to live. . . . Charles is right, he's
heading for trouble. Not his Loyalist sentiments—if he really has them, it isn't a political matter with him, his views
all hinge on one thing. It's an idée fixe—and dangerous. The
Virginians are paranoid about slave insurrections, they see
massacres everywhere. And no wonder. Half the population
is black, enslaved; the other half has good cause to fear the
people they oppress.

The really startling thing about the dreams was their consistency. Everything she discovered confirmed the accuracy
of the visions—the Negro school, the costumes, even the
shape of the pewter tankard from which Charles had drunk
his ale at the Raleigh. One of the books on colonial crafts
had a picture of a similar mug. The Continental flag—she
had seen that before she dreamed of it. It flew over the reconstructed Capitol every year between May 15 and July 4, to
commemorate Virginia's "Prelude to Independence." But she
was certain that many of the other details had not been known
to her before the dreams. Even her subconscious mind could
not have produced that quote from John Woolman. She had
heard of the famous Quaker reformer and theologian, but she
had never read any of his works.

When Camilla knocked at the door she sat up with a start.
Her neck ached from bending over her papers. Incredulously
she realized that the streaks of light were long and golden,
and that the clock said almost five.

"Come in," she called; and her aunt, with scrupulous
courtesy, eased the door open an inch and peered in before
she entered.

"I'm decent," Jan said, forcing a smile. How maddening it
was to be interrupted just when she was trying to get a little
ahead in the story, to find out what happened to Williams-

burg and the rebel cause in the years after the Declaration of Independence. Williamsburg hadn't known of that in May, of course. Jefferson was in Philadelphia, waiting for instructions from home. . . .

"Jan! My goodness, honey, that book of yours must be simply fascinatin'. I don't believe you heard a word I said."

"I'm sorry." Jan leaned back in her chair and stretched her stiffened muscles. "It is interesting, Aunt Cam. I'm going to interview you one of these days, about the family. I never realized how fascinating this period can be."

Her aunt looked pleased, but there was a doubtful tone in her voice when she answered.

"Honey, I think it's wonderful; and I'm so pleased to have such a smart niece. But you shouldn't get too wrapped up in this, you'll get a squint porin' over those thick books, and then what will your beaux say?"

"What beaux?"

"Well, one of them is comin' to pick you up in an hour," her aunt said calmly. "Shouldn't you get ready?"

"Oh, damn," Jan said. "Sorry—sorry, Aunt Cam, it just slipped out. I don't feel like going out tonight. Maybe I'll call Dr. Jordan—"

"Why, honey, you can't do that!" Camilla was genuinely shocked.

"I suppose not. It's too late."

"Don't you like Frank? I can't imagine why a pretty girl like you would rather sit up here readin' than spendin' the evening with a beau."

Jan set her teeth and managed not to swear. If her aunt said "beau" one more time. . . . But of course she would; apparently the archaic word had not died out among the older generation. Was her aunt looking at her rather too sharply? Did something show in her face, some betrayal of matters she would not, could not explain?

"Well, you know how it is," she said rapidly. "Writing is fascinating, Aunt Cam. you get all involved with your characters. But you're right, I ought to go out."

"When are you goin' to let me read it?" Camilla asked, eyeing the pile of papers respectfully.

Jan choked.

"Oh, it—it won't be ready for a long time. I wouldn't dare show it to anyone yet."

"I see." Camilla clearly did not see, but the mysteries of the writer's craft were so alien to her that she didn't question the statement. "Well, I'll just be dyin' to read it when you think it's ready, honey. I don't like to rush you, but—"

"Right. I'll shower and change." Jan wondered how long Camilla thought it would take her to get ready for a date. In her aunt's day, perhaps it had been a full eight hours' work. "Let me get you and Uncle Henry something to eat first."

"Oh, no, honey, we'll just finish up that nice chicken from last night. You run along and don't worry about us."

When the door closed Jan cast a longing look at her books. But the clock informed her that time was running short. If she got engrossed again she might not come out of her trance until Frank Jordan was knocking at the door; and then Camilla really would be shocked.

A cool shower washed the cobwebs from her mind, and with grim determination she decided to behave like a nice proper date. It wasn't poor Dr. Jordan's fault that he interested her less than a big, confused boy who had died—if he had ever lived—almost two hundred years ago. She would dress up in her best and behave like a lady if it killed her.

Prodded by Camilla, she had bought a new dress. Since Camilla had supplied the money—a not inconsiderable sum—and the impetus, Jan chose the sort of dress she thought her aunt would like, and Camilla's delight proved her judgment to be correct. It was longer than any dress Jan had worn for years, and the style was one she did not consider suitable for her slight, rather boyish figure. But when she had slipped the dress on and zipped the long zipper that ran up the back, the image in her mirror really surprised her.

The soft, clinging voile gave her figure curves it didn't ordinarily possess. The dress had full elbow sleeves, with ruffles; more ruffles added an illusion of inches to the bust, and the long scooped neck, trimmed with lace, showed off the fashionable delicacy of her collarbones and throat. It was a frankly romantic dress, and after a moment of amazed contemplation Jan sat down and tried to invent a coiffure that would go with the image. Her hair was long and straight and dull brown, but when she tied the side locks on top of her head with a black velvet ribbon, letting the remainder fall loose on her shoulders, the results were becoming, if unfamiliar.

"I look about sixteen," Jan said aloud, studying the girl in the mirror with contempt. "Oh, well. Aunt Cam will probably love it."

Deciding she might as well go all the way, she selected a pair of dainty white slippers her mother had picked out for her. They had low heels, and Dr. Jordan was not much taller than her own five feet six inches.

Feeling foolish, she lingered in her room, buffing her nails and applying makeup to increase the ingenue look. Her dark eyes looked wider and rounder when she finished; and Jan contorted her pink mouth into a horrible grimace at the face that looked at her from the mirror. Then she heard the doorbell. Picking up her purse and a crocheted "shrug"—another of her mother's contributions—she minced down the stairs.

Her entrance was effective. Frank Jordan stood up with alacrity, and Jan realized that he was surprised as well as pleased. Had she really looked that bad before?

"Honey, how pretty you look," Camilla cried, clasping her hands.

"Pretty as a rosebud," Uncle Henry contributed.

"That doesn't leave me much to say," Frank remarked, with a smile. "Except that I second the sentiments. Is that a new dress, Jan? I had thought you might like to take in a movie after dinner, but we can't hide that dress in a dark theater. How about dancing?"

"Oh," Jan said. "I don't know—"

"Unless you don't like to dance."

"I do," Jan said, resigning herself to the obvious fact that she was not going to be returned home in an hour or two. She would have to spend the evening with this man, and maybe dancing wouldn't take as much time as the movie and the usual drink or snack afterward. She smiled brightly. "I love to dance."

"Just don't keep her up too late, Frank." Camilla said.

Frank's eyes twinkled as he looked at Jan, but he answered solemnly, "Don't worry, Mrs. Wilde. I'll take very good care of her."

He let himself go as soon as they were outside. Jan liked the way laughter lightened his face, but she was too irked to join in his amusement.

"Honestly, she treats me as if I were sixteen!"

"You look about sixteen in that dress," Frank said, with an approving glance.

"That's what I was afraid of."

"It couldn't be more becoming." Frank was obviously pleased at the fact that he could look down at her. "She's a wonderful old lady, Jan; I'm not a bit put out by her."

"That's nice of you."

He did not hear the slight edge of sarcasm in her voice.

"She and your uncle are antiques, like the town," he went on. "Well worth preserving. When they go, an era will have passed. Enjoy them while they last."

"Oh, yes," said Jan. She was wondering if a headache was too banal an excuse to offer for cutting the evening short. With a doctor it was probably unsafe to use illness.

They walked to the King's Arms, since it was just down the street. The restaurant was crowded, but Frank had made a reservation.

"Too many tourists," he remarked, as they followed the waiter up the stairs. "Still the food is good, and I thought you'd enjoy seeing the place."

"It's charming," Jan said. "They've arranged it nicely, haven't they? All these small rooms; one doesn't have the feeling of being crowded."

"Well, I have enough pull to get one of the better tables," Frank said, with a complacent glance around the paneled room with its corner fireplace. "The only disadvantage is that they have no license for spirits. What about a champagne cocktail? I don't know whether I dare offer you that; they may ask for your identification."

Jan gave him a stiff smile and took the menu proffered by the waiter, who was wearing the inevitable knee breeches and waistcoat and white stockings.

During dinner, however, she found Frank an entertaining and considerate escort. He was rather pompous, but perhaps a doctor couldn't help being that way; so many people treated him like an oracle. He talked a little too much, but he was an interesting conversationalist.

She went through the rest of the evening without faltering, although by the time they left the country club where Frank took her to dance, she did have a headache. She admitted as much on the drive home, and Frank was concerned.

"I shouldn't have persuaded you to have that second drink," he said. "I expect you aren't used to it."

"Well, now," Jan said. "I wouldn't exactly say. . . ."

"I'll know better next time. No, dear, thank you, I won't come in; you go straight to bed and take a couple of aspirin."

And call me in the morning, Jan thought.

Frank gave her a pleasant but unremarkable good-night kiss and watched her open the door before he turned away.

Jan didn't take the aspirin, or brush her teeth, or do any of the proper things. She fell into bed as she would have flung herself into the arms of a lover.

II

The room was gray with first light when she awoke, shaken out of sleep by the dawn chorus of the birds. For a moment she lay unmoving. Then a wave of actual physical sickness washed over her. She had not dreamed.

III

If she had been reluctant to keep her date the previous night, the realization that she had agreed to spend the entire day with another "beau" almost drove Jan to distraction. After the sickening disappointment of the night before she was in no mood to be charming to another man. She wanted to huddle in her bed and try to sleep again.

What had gone wrong? Three nights in a row, and then nothing. She was so involved that to miss a single night was a blow; but the fear that it might be more than one night, that the uncanny phenomenon might have ended altogether was a frightful possibility.

She thought seriously of claiming to be ill and spending the day in bed. But she knew that would be a mistake. Camilla would insist on calling Frank. He would come, too. He was probably as averse to house calls as any other doctor, but she was not exactly an ordinary patient. He would poke and prod and take her temperature—of which she had none—and ask stupid questions. . . . Jan writhed. No, that would be worse than going through with the date. After all, she liked Richard. He wasn't a bore, like poor Frank.

The day turned out to be quite pleasant after all. Richard's very presence was soothing.

Uncle Henry obviously liked him, in spite of his disparaging remarks. Richard sat and argued politics with him while Jan packed the picnic basket with her share of the feast. When they stood in the hall, ready to leave, Camilla looked at them doubtfully.

"Richard, do you think Jamestown . . . ? You'll be eaten alive by mosquitoes, and that dress of Jan's . . ."

"It's not a dress, Aunt Cam, it's shorts," Jan said.

"Don't underestimate me, Miss Camilla," Richard said. "I've got some vile-smelling lotion that is positively guaranteed to repel mosquitoes."

"Have a good time," Uncle Henry said. "For goodness'

sakes, Camilla, do you think they care about things like mosquitoes? I wouldn't have, at their age."

The ointment proved effective, and it was certainly needed. As they sat on the grass looking out over the blue water of the James River, Jan was very conscious of the sticky air. It felt like thick cream on her skin. The town site was low, lying only a few feet above the river and the swampland that surrounded it all around. She wondered how the early colonists had endured the unaccustomed heat and the deadly insects.

"They didn't, of course," Richard said, when she expressed the thought aloud. "It's a rotten site, a breeding around for malaria. Two-thirds of the colonists died in the first eight months. And the Indian massacre of 1622 finished off more of them."

"It's beautiful, though," Jan said, gazing out at the tranquil waters, hazed by heat, and the shady greensward, with the low mounds that were the foundations of the first settlement. "Mosquitoes and all."

"It was nicer before they built that stupid Information Center and all the other tourist rot. Even so, it's not usually too crowded; most people prefer Jamestown Park, down the road, where they have replicas of the ships, and souvenir stands, and such other necessities of life. I guess I come here," Richard said musingly, "because those first settlers fascinate me. Imagine the courage it required to set off on that voyage—giving up home and family and all the familiar comfortable things, knowing you'd probably never see them again. The trip took months, and even for the wealthy it was hideously uncomfortable—crowded, unsanitary, dangerous. If the storms didn't get you, the pirates might. And then when they finally did arrive, after weeks of sickness and hunger—this hot swampy wilderness filled with hostile natives. How they had the guts to do it. . . ."

"Not many did, I guess," Jan said, scratching. The lotion's stickiness was almost as irritating as a mosquito bite.

"I couldn't do it," Richard said. He sat up, wrapping his

arms around his bent knees and stared moodily out across the water. "I'm a coward."

"If that's cowardice, then I suffer from it too," Jan said, after a moment. It was obvious that he was sensitive about the subject; she had to choose her words with care. "You said it the other day, Richard; there is a rationale. Keeping an island of sanity alive. . . ."

"Rationale or rationalization? It's easy to find excuses for what you want to do."

"It's the way the world rejects beauty that bothers me most," Jan said thoughtfully. "I teach English. So much wisdom and loveliness—and what do they say in response? 'Shakespeare, what a drag! Keats, who was that cat? Shelley, some kind of queer, man, you know?' And instead, they cultivate ugliness. Ugly faces, distorted with hate. Ugly minds, with vocabularies of two hundred words, half of them obscene. . . . No, thanks. Where do I sign up for that monastery? Or don't you admit women?"

Richard turned his head to look at her. His thin face wrinkled with laughter, and with another emotion that made Jan's heart beat a little faster.

"Jan, you're what the doctor ordered. Thanks. I've had my moment of self-pity, that's all I allow myself each day. How about a swim? Has it been half an hour since we ate?"

They swam in a little cove near a house owned by some of Richard's friends, but spent most of the time lying on the beach, sometimes talking, sometimes comfortably silent. Jan felt her tense nerves relaxing. She was half asleep when Richard said reluctantly,

"I'm sorry, but I have to play at a concert tonight. The harpsichordist got too much sun yesterday; he says he can't sit down. Don't know where he was sunbathing, to get burned in that particular spot. . . ."

Laughing, Jan got up. The sun had dried her suit; she put on her shorts and shirt.

"How about coming to hear us?" Richard asked. "We could go out someplace afterward."

"Thanks, but I'm dopey with sun. Anyhow, I have to get supper for the relatives tonight; I abandoned them to left-overs last night and I can't do it twice."

"Ah, yes," Richard said, as they linked arms and walked toward the car. "How was Dr. Jordan? Don't look so sur-prised; you have to get used to the fact that everything you do is known to everyone in town before it happens. Anyhow, I like to keep tabs on my rivals."

"Poor Frank," Jan said, with a smile. "He's a nice guy, but—"

"Not a rival? That's a relief."

They were driving along Jamestown Road, past the col-lege, when Richard suddenly jammed on the brakes. His out-flung arm caught Jan as she fell forward. Still holding her, he put his head out the window and swore imaginatively.

"What the hell is wrong with you, Miller? Getting blind in your old age, or are you trying to drum up business?"

"Couldn't sue. Too many witnesses," the other man said calmly. "Jan?"

He came around to her side of the car. Jan slid down in the seat, folded her arms and scowled.

"I'll pick you up at noon," Alan said. "Wear something old."

"Wait a minute." Jan straightened. "I've changed my mind, I'm not going to—"

But he was walking away, his wrinkled coat slung over his shoulder, his big ears sticking out like flags.

"Oh, damn," Jan said. "Damn, damn, damn!"

"You have a date with him tomorrow?" Richard started the car. "Sorry; none of my business."

"It's no big secret," Jan said grumpily. "I don't know how he conned me into it. I don't want to go." She looked at Rich-ard's neatly cut profile and added, "He's no rival either."

"All those 'damns' made that fairly evident," Richard said, but he sounded relieved.

He walked her to her door, carrying the picnic basket, and kissed her quickly, mindful of the staring tourists. Jan went straight to the shower. Sand, ointments, and perspiration made her feel as if she were ready for the feathers outraged Patriots had used on their Loyalist neighbors. Wearily, for she was drugged with heat and sun, she prepared an excellent meal and watched her uncle eat it. She pleaded fatigue when Camilla fussed about her lack of appetite, and announced her intention of going to bed early.

"You sure you won't watch some television with us?" her uncle asked wistfully. "Not much fun for you, I guess."

"It's not that, I really am tired. I'm going to read awhile and then go to sleep. I'll be home tomorrow night," she added, feeling guilty. "How about some chess then? I'll beat you this time."

"You sure?" Henry asked, his eyes brightening. "I don't want you to put off any fun on my account."

"I will definitely be home tomorrow night," Jan said, and meant it. She knew Mr. Alan Miller would take her out next day even if she claimed to be dying, but she had no intention of spending both the afternoon and the evening with him.

Her room was beginning to feel like a sanctuary, a quiet cell in that monastery Richard spoke of; when she closed the door her fatigue dropped away and she went eagerly to the desk with its pile of books. She didn't know what had gone wrong the night before, but she could not face the possibility that the dreams were finished. Perhaps they were wholly random; but there was a chance that they had been brought on by some as yet unknown stimulus, something she had omitted the day before. She had been so anxious to get to bed after her date with Frank Jordan that she hadn't done any research. Perhaps reading about the events she hoped to see would help get her mind in the proper receptive state. Charles was going north to join Washington. What would happen to him in the following months?

Some of the story was vaguely familiar to her, but now she read the dry pages eagerly, visualizing people she knew involved in the battles which had once only been questions on boring exams. Charles had not chosen a propitious moment to join the ragged American forces; but then there never would be a good time, only disheartening losses year after year, until the turning point at Yorktown, in 1781. The Continental army never had enough supplies, or men, or money. Many of the soldiers went for years without pay. Really, Jan thought, it's a wonder we won the war.

If Charles joined Washington immediately he would be just in time for the Battle of Long Island in August—a British victory that was followed by the occupation of New York city. Washington retreated across New Jersey into Pennsylvania, his forces thinned by desertion, with the British in hot pursuit. The victory at Trenton, at the tag end of the year, was one she remembered from the history books and the famous painting—Washington idiotically erect in the prow of the overloaded boat, which would have capsized into the icy waters of the Delaware if he had stood up in it. That success had heartened the Continentals; but in the spring of the following year the American loss at Brandywine opened the way to Philadelphia. Congress had already moved out of the capital, pessimistically anticipating the defeat, but the loss was discouraging.

Jan wondered whether Jonathan had been in Philadelphia. It was maddening not to be able to find out anything specific about his background or his plans; but Jan felt sure she could predict what he was going to do. His decision to go to Philadelphia had been sudden, and his excuse specious; it had to be connected with the apocalyptic moment when he had seen the sale of slaves carried on, for the first time, under the new flag of freedom. Philadelphia was the Quaker City, and the Quakers were leaders in the emancipation movement; the connection seemed to Jan to shout aloud. Some of Jonathan's numerous cousins might be Quakers, or might have friends among the antislavery groups, led by such people as Woolman and Anthony Benezet, and Ben Franklin. As Jonathan had pointed out, the Mennonites were among the first to protest slavery and the slave trade. It would not be surprising to find some of them involved in the antislavery movement.

The strength of that movement, as early as 1776, was unexpected. There were even hints that the Underground Railroad, whereby slaves were transported secretly out of the slave states, began at that time. George Washington mentioned the escape of a slave from Alexandria to Philadelphia, "whom a society of Quakers, formed for such purposes, have attempted to liberate." That was in 1786; such a society might have had its beginnings ten years earlier; and although there were no free states to which a slave might escape in 1776, he had a chance of passing as a freedman in the North.

She was still reading when she heard the footsteps approach her door. It must be ten o'clock—the usual bedtime of her aunt and uncle. Suddenly her heart began to pound.

Camilla saw the strip of light under her door. She knocked softly.

"Jan? You still awake, honey?"

"I'm just going to finish this chapter," Jan called. "Good night."

The footsteps went on. When Jan heard the door close she went across the hall to the bathroom that had been assigned to her use.

She made herself take time with her nightly preparations. Suntan lotion hadn't helped her nose; it was considerably redder than the rest of her face, but she had gotten enough sun to look flushed, almost feverish. She could see the pulse beating in her throat.

I can't go to sleep, Jan thought. I'm too excited. What is the matter with me? I've got to calm down.

But she knew she couldn't. Anticipation and anxiety would keep her sleepless.

Then, with a gasp of relief, she remembered the plastic bottle on the top shelf of the medicine chest—the sleeping pills her New York doctor had prescribed. She had not taken them since she got to Williamsburg, but tonight of all nights they were a necessity.

She hesitated for a moment after the little white pill was in her hand. What if the drug affected her ability to dream?

Then, with a shrug, she swallowed it. Better to take that chance than go without sleeping.

Tired as she was, emotionally and physically, the pill took effect faster than she dared hope. She was swaying when she turned out the light, and sleep—or unconsciousness—overcame her almost as soon as her head touched the pillow.

Chapter

7

Autumn 1777

THE HOMECOMING WAS INCOHERENT, TEARFUL, CHARGED with emotion, just as it would have been at any time in history. A Roman family might have welcomed a soldier son, miraculously preserved, with the same embraces and tears of joy. Even Mr. Wilde's reserve broke down and he hugged his tall son.

After the first outburst was over, Charles put his arm around his weeping mother and led her into the parlor. He seated her in her favorite chair by the fire; but when he tried to turn away she caught at him with both hands. Smiling, he dropped onto a footstool, close enough that she could reach out and touch him whenever she wished.

The change in him was rather frightening. It was not unbecoming; the slender, handsome boy had become a bronzed fighting man, all lean bone and muscle. Under its fading tan his face was too thin; his green eyes were hard and wary even when he smiled. His uniform had been patched and brushed, but it had seen hard wear. As he pulled his knees up, his coat fell back; and his mother, with a little cry, indicated the stain on his once-white breeches. Someone had tried to launder it, in an ineffectual fashion, and the tear had been clumsily mended.

"Oh, my darling boy, you didn't say—"

Charles laughed and took her hand in his.

"No, Mother, what was the point of telling you when there was no danger? I was fortunate; it's healing nicely. And you can thank that little scratch for my presence. Do you suppose General Washington allows a soldier to take leave whenever the notion strikes him?"

"Too many of them are doing precisely that, or so we hear," Mr. Wilde said.

Charles's head turned, in a quick warning movement, and his father fell silent.

"Tales like that are wild exaggerations," Charles said cheerfully. "Why, things are going well; one more victory like Saratoga and we'll have them howling for peace."

"You aren't going back?" his mother asked. "Surely now, when you are wounded—"

"Well, not at once," Charles said gently. "Not before I've eaten steadily for a week. Supplies have not been precisely forthcoming of late, and I am thoroughly sick of bread and salt pork."

"And I sit here crying while you are starving," his mother exclaimed. "My poor boy, I'll go and hurry Cook. We have all your favorite dishes, I began preparing them as soon as we got your letter. In the meantime, have some wine and a few cakes, just to stay your stomach until dinner. I shall send one of the maids in with a tray at once. . . ."

She went bustling out, her long skirts swaying, paying no attention to Charles's laughing protests. When the door had closed after her, Mr. Wilde said,

"Let her do it, Charles. Nothing could give her greater pleasure. It was a cruel thing you did to her."

"I didn't do it to hurt her." Charles leaned against the chair, stretching his long legs, and wincing a little as he did so. His father saw the expression.

"We'll have Dr. Pasteur," he said. "I'll send for him at once."

"There's no need, it was just a scratch. Father, I have only a few days. I couldn't tell her, not now. . . ."

"Charles!" It was a cry of pain and protest. Charles's lips tightened but his face remained obdurate. After a moment Mr. Wilde mastered his distress.

"I can't command you," he said. "But I had hoped to convince you. You are the only son, Charles. You have done your duty; can't you leave the fighting to others now, to men who have not your obligations? You haven't even married, so that you might leave a son to carry on the name. . . ."

"And I won't," Charles interrupted. "I know the arrangement with Mary Beth means a good deal to you and Mr. Banister, and I'll honor it—after the war. It's not death I fear, Father. I won't risk burdening any woman with a husband who is less than a man—maimed, blinded, lacking a limb."

"But the family name—"

"I sometimes think the name means more to you than I do."

The words held a bitterness Charles had never expressed. For a moment the two men stared at one another, appalled at the outburst of naked emotion.

"I'm sorry, Father," Charles said finally. "I don't know what made me say that. . . . But the fact remains, I must return. I can't say any of this in front of Mother, there's no need to distress her; but the General needs every man. I know, everyone is a cock-a-whoop over Saratoga; admittedly it was a great victory, but the war is a long way from won. Gates should have insisted on unconditional surrender; the damn fool is getting all the credit for the victory, but it was Morgan and Benedict Arnold who won the battles—"

"Morgan?" His father's lips curled. "That illiterate, brawling backwoodsman with his scarred face?"

"The scar was not acquired in a brawl," Charles said. "It was an Indian who shot out half his teeth and left his face. . . . Well, admittedly he's not a beauty, and his back looks even worse than his face. Five hundred lashes—"

"Standard punishment for insubordination," his father reminded him. "I've no doubt the man deserved it. He would not adjust well to British military discipline."

"He's fighting against the British now," Charles said. "And I'll wager his scars make him fight harder. He's a first rate leader, Father. I'd be honored to serve under him."

"If you must serve, I hope you will remain with Washington. He is at least a gentleman. What are his plans?"

"I'm not sure he has any definite plan," Charles said grimly. "We've lost New York and Philadelphia; the British are settled there for the winter, snug as a bug, and where the hell we'll be I hate to think. We can't winter in York or Lancaster in comfort without exposing both towns and a large section of fertile country to British attack. The army is in wretched shape, Father. The damn militia heads for home after every battle, and the damn Congress can't seem to get supplies to us, not even food. I can't sit here on my backside while my men are going hungry. I wouldn't have come at all, except that someone was needed to carry dispatches."

There was a long, unpleasant silence.

"Has it occurred to you," Mr. Wilde said finally, "that if you survive the war, and we lose, you will be subject to imprisonment, perhaps execution, for treason?"

"It has occurred to me," Charles said briefly.

"And nothing I can say will change your mind?"

"I'm sorry, Father, let's forget it, for a few days. Let me enjoy being home, while I'm here. I suppose you have notified my affianced bride of my arrival?"

"Naturally. She and her father will be dining."

"Good. She's a nice child," Charles said, trying to lighten the atmosphere. "I really am fond of her, you know, Father. And where's our old Puritan? I thought he'd be here to welcome me with one of those bone-crushing handshakes of his. There's a thought, Father; perhaps you can persuade Jon to cripple me a little, just enough to keep me home."

It was not a very good attempt at humor, and Mr. Wilde didn't even pretend to smile.

"I'm surprised Jonathan is not here. I sent word to him earlier, when the boys reported seeing you on the road."

"Oh, you had relays out, did you?" Charles grinned. "But what do you mean, sent word? Isn't Jon here?"

"He is in Williamsburg. But he is not living here. He has a room at some squalid tavern down by the river."

"Why, for God's sake?"

"He has a new position," Mr. Wilde said. "As an agent for a Philadelphia firm of merchants. Apparently it involves a great deal of traveling, and a schedule which is subject to change; he was unwilling, he said, to put your mother to the inconvenience of housing him. And of course we are not in town a great deal. We came from The Folly only this week, in answer to your message."

"Hmm." Charles looked concerned. "I suppose the old fellow feels awkward these days. I can understand why he took a position, Father; he felt the need of appearing active, at some useful occupation, since his principles won't let him serve as the rest of us are doing."

The door burst open and Jonathan stood on the threshold.

Charles got up with a whoop of welcome. They clasped hands and stood grinning speechlessly at each other. Then Charles freed his hand and rubbed the fingers tenderly.

"You haven't changed, Jon—except I think you've grown. How much larger do you expect to get?"

"I can't say the same for you." Jonathan shoved him unceremoniously into the nearest chair. "You're as narrow as a fence rail, Charles. Sit down and spare yourself. Don't they feed you in the army?"

"Not much. God, it's good to see you. What's this I hear about your deserting the family roof?"

"Oh, I'm a man of business now. In and out at all hours. Let's not talk about my dull life; tell us of battles and feats of daring, and your heroism."

In this at least he had not changed; subterfuge never came easily to him, and his constrained tone indicated to at least one listener that he was holding something back. Physically he had altered in ways that were not obvious to a casual eye, but eyes of affection would have noted the new lines on a face too young for such signs of care, and the way his eyelids drooped with weariness, or with a desire to veil the look that had once been as candid as a child's.

"Are you sure you have time?" Charles asked considerately. "The tales of my heroism are of epic proportions; a simple outline may require the rest of the day, without the embellishments such deeds demand."

Jonathan beamed at him.

"Never mind your heroism, tell us about Colonel Washington."

"General, you dolt; he's the commander in chief, you know." Charles's face sobered. "Remember, Jon, the day you told me your Uncle Herman's stories of Fort Duquesne, and how the bullets left Washington unscathed? I agree with your uncle, I could almost believe in witches myself now. The same thing happened at Princeton. It was just a skirmish, not much of a battle; but we needed that victory after the disastrous retreat from New York. The militia is our weak point, Jon. They break and run the minute they see the British advance. Princeton was no different. One volley and the Pennsylvanians took to their heels. Washington rode right into them; you could hear him all over the field, above the shouts and groans and screams and gunfire, calling them 'brave boys' and telling them to stand fast. And, by God, he rallied them and led them straight at the British, waving them on with his hat. He moved so fast none of the officers could catch up with him, and he was smack in between the lines when the British cut loose with a volley, and our men answered it.

"I tell you, my heart stopped. You couldn't see anything for a few minutes, the smoke was so thick; I thought sure we'd find him down, dying, maybe dead. But when I went dashing into the melee there he was, straight as a ramrod as always, squinting into the smoke trying to see what was going on. He turned coolly to me and said, 'Ah, there you are, Lieutenant. Please be so good as to order a troop of the Philadelphia Light Horse over the bridge after them. They are in retreat.' I lost him again after that; it seems he went galloping off after the Pennsylvania cavalry, shouting something about fox hunts."

Jon listened with his hands clenched and his eyes glowing. It was one of the times when an observer could see how difficult it was for him to stick to his pacifist principles. He sighed unconsciously when Charles had finished.

"But it wasn't your first victory," he said. "There was Trenton, too. You were with the General that night, weren't you?"

"Don't even mention it," Charles said, with a reminiscent shudder. "I have never been so cold in my life. It was the worst blizzard of the year. That's how we succeeded, actually; we were behind schedule and dawn broke long before we reached Trenton. But the Hessians never dreamed anyone would be insane enough to cross an icy river and walk eight miles in stinging sleet. They didn't even send out their usual predawn patrols. It was Christmas, too, and half their men were drunk. I still don't know how the hell we did it, though. The men had to tie rags around the firing pans of their muskets to keep the powder dry. Then, after the town was taken, we had to walk back!"

Mr. Wilde had been silent as he glanced from one grinning young face to the other. Now he said sharply,

"Two minor skirmishes won, and a dozen battles lost. . . . Is that Washington's triumph?"

"He is doing an incredible job, with incredibly poor material," Charles said. "None of our men have had professional training, like the—"

"Charles." Mr. Wilde raised his hand warningly as the parlor door opened. Charles turned. When he saw the girl who stood in the doorway he froze, in the act of rising, his hands pressed against the arms of the chair, his eyes wide.

The pale ivory of her skin was perfection. Under the soft

skin of youth superb bone structure gave character to her face. Thick, dark hair waved on her shoulders, in defiance of custom. It was pathetically clear that she had taken all possible means to make herself beautiful; the neat apron had been tied tightly to show off her narrow waist, and the white collar was cunningly arranged to show the shape of her breasts. She was a tiny thing, but so beautifully shaped that she looked taller.

Slowly, staring, Charles got to his feet. The spark that leaped between them and held them locked like an invisible cord was compounded, in his case, of a predictable male response to such miniature loveliness. But there was something of awe in his look as well. The others had seen the gradual change from child to woman. He saw only the astonishing result.

She had had more time to prepare herself, and she had learned to control her emotions in the strictest of all schools. The heavy tray she carried tilted a little; but when she spoke the words were conventional, rehearsed.

"Welcome home, Mr. Charles. It's good to see you safe."

"Leah?" Charles said. He started toward her.

For once Jonathan was ahead of him. He took the tray from the small shaking hands and put it down on a table.

"You've turned the whole household topsy-turvy, Charles," he said good-naturedly. "The front door was standing wide open when I arrived, and here's Leah ready to faint, or cry, or whatever women do to express their emotions. Run along, child, and tell everyone in the kitchen that Mr. Charles is alive, and tougher than ever."

The girl obeyed, her eyes lowered. Charles started to sit down. Realizing that the chair was no longer behind him, he shook his head dazedly and located it with his hand, as if his eyesight had failed.

"I can't believe it," he said. "She's grown up. She—she is beautiful."

"Unfortunately," Mr. Wilde said. He was frowning as he went on. "We've already had one experience that. . . . I must see to finding a husband for the girl. Ordinarily I don't allow the slaves to marry, but in Leah's case—"

"Marry," Charles repeated stupidly. Then he seemed to wake up; his eyes narrowed as he turned toward his father. "You would marry her to one of those—those—"

"You needn't teach me my moral responsibilities, Charles, I hope I am quite aware of them," Mr. Wilde said sharply. "I realize it is not a simple problem. Leah has been raised in the household, she is accustomed to a certain way of life. Clearly I cannot send her back to the quarters at The Folly with some illiterate field hand. She must marry another house servant, or a craftsman. I wish we had someone suitable, but Bob is too old and Billy has a wife."

"So," Charles said, in a voice that sounded like that of a stranger, "you would sell her."

"To a friend, of course; for her own good, so that she might be with her husband. . . . Good heavens, Charles, it would be a sacrifice for me; your mother is fond of the girl and she is quite well trained. But something must be done. That young puppy Walforth has already—"

He broke off, seeing his son's face, and put one hand out as if to ward off a blow.

"What ails you, Charles? Nothing happened; she came to me at once, quite distressed, and told me what he had said; I spoke firmly to him and have taken care, since then, that Leah should not go about freely."

Jonathan, who had been listening with a strange intensity, now decided it was time to interfere.

"Charles, the wine is being neglected and my throat is dry as dust. May I pour it? Sir, may I help you to wine? And I see some of Mrs. Wilde's molasses cakes."

He went to the table, treading heavily on Charles's foot as he passed.

"Damn it, you are as clumsy as ever," said the latter, recovering himself. "Father, we'll discuss the matter later; I have an idea or two I'd like to propose, with your permission."

His voice was as casual as the unimportance of the question deserved. His father relaxed.

"Certainly, my boy. There are a number of matters pertaining to the estate I'd like to go over with you. But that can wait. You'll want to rest and wash off the dust of travel. Your mother is preparing a meal for fifty, so I hope you are in condition to do justice to it."

Charles mumbled through the mouthful of cake he had taken, grinned, and swallowed. He seemed quite at ease— except for his eyes.

"I hadn't realized how hungry I was till I tasted Mother's cakes. Don't worry, I could eat a horse. Come along, Jon, and keep me company while I clean up. It's more than the dust of travel that needs to be removed."

As the two young men climbed the staircase they were conscious of a constant rustle of movement and sound from members of the household who were trying to catch a glimpse of the young master. Charles called out and waved at the grinning faces peering from doorways and dark corners. But when he had closed the door of his room Charles swung on his friend with a cold, unsmiling look.

"Is that bastard Walforth still in town? I thought he would be with the King's soldiers after his prating about loyalty."

"The ones who talk the loudest are usually the last to risk their necks," Jonathan said with a new cynicism. "He's still here. Still talking, too. But not so loudly."

"Good." Charles pulled his worn coat off with an angry movement and threw it at the bed. "I'm glad he's here. I can have the satisfaction of beating his face in."

"Why?" Jonathan sat down on the beautiful embroidered counterpane, which had been put on the bed in honor of the prodigal's return. "To defend the honor of a slave girl?"

His shirt half off, Charles stopped moving and stared at his friend. "I never liked the fellow," he muttered.

"But you never expressed your feelings so vehemently. Perhaps now you have a faint idea of some of the things I have been talking about for years. If Walforth had insulted Mary Beth you might have challenged him—killed him, if you were so inclined—and everyone would have admired your gallantry. But of course he would not have dared to address a lady in such terms. Leah has no such unwritten, unspoken protection; and if you fought Walforth on her account you would be sneered at, condemned as mad. Yet she is as gentle and pure as your betrothed, Charles. I like your indignation. It shows a good heart. It indicates that you don't think of her as a chattel, but as a human being."

Charles tossed his shirt after the coat. He stood with his back to Jonathan, so the latter did not see the smile that curled his mouth.

"Oh, yes," he said softly. "I think of her as a human being. . . . God's teeth, Jon, let's not talk about it. I'm sick of problems. Tell me about yourself. It's been months since I last saw you in Philadelphia. Tell me that you, at least, haven't changed."

Jonathan sat quietly, his hands loosely clasped, his head bent.

"But I have changed," he said. "We all have. You can't go back, Charles."

"I wish I could, sometimes," Charles said. "Back to the days when our greatest worry was how to evade our teachers so we could haunt the taverns and hear the latest news. Do you remember the summer we were fourteen, Jon? You taught me to wrestle."

He threw his shoulders back and stood with his hands on his narrow hips, grinning down at Jon. His green eyes sparkled, and Jonathan, as always, responded to the vein of reckless gaiety that characterized his friend. He looked up, answering Charles's smile.

"Is that a challenge? Don't be so cocky, Charles. You haven't enough weight; I can count your ribs, you poor undernourished—"

The speech ended in a gasp of laughter as Charles jerked him to his feet, one arm wrapped around Jonathan's shoulders in a painful hold.

"I learned this one from a barefoot private from Pennsylvania," he said. "If you can get out of this—"

"Watch out for the washbasin," Jonathan wheezed, weakened by amusement. "Your mother will murder us if we—"

Charles increased his leverage, and Jonathan let out a yelp. He moved, instinct overcoming caution, and they were staggering back, arms wrapped around one another, until Charles came up against the corner of the desk. It was his turn to yell; he bent, grabbed Jonathan by the knees, and tipped him over. The crash shook the room and knocked two books off the desk.

"God's teeth," Charles exclaimed. "That'll fetch Mother, raging."

"Well, who started it?" Jonathan demanded, from the floor.

They exchanged guilty looks; briefly, they resembled the boys of long-past summers. Then Charles smiled and reached down a hand to help his friend up.

"I could set fire to the parlor draperies today and Mother wouldn't say a word. I suppose you're right, Jon; we can't go back, but it's fun to try. . . . You've lost half the contents of your pockets. Here. Knife—four shillings and two-pence—watch—not improved, I fear, by the fall—and—what's this? What's this?"

Jonathan grabbed for the little oval object, but Charles was too quick for him; he jumped back, grinning, and examined his prize.

It was a miniature of a girl's face. Small enough to be cupped in the palm of his hand, it showed a round, smiling face with big brown eyes and demure smile. Her fair hair was coiled neatly around her head, and she wore a ruffled white cap.

Charles let out a shout of amusement.

"So the citadel has fallen! The impregnable fortress has been taken! I thought you looked different; this is the reason. Who is she, Jon? And when does the ceremony take place?"

Jonathan flinched as if his friend had struck him. Charles

looked up. His smile disappeared when he saw the other man's pallor.

"What is it? What have I said? Is she—"

"Dead."

"Oh, God," Charles said softly. He put the miniature gently down and threw his arm around Jonathan's rigid shoulders. "Forgive me, I'll not easily forgive myself. Of all the thoughtless, cruel—"

"No, how could you know?" The instinct that had prompted Charles to embrace his friend was the correct one. Jonathan's face lost its rigidity. "I meant to tell you," he went on. "Someday."

"Don't talk about it if it pains you," Charles said roughly. "If you would like my tongue, pickled, in a jar—"

"Fool. Go, wash yourself and get some clothes on; you're shivering. I can talk better if you are not looking at me. Your sympathy unmans me a little. . . . Yet I would like to tell you."

Obediently Charles poured water from the china ewer into the small bowl provided for that purpose, and began to splash it on his bare arms and chest.

The room was not cold, not to these hardened men who had never known the luxury of central heating. The fire that loving hands had kindled, in anticipation of Charles's return, was not really necessary. The sun was shining outside, and although the bare branches visible beyond the windowpane showed that it was late in the year, Williamsburg was enjoying one of the mellow autumn days that come unexpectedly even in November.

Jonathan went to the window and stood looking out, but it was plain that he saw something other than the scene below. A few golden leaves still clung to the boughs of the maples, and the rich green box and spruce gave color to the view. The garden was dead. Blackened clumps of asters told of a recent frost. From the chimney of the brick kitchen came a coil of smoke where the fatted calf and its accompaniments were being prepared.

"She was the daughter of one of the Philadelphia merchants with whom I do business," Jonathan said abruptly. "I met her—them—through my cousins there. She was only sixteen, and her father's darling, so I did not venture. . . . I did not know she returned my—my feelings until just before I left the last time. We had a few minutes, in the garden, the day of my departure. She gave me her picture and. . . . I'm sorry. The words don't seem to come easily."

Charles said nothing. He did not turn, but stood with his back to Jonathan, rubbing himself vigorously with a towel; but the intensity of his sympathy was as strong as a spoken word.

"It was the smallpox," Jonathan said. "We had been talking about inoculations, while I was there. Her father was in favor of the idea, but her mother feared it, she said it was against God's will, and besides, people were often as ill from the inoculation as from the sickness. I received a letter last month. Her father has occasion to write me on—on business; he apologized for being late in doing so because of—family sorrows."

"Then he didn't know?" Charles asked.

"No one knows. Except you."

"Then no one will, unless you want me to—"

"No, why should it be spoken of? It is past," Jonathan said. Then he added ingenuously, "Do you know, it's odd, but I feel better. I thought I could never speak of her, but now I want to tell you about her. Her name was Patience. It's a pretty name, isn't it?"

"Yes, it is," Charles said softly. "And a pretty face. Gentle and good."

"She was both. But there is a kind of strength, sometimes, in gentleness; she had that, too. We were walking one day when we saw a carter abusing his horse, a poor bony beast with sores on its back. I was about to remonstrate, but she was there before me. She never raised her voice—it was a very soft voice, did I mention that?—but when she finished the man was shuffling and twisting his cap and apologizing.

Can you imagine that? A great rough brute, and she no higher than his top shirt button. I just stood back and watched her, I was so amused and so proud. . . ."

His voice trailed away, but he was smiling; his face had lost its look of patient pain. Charles threw the towel over his shoulder and came to stand beside him.

"How can you bear it? To have lost all that. . . ."

"But it isn't lost," Jonathan said, surprised. "I shall see her again; I know that, of course. It's the waiting that worries me. I thought at first I didn't have the strength to endure long years of it. But I'm beginning to see that I need the time to prepare myself. I'm not worthy of that joy, not yet."

"You really believe this," Charles said.

"I believe it now more than ever," Jonathan said simply. "Charles, our faiths agree on that. You don't doubt . . . ?"

"I didn't. I never thought about it. I went to church and mouthed the prayers. . . . But when you see men blown to bloody fragments, ripped open by bayonets so their guts spill out—what kind of Heaven can permit such horrors?"

Jonathan was silent for a while, as if groping for the right words. This was no casual doubt, to be countered by the platitudes of either faith.

"I don't know," he said diffidently, "what it will be like. Perhaps all our ideas are wrong—simple stories told to children to keep them from being frightened by the dark. All I know is that there is more to man than a physical shape. Love transcends the body; the thing I loved could not die, it was too strong for that. It exists. Somewhere, sometime, under perhaps unimaginable conditions, I'll find it again. I know that. The only thing that frightens me is my own unworthiness."

Charles put his hand on his friend's bowed shoulder.

"You, unworthy? You're the best man I know, Jon."

Jonathan shook his head. "It's so hard," he muttered. "I want to do what is right; but it's so hard to know. Every act has so many sides, some good, some bad. If I could only be sure. . . ."

"You've done me good, at any rate," Charles said. "Tell me more about her, Jon."

"You understand so well. Are you sure there isn't something you want to tell me?"

He glanced up, smiling. Charles turned away and groped in the chest of drawers, looking for a clean shirt.

"No," he said harshly. "Nothing like that. Nothing. . . . Talk, Jon!"

"The Quakers say 'thee,' you know—did I tell you she was a Quaker? You may think it would sound strange, but it didn't, not from her, it sounded—well, friendly and concerned."

He went on, enjoying the release of emotion he had not been able to express in tears; and Charles, struggling into clothes that were too short in the arms and too tight across the shoulders, and too big everywhere else, listened with a face like stone.

II

The dreamer stirred restlessly. One hand lifted, the fingers curled as if to grasp some elusive object. Then the hand fell, the lines on the sleeping face smoothed out. The body on the bed lay still, so still that a watcher might have thought the quiet breast did not move at all.

III

The ballroom at the Governor's Palace was of good size—forty-seven and a half feet long, twenty-six feet five inches wide, according to the plan drawn up by a man who was a fine architect as well as Virginia's second state governor. He was among the guests that night; his reddish hair was whitened with powder, his freckles faded by winter, but his height made him stand out over the crowd and his "mild and pleasing countenance," as a foreign visitor once described it, attracted even the eyes of those few who did not recognize the young author of the Declaration of Independence.

He was there as one of the delegates to the Assembly; the man who stood at the door, welcoming his guests, had a sallow wedge of a face and the long tight mouth of a Puritan. No one had ever accused Patrick Henry of puritanical tastes, however. His twenty-one-year-old bride stood at his side. His first wife had finally succumbed to the illness that had earlier robbed her of her reason.

He greeted Charles warmly, with a neatly turned compliment about his gallantry in battle before passing him on into the room. Jonathan got a stiff bow and a disparaging glance.

"I told you I shouldn't have come," the latter muttered, as he and Charles moved on.

"It's your clothes," Charles said with a smile. "Mr. Henry has turned into quite a dandy, and that god-awful snuff color you insist on wearing, without so much as a gold button . . ."

"It's a new suit," Jonathan said indignantly. "And I let you tie my neckband."

His hand went up, as if to loosen the white folds. Charles knocked it away.

"Leave it alone, just for one evening, can't you? It would be a sin to mar such artistic perfection. Relax, man! You look the way I felt the night before Trenton."

"I'd almost as soon be in a battle," Jonathan mumbled.

The room was ablaze with candles, hundreds of them, in sconces and silver candelabra. They gave an illusion of heat, but no warmth, and some of the older women were wearing shawls. The younger ones braved the chill, displaying white throats and arms framed by delicate lace. The night was cold; frost spangled the windowpanes, reflecting candle flames in translucent silver.

Charles was magnificent in sapphire-blue velvet, with gold buttons and Mechlin lace at his throat. The coat was new, a gift from his mother, who had been horrified at the fit of his outgrown wardrobe.

The dancing had not yet begun. They made their way through the crowd to the supper room, where a number of the men had already assembled to sample the governor's punch. Here Charles was stopped by a gentleman in a bag-wig and a salmon-colored coat, who greeted him familiarly.

"So it's back to the war tomorrow, eh, Lieutenant? I don't know why you're in such a hurry. Nasty cold place, Pennsylvania. And Lord knows we need our men here, with those cursed British stirring up the slaves."

The magic word turned heads in their direction. Charles, looking exasperated, was soon surrounded by men, all arguing violently about the subject that was their constant fear.

Finally he managed to get the floor.

"Gentlemen, I don't understand your concern. As we all know, Lord Dunmore's plan to enlist Negroes proved a failure. Many of them died of disease; and it's been over a year now since his lordship gave up and sailed to Bermuda with the remnants of his Ethiopian regiment."

"It isn't only the British," said a red-faced man. "I hear that Washington is now recommending the enlistment of blacks."

Charles glanced at Jonathan, who had not said a word. His face was as blank as an Indian's.

"We've got to have troops," Charles said. "Some states claim they can't supply their quota without enlisting blacks. But Washington doesn't advocate arming slaves, he only wants to allow enlistment of free Negroes—"

"Ha," the red-faced man said explosively. "He may say that now; but wait, just wait. There are traitors within our own ranks, my boy; within our own class." He nodded portentously, and the circle of white heads nodded too, like Punch and Judy puppets. Charles, who found the discussion frustrating as well as amusing, bit his lip to keep from laughing.

"Yes, that young fool Laurens, for one," added another

man. "A South Carolinian and a plantation owner, and yet he's been bending Washington's ear with wild proposals for black regiments."

"What can you expect from his father's son? Henry Laurens gave up the slave trade in 1770, and has been preaching about it ever since. Why, I hear he has freed many of his own slaves. And we elected a man like that head of the Continental Congress!"

"Laurens' policy has one conspicuous advantage," a new voice said. "Not one of his slaves has run away. I believe all of you have lost several, and it is costing you a considerable sum to patrol the estuary to prevent escapes. As for the slave trade—many of us share Mr. Laurens' views, Fleming."

The speaker was a slight man with a prominent bony nose and thoughtful dark eyes. It was obvious that the others held him in deference; the brawling voices stopped and Fleming looked embarrassed.

"The trade is one thing, Mr. Wythe," he said doggedly. "But arming our slaves—"

"I assure you, it won't come to that." Wythe turned to Charles. "I'm sorry not to have seen more of you, my boy; but I know your time is short. If you have a moment before you leave, it would give me great pleasure to see you at my house. The Jeffersons are staying with me now, you know."

"Thank you, sir. I should be honored."

"Tomorrow, then. If you will excuse me, gentlemen?"

There was a moment's pause, in deference to one of Williamsburg's most respected elder statesmen, but before Charles could make his own excuses and retreat, Fleming burst out again.

"It's all very well to talk, but the fact remains we are still losing slaves. The black rascals are constantly escaping to the British. We're patrolling the waterways and guarding all the boats, and yet they manage to get through. Mark my words, gentlemen, there is a conspiracy afoot!"

"The ingratitude of it is what hurts me," said a lean, stoop-shouldered man, with a sanctimonious sigh.

"Do you feel they owe us gratitude, Mr. Johnson?" Charles asked sardonically. "For robbing them of their liberty and the ownership of their persons?"

Johnson's ferret face sharpened.

"If you are such a Christian, Wilde, I suppose you will take no steps to recover your own property. Was it not your valet that ran away recently? A fine way to welcome you home, I must say."

"Martin was a faithful servant," Charles said coldly. "He gave me excellent service in the North until he took ill and I had to send him home. I don't believe he has gone to the British."

"Then where has he gone, eh?" Fleming asked, jabbing Charles in the ribs. "You don't know what goes on in their minds, young Charles."

"And what will you do with him if you recover him?" another man asked curiously. "You have advertised, I suppose."

"My father has taken steps," Charles said. "Pardon me, gentlemen, but I must—"

"Hang the rascals," Fleming said. "That's what I say. It's the law, isn't it? Treason—hanging—"

Jonathan, who had controlled himself longer than his friend had expected, finally lost his temper.

"How can a man commit treason against a state in which he has none of the privileges of a citizen? Where there is not voluntary allegiance, there cannot be treason."

"Furthermore," Charles said affably, "we have given them good precedent, have we not? 'If this be treason, make the most of it.'"

And, taking advantage of their speechless surprise, he made a courtly bow and backed away, pulling Jonathan with him.

"Will you ever learn to keep your mouth shut?" he muttered.

"But you—but I—you said more than I," Jonathan protested. "Faith, Charles, I was surprised—and very pleased, of course."

"Don't suppose you have converted me," Charles said dryly. "I would sing Satan's praises to that group of sanctimonious asses if they were on God's side. The point is, Jon, that I can express sentiments with the prestige of my uniform invisibly on my shoulders, where you cannot. You were not greeted with much warmth, I observed."

Jonathan changed the subject, but not tactfully.

"What are you planning to do about Martin?"

"I don't know what to do. I almost hope we don't catch him, that would solve the problem. Damn it, Jon, it was a rather pointed insult, wasn't it—to run away the day after I got home?"

"You might rather say that he waited to see you before he left," Jonathan said.

"Perhaps you might. . . . Let's not talk about it. This is a night for pleasure, my boy. Let's make the most of it."

He followed his own advice, dancing every dance and partaking freely of food and wine. Jonathan wandered rather aimlessly around the room; he did not dance, but he made himself agreeable to the ladies, with whom he seemed to be a favorite. He sat out one dance with Mary Beth.

She had a bad cold and kept mopping at her streaming nose with an elegant lace-trimmed handkerchief. Her red eyes and nose made her look quite like a distressed albino rabbit. But she was magnificently dressed, outshining even the governor's lady. The fashionable *robe à l'anglaise* was of apple-green brocade, with a pattern of flowers in silver thread, the skirt open to display the petticoat embroidered richly in bright silks. The full elbow ruffles were of lace; more lace trimmed the low U-shaped neckline, and goose pimples adorned the expanse of skin thus displayed. The rigidity of her bosom made one suspect that its curves had been augmented by a pair of the bust enlargers that have been used by women probably since prehistoric times.

Her blue eyes lit up when Jonathan ambled up to her and greeted her with the warmth of old friendship. Apparently he had dismissed Charles's insinuations; his innate modesty prevented him from seeing the truth that was written plainly on the girl's face whenever she looked at him.

It would not have been proper for her to express even a hint of such feelings, however; she looked modestly at her satin slippers with their glittering buckles as Jonathan sat down beside her.

"Forgive me for not asking you to dance," he said. "You know how clumsy I am; and those slippers are too pretty to be trodden upon."

"I don't mind. The dancing is getting too wild for me; I prefer a minuet to these contra dances."

Jonathan smiled as he watched the vigorous reel then in progress. Charles, conspicuous by his height and grace, advanced into the center, where he caught his partner's hands and swung her clear off the floor before they both retreated to their places.

"You'll have to tame Charles, then," he said. "I don't see how the ladies bear with him, he's boisterous enough to wear anyone out."

"I doubt that any woman could tame Charles," Mary Beth said. It was a simple statement of opinion, without sarcasm or any particular warmth; and Jonathan looked at her interestedly.

"You two are still—"

"Oh, yes. Someday."

Jonathan looked as if he wanted to say something, but the subject was too sensitive even for friendship. Instead, they talked of music, which was one of their shared interests. After a time Mary Beth said curiously,

"Jonathan, what are you looking for? You keep gazing around the room. It—it isn't a lady, by any chance?"

"Good heavens, no," Jonathan said. "I'm not looking for anything in particular, just watching the dancing. Forgive me if I have been rude or inattentive."

"Of course."

The dance ended; Charles, flushed and breathless, came

laughing up to them and claimed Mary Beth. She protested, but was overruled, and before long Jonathan caught glimpses of them as Charles swung and tossed and bounced his limp companion through the measures of a vigorous country dance. Mary Beth's expression of grim resignation made Jonathan smile, but then he sobered and shook his head. They were such opposites, fire and water, brandy and milk—watered milk. But then he supposed good marriages had been made of equally unpromising material. Few people had the rare blessing he had known, if briefly—the magical meeting of spirit and flesh in a unity that hints of the eternal.

He lost sight of Charles for a while as he wandered back and forth between the supper room and the ballroom, even taking a turn in the frostbitten garden. When he came back into the supper room he realized, from the way heads were turning and voices dropping into silence, that something was happening; and as soon as he saw whom Charles was talking to, he headed for them as fast as he could without actually running.

Henry Walforth was dressed like a London fop; even his clothing flaunted his political opinions. His cuffs were a little too wide, his coat skirts too long, and the embroidery on his waistcoat too ornate even by the standards of that day. There were diamonds on his coat buttons and red heels on his shoes. It was with regret that Jonathan admitted that he did not look ridiculous. He was not quite as tall as Charles, nor as muscular, but he had a good build, all the same, and was an expert swordsman and rider. He was also an expert at inciting people to riot, and it was clear that he was exercising this skill on Charles.

Charles had been indiscreet. He had not, of course, been stupid enough to express the reason for his anger outright, but apparently he had slipped once or twice, and Walforth's keen, malicious mind had made the connection. It was all the more easy for him to do so since he had been preoccupied with the same subject.

"Well, well," Walforth was saying, as Jonathan came

panting up. "So that is how the land lies. How nice to have my tastes confirmed by an expert."

Charles pronounced, very softly, a word that made Walforth's cheeks turn red with anger.

"Excellent," he said, in an equally quiet voice. "We'll need an excuse, won't we, for crossing swords. Something more than an exchange of epithets, though, I think."

"In heaven's name, Charles," Jonathan exclaimed, grabbing his friend's sapphire velvet sleeve. "Control yourself! People are staring—you are supposed to leave tomorrow—"

"This won't take more than ten minutes," Charles said. He was smiling. The lines in his cheeks looked like scars.

Horror gave Jonathan an unwonted eloquence and made him forget his reluctance to employ profanity.

"Ten minutes, hell. Even a rotten swordsman—which Walforth is not—may have a lucky moment. Do you want to limp back to General Washington and explain to him why you're unfit for duty? And your mother—"

Charles's arm lost its iron stiffness. Seeing that he was gaining ground, Jonathan turned to the other man.

"Haven't you more important matters to attend to, Walforth? Save your quarrel, both of you. You can always kill one another at a future time," he added bitterly.

"True." Walforth flicked at an imaginary bit of dust on his immaculate cravat. "Dear Jon, always sensible. Perhaps we'll meet on the field, Wilde."

He turned away, the curve of his back an insult in itself, but by sheer brute strength Jonathan managed to drag his friend out of the danger zone.

"You're a fool, Charles," he said. "Are you drunk? It's getting late. Why don't you go home?"

"You said you'd come back with me," Charles muttered. "You aren't going to that filthy inn and leave me to spend my last night drinking alone, are you?"

"I'll come. Find your mother, say your farewells; I'll meet you in the hall in a few minutes."

Charles walked away. Jonathan watched him pass into the ballroom and then turned to the corner where Walforth had ensconced himself, his back against the wall, a full glass in his hand.

"Can we talk here?" Jonathan asked softly.

"It's as good a place as any," the other man replied negligently. "And we have an excellent excuse now; everyone will suppose you are lecturing me for trying to pick a quarrel with your friend."

"What news? Did Martin escape safely?"

"Martin? Oh, yes; the mahogany-colored creature you said farewell to so touchingly. He's safe aboard the *St. Albans* now; soon he'll be handsomely fitted out with a bright-red uniform. It will become his black face enormously, I don't doubt."

"Why do you do this, when you despise them so?" Jonathan asked, his hands clenched.

"You know quite well why I do it. Isn't it odd that we are acting in concert—reluctant yoke mates, if ever there were—with precisely opposite motives? You hope to free these swine, I hope to see them spill their blood and brains for the King. Very odd indeed. But I shan't be doing it forever. I don't fancy the name or the inconveniences of our temporary profession. They hang spies, you know."

"I'm no—"

"Oh, aren't you? I fear your Patriot friends would think otherwise. The men you send me carry information; don't pretend to be unaware of that. Their thick black skulls are emptied when they arrive—troop movements and dispositions, defense plans. . . . At any rate, you'll have a new contact soon. It's an unsavory occupation, and if I were suspected I doubt that even my father's ardor for the rebel cause could save my skin. I shall lie low for a while. I'm not quite ready to go to war officially. But when I do—what a pleasure to return in the uniform of the conqueror and deal out some good strict military justice."

"Damn you," Jonathan said.

"How shocking! I thought you German Quakers were careful not to use bad language. Well, this is beginning to bore me; I have, as you pointed out, better things to do. Where and when do I meet you for the next cargo?"

Jonathan's facial contortions, as he struggled with his temper, would have been comical if the matter had not been so deadly serious.

"Speedwell's Ordinary, on the Richmond road," he said finally, in a smothered voice. "Ten days. There will be three, possibly four."

"And you are leaving—"

"Tomorrow. They will have to lie over at least one night, and there are other matters to arrange. And you?"

"Oh, not for a few days," the other man said, with a sly glance at Jonathan. "I have matters to arrange here. Private matters, and a good deal more pleasurable than the ones you and I share. Although they have one shade in common. . . ."

Jonathan's wits were not slow, but he was not quick at comprehending such innuendos. When he realized what the other man was referring to, his face darkened.

"I hope I fail to understand you," he said. "You have already been warned; if you persist I'll denounce you myself, and take the consequences."

"Such heat!" The other man raised amused eyebrows. "I vow, I have never seen such a turmoil over a wench, you would think her a lady of consequence. Very well, I'll not honor your sable Venus further. Though, come to think of it, the word does not apply too well, does it? A splendid result of one of our most delightful Virginia customs. She's a beauty, but she isn't worth fighting half the town for. Which is it, the old gentleman or the son? Or do they share her favors, turn and turn about?"

Jonathan's face slowly cleared. A smile of genuine pleasure curved his lips. He lifted the other man up and threw him into the middle of the refreshment table.

*   *   *

Charles was hysterical all the way home. The two men walked—Charles stopping occasionally to lean against a tree or a fence railing, and catch his breath—since Jonathan had refused to share the Wilde carriage, or face Mr. and Mrs. Wilde. He wouldn't enter the house until Charles had assured him that his parents had both gone straight upstairs.

Charles was still wheezing with laughter when they settled down comfortably in the dining room, with the decanter on the table between them, their coats slung over the backs of the chairs and their elbows on the table. Jonathan's face was hidden in his hands.

"What makes it so magnificent," Charles said, for the fifth or sixth time, "is that *you* kept telling *me* to keep *my* temper. When I remember your pious face as you dragged me away from that bastard—"

"The terrible thing is that I enjoyed it," Jonathan said. "Just before I picked him up I was filled with the most glorious feeling of peace and satisfaction. It was heavenly." Then he groaned heartily. "God forgive me, how can I use such words about an act of violence? Will I never learn? I think I am making progress and then something like this happens."

"Don't worry about it," Charles said. His eyes were still dancing, but he kept his voice sober in deference to his friend's distress. "You only did what most of the men in the colony have been longing to do. Have some wine, it will drown your unnecessary remorse. Unless you feel you must give up wine, along with other harmless vices."

"I should," Jonathan said gloomily. "You have no idea, Charles, how confusing it is to come from a family that practices half a dozen different religions. Mennonite, Lutheran, Reformed, Anglican . . . and there was Great-Aunt Sophronia, who decided that the Second Coming was imminent, and went up to the top of a hill near the house on Christmas Eve to wait for it, and froze solid to the ground. She was extremely fat and it took two of my uncles to pry her loose and carry her down next morning, because naturally she was stiff from sitting so long—"

Charles exploded with laughter, and Jonathan looked at him reproachfully.

"It isn't funny, Charles. It's damnable. Damnable and dangerous."

"You aren't afraid of that little weasel, are you?" Charles asked contemptuously.

"Not of him. Of what he can do." Jonathan's voice was barely audible.

Charles found a meaning in the words Jonathan had not intended; his face sobered.

"This isn't London, Jon, where bullies and assassins can be hired for sixpence. All the same—it might be wise to avoid dark streets late at night. You humiliated Walforth, and that is more dangerous than injuring him."

They talked for a while longer, of trivial things; and then Jonathan rose.

"There are too many things to say and too little time. It troubles me to see you go, Charles. Truly. I suppose it would sound stupid to say 'Take care.' . . ."

"You, too." Charles rose and held out his hand.

Jonathan looked at it with a strange expression on his face. Then he extended his own hand.

"Good-bye," Charles said.

"Let's say 'Auf Weidersehen.'"

"Oh, yes, your Dutch expression."

"Till I see you again," Jonathan repeated. "Don't come to the door, Charles."

He left the house, but instead of walking to the gate he stood looking up and down the deserted street. The moon was out, and frost glittered coldly on the frozen mud, whose curving, baroque patterns were made even more fantastic by shadows. Jonathan was hidden from sight by the shadow of the house; he stayed in its concealment as he slipped along the side, moving very quietly for so big a man.

The ruddy glow of firelight showed in several of the out-buildings, and from one came the sound of a rude stringed instrument and a voice singing. The words were indistinguishable, but the melody was poignantly melancholy. At first the courtyard appeared to be deserted, which was not surprising on such a chilly night, but after a while Jonathan made out the slim dark figure, almost invisible against the evergreens at the back of the house.

He was about to leave his concealment when the back door opened. No light showed, but someone came out, walking slowly, with head bent and hands clasped behind the back. Moonlight glimmered in the thick fair hair, whitening it; but Jonathan would have recognized his friend's outline anywhere.

Charles might well have passed the figure in the shadow without seeing it, had it not moved. He whirled around, his hand going instinctively to his side; but sword belt and scabbard had been discarded with his coat.

"Who is it?" he asked sharply; and then: "Leah . . ."

She came to him, her head lowered submissively, the dark cloak falling open as her hands dropped to her sides.

"What are you doing out on such a night?" Charles asked. "That cloak is too thin, you'll take cold. Is it Martin? I know you must be worried about him, but you needn't, not as far as I'm concerned; you know I would never do anything to harm him."

"I know," she said softly.

"Then what's the trouble? If there is anything I can do to help. . . ." He had done very well so far; his face and voice expressed kindly, almost paternal concern. But as she turned away, her shoulders shaking, he looked like a man gasping for the air he needs to stay alive. Reaching out he pulled her into his arms.

"You're so small," he said wonderingly. "So small and cold. . . . Leah, tell me why you're crying."

Her hands twisted in his shirt front, her head tipped back, she looked up into his face. The tears on her cheeks looked like crystal beads on ivory.

"You're going away," she whispered. "I can't stand it. I'll die if they hurt you—"

And then she said no more, because Charles's lips were on hers and their bodies were straining together.

The watcher in the shadows closed his eyes. Rigid with shock, he was unable to move for fear of making a noise, but his lips moved silently, as if he were praying.

Chapter

8

Summer 1976

JAN WOKE UP, FEELING HER AUNT'S CLAWLIKE FINGERS digging into her shoulders. Her head rolled on the pillow as Camilla tried to shake her.

"What's the matter?" she demanded, opening her eyes.

Camilla sat back with a gasp.

"Child, are you all right?"

"Of course. What's wrong? Why, Aunt Cam, you're blue. Here, lie down. Is Uncle Henry . . . ?"

"No, no. It was you I was worried about." Camilla passed a trembling hand across her forehead. "I've been tryin' to wake you for ten minutes."

"There isn't a thing wrong with me," Jan said. "I feel great."

And she did; exaltation filled her as memory returned.

"You don't look great," her aunt snapped, shrewish in her relief. "You've got big black circles under your eyes. My land, child, do you always sleep so hard?"

"No, of course not," Jan said soothingly. Camilla was exaggerating, as old people did; she had probably called her twice and then gotten panicky. "I took a sleeping pill last night; couldn't drop off. I was so tired. I haven't taken anything for a week, it must have been more effective than I expected."

"Oh." Camilla looked relieved. Then her face clouded. "I do wish you wouldn't take that stuff, Jan. A girl your age shouldn't need drugs to sleep."

"I won't take any more," Jan said, ready to agree to anything that would get Camilla out of the room, so she could revel in her success.

"Well, I would have let you sleep. Only it's getting late, and your uncle says that Alan Miller is picking you up at noon, and it's almost eleven, so—"

"Oh, gosh." With some difficulty Jan had reverted to the expletives of early childhood in order to spare her elders' feelings. "I had better hurry. I'm sorry, Aunt Cam, it won't happen again."

Her aunt trailed out, muttering, and Jan headed for the shower.

She felt like singing and dancing. She did sing, a few bars, and giggled gleefully at the amplified echo that came back at her.

The dreams weren't ended. Last night's had been bigger and better than ever. It was the first time she had experienced two separate episodes, though both seemed to date from the same few days. Days in November, 1777, when Patrick Henry was governor of Virginia and Thomas Jefferson was helping to write the new state constitution, and Charles was about to return to the fighting in the North. No, he wouldn't find it very comfortable in Pennsylvania. This was the winter of Valley Forge.

The discomforts of that bitter camp were no worse than the problems Charles was facing at home. His personal life was getting to be as complicated as Jonathan's.

Strange it had never occurred to her before that Leah was Martin's sister and, like him, a slave. Not so strange, really, considering the girl's fair skin and delicate features; but by Virginia law she was black and would die as she had lived, in bondage. Insane, Jan thought wonderingly. They were crazy. And are we any better, with our riots and our bigotry and the distorted faces of the "ladies" of New Orleans and Boston, screaming obscenities at six-year-olds going to school?

The thought of the only possible consummation for the love between Charles and Leah sickened her, not because she had any outdated qualms about extramarital sex, but because this relationship only degraded the girl, emphasizing her status as a piece of property. That she returned Charles's passion didn't change a thing. And yet the scene in the winter garden had been touching and beautiful, like any lovers' meeting.

Jonathan's problems were more serious. His sneering enemy had been quite right about the dangers of their job; Jonathan was risking his neck helping his neighbors' slaves escape. Jan wasn't surprised to learn he was doing this, but somehow it had never occurred to her that the slaves would escape to the British. Yet what other choice was there? Virginia wouldn't enlist free Negroes, much less offer freedom to a man who would fight for the country that had enslaved him. Whether or not the British would keep their promises to free the men who fought for them was another matter; at least the gesture had been made, and it held more hope than anything the Patriot cause had to offer.

But Jonathan was such a rotten conspirator. His warm heart and quick temper were constantly getting him into trouble, and it was obvious that his touchy conscience was giving him hell. No wonder. He was supplying aid and comfort to the men who were shooting at his best friend, and he had a genuine sympathy for the American position. He was discovering what some young revolutionaries refuse to admit: that right and wrong are not as clear-cut as they would like to believe.

Jan realized that she had been in the shower too long. She could have washed an elephant with the amount of water that had flowed down the drain.

She was in such a good mood that even the thought of a date with Alan didn't disturb her. There was not much time to brood about it; when she had dressed and taken a quick cup of coffee—over the strenuous protests of Camilla, who wanted her to eat something—Alan was knocking at the door.

He gave her white slacks and sleeveless navy top a disparaging look.

"I told you to wear something old."

"This is old. You could at least say hello."

"A meaningless social amenity."

"It takes less time to say 'hello' than 'a meaningless social amenity.'"

"Good," Alan said approvingly. "I see you're in a fighting mood. We'll have a nice day."

"Where are we going?"

"To a carnival," Alan said.

II

It was a county fair, actually, and not a very fancy one. The roller coaster had the alarming, rusted look of machinery that has been run too long without repairs. The sun beat down on the fairground, with its stretches of brown burned weeds and dust as hot as white steel. The fair buildings were badly in need of paint. Barkers shouted the attractions of the freak show, garish signs invited spectators to win a stuffed teddy bear, and children daubed unwary adults with sticky streaks of pink cotton candy.

Jan had a wonderful time.

She rode on the merry-go-round, a good one, with bears and zebras and lions as well as horses. She rode on a bear and a unicorn and two different horses, before Alan dragged her away to more active sports. They rode the Ferris wheel twice, and all the other rides at last once, including the one where you drive a little car into other little cars. They admired the pigs and the fancy breeds of chickens; they ate hot dogs and peanuts and drank warm Coke, and then ate cotton candy and crackerjack. Jan won a ring with a skull on it and

Alan won a Dracula mask. By five o'clock Jan was feeling a bit queasy, what with the heat and the cotton candy, which had been the last straw, but she had to be forcibly removed to Alan's car.

"I want to ride the roller coaster again," she said sulkily.

"Uh-uh." Alan looked her over. "You do look better than you did this morning; but I don't think the roller coaster is a good idea. We'd best get you some dinner."

"I couldn't eat."

"You'll be sick as a dog," her companion said crudely, "if you don't get some solid food in your stomach. How do crabs strike you?"

"That ought to do it," Jan said. "One way or the other."

"Maybe so. Well. . . . I happen to know the best French restaurant in the Tidewater."

Jan looked at her sticky hands with dismay.

"I can't go to the Inn, or someplace like that, looking the way I do."

"I wasn't thinking of the Inn, or someplace like that. You are a little overdressed for Gus's place, actually."

They were on the highway by this time and the wind was blowing some of the stored heat out of the car. It was also blowing Jan's hair all over her face, but she ignored this.

"What do you mean, I look better than I did this morning?" she demanded indignantly.

"Think fast, think fast," her escort said nastily. "That was five minutes ago. Can't you keep up with the conversation?"

"Not with yours; you can cram so many insults into a single comment it takes five minutes to catch up with them."

"I just meant that you looked a little hollow around the eyes," Alan said, with one of his quick changes into relative courtesy. "Have you been sleeping?"

"Have I. Cam had to shake me awake this morning."

"Then you must be burning the midnight oil. It can't be your ardent suitors who are keeping you up; the doc never stays out past midnight and Richard was playing tinkly music at the Center last night. So," he swept on, over Jan's outraged response, "you must be studying too hard. I hear you're writing a book."

"Uncle Henry is the worst gossip!"

"I hope it's not another of those Revolutionary War epics."

Jan started.

"I was afraid of that," her tormentor said with a sigh.

"What have you got against the Revolution?"

"After two weeks in Williamsburg you can ask me that? Imagine what it feels like after five years. I'm sick of the subject. However, when all is said and done, I am slightly less nauseated by the Revolution than by the Civil War—or the War Between the States, as we call it in these parts. Have you ever gotten Camilla onto the subject of Yankees, and how they burned down Great-Granddaddy's dear old plantation house? She drags poor Henry out there once a year and they stand amid the ruined walls and mourn the passing of beauty and gracious living. Talk about throwing up—"

"Why do we have to talk about throwing up?" But the riposte was halfhearted. Jan had been struck by a dazzling new thought. "You mean the plantation is still there? Patriot's Dream?"

She could have clapped her hands over her mouth when she realized what she had said. Charles had talked about changing the name of the family homestead, but she didn't know whether it had actually been done. But Alan only nodded.

"Touching name, isn't it?" he said, in the mocking tone Jan found so annoying. "For a family that sent two sons to assist the breakup of the Union. . . . By some machinations or other, probably illegal, they managed to hang on to the estate after the war. Most of the land is gone, of course; sold off in chunks and pieces over the years as the family sank into genteel idiocy and incompetence. But they still own about fifty acres. It wasn't the Yankees who burned the house; one of your ancestors set fire to it in a drunken fit, somewhere in the eighteen seventies."

"How far away is it?"

"An hour, three-quarters of an hour," Alan answered, in the measurements of modern transportation. "I'm not going to take you there, if that's what you're about to ask."

Jan was intrigued at the idea of seeing the place where Charles and his family had spent most of their time. The weeks in Williamsburg were interludes only, visits made for business or social reasons. . . . And it was odd, come to think of it, that her dreams had only shown the family when they were in town. Or did it have to do with the house as a focusing lens for ancestral memory? She had not tried to analyze the methodology of her dreaming. Yet perhaps there was a pattern. There must be something significant about the one night she had not dreamed, something missing, that had prompted the earlier dreams. And why had the dreams not begun until after she had been in Williamsburg for a week? Something building up, like an electrical charge. . . .

Alan jabbed her in the ribs.

"Wake up. I said, I won't take you to Patriot's Dream, if that's what—"

"No, that's okay. I'd like to go sometime, though. Tell me more about it. Didn't it have another name, a long time ago?"

"How would I know? Your family history is of no interest to me. Ask Camilla. She'll love it. Is that the idea behind your newborn interest in the past, winning the old lady's affection—and her expensive antiques? Maybe she'll leave them to you, now that she has learned to love you, instead of willing them to the Foundation."

Jan had to clench her hands to keep from slapping the dark, sneering face. He had been nice, really nice, most of the day. Did he still harbor suspicions about her mercenary motives?

She said nothing. Alan did not apologize; she had not expected that he would. His heavy brows were set in a scowl.

Finally they stopped in a graveled parking lot and Jan looked with utter disbelief at the finest French restaurant in the Tidewater.

It was a typical tavern or roadhouse, built of cinder blocks painted pale blue, with a huge neon sign—unlit, of course, at this time—that read "Gus's." There were three other cars in the parking lot, presumably those of the help. Jan locked at Alan.

"It's early yet," he said. "That's good, we won't have to wait for a table."

His good humor had returned; probably, Jan thought, because he was pleased at the success of his weird joke.

The inside of the place was clean, at least. But the red plastic on the booths was cracking and the formica tabletops bared their scars shamelessly. The jukebox was going full blast and the girl behind the counter, snapping her gum in time to the music, looked as if she were about to burst out of her low-cut dress.

"Turn that damn thing off," Alan shouted, in a bellow that made Jan jump.

The girl complied.

"Hi," she said, grinning broadly.

"Hi, Doreen. This is Jan."

"Hi," said Doreen.

"Hi," said Jan.

"What's on the menu tonight?" Alan asked, taking the nearest booth and waving Jan to a seat.

"The usual." Doreen tittered. "Patty dee maysen and ham and mushmelon—"

"That's *prosciutto e melone,* you dumb broad," Alan said, in a passable imitation of Humphrey Bogart. "We'll have the pâté. Now move it, sister."

Doreen tittered again and ambled toward the kitchen. Evidently she considered Alan a first-class comedian.

When she returned with the pâté and a slim, frosty bottle, she informed Alan that Gus recommended "that veal thing" and this wine, to go with it. He gave her another speech from a gangster film and she tittered all the way back to the kitchen.

The pâté silenced any comment Jan might have thought of making. The wine, a pale rosé, reconciled her to the fact that Alan hadn't offered her a cocktail. And the "veal thing" turned out to be a superb cordon bleu, with an elusively seasoned, delicate sauce. The place began to fill up as they ate, without affronting the food with conversation, and when Doreen brought their coffee Jan saw that there were indeed people waiting for tables.

Like any master chef, Gus came out for compliments. He was a man who obviously appreciated his own talents. The white apron tied over his bulging stomach was spotlessly clean, although his bald head shone with perspiration. He greeted Jan in the unmistakable accents of the Bronx and held out a moist pink hand.

"Where did you learn to cook?" she asked respectfully.

"Paree, where else? I was in the war."

"But you could be working in New York—some fancy place—"

"I hate cities," Gus said simply. "Grew up in one. After the war I decided the hell with it, life's too short; I found this place. Only open weekends. The rest of the time I fish. Come back anytime. Next week it's tournedos Abrantes."

He passed on to the next table, where he was received like royalty, and Jan shook her head in amazement.

"What a character!"

"Most people are, when you get to know them," Alan said pompously. He added, "I'm writing an almanac, la Franklin. That will be one of my chapter headings."

The first stars came out as they drove back. Alan took it easy; they idled along the country roads, high-walled with tangled greenery, where honeysuckle drowned the night with sweetness. Alan didn't talk and Jan leaned back and relaxed.

She was not at all sleepy, but she was conscious of a quiet contentment.

But as they neared Williamsburg and the back lanes turned to broad highways lined with hamburger stands, she felt a growing impatience. The day had been a nice interlude, far more pleasant than she had anticipated, but now she could hardly wait to get home. Last night's revelations had merely whetted her appetite for more.

As dark deepened and the town came closer she began to be uneasy as well as impatient. Surely she would dream again tonight. And this time, if possible, without the help of sleeping tablets. She had frightened Camilla that morning, she couldn't risk repeating the stunt. What had she done—what had she left undone—that might affect the dreams? The phenomena might be random, but if there was a cause. . . .

She was sitting bolt upright, her hands folded tightly in her lap. Alan glanced at her.

"What's the matter? Leave the iron plugged in or something?"

"What?"

"You look as if some frightful thought had just occurred to you."

"Well—I did promise Uncle Henry I'd be keeping him company this evening. I shouldn't have gone to dinner. But," she added cunningly, aware of his intent scrutiny, "I don't regret it. Thank you, Alan. It was a lovely day."

"Don't mention it, ma'am. I am amply repaid by the joy of your company. Especially," he added, pulling up at the curb, "as it looks as if that's all I'm going to get."

He turned toward her, his arm over the back of the seat. It was not so dark but that Jan could see the breadth of his smile and the way his eyes had narrowed.

"You're absolutely right it is," she said, as the sense of his comment finally penetrated. "After a clumsy pass like that one."

"Next time I won't ask," Alan said. "I'll just grab you.

My buddies tell me that's what women really want, caveman stuff."

He made no attempt to come any closer, however; and after waiting a moment—so he wouldn't get the impression she was intimidated—Jan gave a disdainful grunt and opened the car door. As soon as she had closed it the car started off.

Jan watched the taillights brighten as the car turned. She was feeling a little guilty. If he hadn't shot off like that, she would have thanked him again. The meal alone had been worthy of courtesy. But she didn't waste much time thinking about Alan Miller.

The blue twilight deepened, jeweled with fireflies, as she stood in thought. There was one thing. One possible connection.

She was about to turn when she saw the flicker of a window shade, and realized that of course Camilla would be watching for her return—ready to rush to the rescue in case Mr. Miller had the audacity to embrace her in front of the family mansion. Jan ran up the walk and opened the door.

"I'm home," she announced—and was not deceived by the casual voice that answered from the parlor.

"Oh, honey. I declare, you took us quite unawares."

"I've got to go out again for a minute," Jan said. "I left my purse in Alan's car. Wasn't that dumb? I don't suppose he'll notice till tomorrow morning, it's probably on the floor of the car. I'll just run over and get it; I won't be half an hour."

"Honey, you can't go to a man's apartment at night, alone," Camilla exclaimed.

"Now, Cam, don't be such a fuddy-duddy," Henry said. "They've been together all day, what do you suppose he's going to do to her in the next fifteen minutes? But you must be tired, honey, why don't you call Alan and ask him to bring your purse here? Easy for him, with the car."

"I don't mind the walk," Jan said. "It's a nice night, I'll be right back."

Retreating as she spoke, she was out the door before they could think of any more arguments.

She knew where Alan lived; he had pointed out the block of apartments near the college as they passed it that morning. She turned in the opposite direction.

Richard's house was only ten minutes away. She was relieved to see there were lights in the windows; it would have been terrible if he had been out.

He was surprised to see her, but obviously pleased.

"Jan! What a nice surprise. Come in, honey. Did you want something, or do I dare assume it was merely me you wanted?"

"I just wanted to see you." Jan was in no mood for conventional male-female compliments. "I can't stay but a minute, though. Uncle Henry is waiting to play chess with me."

"Can I get you some coffee? Brandy? You've had dinner?"

"Not a thing, thanks." Jan turned toward a chair. Still holding her hand Richard led her toward the couch and sat down beside her. He had been listening to music; the delicate icy web of a Vivaldi sonata hung invisibly across the air. Although Richard had been relaxing, all alone, everything was in immaculate order. The shining surface of the three-tiered dumbwaiter, Richard's latest prize, held a formal arrangement of blue-and-white chinaware and a single slim crystal glass, carefully set on a coaster.

After a moment Richard put his arm around Jan. He moved tentatively, but when she said nothing his hold tightened and he turned her face up toward his.

The kiss lasted a long time; but when Richard let her go his face was puzzled and a little angry.

"Am I boring you?" he asked.

"I'm sorry." Jan stood up. "This was a crazy thing to do, Richard. I didn't mean—"

"Obviously you didn't." Richard rose too. She was very conscious of his height and of the strength of the broad bands of muscle that showed at his open shirt front. "What's the matter, Jan? I'm sorry if I was out of line; I should have seen that something was bothering you."

She almost loved him in that moment for his gentleness; but she couldn't assuage the trace of injured vanity in his voice by telling him the truth. It would hardly have salved his ego; for she had sought his embrace because of an insane hunch that it might be the catalyst for her nightly trysts with the dead. Nor could she explain that she was rejecting him for a man who was at best a figment of her imagination, and, at worst, two hundred years in his grave.

"Is it Miller?" Richard asked, when she did not reply. "Honey, if he—"

"Oh, no, don't be silly," Jan said irritably. "Richard, I'm so sorry. I'm just in a weird mood tonight and the best thing I can do is go. You'll do me a favor if you'll forget this altogether. I'm ashamed of myself."

He followed her to the door, gently persistent; Jan *was* ashamed, all the more so because his questions made her want to shriek with vexation. She ran almost all the way home, as if trying to run away from her reproachful thoughts.

The cool-blue air was still quite warm; when she stopped running she felt sweat trickling down her cheeks and neck. She had reached the front gate before she realized that she had left her purse at Richard's house.

There was nothing to be done about it. Maybe Richard would have the tact to return her property privately, maybe he wouldn't. Now she had to lie again. Sooner or later the growing pyramid of prevarication would tumble down on her; but she didn't care, all she was worried about was the interminable hour and a half that must pass before she could go to bed. It serves me right, Jan thought wearily. I'll give Uncle Henry a good game, that's the least I can do.

In spite of her best efforts she lost miserably, three quick games in a row. She had told her aunt and uncle that Alan had not been at home, to explain the missing purse, and they both seemed to accept it. After the third game Henry tactfully suggested they watch television, and Jan sat, with clenched teeth, through one of the private-eye programs her gentle uncle adored. Camilla professed to despise them, but Jan noticed that her embroidery made very little progress during the wilder chase scenes. There was always a chase scene.

And then, finally—thank God—it was time for bed.

Chapter

9

December 1778

CHARLES CAME OUT OF THE ROOM AND CLOSED THE door behind him very gently. He stood for a moment, his hand on the knob and his shoulders bowed. Then he went slowly down the stairs and into the library, where his father was waiting for him.

The room was chilly, despite the fire roaring up the chimney. Snow made polka-dot patterns at the window, white on the background of somber evergreens. The warm turkey-red draperies and thick carpet did little to dispel the chill that pervaded the room except in the area near the fire.

Mr. Wilde was wearing a thick dressing gown. He had removed his wig and covered his cropped head with a turban-like scarf. Seated in his favorite chair, which had an attached swinging arm that could be used as a lap desk, he looked up from his papers when his son entered.

"How long has she been like this?" Charles asked.

"She has been bedridden for only a month. But she began to fail after you left the last time."

Charles turned to the fire. The ruddy light showed the sorry state of his once elegant uniform. The white was a muddy gray and the blue had faded to a darker shade of the same gray. It was not possible to make out separate bloodstains now, there were too many other marks. His hands braced on the mantel, Charles leaned forward, staring at the flames.

"Well, go on," he said. "Why not make the argument explicit? As you said before, I have done my duty. I am the only son. Now tell me that if I go back to the war it will kill my mother."

"Charles! Do you think me capable of—"

"No." Charles's body sagged. "I beg your pardon. You are an honorable man and would never use unfair means to turn me from my duty."

His father accepted the words at face value. He pushed the wooden desk arm out of the way and stood up, rubbing his stiffened fingers.

There was a knock at the door.

"Gentleman to see you, Mr. Wilde," the butler said.

"Jon?" Charles asked.

The grizzled old servant laughed. "No, Mr. Charles, do you think I announce Mr. Jonathan that way? No, suh, it another gentleman, that friend of Mr. Pendleton's."

"A business matter," Mr. Wilde said. "It won't take long. I'll see him in the parlor. Charles, you remain here. The fire is better and Jonathan should be along shortly."

He left the room. Charles continued to stare into the fire. Before long there was a sound at the little door through which a child had come with her tray on a summer night four years earlier. It opened and Leah slipped in.

They came together like iron to a magnet. But after a short time Charles loosened her clinging hands and held her off at arm's length.

"You shouldn't have come here," he said in a harsh whisper. "If my father finds you—"

"I couldn't stay away. I've hardly seen you; never alone—"

He bent his head to kiss her again. His voice muffled against her hair, he said, "I've only been home a few hours."

"But you wouldn't have come to me. Would you?"

"How can I? There is no future for you in this, nothing but shame and pain. . . ."

"Do you think I haven't suffered this last year? Every day has been like starving."

"Yes," Charles said in a wondering voice. "That's how it has been. . . . I didn't believe it could last so long. . . ."

"It will always be this way for me," she said. "Always."

"What can we do? If my father finds out he'll sell you. I couldn't stop him."

"We can be careful." Her slim fingers stroked his cheek. "Someday. . . ."

"Someday," Charles repeated bitterly. "When he's dead, and I'm master? Would you really assume the role of my black concubine—that's the term, you know. Could I endure to hear you spoken of familiarly by my friends? To see my children slaves?"

"But my children will be slaves whoever their father is," she said quietly.

Charles's face went ashen.

"And I'm a slave," she went on passionately, too hurt to care about anything except hurting back. "Or had you forgotten? You can sell me—or take me—or give me to one of your friends, anything you like. I have no choice, and you are refusing me the only chance I'll have to give, instead of being given. Would you rather see me married to old Bob, or to one of Mr. Jefferson's Heming family?"

She broke off, seeing the misery in his face; with a cry of remorse she flung her arms around his waist and hid her face against his breast.

"I'm sorry. Forgive me, I'm making it harder. . . . You were trying to think of what is best for me."

They stood locked together in an embrace as tender as it was passionate. The room was silent, except for Leah's muffled sobs and Charles's quick breathing. Neither of them heard the door open.

Charles was the first to see his father. He thrust the girl away from him, so that she fell back against the wall. Behind his father he saw the horrified face of his friend.

Mr. Wilde went white, then mottled red. After the first

moment of shock Charles recovered himself; only the glitter of his eyes, darkened to emerald, betrayed his feelings.

"I'm sorry," he said to Leah. "I didn't mean to hurt you. I think you had better go now."

Tears stained her cheeks but she did not break down or cry out. There was pride in the smile she gave him before she went out, closing the door quietly behind her.

"I'll go," Jonathan stammered. "I'll come back later, Charles—"

"No." Mr. Wilde made a peremptory gesture, without turning. "Come in. Close the door."

Jonathan obeyed. It was obvious that he wished himself a hundred miles away. Mr. Wilde walked slowly to his chair and sat down. His movements were clumsy; Charles's grim face softened as he watched. He went to the table and poured a glass of wine.

"Here, Father. You had better take this."

The older man struck the glass out of his hand. Then he looked with horror at the spreading stain on the floor.

"Your mother's new carpet," he muttered. "So proud of it."

Charles dropped to his knees and scrubbed at the stain with a napkin.

"It won't come out," he said. "I'll call someone to fetch water and—"

"No. You will sit down, and we will discuss this."

Jonathan opened his lips and then closed them again. Mr. Wilde was taking the wrong approach; the older Charles got, the less amenable he was to a direct command. But there was no use interfering, neither father nor son would listen to him. He could only remain a helpless spectator as two people he loved tried to destroy each other.

Sitting back on his heels, composed and dangerous as a leopard, Charles returned his father's unblinking stare.

"Very well," he said, rising, "But I'll stand, thank you. What do you want to say?"

"I know now why you were so hot, last time you were

home, at the idea of my finding a husband for Leah. Why didn't you—"

"You don't understand. At that time my feelings—"

"A pretty word for the reality," Mr. Wilde said sarcastically. "If that is true, then why has she resisted my attempts to find a home for her? I believed her when she pleaded her affection for us, her unwillingness to leave your mother."

"She is not to blame," Charles said.

"I don't blame her. I hold you completely responsible."

"Thank you."

"I shall, of course, take steps to send her away at once."

Charles's laugh was not a pleasant thing to hear.

"Why trouble yourself? I shall be gone in a few days. The chances are fairly high that I won't return. That will solve your problem."

"Charles," Jonathan protested. His friend gave him a blank, unseeing stare.

"Shut up, Jon. This isn't your affair. Father. I'll give you my word that nothing—nothing of what you fear will pass between me and Leah. But you must promise not to force her into a marriage she doesn't want."

"You are that deeply infatuated?" The older man's voice was incredulous. As Charles turned away he tried another tactic. His voice became pleading. "My boy, I understand these things. I was young once myself. The lure of the flesh is strong. Why, even I—"

Charles whirled around.

"Father! You don't mean— Not her mother!"

The old man's lips drew back in a snarl of disgust.

"How dare you suggest such a thing? Certainly not. How strange it is that you are shocked at the thought of incest, but not at—"

"Why should I be? The other gentlemen of our class are not. Leah is the product of several of these alliances you mention with such loathing—and if you did not share in the last of them, one of your friends must have done. That family of mulattoes whom Jefferson acquired from his father-in-law is close kin to Mrs. Jefferson, if rumor is correct. Walforth brags of his half-black bastards—"

Mr. Wilde choked, clutching at the folds of his neckcloth.

"Stop it, both of you," Jonathan said sternly. The authority in his voice so surprised his hearers that they obeyed. Jonathan went on, "You are both angry and hurt and are saying things you will bitterly regret. This is a distressing situation—not the least for Leah," he added, glancing at Charles. "It must bring pain to someone, whatever is decided. Can you not try, in love, to settle the matter so that it will cause as little pain as possible?"

The older man rose. He had just enough control left to know how close he had come to a fatal error, but he could not bring himself to be conciliatory.

"Speak to him, Jonathan. He seems to heed you, when he will not heed his father. I trust you to show him the dire consequences of his attitude."

The door closed behind him.

Charles dropped heavily into a chair.

"Well," he said staring at the floor, "go on. Show me the errors of my ways."

"You know them yourself," Jonathan said. "You needn't strut and roar at me; you will do what is right."

"What is right?" Charles's inflection gave the repetition a new meaning. "I remember your saying to me, the last time I was home, how difficult it is to know the right path; there are so many sides to every question, you said. I didn't understand you then. . . ."

"There are no doubts in this case," Jonathan said. "You know what must be done, Charles, and if your father hadn't baited you—without meaning to, he can't help it—you would have made the decision yourself."

Charles leaned back in the chair, stretching his legs in their scarred, scuffed boots. He closed his eyes. He looked deadly tired, and with the predatory eyes hidden, very young—as young as he really was. Jonathan's face reflected his sympathy, but he kept quiet.

"You're a comfortable sort of person, Jon," Charles said, with a sigh. "You don't preach, you don't express righteous horror; you don't even seem surprised. Did you know about—about this before?"

"I saw you together," Jonathan said. "The night of the governor's ball. I was—"

He stopped abruptly, realizing the pit into which he had let his compassion lead him, but Charles was too absorbed in his own feelings to question the statement.

"And you didn't rush out and denounce us?"

"You were leaving next day," Jonathan said. "I hoped it was just a—a temporary thing. I saw her more often than you did; I thought once or twice what a pretty girl she was getting to be, but for you, seeing her so changed. . . . Well, I mean, I know how it is. . . ."

"Old Puritan," Charles said, smiling faintly. "I wonder if you do know. . . ." He sat up with a sudden air of decision. "I've just had a brilliant idea. Let's go get drunk."

"There's wine here," Jonathan said.

"I can't get drunk on wine. Anyhow, I need to get out of the house."

The old butler appeared out of nowhere, as a well-trained servant does, to swathe them in the long cloaks that made them both look ten feet tall. Charles clapped his tricorn hat on his head; battered as it was, he wore it with a dashing air. Jonathan looked vaguely around the hall, as if he expected his own hat to materialize, and the butler shook his head.

"You didn' have no hat, Mr. Jon. You gonna catch your death someday, runnin' around without it."

"My hair is thick," Jonathan explained.

"I'll be back in an hour or so, Bob," Charles said.

The snow was still falling when they stepped outside, a gentle, feathery-dry whiteness that didn't feel very cold. Several inches had accumulated; in the street it had been trampled into slush, but elsewhere the velvety white blanket had laid a beautifying cover over the piles of human and animal refuse, and the Duke of Gloucester Street looked like one of the Christmas cards a later world would consider so charming. The snowy sky had a strange, unnatural brightness, as if the sun were struggling to break through, and isolated patches of color shone luminous against the gray and white mingling of ground and sky—a woman's bright-red cloak, the ruby globes of the holly berries, and the pastel fronts of the houses, saffron and blue and barn red.

As they passed one house they heard music. A woman's voice was singing an old carol, and Charles's tight face softened. A group of boys were reveling in the piled snowbank that had drifted up by the steps of the courthouse; when the two men had passed, one of the urchins threw a snowball. It hit Charles in the back, having been aimed at the irresistible target of his hat. The boys scattered, whooping, as he whirled, but they were not quick enough to avoid the snowball he hurled back. A howl of pain floated on the air as the missile hit one tattered child.

"Come on, you bully," Jonathan said, grinning. "Pick on someone your own size."

In another lithe blur of motion Charles gathered a second handful of snow.

"Is that a challenge?"

"If you like," Jonathan said, prepared to engage in any form of idiocy if it would keep the smile on Charles's face. After a moment, however, Charles tossed the snowball away.

"No; we're not boys, are we? And going back doesn't work. Brandy works better. . . . Remember the Christmas you stayed here, Jon, when the roads were too bad for you to go to Fairhill? Remember the way we decorated the house with branches and holly? And the party, when I got sick on too much roast goose? Mary Beth and her father came for dinner, and afterward we sang all the old songs. The servants came in for that part of it. Leah had a little, high voice, like a bird cheeping. . . . Jon. Martin is dead."

Jonathan stumbled. The path was littered with deceptive, anonymous piles of whiteness, and it is possible that he tripped over one of these. Charles reached out to steady him but he shook off his friend's hand and went on walking.

"Killed?" he asked.

"No, it was the smallpox. You must have heard how bad the British ships were, and Dunmore's temporary camps were worse. I suppose one can't accuse the British of deliberate neglect; their own men suffered too. But I heard one story that turned me a little sick: that they planned to send the infected slaves back to their owners—spread the disease. That seemed a trifle callous, even for a Tory. I . . . we grew up together, Martin and I."

"How did you find out?" Jonathan asked. The snow, melting as it touched his face, left spots like tears.

"There were two runaway slaves in a patrol we bagged last month," Charles said. "One of them recognized my name. Martin had mentioned it while he was ill. . . . Why did he run away, Jon? He was well treated—protected, comfortable, with people he loved. . . ."

"For freedom," Jon said. "Remember that word? The same word that moved you to abandon your comforts and the people who love you. He had less to lose, and more to gain than you. Did you think him less of a man because his skin was dark?"

"I suppose I deserved that," Charles said slowly. "But don't hit me again, Jon, I'm already down. . . . At any rate, I suppose poor Martin hoped that one of his comrades could get word back to Leah. I couldn't tell her, Jon. I meant to, but—well, the thing went right out of my head, can you believe it?"

"I can believe it. You were thinking of other things."

"I hate to ask you," Charles said, with a new humility, "but I probably won't be allowed to see her again before I go. And I won't let Father break it to her. He wouldn't be . . . gentle."

"I'll tell her."

"Poor old Jon." Charles clapped his friend on the shoulder. "You always get the dirty work, don't you?"

"I don't mind. It is fitting that I should do this job. Where are we going, Charles?"

"I don't know." Charles stopped and looked around. They could see the Capitol ahead, its once brave new flag hanging in damp, disconsolate folds. Their end of the street was full of taverns and ordinaries, conveniently located near the area where most of the town's business, legislative and otherwise, was carried on. "What about Mrs. Vobe's?"

Jonathan agreed listlessly, and they crossed the street toward the low, rambling white building that would one day be carefully reconstructed to give visitors a slightly misleading impression of gracious living in colonial times. It was one of the better inns, but that day the most meticulous housekeeper could not have kept the hall free of muddy water, or dispelled the smell of dirty wool steaming as it dried. The taproom was not as crowded as it might have been; most of the legislators were at home for the holidays, and the younger men had gone to war.

Charles found a table in a corner and summoned a waiter.

"Perhaps we should find someplace more private," Jonathan said, glancing at the men who jostled one another for a place near the fire.

"A crowded room is the best place for a private conversation," Charles said. Jonathan gave him a startled look.

"Yes," he muttered. "There is some truth in that . . ."

"Besides," Charles went on, "what more is there to say? As you pointed out to me, I know my duty as a man of honor, and I shall do it. I haven't time to do anything else. I'm leaving tomorrow."

"So soon? Your mother hoped you could stay for Christmas."

"I'm afraid the war won't wait on my mother's hopes."

"I hope you won't spend this Christmas the way you did the last one," Jonathan said.

"There are worse ways," Charles said, unsmiling. "We won at Trenton. It was worth the physical misery. Our winter quarters this year are more wretched than Valley Forge ever was. The men have a single thin blanket apiece. Some of them don't have shoes. You'll think me insane, but—well, I'd rather be with them than eating roast goose with my loving family."

"You're not insane," Jonathan said gently. "It is natural, and praiseworthy, to feel affection for the men who fight at your side. Things haven't improved at all since last year, then? That's discouraging."

"Oh, yes, things have improved. We're an army now. We keep losing—and we keep coming back to lose again. You've heard of von Steuben—the Prussian who served under Frederick the Great? He joined us last year at Valley Forge, and drilled us off our feet—officers as well as men." Charles grinned. "It was the first time I was glad I had learned French. To hear that man swear was an education! He couldn't speak a word of English, so one of his aides translated his curses for the benefit of the troops. But von Steuben says an officer must win the love of his men, as well as their respect; he must be sincerely concerned for their welfare."

"He sounds like a fine man," Jonathan said encouragingly.

Charles laughed.

"He's not a fine man; I suspect he's something of a rascal. But he's a fine officer. Thank God, we have several—and some excellent men. If we can get through this winter without starving, or freezing to death, next year should be better. I have a feeling the war is going to move south."

"Will you be sent south, then?"

Jonathan spoke without thinking; he was trying to keep Charles talking about the war, instead of more imminent problems. But this question was a mistake.

"I hope not," Charles said harshly. "I plan to stay as far away from Virginia as possible, with Washington's cooperation."

"But you speak as if this—this unhappy situation were the end of the world," Jonathan protested. "It isn't the only thing in your life. The affection of others—your parents, Mary Beth—"

And then he stopped speaking, struck dumb by the look on Charles's face.

"Is it—like that with you, then?" he stammered.

"Yes." Charles looked almost as stunned. "I didn't realize, until you made me think of marrying someone I don't. . . . Jon. What am I going to do?"

"If you feel that way," Jonathan said, recovering himself, "then the only thing to do is whatever is best for Leah."

"You make it sound so damn simple," Charles said. He groped for his glass and swallowed the fiery contents in a single gulp. He gestured to the waiter, his cheeks flushed as the brandy took effect. "Why don't you take Mary Beth?" he asked flippantly. "She's still in love with you, she always has been." Then it was his turn to stop speaking, in response to the look on Jonathan's face.

"You see?" he said simply.

"How did it happen?" Jonathan asked dazedly.

"It's partly your fault, you know." Charles's head was bowed over the glass he held in his clasped hands, so that he didn't see Jonathan's face. He went on, "Your talk, your quotations, your . . . indignation over all these years. Water wears away a stone, give it long enough. And you weren't a gentle babbling brook, my boy—more like a flood. We all feel guilty, deep down underneath. Men like my father are genuinely tormented by guilt. He's a good man, really, and he is not stupid. He feels the cruelty of slavery, and the injustice. That's why this has hit him so hard. He can't admit, even to himself, that my feelings are right and natural; it's the whole situation that is wrong. It's not to my credit that it took a personal cataclysm to make me see the truth, but at least I can see it. The only trouble is, I don't know what to do about it."

Jonathan's eyes had a stunned look, like those of an animal caught in a trap.

"You are not alone in that," he said.

"I can't change the system," Charles went on, still staring into his glass. "Oh, someday—when this damn war is over—if I'm not hanging at Tyburn, next to Jefferson and the others—then, maybe, we can start working on it. Jefferson has ideas about gradual emancipation. I've heard some of the talk. It's stronger in the North, of course. I can't even think about it now, it's too complicated. And whatever I do five years from now won't help Leah, will it?"

He looked up, his eyes candid and questioning. The discussion had helped him. It had left Jonathan shaken to the core, but Charles was too selfish in his distress to see that in his friend.

"No," Jonathan said stupidly.

"Then what I think I must do," Charles said, "is come to an agreement with Father. The important thing is that Leah shan't be forced into anything. I couldn't endure thinking of her with—"

"You're jealous," Jonathan said harshly.

"Yes, of course. Are anyone's motives ever entirely pure? But, Jon, she feels the same way. I know she does. She might try to do something desperate if Father forced her. Run away, or. . . ."

"She wouldn't do that," Jonathan said. But the dark fear in Charles's eyes was reflected in his own. "Charles, don't worry. I'll look after her."

"Would you? I was about to ask, only I feel ashamed, putting so much on you. You see, when I go away there won't be anyone to help her. And yet I wouldn't help her by staying; I would only make matters worse. I'll agree to stay away, not try to see her, if Father will promise not to sell her, or marry her against her will."

"What if she should want to marry?" Jonathan asked.

Charles drained his second glass; Jon caught his arm as he raised it to call the waiter.

"That won't help," he said. "Face it, Charles. Leah's only hope for a decent life is in such a marriage. Someday—"

"We're not talking about someday," Charles interrupted. "We're talking about now. Will you be my emissary to Father, Jon? Put the proposition I offer? I can't speak with him, I'd lose my temper. I'm going to be fully occupied elsewhere for some time to come. I may be killed, in which case I won't have anything to worry about, will I? If we lose the war, Papa George will solve my problem for me, at the end of a rope. If we win. . . . Well, that won't happen soon, not by a damn sight. I'll worry about that when the time comes; right now I'm worried about Leah."

"All right," Jonathan said wearily. "I'll talk to your father."

"I knew I could count on you. Poor Jon," Charles said again. "You must be sick of us and our troubles. What about yours? I've been so selfish I haven't let you talk about them."

"Mine? I have none."

"You must. Everyone does. How is your job?"

"I gave that up. At least—it's not quite the same as it was."

"Didn't work out, eh?"

"No," Jonathan said. "Not as I expected."

"What are you going to do with yourself, then?"

"I wish I knew. I had thought of going into the ministry, but it's difficult just now to study; and I'm not sure I'm worthy of that calling. Yet if I don't find something to do, something worth doing. . . ."

He broke off, for Charles was obviously not listening, although his head was bent in a polite imitation of interest. Jonathan, who had been on the verge of exposing a long-festering sore, drew a deep breath of anger. After sympathizing with his friend, he felt he deserved some attention in return. But his mouth relaxed as he studied Charles's face, which looked very young and vulnerable as he struggled with his painful thoughts. This added grief was almost too much for a man who faced death, in various unpleasant forms, every day of his life. He couldn't burden Charles with his worries too.

"I'll watch over Leah," he said gently. "You can take that fear off your mind, Charles. As you say, who knows what will happen in the next year or two? Your feelings may change. Hers may change."

Charles nodded, in seeming agreement. But of course both of them were too young to believe it.

Chapter
10

Summer 1976

GROCERY SHOPPING HAD NEVER BEÈN ONE OF JAN'S favorite occupations. And on this particular morning the familiar rows of canned goods and packages were a torment to the soul. How could she decide between applesauce and peaches when there were so many things on her mind? She had a headache, too. Every step she took, even in her rubber-soled sneakers, sent a jab of pain through her skull.

So Jonathan had given up his "job." That was good—if he had been speaking the truth. If he had not already done so, the news about Martin could have been the deciding factor. He would blame himself for sending the boy to a miserable and futile death. People were always accusing the younger generation of having no sense of responsibility. The absence of that quality was certainly a moral failing, but Jonathan had gone too far in the other direction. He blamed himself for everything; and his friends didn't help. Charles's remarks about Jonathan's influence on his changed attitude toward slavery in general and Leah in particular. . . . It had been made in all innocence, but Jonathan's stricken look had showed how hard the statement had hit him. He didn't need that burden, he already had enough on his shoulders. And he had so little comfort—his sweetheart dead, his friend in constant danger, his conscience torturing him.

Jan was no longer aware of the fact that she thought of Jonathan—and the others, but especially Jonathan—in the present tense. The intensity of her empathy was beyond logic; but she had reasonable grounds for believing that the dreams were more than a creation of her imagination. Somehow, for unknown reasons, she had been given a vision of the past. It had become more real to her than the world into which she had been born. There were moments when her aunt and uncle seemed like shadows, mouthing words she scarcely heard. As if the present were receding, with all the people in it. Even Richard, Alan . . .

No. Not Alan. Jan grimaced, and selected a package of frozen fish. He was too crudely, violently alive to lose his identity. But he presented her with no incentive to remain in the world he inhabited.

Richard was different.

He had returned her purse that morning, on his way to work. Luckily she had been the one to answer the door, so she didn't have to invent more lies for her aunt, and his luncheon invitation, promptly accepted, would explain to Camilla why he had stopped by. There wasn't time for conversation; Richard was late, and Camilla's footsteps, pattering around upstairs, warned them that she would soon be down, overflowing with hospitality and curiosity. But Richard had seemed perfectly at ease. Nothing in his manner indicated that he resented the way she had acted the night before.

And he had a right to, by the standards of his sex. A tease—that was the polite term; there were others, for a girl who led a man on and then turned him down. Although Jan rejected the assumption behind that arrogant male attitude, she didn't particularly relish being thought of in such terms.

She was staring at a shelf of canned vegetables when a voice spoke behind her.

"Ill met, if not by moonlight. . . . Why do you always jump when I say hello to you?"

"Because you sneak up on me," Jan said angrily. "What are you doing here?"

"I eat, like everybody else," Alan said. "Want a ride home?"

"No."

"It's ninety in the shade, and that looks like one big bagful."

"Oh, all right," Jan said ungraciously. "I might as well get some more stuff, then."

She tumbled cans, at random, into the shopping cart. Alan's eyebrows went up, but he did not comment. If the Notre Dame gargoyles had beards, Jan thought, they would look like relatives of Alan. He hadn't shaved that morning; he had a heavy beard, and the overnight growth was as much as some men get in a week. He looked as if he were still wearing last night's shirt, too.

He turned abruptly as she was about to comment on his dishabille, and wandered off down the aisle, pushing his own cart. She didn't see him again until she had checked out and found him waiting outside the store. He had already picked up his groceries. They filled four bags.

"Expecting houseguests?" she asked.

"Nosy, aren't you."

Jan subsided. Her headache was getting worse, and she was in no mood to defend herself against Alan's ungallant comments.

Alan's old car was not in the pink of condition. When Jan got in and closed the door it failed to catch; Alan leaned across her to slam it again. His shirt sleeve, rolled to the elbow, caught on one of the knobs on the dashboard and exposed a long, barely healed scar that ran down the outside of his upper arm.

"War wound, no doubt," Jan said.

Alan put the car in motion.

"Drunken brawl," he said. "Switchblade."

"I thought that's what it looked like."

"And how would you know?"

"I taught high school, remember?"

"I remember, my dearest, as I remember every tiny detail about you," Alan said. "But I did not realize that it should necessarily follow that you had seen a switchblade." He slid neatly past an idiot trying to make a left turn from the right lane, and then said soberly, "Bad?"

"Awful." Jan shivered. "They cut each other terribly before the police arrived."

"I expect they did, if you waited for the police to get there." The sardonic note was back in Alan's voice. "Do you mean you stood around with a bunch of other ineffectuals and watched two kids slash each other?"

"What could I have done?"

"Grab a baseball bat or a chair or a fire extinguisher and knock 'em both silly," Alan said. "Good God Almighty, I never heard of such crap. No wonder the kids are in such a mess if the teachers can't—"

"Shut up," Jan said.

"I can't shut up, I'm constitutionally incapable of keeping quiet. But I will change the subject, although you were the one who introduced it. . . . Mind if we stop by my place first? Some of that food is for one of my neighbors, and she's waiting for her baking soda, or whatever the mystery ingredient is."

"Fine with me," Jan said. She had an illogical desire to see what the said neighbor looked like. Blond and blue-eyed and cuddly, no doubt, with one of those sickening Southern drawls.

They drew up in front of Alan's apartment and walked into a small war. The combatants were a whirling, furry mass in the middle of the sidewalk. Barks and growls and snarls came from the fighters, and a variety of shouts from the circle of spectators, punctuated by the shrieks of a little old lady in tennis shoes, with pale-blue hair and a pair of regrettably tight culottes.

Alan plunged in with both arms, and emerged with a dog dangling from each hand. One was an aged Pekinese, white hairs frosting his amber muzzle; his pop eyes protruded even more than usual, thanks to the stranglehold Alan had on his collar. He was still trying to bite something. The other dog was a black Labrador, half grown, but of good size, who had already seen the error of his ways.

As might have been expected, the lady with the blue hair was the owner of the Pekinese. She caught at her pet.

"He's choking," she screamed. "Alan Miller, you awful man, how dare you strangle poor Nanki Poo? Let him go at once! Poor baby, he's bleeding."

"He is," Alan agreed, relinquishing his hold. "Goddamn it, Mabel, will you ever learn to keep that superannuated Casanova on a leash? Someday he'll meet a Saint Bernard who'll swallow him in one mouthful. Wait a minute, let me get rid of this monster and I'll have a look—"

"You certainly will not." Mabel retreated, clutching her wriggling, snarling dog to her bosom. "I'll take him directly to Dr. Smithers. I never knew you were so cruel, Alan. You will certainly have to apologize to Nanki Poo before either of us will speak to you again."

She stalked off, her haunches shaking with indignation.

Alan sent the Labrador on its way with a well-placed boot to the tail and then turned purposefully toward the cause of it all—a demure poodle who had been watching the duel from the sidelines with ladylike interest. Before he could grab her, her owner—a big, burly man in a ragged undershirt—rushed up and gathered her into his arms. From this safe vantage point she looked at Alan and smirked.

"Okay, Miller, okay," the man babbled. "I know what you're gonna say—"

"But I'll say it again, since you don't seem to get the message. If you're too cheap to have that bitch spayed, at least keep her inside when she's in heat. Jesus Christ, what a neighborhood! Can't even bring a lady here for five minutes without getting into a brawl!"

The spectators had dispersed during this tirade, except for a middle-aged black woman wearing an apron on which she was wiping floury hands.

"Thanks, Alan," she said with a smile. "Miss Mabel have a fit if anything happen to that damn little dog. He getting too old to fight, but she won't keep him on a leash when he yells to get loose."

"Pekes are fighting dogs," Alan said. "Is it stupidity or courage that makes an animal tackle something four times its size?"

"It's plain ole sex this time," the cook said dryly. "You got them groceries, Alan? Never mind, I fetch 'em. Thank you kindly." She lifted two of the bags and, on her way back to the apartment, paused to add, "Looks like one of them dogs bit you. If it was Nanki Poo, ain't nothing wrong with him but meanness; but if it was that other, maybe you better make them check for rabies."

"He hasn't got rabies," Alan said. "Just overactive gonads. Come on, Jan, I'll take you home."

He wiped his bleeding palm on his shirt. Jan got up from the lawn, where she had been sitting cross-legged watching the show.

"Don't you want to unload your groceries?"

"No, I want to get you off my back," Alan said rudely.

"Want me to drive?"

"For God's sake, I haven't lost an arm. Get in."

He looked amused, though, and as they drove back toward the center of town he started to laugh.

"See why I love that place? Something going on every minute. It's like a bloody soap opera, even the dogs get into the act. Will the little guy beat Black Bart and win the fair lady—who is, in the manner of bitches canine and human, standing safely on the sidelines after inciting mayhem. . . ."

"If they're dumb enough to be incited, it serves them right," Jan said.

"You have a point there," Alan said, losing his smile.

Traffic on the Duke of Gloucester Street was prohibited during the day. Alan parked as close to the house as he could and they proceeded on foot, with Alan carrying two of the bags and grumbling every step of the way. Jan considered whether she ought to ask him in for coffee, but he didn't give her time to frame the invitation; he simply dropped the groceries on the porch and walked off. As Jan reached for one of the bags he had carried she burst out laughing. Alan had left his mark, in the form of a bloody handprint on the coarse brown paper. She carried the groceries into the house. The incident, ludicrous as it was—so ludicrous that it had offended Alan's touchy male dignity—had impressed her a little. Maybe his advice on how to stop a fight had been based on personal experience.

Camilla exclaimed over the bloody print, and Jan had to explain how it had got there. Uncle Henry, who was helping to put the groceries away, chortled with amusement.

"Just like Alan," he said. "If there's a fight, he's in the thick of it. Like that brawl last month. Got himself cut up that time, too."

Camilla, her nose high in the air, was ostentatiously ignoring the discussion. Jan looked up interestedly.

"Is that how he got that cut on his arm?"

"Yep. One of those—er—dives, as your aunt calls 'em. He goes to places like that all the time," Henry said wistfully. "Couple of the boys got a little tipsy—"

"Nigras, I suppose," Camilla said, forgetting that she was not supposed to be listening.

"One of each," Henry said with another chuckle. "How's that for integration, eh, Jan? Alan had a few himself, I guess, or he wouldn't have been stupid enough to jump two guys with knives. It worked, though. He got 'em calmed down, and out, before the police arrived."

"That's his story," Camilla said. "He probably started the fight himself. Goodness, Henry, it's bad enough that you consort with that man; do you have to egg him on with those wild stories? And him a hero in every one of them."

The telephone interrupted her, and Jan watched with amusement as her aunt and uncle started their customary race to answer it. Neither was willing—or able—to run, so it became a question of who could shuffle faster. This time Henry won by a nose, and Camilla came back into the kitchen, trying to look as if she hadn't wanted to answer the phone anyhow. When Henry returned he was grinning broadly.

"Speak of the devil," he said, rubbing his hands together. "That was Alan. He's coming over for some chess tonight."

"He was only here a few days ago," Camilla exclaimed.

"Well, we aren't on any schedule. He comes when he can. It's nice of the boy to spend so much time with an old codger like me."

"He never came this often before," Camilla said, with weighty significance. She and Henry both looked at Jan and then hastily looked elsewhere.

"Oh, stop it," Jan said crossly. "You're wasting your time attributing romantic motives to Mr. Miller. He can't stand me. Now here's a nice ham-and-potato casserole, enjoy your lunch. I'll see you later."

She could hear them muttering to one another when she went through the hall on her way out, and she smiled to herself. Poor old things, they got a vicarious kick out of her romances—imaginary and otherwise. But Uncle Henry was in for a disappointment if he thought she and Alan were ever going to hear wedding bells.

She walked along the palace green toward Nicholson Street. As usual, it was crowded with tourists of all shapes and sizes, and there was a long line waiting to be admitted to the Governor's Palace. It was a stately building, with its cupola and balcony and handsome wrought-iron gate, with the brightly painted unicorn and lion supporting the royal arms. Jan wished she had paid more attention to the details when the palace had made its appearance in her nighttime sightseeing; but it had been dark, and the only lights had been those of the lamps on the carriages and the torches borne by servants escorting departing guests. The reconstruction was accurate, though. It was based on contemporary drawings and descriptions, including the plan drawn up by Jefferson when he was governor. Even the marble and tile of the interior was copied from fragments of originals found when archaeologists excavated the basement. A military hospital after Yorktown, the palace had burned down a few days before Christmas of 1781, and since the capital had already been moved to Richmond there was no need for a governor's residence in Williamsburg.

Jan wondered what the reconstructed ballroom looked like. It would be interesting to take the tour someday and compare. But she knew she wouldn't do it. It was hard enough now to keep track of what was real and what was not.

Before she turned into Nicholson Street she paused to look at the Wythe house, cool and white under the sheltering trees. It was another of the historic buildings open to the public, and the usual patient line was waiting for entry. It was being entertained by one of the lads who marched with the fife and drum corps; wearing the regulation costume and tricorn, the boy was playing a lively march tune on his fife. He was black. How Jefferson, and Charles Wilde, and Mr. Wythe—who had owned that very house—would have stared to see him marching side by side with white soldiers, imitation or otherwise. Negroes did serve in the Continental army, there were even a few black regiments. But not in the South.

Applause greeted the end of the selection, and the entertainers moved on, to amuse other lines elsewhere. The Foundation did its best to mitigate the inevitable waiting time for its most popular attractions. All the same, Jan thought, there are too many people in the world. And most of them are waiting in lines.

Someday she really ought to stand in that particular line and go through the house where Mr. and Mrs. Tom Jefferson had stayed in the winter of 1778. Wythe had been Jefferson's teacher. Indeed, he had probably had as much influence as any man in the process of thinking that culminated in revolution. Not only as a mentor of two generations of Virginia's aristocrat-intellectuals, but as a statesman, he had consistently supported the cause of independence. Like many of his friends he was against slavery, and had manumitted his own slaves when he died. Although he was a signer of the Declaration of Independence, he was one of the forgotten men of the Revolution, honored in his home town of Williamsburg, but almost unknown in the history books.

Jan knew, though, that it would be a long time before she did any conventional sight-seeing. Accurate as they were, the reconstructions held little charm for someone who had seen the reality, with the original actors playing out their roles.

The music instrument maker's shop was not as popular as some of the attractions, but there were people waiting to get in when Jan crossed the bridge over the little stream. The ticket taker recognized her with a smile. Jan indicated, by gestures, that she would wait outside.

It wasn't long before Richard came out, and they had lunch—hamburgers and french fries—at a restaurant near Merchants' Square. Richard was apologetic about the cuisine.

"I'm sorry we haven't time to go someplace decent. Things are really crowded this summer, and this is a particularly busy time for me. One of the other guys is sick with summer flu—selfish man—and we've got a recording next week, so we have to practice every night. Put some mustard on that hamburger, Jan, maybe it will kill the taste."

"It tastes fine," Jan said, chewing valiantly. "Richard. About last night—"

"Let's forget it." Richard smiled, his eyes crinkling. "Crossed signals, right? The yin and the yang didn't mesh. I feel as if I ought to apologize, and apparently you do too. We're two of a kind, you know that? How's your book coming?"

"You, too, Brutus," Jan said resignedly. "I'd sure hate to try to carry on an illicit love affair in this town."

"It wouldn't be easy," Richard agreed. "But Williamsburg isn't the usual small town. The college adds another dimension, and so does the Foundation. I was delighted to hear that you're getting interested in history. If you need any information I could give you—"

"I was thinking about George Wythe when I passed his house this morning," Jan said. "What extraordinary men they were! That one small area could produce so many outstanding human beings is really amazing."

Richard nodded. "Jefferson is my personal hero," he said. "All those skills—even with slaves to do the manual labor, how did he find the time? Did you know that Jefferson was a first-rate violinist, in addition to being an architect, statesman, author, archaeologist, historian, lawyer, and botanist?"

"No," Jan said, a little dazed. "Was he really?"

"And," Richard added, "a devoted husband and father. He adored his wife. Adams and Washington kept complaining because he would run off to Monticello every chance he got, instead of staying on the job."

"I haven't had time to read about Jefferson. Maybe I should."

"Yes, you should, he is an amazing character. Read Dumas Malone, he's the authority. A little heavy, but well worthwhile. There are a lot of popular biographies, but they love to repeat scandal and gossip."

"About Jefferson?" Jan was intrigued. "That's rather like gossiping about the Roman Forum, isn't it? I mean, he's monumental. What kind of gossip?"

"Oh, that same old scandal about his black mistress," Richard said disgustedly. "His political opponents raised it in the early eighteen hundreds. Smear techniques aren't new to politics, you know."

Jan propped her elbows on the table, forgetting manners and mustard stains.

"Did he have a black mistress?"

"You, too, Brutus?" Richard grinned. "I don't know. And I don't think anybody does. There was a girl—a very young, very pretty girl—named Sally Hemings. She went to France with Jefferson's young daughter, as her maid, when Jefferson was ambassador. Sally and her brothers and sisters, and her mother, came into Jefferson's possession through his wife; they had belonged to her father. The family held favored positions in Jefferson's household, but that can be explained by the extremely high probability that Sally and her brothers and sisters were the children of Jefferson's father-in-law."

"So Sally was Mrs. Jefferson's half sister," Jan said.

"It did happen."

"Then why couldn't it happen to Jefferson?"

"He wasn't that kind of man."

Jan was tempted to ask "What kind of man is that?" but decided Richard wouldn't appreciate the question. The subject intrigued her, though, because of Charles's relationship with Leah.

"Tomorrow?" Richard asked, when they parted at the bridge. "Same time, same place."

"I can't have lunch with you every day," Jan protested.

"Why not? Sounds like an excellent arrangement."

He didn't kiss her good-bye, but she knew he would have if there had not been so many people watching. She wondered what Williamsburg was like in the winter and fall. She was getting used to the tourists, who were amazingly well behaved, on the whole; but they made her feel a little like a fish in a glass bowl. Too many eyes.

And as she walked toward home she thought, There, that's that; and despised herself for using Richard as a means to reach Jonathan.

And the others, of course.

But if she had hoped that the meeting would produce a dream at naptime she was disappointed. She rested on her bed for a while, without feeling the least bit sleepy. Then, disappointed but not disheartened, she went back to her books.

Her uncle's library included a biography of Jefferson, but it was a dull tome, stressing his political philosophy and his legislative reforms. The tall, redheaded student who played the fiddle and flirted and joined in the pranks of the Flat Hat Club had no part in those austere pages. The Sally Hemings story could not be omitted, since Jefferson's political opponents had used it in a way that made modern campaign smears sound like Elsie Dinsmore. But the author dismissed the allegation with a shudder of well-bred distaste: "Totally contradictory to everything we know of Jefferson's character."

But Jefferson's views on slavery were rather contradictory too. It was clear that he considered the black race inferior in intelligence, although he was somewhat cautious about stating that untested conclusion without qualification. On the moral issue he was definite: slavery was wrong. He believed in emancipation, but he had no vision of an America in which white and black worked side by side, sharing the responsibilities as well as the rights of citizenship. The freed slaves would have to emigrate, there were too many of them to be assimilated peacefully.

But how the man could write! The great speeches sounded like trumpets.

"Indeed, I tremble for my country when I reflect that God is just; that his justice cannot sleep forever; that considering numbers, nature and natural means only, a revolution of the wheel of fortune, an exchange of situation, is among possible events; that it may become probable by supernatural interference! The Almighty has no attribute which can take sides with us in such a contest."

A passionate awareness of moral failure sounded in the words; and so did another, more selfish, fear. Like his fellow Southerners, Jefferson was in terror of a slave uprising.

By the time Jan reached this point in her reading it was time to get supper. She had never before been in a situation where she had to regulate her life by those three meals a day. She and her mother nibbled as they pleased; Ellen was always on a diet and Jan stayed away from the apartment as much as possible. But she felt she ought to cook proper meals for her aunt and uncle, and she was surprised and annoyed at the amount of time the whole process required. Really, she thought crossly, it would be so much more sensible if people just took pills. If this is what a housewife has to do for fifty or sixty years. . . .

She washed dishes with a careless speed that would have made Camilla protest—if that lady had not already been banished to the TV set in the parlor—and then she escaped upstairs before Alan arrived. To see him once a day was enough for her. As darkness fell, Jan watched the clock as anxiously as a girl awaiting her lover.

At nine-thirty she decided to sneak downstairs for a snack. The chess game would still be going strong, so there was no danger of running into Alan. Some warm milk might help her sleep. She was reluctant to resort to sleeping pills again, but she could feel her excitement mounting.

Her book tucked under her arm, she reached the kitchen without being seen. Camilla had gone to bed—probably as a silent protest against Alan's presence.

Jan put the milk on to heat and sat down at the kitchen table to read a few more pages. When she heard the door open she did not look up.

"I don't want to talk to you," she said flatly. "Go back and play chess."

"Can't. Henry's gone to bed. Said he was tired."

"Drunk, you mean. I know what those chess games are an excuse for."

"Henry never gets drunk. He's got a head like a rock. Keeping up with him is hard on an innocent lad like me, though. I thought maybe I could talk you out of a glass of milk before I leave. You wouldn't want me to stagger down the Duke of Gloucester Street singing rude songs in a loud voice, would you?"

Jan looked up from her book and encountered an affable smile. She sighed and closed the volume.

"I can't keep up with you. Is this one of your good nights?"

"I'm too tired tonight to fight," Alan said. "Go easy on me. What are you reading?"

He perched himself on a tall stool. With his feet on the lowest rung, his knees were on a level with his chest. He leaned his elbows on them and smiled ingratiatingly.

"Oh, all right," Jan grumbled. "One glass of milk and then out you go."

"Fair enough." Alan picked up the book and glanced at it. His bushy eyebrows lifted. "Heavy, girl, heavy. What's this you're writing about?"

"It is not about Jefferson." Jan brought the milk to the table, added a plate of cookies, and sat down. "I got interested in him because of something Richard said today."

"And what did your Richard say?"

"About Sally Hemings. Richard doesn't believe it, though."

"He wouldn't."

"I suppose you do."

Alan shrugged. "What difference does it make?"

"It does make a difference, if you want to know what kind of man he was." Without realizing it, Jan used a phrase she had heard elsewhere. "It's the monstrous inconsistency of their attitude that is hard to understand. Not just Jefferson, all of them—all the big heroes and framers of the Constitution. How could they talk about freedom with such eloquence, and own slaves?"

"Who the hell ever said human beings were consistent? It's an attribute of machines, not people."

"They were hypocrites," Jan insisted. "Saying one thing and doing another—"

"I keep forgetting how young you are," Alan said infuriatingly. "One of these days you'll find out that right and wrong aren't as clear-cut as you think. Our heroes didn't create the world they lived in; they inherited its problems from their fathers before them, and some of the problems couldn't be solved by a stroke of the pen. Jefferson did believe in freedom. He risked his life by being a rebel. And he kept a slave concubine and had half a dozen slave children by her."

"I thought you didn't believe that," Jan gasped.

"The evidence is inconclusive," Alan said calmly, taking the last cookie. "But it leans toward the positive side. Jefferson wasn't at Monticello all that much; but Sally Hemings's

children were born nine months after each of his visits. If
someone else had been the father, you would expect at least
one discrepancy. The counterargument, that he wasn't that
kind of man, is no argument at all. If he did get involved
with Sally, it wasn't until after his wife died. He didn't marry
again. I find it difficult to believe that he was celibate all
those years. . . . He—look at your lip curl. You find that
disgusting?"

"Yes!"

"Even if he loved Sally, and she loved him?"

Jan was silent. Watching her face, Alan snorted in
disgust.

"That's how the professional historians react, too. The
great Tom Jefferson, founder of the republic, in love with a
slave? Your prejudices are showing, Jan. Why does it strike
you as so impossible? Because she was black—a slave—unsuitable in every way? You poor little klutz, don't you know
that's how love works? The girl was pretty, even by stuffy
white standards. Perhaps she also had warmth or gaiety or
charm; perhaps she looked like Jefferson's wife. They were
probably half sisters, after all. And if she and Jefferson did
love one another, then he acted in the only way he could to
keep faith with that love. He couldn't free her; how could
she support herself and the children? By Virginia law a freed
slave had to leave the state within a year. Even a free white
woman without a man had a hard time of it in those days. He
couldn't settle money on her without creating a huge scandal
that would have blackened—excuse the pun—her name as
well as his. Anyhow, he didn't have the cash. Those Virginia
planters were on the verge of bankruptcy all their lives. Jefferson even had to sell his library.

"No. From a practical point of view emancipation was
out of the question, and if they cared for one another, it was
emotionally unacceptable. If there was an affair, it lasted
longer than most marriages; Tristan and Isolde were cheap
adulterers by comparison. It wasn't Jefferson's prejudices
that trapped Sally, it was the stupid social and legal conven-

tions of their time—conventions he did his best to change. If that's inconsistency—make the most of it. Got any more cookies?"

Jan started and closed her mouth. It had been hanging open as she listened to this astonishing speech.

"I didn't realize you knew so much about it," she said.

"I am a mine of useless information," Alan explained, in the old mocking tone. "And what I just said is a pretty fable. Maybe it was that way, maybe it wasn't. No one will ever know, unless a new batch of Jefferson papers turns up."

"It's an interesting theory, though," Jan said, putting the cookies on the table. "I must admit you've made a point or two I hadn't considered."

"The trouble is, most people insist on judging Jefferson and the other boys by modern standards," Alan said. "It's like sneering at Harvey because he couldn't do open-heart surgery. Sure, you can find a lot of ambiguous statements about slavery and blacks in Jefferson's writings. I'd hate to have anybody check my collected works for consistency. The important thing is not what the man said, but what he did. And for a Virginia aristocrat and a slave owner, Jefferson's record is impressive. When he was a cocky young upstart of a lawyer he defended a man who claimed to be free because his great-great-grandmother had been white. Later, he tried to get a bill through the Virginia legislature allowing men to free their slaves without special permission. When he worked on the revision of the Virginia constitution he had an abolition bill prepared, but his other legislative reforms caused such a storm of conservative protest that he didn't dare propose it. In 1784 he proposed a bill to the Continental Congress that would have outlawed slavery in every new state. Can you imagine what that would have meant? The Southern states would have been isolated, and slavery would have died a natural death. The Civil War might not have happened. The measure failed—by a single vote. Every Northern delegate voted for it. Only two Southerners did. One of them was Jefferson."

"I didn't know that," Jan said meekly.

"Well, now you do. How did we get onto this subject, anyhow?"

"I don't know." But she did know. It was the relationship between Charles and Leah that had aroused her interest in the subject. She had not realized how tragically common the situation might have been. "I've never heard you talk so seriously about anything," she added.

Alan's face wore its familiar look of cynical amusement.

"You mean you haven't been struck by the resemblance between me and Jefferson? Rising young lawyers, admired by all? I haven't picked out the lucky girl yet; but when I do, that won't be a consideration. It won't have to be. We've got a long way to go, but we've made it this far."

"Pollyanna," Jan said. "Go home."

Alan left. He didn't say good-bye. He didn't say anything. He simply went. He took the rest of the cookies with him.

Jan had had enough of Thomas Jefferson for one night. She got into bed with her *Outline of American History* and looked up 1779.

It was a slow year, as war years go. Charles had been right, the war was moving south. Virginia got its first taste of invasion with a raid, launched from Portsmouth, that did ten million dollars' worth of damage to the Tidewater area. But the major British effort was aimed at the Carolinas and Georgia. Savannah was taken, and the American general, Benjamin Lincoln, was unable to get it back, even with French help. He settled down at Charleston.

There were raids in the north, but if Charles was still with Washington he wouldn't see much action.

The dull narrative, or the milk, or both, had their effect. Jan's eyelids grew heavy. She turned out the light.

Chapter

11

March 1780

"SOMEDAY THEY WILL COVER THESE ROADS WITH A HARD surface," Jonathan said. "The streets in Philadelphia are paved with brick, but I suppose that wouldn't be feasible over long distances. Stone? The Romans did it; miles and miles of Roman roads, cutting through wilderness, fording streams. We consider ourselves more civilized, but we can't even build roads the way the Romans did. I'm sick and tired of red mud."

There was some justice to his complaint. The horse's legs were red, and Jonathan's boots were splashed. He was apparently talking to the horse, since there was nobody else in sight, but the horse was not interested. The new grass was delicious.

The tree branches were bare against the pale-blue sky; but the promise of spring was there, in swelling buds and in the sun's tentative warmth. The fields were ready for the spring sowing. Plowed earth stretched away to right and left of the narrow road, and in the background the roofs and smoking chimneys of the town could be seen.

Jonathan sat slouched in the saddle, the reins loose; either he had reached the place he was heading for or he was in no hurry to get there. The former alternative seemed unlikely, for there was no house nearby, only the empty fields.

"I wonder what it will be like," he went on; the horse was an unresponsive audience, but at least it didn't interrupt. "A hundred years from now—two hundred. . . . Supposing we win—and we have to, any other idea is inconceivable—what will happen in the next centuries? What sort of nation will come out of these birth pangs? I hope it will be a good world, better than this one. There are so many things that need changing! Slavery, of course, that's the most important. Surely it won't last much longer, not with so many people working to end it . . . What about war? Maybe that's hopeless, men like to fight. Even I. . . . But I couldn't kill anyone, Jenny. I can't even hunt now, not since *she* taught me that animals feel pain too. . . . Maybe they will learn more about sickness in the future, so people don't have to die from things like smallpox—or wounds. Charles. . . . I worry about him. He is so unhappy. Do you suppose, Jenny, that there will ever be a world in which people like Charles and Leah can fall in love and marry? A world where *she* wouldn't have to die at sixteen because doctors are too ignorant to save her? It's no use, Jenny, I can't imagine such a world; it would be like heaven. At any rate, maybe they will pave the roads. . . ."

The mare, who had pricked her ears at the sound of her name, returned to grazing. Jonathan straightened. A rider had appeared on the road that led from the town. He came slowly. The footing was bad, but there was a deliberate procrastination in his approach, as if he realized Jonathan's anxiety and wanted to prolong it. As soon as he was within hailing distance he raised his arm.

"Greetings, Cousin! What a coincidence to meet you here."

Jonathan waited until the other rider had reined up next to him before he answered.

"Not such a coincidence, considering that I am here in response to your message. You didn't have to threaten me, you know."

"Really?" Walforth raised a languid eyebrow. His mount, a handsome bay gelding, pranced nervously, and Walforth reined it in with a brutal jerk. "I thought I did. You've avoided me rather consistently this last year, Cousin Jonathan."

"You know why. I haven't time for your innuendos, Henry; I must get back to town. Come to the point."

"Ah, yes. Charles is coming home, isn't he? Dear Charles; he's been amazingly lucky. I expected he would have been picked off long before this."

Jonathan didn't answer. His lips compressed, he waited, his dark eyes fixed steadily on Walforth's face. The latter shifted uneasily.

"I'm off myself," he said suddenly. "Next week."

It was Jonathan's chance to be sarcastic, and he was unable to resist the opportunity.

"And you wanted to say good-bye? How touching, Henry. Where are you off to?"

"Charleston. I've a commission in Tarleton's Legion."

"Tarleton. Yes, I've heard of him. Fine young officer. Libertine, brawler, bully. The Legion is composed of New York Tories in the main, I believe. You should fit in nicely."

Walforth's eyes narrowed. For a moment his face expressed such naked hatred that Jonathan recoiled.

"Are you enjoying yourself, Jon? Do so while you can. Yes, I think I shall be very happy with Tarleton. I shall be with the dragoons, not the hoi polloi of the Legion, and I plan to specialize in the gathering of intelligence. I expect to be well received. You see, I don't mean to go empty-handed."

He was far more experienced at this sort of repartee than Jonathan. The latter looked warily at his adversary.

"Black soldiers for the young bully?" he said. "You'll have to persuade them yourself, Henry. I gave up that business some time ago. But I doubt that you will be very successful. They don't trust you."

"Nothing so useless." Walforth brushed at the sleeve of his fine broadcloth riding coat, and lingered over his words. "Washington is sending troops south to reinforce Lincoln in South Carolina. I want to know how many, and what route they are taking."

"Of course you do," Jonathan agreed, in a pathetic attempt to imitate Walforth's smooth tone. "How do you propose to find out?"

He knew what was coming; the horse looked up inquiringly as he shifted his weight.

"From you, of course," Walforth said. "Charles will be here today or tomorrow. I expect he will be carrying dispatches. He usually does. If not, he will know, as one of Washington's trusted officers, what the plans are. The information I mentioned is minimal; the more detail the better, of course."

"Go to hell," Jonathan said.

"If I go, I'll take you with me. Don't put on a show of virtue, Jon, you're a terrible actor. I have you just where I want you. And, by God, I relish it!"

"Charles told me once I had made a mistake by humiliating you," Jonathan muttered.

"Yes, you made a mistake." Walforth had let down all the barriers; his lip curled up like that of an angry dog. "I've hated you and that arrogant swine Wilde ever since we were children. You sneered at me then, and made fun of me; you had secrets and kept me out of them. I'd like nothing better than to see Charles Wilde dead at my feet; and with any luck I may yet have that pleasure. If he is sent south I'll make sure we meet. But my feelings for him are pale beside the hatred I feel for you, Cousin Jonathan. You'd have done better to kill me that night at the palace. But you wouldn't do that, would you? You're too noble, you and your high-sounding principles. . . . Charles admires those principles, doesn't he? How surprised he'll be to discover that you are a hypocrite as well as a traitor to his precious cause!"

He had been watching Jonathan like a hawk, and was ready. A quick twist of the wrist pulled his horse up on its hind legs, and Jonathan's fist passed through empty space. When Walforth had the rearing, snorting animal quiet again, his sword was in his hand.

"You had better hear me out," he said. "I could hide your body in those woods and be gone, long before you were found. Perhaps you don't mind dying, but you wouldn't like what would happen to your honorable name afterward."

Jonathan's mare was prancing nervously. He stroked its neck and it quieted.

"You needn't go on at length," he said. "I think I understand your proposition. You want me to get information for you—not only this, this is just the beginning, isn't that right? I must act as your spy or you'll tell Charles about—about—"

"Your activities on behalf of his enemies in seventy-seven and seventy-eight, yes. I mention Charles because you have a strange regard for his opinion, but of course he won't be the only one I'll inform. You've ingratiated yourself with the old man too. If anything should happen to Charles, Mr. Wilde might be induced to make you his heir. That's quite a tidy estate—what is the absurd name Charles gave it? Oh, yes. Patriot's Dream."

"But this is fantastic," Jonathan said helplessly. "You're behaving like a stage villain again, Henry. You can't possibly believe you can influence me this way."

Walforth's hand did not relax its grip on his weapon. The feel of it seemed to give him courage; when he spoke again there was a wheedling note in his voice.

"All I'm asking you to do is consider your own advantage. The King will win, Jon; how can he fail, against this rabble? You'll be on the winning side. If Charles survives, he'll be outlawed, imprisoned, his property forfeited. . . . Should you serve us faithfully you can end up as the wealthy, prosperous owner of Patriot's Dream. Of course you'll have to change the name." He laughed.

Jonathan bowed his head. As usual he was hatless, and agitated emotion had loosened his hair from the ill-tied ribbon. A thick brown lock fell across his cheek, veiling his face from Walforth, who had the sense to remain silent instead of trying to reinforce his argument by further speech.

As the two men sat motionless, a bird burst into song. A flash of blue crossed the field, flying low, and settled on a tree branch nearby. Jonathan looked up.

"Courting time," he said in an abstracted voice. "They will be nesting soon. . . . I think these Virginia bluebirds are among nature's loveliest creations, don't you?"

"I haven't given the matter much attention," Walforth said. "Well?"

"Well what?" Jonathan looked surprised.

"What about my proposition? I prefer to call it that; threat is such an ugly word, don't you think?"

"Oh, that." Jonathan patted his horse's neck. "Yes, I'll do it."

For a moment Walforth's face was a ludicrous mask of astonishment.

"You have better sense than I expected," he said. "Meet me here tomorrow at the same time, then. With the information."

"Make it three days from now," Jonathan said. "I can't very well walk up to Charles and say, 'Welcome home, what are Washington's plans?'"

"You have a natural aptitude for the profession," Walforth said, with an unpleasant smile. "Very well. But no later. I plan to go south within five days. And, Cousin—don't try to trick me. It won't do you a particle of good to denounce me. It would be your word against mine. And if you have any illegal ideas, forget them. I carry a pistol as well as a sword, and I don't go out alone at night."

Jonathan listened with interest.

"What a mind you have," he said. "I hadn't thought of either of those possibilities."

"Don't play the hypocrite with me," Walforth snarled. "I understand you now. In fact, I believe I have underestimated you. No wonder you have been so assiduous in your attentions to the Wildes. Only one son, and you with half a dozen brothers and sisters to share that overgrown farm in the Piedmont. Well, Cousin, stick with me and you'll get what you want. If you are a good boy, I'll see if I can't clear the way for you. Nothing easier than to shoot a man during a scrimmage, when so many bullets are flying. . . ."

"No," Jonathan said slowly. "I'll take care of that myself. Perhaps later, if he survives the war. . . ."

Walforth shrugged. "Suit yourself. I have more important matters on my mind. But don't expect me to leave him for your attentions if we should happen to meet on the field. I have a grudge to settle with him too. As for our old grudge— why, in truth, Cousin, I find myself growing quite fond of you. To think we have been at odds all these years, when we have so much in common."

But he did not sheathe his sword or approach Jonathan more closely. The latter sat quietly, his eyes fixed steadily on Walforth's face, his own face showing no emotion. After a time Walforth spoke again.

"You'll have to make arrangements to travel south from time to time. I can't very well take leave to ride to Virginia when I want to meet you. Can you resurrect that fictitious business position of yours?"

"Leave it to me," Jonathan said.

"Very well. We'll make plans when next we meet. In three days. And, Cousin—I am inclined to believe in your change of heart because your motives make good sense. But don't try to trick me, you haven't the skill. If you betray me you'll live just long enough to regret it."

He yanked at the reins; the horse set off at a gallop as Walforth drove his spurs home. Jonathan winced.

"What a theatrical swine he is," he muttered. "Every movement calculated. . . . But he's dangerous. What am I going to do, Jenny?"

The horse made no suggestion. Jonathan sat still, his hands folded on the pommel, and watched his enemy until he was out of sight.

II

It was as well for the conspirators that they had allowed three days for Jonathan to gather the information he needed.

Charles did not come that day, and Jonathan grew more and more anxious as the following day passed without word. Late in the afternoon he rode down to the college, where the Jamestown road branched off, in the hope of finding some traveler who might have word of his friend. He had been there for several hours when he saw a rider approaching and recognized Charles. A few years earlier he would have galloped off to meet him. His hands gathered up the reins; but then he thought better of it and waited till the other rider came close enough to recognize him.

The two men greeted one another with a new restraint. Jonathan, who had his own reasons for feeling awkward, studied his friend out of the corner of his eye and realized that Charles was in a state of exhaustion—physical or mental, he could not tell which.

"What is it?" he asked. "Your mother?"

"No." Charles shook his head, and the movement seemed to rouse him. "It's good to see you, Jon. What are you doing here?"

"Waiting for you, or for word of you. I went to the house this morning, and Bob told me your parents weren't coming to town. So I thought—"

"That I might have gone to Patriot's Dream? You were correct. I've just come from there. I would have gone on, but I thought you might be here; and I wanted to see you."

"I'm glad."

"I'm stiff as a ramrod," Charles said, stretching. "Let's walk."

Both men dismounted. It was a bleak day. The sun still shone feebly, but the masses of dark clouds building up in the west were a portent of a stormy night. Gusts of chill wind rattled the branches of the elms that, in another month, would shade the grassy grounds of the college.

Charles glanced at the buildings as they passed, leading their horses. The red brick structure that was supposed to have been designed by the great Christopher Wren himself looked deserted.

"It seems like a million years ago that we were students, doesn't it?"

Jonathan was in no mood for nostalgia or the melancholy contrasts it suggested.

"How are your parents?"

"As usual. Mother recumbent and sighing, Father even more—perpendicular. He is as rigid and unbending as a sword blade."

Jonathan cleared his throat but could think of nothing to say. Charles went on in the same hard voice.

"He refuses to come to Williamsburg. Last year's raid put him into a panic. He is afraid that if he leaves the plantation the British will swoop down again. He has already lost a number of slaves."

"He might be safer here," Jonathan said. "The plantations are too accessible from the river."

"He is calling it 'The Folly' again," Charles said.

"Well, but he may be right to stay," Jonathan said, deciding he had better overlook the last comment. "Williamsburg is also exposed to invasion; and heaven knows we've little to defend it with. Jefferson is moving the capital to Richmond, you know."

"You ought to hear Father on our new governor," Charles said, with a smile that held no amusement. "He says Jefferson is an incompetent executive and a radical. The bills he and Mr. Wythe submitted to revise the state constitution have Father in a rage. Is it true that they prepared a statute providing for emancipation?"

"I did hear rumors to that effect," Jonathan said cautiously. "But they decided this was not the time to propose it. The statute on religious freedom had the house in an uproar for days."

"Naturally."

There was little traffic on the street. The threat of rain had sent most of the townspeople indoors. The sky was darkening. Lightning crossed the rolling clouds like a bright spear and thunder muttered, still distant but coming closer.

They were opposite the Wilde house and Jonathan turned toward it. Charles caught his sleeve.

"No. Let's go on."

The house did not have a welcoming air. No lights showed in the windows. The white paint and black shutters had a queer dead look in the dismal light. Charles walked on without a second glance.

"What is it, Charles?" Jonathan asked. "Something has happened."

"You, of all people, ought to know."

Jonathan sighed. "I had hoped your feelings had changed."

"You're an unromantic fellow, Jon," Charles said fliply. "Don't you know true love never changes?"

"Don't."

Charles's shoulders sagged.

"I can't help it. If I start taking myself seriously I'll rant and rave like some jackass in a play. It's disconcerting, isn't it, that when one tries to express a profound emotion the words come out sounding like bad prose?"

"I suppose that's because the feelings have been expressed so often," Jonathan said. "But what is wrong? I visited Patriot's Dream last month; Leah was all right then, I talked to her."

"Did you?" Charles turned to him, his face alight. "Then tell me about her. How does she look? What did you talk about?"

"Didn't you see her?"

"No."

"But—"

"Father locked her up," Charles said. "In one of the empty cabins. There are several empty now, he's lost so many slaves. Oh, she wasn't mistreated, he made sure she had food, even a fire. He told me she could go back to her normal duties when I left."

"You're joking."

"Yes, it's the sort of thing I would joke about, isn't it? The situation was rather amusing, actually. Mother knows nothing about the problem; she was quite vexed at Leah for being so inconsiderate as to take an ague. I don't know whether her fussing was the worst, or whether it was Father's sanctimonious air. He feels that he has acted honorably; he has kept his word about not forcing Leah into marriage, or selling her. He couldn't see that this action deprives me of my chance to be honorable. How can he treat me like a naughty child?"

"But what does he propose to do about this?" Jonathan asked in bewilderment. "He can't incarcerate the girl whenever you're around. It's ridiculous."

"He proposed an alternative," Charles said. "You could never guess."

"I think I could. Marriage—for you?"

"I forgot how well you know him. Jon, he had her there—Mary Beth—"

"She has spent much time with your family since her father died last fall," Jonathan said.

"Reverend Willis's father didn't die last fall. He happened to be visiting as well. Father was quite explicit. I was to agree not only to marry the girl on the spot, but to stay for a week." Charles began to laugh helplessly. "Not too complimentary, is he? He thinks it would take me a week to beget a child—a son, of course—on that poor limp creature. If anything could put me off, it would be the knowledge that Father was standing outside the door of the bedchamber with his ear pressed to the panel."

Laughter choked him. He stopped, leaning against the horse's side.

They had reached the Market Square. The rising wind swept cold across the open space. The militiamen who kept a casual guard over the powder magazine were standing close against the walls for shelter. A woman hurried past, a basket over her arm, one hand clutching her hat as the wind threatened to pull it loose.

Finally Charles straightened and wiped his eyes.

"It's all right, I'm not having a fit of the vapors. I can

understand why women do, though; it must be a relief. Jon, my father hates me."

"Now, Charles—"

"No, he does. I've been thinking about it all the way here, and I understand the way his mind is working. He never cared for me as a person, an individual. All he wants is an heir for the name and the property. So long as I behaved the way a proper Wilde should, he was able to love . . . not me, but the image he had made of me. Why do parents do that, Jon?" Charles's face was genuinely bewildered. "The day you are born they picture you the way they want you to be—glorified reflections of themselves, but stronger and more successful. And when you turn out to be something quite different, they resent the slightest sign of nonconformity or independent thinking."

"Aren't you exaggerating just a little?"

"Not much, no. I can see why he's angry. It isn't just Leah. I've threatened many of his cherished beliefs. He'll turn Tory next, Jon."

"How can you say such a thing?"

"It's true. If a troop of dragoons comes riding up to Patriot's Dream, they'll find Father on the veranda waving the Union Jack. His heart was never in the war, or the ideals it stands for. It won't be a betrayal of anything for him—and it would be eminently practical. A foot in each camp. If we win, the gallant officer Charles Wilde will save the estate. If we lose, Father still has the estate. He might even put in a good word for me—if I have not engendered another heir for him."

Jonathan was speechless. He might have found words to soothe hurt or combat bitterness, but Charles's cool statement left him with nothing to say.

"Anyhow," Charles went on calmly, "Leah is out of prison now, tending on Mother's whims. And I'm off south in the morning. Washington is sending the entire Virginia Continental line to reinforce General Lincoln. Clinton means to take Charleston, and if he does—"

"Don't tell me this," Jonathan exclaimed.

"Why not? It's no secret." Charles hesitated, glancing at his friend. There was no suspicion in his face, only the embarrassment friends feel when they touch on a topic that may hurt another friend. "I hope I didn't offend you, Jon, when I criticized Father for his political opinions. You haven't been exactly forthcoming about yours lately—"

"Charles, it wasn't because—"

"It wasn't any of my business," Charles interrupted. He put his hand on Jonathan's dusty brown sleeve. "I wouldn't question any decision you made, Jon, because I know it would be based on the best of motives. Even if I didn't agree with you I would respect your choice. It hasn't been easy for you, has it?"

Jonathan shook his head dumbly, moved by Charles's new understanding.

"I guess I've grown up this last year," Charles went on thoughtfully. "Or else my own problems have made me more aware of the problems of others. I've been selfish, Jon; I haven't tried hard enough to understand your point of view. But now I see that the path I took was the easy one—marching off to war in a handsome uniform. It's a lot harder to stay at home and fight your conscience. Are you—I mean, are people decent to you, or is that another burden?"

"I'm not exactly popular," Jonathan admitted. "My people have been officially exempted from military service, but Williamsburg isn't Philadelphia, they aren't accustomed to pacifists down here. I can't blame people for thinking I'm a coward, or a Tory—or both. Sometimes I'm not sure myself."

"You're not a coward," Charles said firmly.

"I'm not a Tory either."

"Truly?" Charles's eyes lit up. "Is that true, Jon? I've wanted to plead our case; but I didn't want to influence you against your conscience. You're so much wiser than I."

"I'm not as wise as you think," Jonathan said, trying to smile. "But you needn't plead your case. I've always been sympathetic to the basic ideas. Now I've come to feel that the Patriot cause is the one that will serve my own ideals best. I was in Philadelphia at the beginning of the month, when the state legislature passed the emancipation bill. It's limited, but it's a step in the right direction. If Pennsylvania does it, other states must follow."

"They must," Charles said. "The only alternative to emancipation is catastrophe."

"That's what Jefferson believes. I have discussed the matter with him and with Mr. Wythe. I don't agree with all their views, but they are on the right track. It will be a long, hard struggle in the South, of course—"

"But worth fighting for," Charles said.

"Sometimes I think it's the fight that interests you, not the victory," Jonathan said with a smile.

"The fight *is* the victory," Charles said; and they stood smiling at one another under the storm-darkened sky, their other difficulties forgotten.

"This is wonderful," Charles said, after a moment. "It's good to feel that we are in agreement again. I don't know that I've ever told you, in so many words, what your friendship has meant. I sometimes think it's the only relationship that has never betrayed me. Why—what's the matter? Are you cold?"

"No," Jonathan said, rigid with the effort to control the long shiver that had passed through him. "Someone must have walked over my grave."

Chapter
12

Summer 1976

CAMILLA CAME INTO THE KITCHEN WHILE JAN WAS SHELL-
ing peas.

"Good gracious, honey, you've got them all over the
floor," she exclaimed. "I don't know why you insist on getting us a regular meal every day, we could eat soup and sandwiches for lunch just as well. Aren't you having lunch with
Richard? You had better run up and get dressed."

"I am dressed," Jan said. "We're not dining in style at the
Inn, we're just having lunch at his place. And I am getting
you a proper lunch because Frank Jordan said Uncle Henry
shouldn't eat all that canned junk, it's bad for him. It won't
take me fifteen minutes, Aunt Cam . . ."

If you get out and leave me alone, she added silently.

Her aunt got the message. She retreated with a sniff. Jan
got down on hands and knees and picked up stray peas. There
were quite a lot of them on the floor. Peas were such vehe-
ment vegetables, popping out like bullets. Especially when
your mind wasn't on the job.

She rinsed the peas and put them on the stove, but she
still wasn't able to concentrate on what she was doing. The
previous night's dream had been worrying her all morning.
It had confirmed something she had already suspected—that

Jonathan was related to the Wilde family, closely enough to be considered a possible heir in case of Charles's death. But Jan didn't believe for a moment that he had really agreed to Walforth's infamous proposals. Even if he could be persuaded to spy for the British, he would never connive at Charles's murder. Walforth himself was a little suspicious, but Walforth wanted to believe in Jonathan's selfish motives; he couldn't understand any other kind, and like most self-seekers he thought everyone else was a crook at heart.

Yet a nagging doubt underlay Jan's assurance. That was why she was so worried. How could she be sure of what was in Jonathan's mind? In the latest dreams it had seemed to her that she could sometimes sense what he was thinking, so acute was her empathy with him. The same thing was true of the other characters, to a lesser degree. Her own identity was becoming submerged, not in any single personality but in the events themselves. But she knew it was impossible to be certain of anyone else's private thoughts. People are always doing things that astonish their nearest and dearest friends, who respond with incredulity—"No, sir, good old Harry would never do such a thing!"—even when incontrovertible evidence proves that good old Harry has done precisely that.

What was the point of the whole thing, anyhow? She could not alter the past; from the first she had been invisible and inaudible to the actors. She could not tell Charles that he would survive the war, to face the agonizing problem that awaited him afterward, or warn Jonathan that he was risking his reputation, perhaps his life, for a futile cause. Would he go on with it if he knew that a terrible war and a century of bigotry would not solve the problem that had started with the first boatload of blacks landed in Jamestown in 1617? The Utopia he envisioned would never come about, and the brave new world would appall him if he could see the reality.

Charles had been won over to his friend's belief in emancipation, not because of abstract idealism but because he had been so desperately inconvenienced by the reality of slavery.

Well, Jan thought cynically, that was how most people were converted to an idea, by personal discomfort. But if Charles found out that Jonathan had been giving aid and comfort to the enemy, their friendship—Jonathan's last consolation— might not survive the disclosure.

A sizzle and a pop brought Jan back to the twentieth century. She snatched the peas off the stove and picked out the scorched ones. Quickly she spread the fish fillets onto a pan and put them under the broiler. She stood in front of the open door with her eyes fixed on the pan, determined not to let this food burn, but it was hard to keep her thoughts from wandering. She still had no answer to the most important question.

If she could not affect the past, then perhaps the past was meant to affect her. Was she supposed to learn something from the dreams? If so, the lesson eluded her. It seemed more likely that that assumption was a product of the unconscious egotism that guides human beliefs—the assumption that somebody, somewhere, gave a damn. Probably the phenomenon was random, without purpose or meaning.

The fish was burning. Jan swore.

She served a scorched meal and escaped, leaving her relatives eyeing their plates without conspicuous enthusiasm. Her head was aching again. It ached all the time now.

The muggy heat outside didn't help, and she was in a mean mood by the time she reached the shop where Richard worked. Why had he asked that she meet him there? She could have gone to his house instead of standing around in the broiling sun waiting on his pleasure like a docile slave. . . .

Richard didn't seem to notice her evil humor, and his gentle manners mellowed Jan slightly. He did everything with such grace. The wine was chilled, the table was beautifully set with fresh flowers in the center. Gradually Jan realized that the elegance was even more pronounced than usual. She looked at her glass of wine.

"Champagne?" she said uncertainly. "What's the occasion?"

"I'm not sure yet," Richard said mysteriously.

Jan let the comment pass. It was not until after lunch, when Richard had settled her on the sofa and taken a seat beside her, that her instincts began to twitch.

"Don't you have to get back to work?" she asked.

"I told them I might be late." Richard shifted a little closer.

"Don't be late on my account. I'd be happy to clean up the dishes, if you trust me with that lovely old—"

"With that and everything else I own," Richard said.

"Richard, I don't think—"

"I know it seems premature," Richard said. "I never thought I'd be so precipitate. I'm thirty, Jan; no longer an impetuous youth. This isn't as impetuous as it may sound, though. I've given it a lot of thought. It isn't only that I love you. I do; you must have felt that. But it's more. We're ideally suited. We agree on so many things, and most important of all, on the kind of life we want. I can give you that life, Jan—peaceful, full of beauty. Will you take it—and me?"

Jan's mouth was hanging open unattractively. If she had ever pictured a proposal from Richard, it would not have taken this form; and yet it was typical of him, gentle, logical, without unfair emotional pressure. Yet the emotion was there; the look in his eyes told her that, and the tension of his left hand, which was clenched tightly. She stared at it, and saw it move slowly toward her. All his movements were slow, giving her time to pull away or protest; but she did neither, and when his mouth found hers she felt the first surge of genuine strong emotion she had felt for days.

Then, against the darkness of her closed eyelids, a face took shape.

It was not the first time Jan had been aware of the resemblance between Jonathan and Richard. It was not a physical resemblance, but one of personality—the same gentleness and dislike of violence, the same sensitivity to beauty. Was this the reason for the dreams?

Since certain instincts are stronger than conscious thought, she had responded adequately to Richard's embrace. When he raised his head there was triumph in his look. Apparently he had felt nothing wrong.

"Darling," he said.

"Wait," Jan said breathlessly. "Wait, Richard, I'm not—"

"Of course." He immediately let her go. "I'm sorry, dearest, I'm pressuring you. Tell me I swept you off your feet."

His smile was very charming. Jan never knew what gave her the strength to resist.

"You'll have to give me time," she muttered, feeling like a fool.

"All you want. I know I'm jumping the gun, we haven't known each other very long. But I'm sure, Jan. I want you to be sure too."

"I'm not. I mean, I think. . . . But I don't know."

Good lord, I'm stammering like a schoolgirl, she thought disgustedly.

"All right. We'll leave it at that for now." Richard leaned toward her and then shook his head, smiling. "No fair, eh? I want you to think about it rationally, darling. I'd better go. I can't sit here next to you and keep my head. Would you like to stay? Sit quietly for a while and think?"

"Yes. I guess so."

"Just close the door, it locks itself. And leave the dishes."

The house was very quiet after he had gone. Jan sat without moving. She was trying to think, but she couldn't seem to concentrate.

Gradually she found herself listening—for what, she did not know. The silence was a positive thing, not the absence of sound but a quality in itself. It filled the room like a gas, as if an invisible barrier blocked the doors and plugged the air vents. The pressure built up. Jan could feel it against her ears, pushing against her body, squeezing her in, pressing her elbows against her sides, bending her head. . . . She jumped to her feet, flailing out with both arms. Staggering toward the door, she felt as if she were trying to run underwater.

She burst out of the house into the heat and sunlight and

leaned against the wall, gulping for air. The pressure of the house still seemed to reach out for her, through the closed door, and she started walking, at random. She wondered if she was going crazy.

She paid no attention to where she was going, or to the curious stares she received from passers-by; but when a hand caught her arm and spun her around she realized that a motorist was honking his horn loudly. The fingers on her arm squeezed painfully. It was, of course, Alan.

"Are you following me?" she demanded.

Alan's scowl was formidable.

"Somebody should. You almost walked out in front of that car. What's the matter with you?"

"Richard just asked me to marry him," Jan said.

Alan's face congealed, like a quick-drying plaster mask.

"Oh, well," he said. "No doubt that accounts for it. But if Richard's embraces turn you into a mindless idiot he ought to consider whether he can afford to hire a keeper for you."

"Let go of me," Jan snarled.

"No. Even the rapture of being proposed to by Richard doesn't account for your present condition. Are you high on something? Never mind; you'd better come along with me."

Jan would have protested more strenuously if she hadn't felt so peculiar. Her knees had the same wobbly feeling that sometimes followed a bad attack of flu. Alan kept his grip on her arm as he moved her along, and she realized that they were not far from his apartment. He led her into the building and up the stairs and thrust her into a chair.

To call Alan's decor eclectic would have been to give it undeserved praise. It was belligerently chaotic. The only era of style not represented in the furnishings was the eighteenth century. Over the worn early Grand Rapids sofa hung a huge painting, an impressionist swirl of yellows and browns, with two red spots that conveyed the image of a feral animal within the mist about to leap out. The most conspicuous object in the room was the hi-fi; most of the pieces were unencased, and the collection suggested a writer's conception of a mad scientist's laboratory, all tubes and wires and mysterious glittering objects.

While Jan sat with her legs stretched out like a doll's, Alan put a record on the turntable, switched on the machine, and disappeared into the kitchen. The music came out of the quadruple speakers like a cavalry charge. Jan sat up with a start. It is difficult to ignore Beethoven at any time, and impossible to be indifferent to him when he is coming at you from four directions at once.

She drank the coffee Alan slapped down in front of her. It was so strong it almost scarred the roof of her mouth. Neither of them spoke until the last movement of the concerto had risen to a monumental crescendo, and died.

"Don't your neighbors complain?" Jan asked, as Alan moved to take the record off.

"Frequently."

"What was that supposed to prove?"

"Nothing."

"I thought you only liked loud vulgar music."

"Beethoven is generally loud and occasionally vulgar."

"Would you care to initiate a subject?"

"No."

"Then I'm going home." Jan stood up. She felt better. Not good, but better. Astonishingly, her headache was gone, although the sheer volume of the music had been enough to bring on a migraine.

"Wait, I've changed my mind. I will initiate a subject."

Alan was standing in the doorway. Jan looked at him uncertainly. He was quite capable of stopping her if she tried to leave. It is as well to face the inevitable with dignity.

"Go ahead," she said.

"Are you going to marry Richard?"

"None of your business."

"If I only asked questions about things that are my business, I'd never find out anything interesting."

If he had been disturbed earlier, there was no sign of it

now. Alan's face was as bland as his dark, strongly marked features could be.

"Oh, well," Jan said, with a show of indifference. "I'll answer your question, although you don't deserve an answer. I don't know."

"Hmm."

"If there are no more questions . . ." Jan edged toward the door.

"No questions. But . . ." Alan's face registered emotion, but Jan was unable to interpret it. When he went on he sounded unusually hesitant. "I know I'm not exactly the type sweet young things confide in. But if there is anything I can do . . ."

"About what?"

"Oh, hell, girl, there's something wrong with you. Do you think I'm so stupid I can't see it? The change in you this past week is terrifying; you look as if something is eating out your insides. Only it's not a physical illness, at least I don't think it is. What's bugging you?"

Suddenly, without warning, an irresistible urge to talk enveloped Jan. The words felt as if they were pushing against her closed lips, frantic to get out. She dug her nails into her palms and managed to control herself. The impulse retreated as suddenly as it had come, leaving Jan aghast and astounded. Of all people to unburden herself to . . .

"Nothing is bugging me," she said coldly. "You've got a lot of nerve. Now move and let me out of here."

"Want to go for a ride?"

"What?" Jan stared.

"I said I'd take you out to Patriot's Dream sometime. I don't have anything particular to do this afternoon."

Jan hesitated. Pride demanded that she walk out, her nose in the air. However, she was very anxious to see the ruins of the plantation, and this might be her only chance. Alan had chosen the one lure that might have held her; that he was aware of this, and of her struggle, was apparent as he watched her with sardonic amusement.

"All right," she said at last. "But no more impertinent questions."

"Is that a condition? If so, I refuse. I'll ask any questions I please. There's no reason why you have to answer them," he added, with a wide-lipped smile. "Tell me to go to hell if you like. My God, if you can't even handle nasty impertinent questions you are too delicate for this world. Maybe you had better marry Richard."

"Go to hell," Jan said.

"Do you want to go or not?"

"Yes."

"Then let's go."

II

The great Virginia manor houses of the eighteenth century were built on the riverbanks; each estate had its own private pier, so that ships could stop to collect the precious tobacco that was the lifeblood of the Virginia aristocracy. Several of the great houses still stand. A few, like Shirley and Berkeley, are open to the public.

The drive took less than an hour. The narrow two-lane road made it necessary for Alan to drive sedately, although there was not a great deal of traffic. It was a rural region, with only a few crossroads communities along the way. Finally Alan turned off onto a narrower graveled road that rapidly deteriorated into a rutty track. The trees that lined both sides were old and ill-tended; dead branches hung threateningly low; but the ancient evergreens were tall enough to form walls interlaced with creepers and vines of all kinds. In some places the boughs met overhead. It had not rained for some time, but the ground was still slippery and the air was as close and dank as that of a tunnel. Unlike an underground tunnel, it was hot. Jan pushed the damp hair back from her forehead. Alan's old car was not air-conditioned. It was one of the indications of his financial status, like his shabbily furnished apartment and his unimpressive wardrobe. Of course, Jan thought, with Alan you could never be sure whether shabbiness was a sign of indifference, arrogance, or poverty. She suspected, however, that he was not very successful in his profession. He certainly seemed to have plenty of free time.

"You say Aunt Cam comes out here?" she asked, as they bounced along over the ruts and potholes. "How does she stand it?"

"One of the local handymen runs a bulldozer through a couple of times a year," Alan answered, wrestling with the wheel. "But don't kid yourself, Camilla is plenty tough when there's something she wants to do."

One last bounce, and they were out of the trees, onto a level stretch. With a thrill Jan saw the crumbling remains of a stone wall ahead. One of the gateposts was still more or less intact; on it sat a blob of stone that had once been a heraldic figure. It was so worn by time and weather that its shape could no longer be made out.

Alan stopped the car by the wall.

"Here we are," he said. "This is the best-preserved part, so don't get all excited. There were gates at one time; they went for scrap long ago, of course."

The local handyman with the bulldozer had not been around recently. The weeds were hip-high in some places. Wild daisies and black-eyed Susans made spots of color among the yellowing stems, and there were patches of red and white clover.

There was no way to get through the weeds except to plunge straight ahead. The former lawn area was bare of trees and the sun beat down. The prickly weeds stung Jan's skin, and clouds of mites swarmed, getting tangled in her eyelashes.

The house had been built on a rise of land. When Alan neared the top he stopped, taking Jan by the arm.

"Watch your footing. The foundations are overgrown and there are some sunken places where the cellars used to be."

It was not long before they found the first ruins—a stretch of foundation stones, rough and crumbling. There were no walls left. They had been of brick, Alan explained, and the material that had survived the fire had been carried away by local builders. She realized why Alan had cautioned her to go slowly. In two sections the sunken cellar rooms remained, half filled with rubble, but deep enough to be dangerous. The walls were slimed with lichen. Not even the ubiquitous honeysuckle and poison ivy could grow in the lightless sub-terrene. As she stood on the edge looking down, Jan saw a gleam of water far below.

From the top of the ridge she could see the river, its shining surface dimmed by heat haze. The fields of weeds ran down to the shore, a rippling, golden-green sea. Despite the sunlight and the heat the site had an inexpressible air of desolation. There was no sound except for the noises of nature—birds, insects, the rustle of leaves stirred by a breeze.

Alan stood several feet away, looking out at the river. His shirt was open and his sleeves were rolled above the elbow; the pale fabric showed off his heavy tan. He looked taller than ever, and somewhat formidable, like a buccaneer surveying a site he meant to take. There was something distinctly piratical about his swarthy complexion and tall, muscular body, and his air of being in control of any situation.

Jan moved closer to him.

"It's awfully quiet out here," she said.

"Yes, I wouldn't advise you to come here alone."

"Bears?" Jan said with a smile, indicating the heavily wooded area that surrounded the rise.

"Snakes," Alan said calmly. "Foxes, badgers, skunks. . . . There's a lot of rabies this time of year."

"Good Lord!" Jan realized that she couldn't lift both feet off the ground at once, although that had been her first impulse.

"Don't get excited, city girl. There's only one poisonous variety of snake, and you won't run into one of them unless you go sticking your hands into holes in rocks. If you should get bitten, I can probably get you to a hospital before you die."

"Thanks a lot," Jan groaned.

Alan grinned and then relented.

"It takes quite a while for copperhead venom to reach the heart," he said consolingly. "The local hospitals all have the antitoxin, and I carry a snakebite kit, just in case. As for the rabies, just watch out for unusual behavior. If a rabbit tries to attack you, you know something is the matter with it. The only real danger in either case is if you panic."

"Oh," Jan said, slightly reassured. She had no intention of telling Alan that his presence helped to reassure her. He gave her a sharp look and went on.

"That isn't the only danger. There are some wild human types around too, and some of them are nastier than any animals you'll meet. The older ones come out here to hunt and fish and drink; the kids come to drink and smoke pot and fornicate and rip off anything that is lying around loose. It would not be a good idea to run into any of them, drunk or sober."

"Why are you trying to frighten me?"

"You're so nutty I don't know what you're apt to do. It would be just like you to take a notion to make a sentimental pilgrimage to the old homestead by moonlight. That's why I brought you out today, to show you there's nothing to get sentimental about."

Jan decided to ignore the insult, especially as there was more truth in it than Alan realized.

"There sure isn't much left," she agreed. "You say it burned down?"

"Uh-huh. The family was in bad shape financially when it happened; there wasn't enough money to build again."

"I suppose without slaves they couldn't make a financial success of the plantation."

"They never did make a success of it, even with slaves," Alan said. "The system was a colossal fraud from the start;

most of the planters were in hock up to their eyeballs. The gracious, elegant way of life that Southern writers sentimentalize about was a fraud too. They liked to compare their system to medieval chivalry. Well, they were right—but they weren't thinking of the reality of life in the Middle Ages, they meant the fictitious glamour world created by writers like Sir Walter Scott. There was very little chivalry about either system. Southern plantation life was a system of oppression that exploited the land and the people who worked the land. And it didn't have a very good effect on the owners, either. It has been said, correctly, that slavery degrades the slave owner more than it does the slave. No, the system never worked; it was a mummified anachronism, and it should have died of its own waste long before the Civil War killed it off. If you and Camilla want to come out here and moon over the magnolias and the happy darkies singing in the quarters, go right ahead. It makes me want to vomit."

"Me and Camilla!" Stung to the quick, Jan forgot grammar in indignation. "My God, do you think I approve of that—that—"

"Oh, dear, oh, dear, I have been unfair again," Alan said, rolling his eyes. "Do forgive me. Why did you want to come out here, then?"

"Idle curiosity," Jan said coldly. She hated Alan Miller. She had never hated anyone so much in her whole life.

"In that case . . ." Alan turned and extended a long arm toward the south. "The main house lay that way. This part was the office, a separate building. A plantation was a big-time operation, hundreds of workers, half a dozen industries going on in addition to the farming. So . . . within these fallen walls the master met with his overseer to go over the accounts and decide on the week's work. The main house was a handsome place: two stories, brick. The interior paneling, staircase, and so on were of local walnut. They would be worth a fortune today. Black walnut is getting scarce—like everything else. On the far side of the house was another one-story brick structure, corresponding to the office. It was the schoolhouse. There's one like it, still standing, at Berkeley; the kids were educated at home, until they got big enough to go abroad to Cambridge or Oxford, or were sent to William and Mary."

"What about Harvard?" Jan had forgotten her anger; the only way to deal with Alan was to go along with his changes in mood. "I thought it was the oldest school in the U.S."

"Technically, it is. I guess it was too Yankeefied or something. Anyhow, few Virginians sent their kids north. The founders of the Republic—Washington, Jefferson, and the rest—either went to Williamsburg to college or didn't go at all. Interesting to speculate on how the independence movement might have developed if Washington had gone to Oxford. . . ."

"It might not have mattered. Do you think individuals have that much effect on the course of history?"

"Hell, yes. Other things shape history, of course, and not all men affect it. But Washington was one of the rare birds who was really as great as posterity has made him out to be. The truth is even more impressive than the legends. Do you realize what an extraordinary thing our particular revolution was? It's one of the few that didn't end up in a dictatorship of the mob or the military. We came very close to the latter, you know. Washington stopped it—single-handed."

"Oh, come on," Jan said.

"He did. Honest. The army had cause to complain: they were about to be sent home in their ragged pants, without a nickel to show for six years' sacrifice. No G.I. bill, no disability pay—no pay, period. The officers decided they should march on Congress and demand their rights at swordpoint. They wanted Washington to lead them. No man in history had a greater chance to proclaim himself dictator . . . king . . . emperor—you name it.

"Washington went to meet the plotters. He made his speech. It expressed his sympathy for their needs, and his horror that they could consider turning their swords against their own people, under any circumstances whatever. Then he started to read a letter from a member of Congress telling what they hoped to do for the soldiers." His hands in his pockets, Alan stared out across the river. He was smiling faintly. "He couldn't read it. He couldn't see. None of them knew he had to wear glasses. They sat there, all the disaffected young officers, and watched him fumbling in his pockets; and then they heard him say, 'You see, gentlemen, I have not only grown gray, but almost blind, in the service of my country.'"

"And that was the end of the plot," Jan said.

"That was it. They were all in tears." Alan grinned. "I've often wondered whether he did it on purpose. But that's not the point. How many men would have used that kind of charisma to negate power, instead of claiming it?"

"'Thrice they proffered him a kingly crown,'" Jan murmured.

"Caesar refused the crown but took the power. So did Cromwell. Napoleon took the crown. None of them had done what Washington had done—made an army out of a starving rabble. He wasn't a genius; he wasn't even unusually brilliant. But he had unshakable integrity."

"You're a fraud," Jan said, after a moment of respectful silence. "You talk tough, but underneath you're a big sentimentalist. I think you're worse than Richard."

She had not spoken with malice aforethought, but Richard's name was not one Alan wanted to hear. His mouth shrank to a thin line.

"I meant it as a compliment," Jan said.

"Did you? You don't know what you mean yourself half the time. Just don't compare me to Richard or I'll leave you here with the snakes and the rabid rabbits. Come on, let's get out of this wilderness. I could use a beer."

Chapter

13

February 1781

THE NIGHT WAS COLD AND RAW. THIN SLEET DROVE DOWN onto the road, icing the surface but not freezing it through, so that a walker's feet broke the crust with every step and sank into the cold mud beneath. The lights of the Raleigh were welcoming orange blooms against the darkness. Charles slipped on the steps, but recovered himself and went in.

He took off his hat and stood dripping in the hall. Water trickled from every fold of the heavy caped cloak that covered him from his throat to his muddy boots. It was a little warmer inside, but not much. He shivered.

The door on his right led to the Raleigh's billiard room, which was often reserved by local gentlemen as a private clubroom. It opened as Charles stood glancing around with an uncharacteristic uncertainty. The man who stood in the doorway, with a steaming mug in his hand, recognized him with a shout.

"Wilde! When did you get back?"

Charles blinked at him, shaking icy slush from his lashes.

"Oh, it's you, Pendleton. I—just today. I came back with General Morgan. He's been sent home ill."

"You don't look too healthy yourself," Pendleton said.

"Come in, man, come in; a glass of hot punch will stop that shivering. No, no I insist; you must tell us about Morgan, and that brilliant victory of his at Cowpens. The town's been buzzing with it." Seizing the reluctant Charles by the arm, he turned and shouted, "Gentlemen, here's Charles Wilde come back, with Morgan."

The news brought a rush of faces to the door—all friends or acquaintances, all voicing eager questions. They were not to be gainsaid; with a shrug that was half shudder, Charles allowed himself to be tugged into the room. A mug was thrust into his hands and a red-hot poker plunged into it. He applied himself to the contents. The warm, heady beverage did him good; a little color came into his gray cheeks and his eyes lost their dull glaze.

"Yes, I'm afraid the war is over for General Morgan, at least for a while," he said, in answer to their queries. "His health was shattered by the Quebec campaign in seventy-six, you know. That's why he resigned in seventy-nine, because of ill health, although God knows he had a right to be bitter. He was as responsible as any man for the victory at Saratoga, but General Gates carefully omitted his name from the official report. After that ghastly defeat at Camden, Gates had to eat humble pie. He wrote to Morgan, and although Morgan could barely sit his saddle he went south at once. I was lucky enough to be appointed to his staff."

"He's getting credit now." One of the men, perched on a corner of the long billiard table, broke in. "I find it hard to believe the tales I hear of his generalship. Another Caesar, another Hannibal—he's only a backwoodsman—"

"Those tales of his illiteracy and uncouth breeding are exaggerated," Charles interrupted hotly. "It is true he is self-educated; all the more credit to him. His knowledge of the classics is as great as mine, despite my expensive tutoring. . . ."

"That isn't a great recommendation," Pendleton said. A ripple of friendly laughter ran through the group and Charles grinned.

"Perhaps not. But Cowpens was a classic battle, gentlemen, perhaps the most brilliant of the war."

"But to select a battle site with an unfavorable river at his back," the skeptic on the billiard table protested.

"If you had seen our motley collection of militia, you would understand why Morgan selected that site," Charles retorted. "It concentrates a man's courage considerably if he knows he has nowhere to run. But he didn't rely solely on fear; he is a master at encouraging men." Charles smiled reminiscently.

"The evening before the battle I went with him as he made the rounds from campfire to campfire. He could barely walk because of rheumatism, but he wouldn't take my arm; he said it would cheer the men to realize he was so crippled he couldn't run away. He told them that, and joked with them, and he kept repeating, 'Just hold up your heads, boys; three fires and you are free.'"

"But the battle," Pendleton said eagerly. "Tell us about the battle."

Charles looked at his mug, which one of the audience had quietly refilled.

"Never ask a man who has been in a battle to describe it. In the end it comes down to one thing—a few men shooting at you while you try to shoot them first."

"But it was Bloody Tarleton's men who were trying to shoot you," one of his audience said. "Beating those greenbacked butchers made the victory doubly important. They had a reputation for invulnerability."

"I was at Waxhaws, where Bloody Banastre Tarleton won his nickname," Charles said quietly. "I watched his dragoons cut down unarmed men as they tried to surrender. There were many of us who had personal reasons for wanting to meet Tarleton. . . . But he's a damned good military man. He broke camp soon after midnight. He didn't catch Morgan napping, though; I don't believe the general slept a wink that night. At four A.M. he woke the men, bellowing. 'Get up, boys; Benny is coming.' He made the rounds again in the dark: limping, making rude jokes, telling the men what heroes they were, and calling Tarleton by that absurd nickname that made him seem smaller and less frightening. . . ."

Charles had his listeners spellbound; they waited, breathlessly, while he drank. He continued.

"It was cold that morning, the men had to keep breathing on their trigger fingers to keep them limber. As soon as the sun was full up, Tarleton ordered the advance. Morgan was riding up and down yelling, 'Don't fire yet, don't fire.' But when he gave the word he got the three volleys he'd asked for. The first line fell back then, and the second line fired their three rounds before they broke. Tarleton probably thought he had us then. But as the dragoons were slashing at the stragglers, down came Colonel Washington's cavalry at the full charge. He's a fine officer, the commander in chief's cousin. The British cavalry broke. It was their turn to run, with Washington close behind.

"In the meantime our militia made hell for leather for the place where the horses were kept. I don't think they were planning to ride back into battle, but Morgan was ahead of them, as he was ahead of everything that day. He turned those running, panicked men, and formed them up again. Then he went bolting off to find Howard's boys—our Virginians, gentlemen—also in retreat. But it was an orderly retreat, not a rout, and when Morgan told them to face about and fire a volley they obeyed like veterans. It was then that Washington returned and hit the British from the rear—and it was done. The whole damn British line fell apart. Tarleton tried to rally them, but it was no use; we captured the lot except for Tarleton and a few of his dragoons. Washington went after him. That was the part I missed; I heard about it afterward and I'm sorry I didn't see it. Washington and Tarleton had a hot saber duel, in the midst of a general melee. Tarleton broke away again and escaped. But we took over eight hundred prisoners, and killed one hundred and ten. Our losses were twelve killed and sixty-one wounded."

"Well," said Pendleton, drawing a deep breath, "you've converted me. Here's to Morgan, gentlemen!"

"But we've lost him," another man said. "That's a blow."

"He had to be carried home by litter," Charles said. "General Greene was reluctant to release him, but he couldn't even ride."

"And what about Greene?" someone asked. "We heard of that wild ride of his to join Morgan—straight through Tory territory with only a handful of men. If he's that foolhardy—"

"That wasn't foolhardiness, it was necessity," Charles retorted. "He knew Morgan's state of health, and he reached him just in time to take over command. Greene's tactics have been the reverse of foolhardy. He's been drawing Cornwallis farther and farther from his supply lines, while avoiding a battle we can't possibly win."

"Let's drink to Greene, too," suggested the skeptic. "And Colonel William Washington—and what about a round to Captain Wilde?"

There was a shout of inebriated acquiescence. Smiling faintly, Charles glanced at the door, where a neatly dressed man stood trying to catch his eye. Charles nodded, and then turned from the fire where he had been steaming like a lobster.

"I must leave you, gentlemen. An appointment—"

"A lady, no doubt," someone said slyly. The drinkers settled back to their employment.

Outside in the hall Charles turned to the man who had summoned him.

"Good evening, Mr. Southall. Is he here?"

"Yes." The landlord's face was sober. "I arranged a room, Captain, as you requested. I hope you'll take—your friend—out the back stairs, as he came. I wouldn't want any disturbance here."

Charles nodded. His forced good humor had vanished; as he ascended the stairs, dragging himself up step by step with his hand on the railing, his face was a stern gray mask.

The room was lighted by a single candle. It was a tiny corner cubbyhole, without a fireplace, and the air was cold enough to keep food fresh. Jonathan stood in the center of the room. It was the only place he could stand, the sloping ceiling came down so sharply on both sides.

Charles closed the door. For a few moments the two contemplated one another in silence—two shabby, tired men whose drawn faces had a strange new look of kinship in their expressions of weary endurance. The dark little room was haunted, briefly, by ghosts—the brilliant, laughing shades of the boys who had sworn eternal friendship on a summer morning in a past that seemed unbelievably remote.

Apparently Charles had, until that final moment, cherished a shred of hope that his suspicions might be wrong. One look at Jonathan's face told him all he needed to know. His shoulders, broadened by the double capes of his cloak, sagged.

"So," he said. "It was you."

"Yes," Jonathan said. He added simply, "I saw you too. I didn't get out of sight quickly enough."

"You saw me," Charles repeated, "and the rest of Colonel Buford's regiment. You must have been surprised to see me. I was supposed to be in Charleston, with the other five thousand prisoners the British took when Lincoln surrendered. Unfortunately for you, the general had sent me out to meet Buford's regiment. It was just as well for him that they didn't reach Charleston; they would have been captured along with the rest of the Virginia line. But their luck didn't last—thanks to you. We didn't believe there was a British regiment within fifty miles. And there wasn't, was there? Not until you got the word of our whereabouts to Tarleton. He's a devil for forced marches, Tarleton. . . . You know what happened at Waxhaws, Jon. One hundred and thirty dead, more than that number wounded so badly they could not be evacuated. It's a miracle I wasn't one of them. Our near and dear relation Walforth did his best to split my skull. He looks very dashing in his pretty green coat, but he's not that good a swordsman. . . . He might have succeeded, though—since he had quite a few assistants—if one of my men hadn't taken the thrust that was meant for me. Remember Peter Forest? He was a few years behind us at the college. He had a pretty sister, Rebecca; you used to say she—"

"Stop!" Jonathan's hand went out. "Charles, you're wrong. You can't think I—"

"It's taken me a long time to see it," Charles went on in a monotone. "I was extremely stupid, wasn't I? Twice I saw you with Walforth—not to mention the encounter at the palace two years ago, when I thought you were speaking on my behalf—that was a clever bit of pretense, your attack on him. It would have disarmed suspicion in any man, much less a friend. . . . Your mysterious business should have made me suspicious too. All that traveling. . . .

"But the damning proof was something I've known for— a year? More than that. When you told me you had seen me with Leah, the first night I. . . . I was a trifle preoccupied with other matters, admittedly. But I might have wondered, if I had not been so naïve, why you were lurking around the house on a winter night. I might have wondered why she was there. She couldn't have known I would come out, it was an impulse on my part. You were meeting her by appointment, were you not?"

Jonathan made no attempt to interrupt him, although his face reflected every blow as Charles delivered it. When Charles paused he said,

"If you think—"

"No, I don't think you had a romantic assignation. That's one kernel of comfort, I suppose; that you weren't my rival in love." Charles's laugh was very soft. Jonathan closed his eyes briefly and then forced them open, as if he would not spare himself anything.

"No," Charles repeated. "Again, the truth was plain to see if my eyes had not been blinded. You had a chance to speak with Walforth that night at the palace. You came to reassure Leah that her brother had made his escape in safety. She must have been worried about him. It was thoughtful of you. But then you have always been a kind man."

"Charles, listen. You're right, that's why I was there. But I didn't—"

"Spare me that, for God's sake!" Charles's voice rose. "Spare me your lies! You know what I have to do now, don't you? If I could forgive you for the rest, I can never forgive you this—that I must turn you in. They'll hang you, Jon, and I'll have to live with that all my life. I saw a man hanged last year—a deserter. The fall didn't break his neck. He strangled to death, it took almost—"

"Charles—"

"No, there is no use dwelling on that, is there?" Charles passed a shaking hand across his face. It was slimy with sweat, even in the chill of the room, and Jonathan, realizing what was wrong, took a step forward.

"Charles, you're sick, you are not yourself. You should not have come out. We can talk later, let me—"

Charles flung himself back from the outstretched hand as if it had been raised for a blow. Flat against the door, his hands pressed against the wood, he shook his head.

"We won't talk again. If God is merciful I'll never see you again. I shouldn't have come, you're right about that; I should have made my report without giving you a chance to . . . to explain. That's what I told myself all the way here. I can't act without giving Jon a chance to deny this foul thing. But you don't deny it, do you? And that wasn't my real reason for coming. I can see it now. Now you are warned. If you don't get away it won't be my fault. I didn't even have the guts to do my duty and face the consequences."

The pitiful rambling monologue died away, not because Charles was finished, but because his lips would no longer shape the words. He was shivering violently, and Jonathan, who had forgotten everything except compassion, tried again.

"You don't know what you are saying. You're delirious. Let me get you home."

"Home," Charles said. "Where is that? The house on the

Duke of Gloucester Street, where my mother lies dying and my father sits wrapped in his hate? There's no comfort for me there. No. I'm going to Patriot's Dream. Leah's there. They made sure she wouldn't be here, just in case I came back. They were unlucky, weren't they? I did—come back. . . ."

Jonathan caught him as he fell, dropping to his knees with Charles's head against his shoulder. It was all done without a great deal of noise, but apparently Mr. Southall, hovering nervously outside the door, had heard enough to arouse his concern. Jonathan looked up as the door opened.

"He's ill," he said, before the landlord could speak.

"Malaria." Southall needed little time for the diagnosis. "I thought he looked poorly when he came in. It's the cold that's brought it on. He needs his bed, and quickly. I can find a room for him here, but—"

"That's not necessary," Jonathan said quietly. "I realize that my reputation is none of the best nowadays, but Captain Wilde has nothing to hide, and his family will be anxious to give him proper care."

The landlord looked relieved.

"I'll arrange for a litter. He has friends downstairs who will see him home. If you—that is, perhaps you should—"

"I understand. You want me out of the way. Hurry, then. I'll be gone before you get back."

Gently Jonathan lowered his friend's limp body to the floor. He fumbled in his pockets, and then realized that, as usual, he had no handkerchief. He used his sleeve to wipe the icy sweat from Charles's face, and arranged the folds of the cape as a clumsy pillow. Then, as excited voices rose from the floor below, he rose and made his way toward the narrow back stairs the servants used.

Shortly thereafter, a reluctant horse left the stables behind the Raleigh and took the road that led toward the river and the riverside plantations. The rider was bareheaded, but he paid no attention to the driving sleet.

Chapter

14

Summer 1976

LATER, WHEN SHE TRIED TO RETRACE THE DARKENING path her mind had followed, Jan could not remember precisely when the strangest idea of all had come to her. It did not grow slowly from a seed into a plant, but appeared out of nothing like an Indian juggler's magical tree, full-fruited and familiar, as if it had always stood there.

But the fruit was poisonous, and there was never a time when Jan did not realize the fact. She was both frightened and fascinated; and for a while fascination overcame both fear and common sense.

Perhaps the plan had first occurred to her after the 1777 episode, when she learned of Jonathan's short-lived and tragic love affair. The feelings he expressed about his dead sweetheart struck Jan all the more forcibly because she had never heard such ideas voiced by a man who believed them with his whole heart—a man of profound religious faith and the unselfconscious sensibility which a later age mistakenly labels sentimentality. He believed in a hereafter, where true souls would meet again, and where such reunion was the reward of honorable living—concepts that had been out of fashion for so long that the expression of them in the twentieth century is a subject for farce or "camp" fiction. It is impossible for a modern, even a historian of the period, to comprehend the living force of such ideas. But Jan had a unique advantage over historians. She had been there. She had seen Jonathan's face and heard the ring of conviction in his voice.

She woke early after the vision of the terrible encounter between Jonathan and Charles. She was crying when she awoke, as one sometimes does after a particularly vivid and terrifying nightmare. The usual release of the dreamer was not hers, for she could not tell herself that "it was only a dream." Nor was it of any value to remember that if the events she saw had actually transpired, they had long since ended. To her, the actors were not only real and actual, they were contemporaneous. When she awoke after a dream episode she thought of them as carrying on their lives elsewhere. Or elsewhen?

The room was too dark for Jan to see the portrait, but she didn't need to see it. She could visualize Jonathan's living face as clearly as if it hung in the air before her, and the memory of the agony it had expressed made her eyes overflow again.

It was then that she recognized the idea. The arguments marshaled themselves so neatly in her mind that they must have been present, if unacknowledged, for days.

Perhaps, after all, she was not the first person who had walked into another time. There were stories. . . . The one about the two ladies, tourists, walking in the gardens of Versailles, who had come upon a crowd of people wearing the elaborate costumes and high powdered wigs of the court of Louis the Fourteenth. . . . That was supposed to be a true story. The theme was common in fiction, from the popular play *Berkeley Square* to a number of modern novels. How many others had experienced a similar slip in the fabric of time and, like herself, had kept quiet about it for fear of being committed to a mental institution? In earlier centuries such an experience would have been regarded as communication with the devil, and would probably have brought the unfortunate dreamer to the stake.

The Versailles case was not really a parallel. The ladies had stumbled over a crack in time, but Jan's involvement was neither casual nor fortuitous. Something had drawn her to a particular time and place, to a particular group of people. Was it a case of reincarnation? That theme was so common, in both fiction and so-called fact, that there had to be some basis for it.

There was one difficulty. Jan couldn't honestly feel that she had once shared the identity of any of the actors in her dreams. The feeling she had for Jonathan was certainly not that of identity, or, if it was, she was suffering from narcissism of the worst kind. She loved him. The only reason why she had responded to Richard was because he reminded her of Jonathan. She was obsessed by the dream image of a man who had died almost two hundred years ago.

Yet the concept lost its aura of abnormality and became almost sensible if one accepted a dogma held by mystics and divines for thousands of years: that the soul is eternal, the body meaningless. Souls might recognize one another across time. . . .

Jan had enough common sense, or enough cynicism, to grimace slightly at this sentiment. Well, why not? she asked herself. It might sound corny. So did a lot of basic beliefs when you expressed them so baldly. Honor, love, patriotism—all corny ideas in the terms of her own time, but then her time was sick, everyone admitted that. A century earlier people hadn't thought things like that were subjects for humor. Why should she judge ideas by the passing fashions of a corrupt era?

It had occurred to her, of course, that she might have lived briefly as Jonathan's beloved. Patience. . . . Neither the name nor the childish, smiling face had struck her with any shock of recognition. But it was possible. Perhaps she had lived, and died too soon; perhaps Patience's death had been a flaw in the pattern that had been designed to give Jonathan the happiness he deserved. And if the pattern had gone wrong. . . . Why shouldn't someone try to mend it? Was that the reason why the dreams had been sent to her, the reason that had eluded her so far, but which she instinctively knew must exist?

It was only one short treacherous step from that idea to the next.

Go back.

A few days earlier Jan would have recoiled from the idea as from a snake in her path. Now she leaned back against her pillow and contemplated it with increasing favor.

There was no clue in any of her casual reading as to how—or even if—such a thing might be done. Besotted as she was, a faint quiver of uneasiness stirred as she thought about it. Granted that there might be some Plan, some Pattern—didn't that presuppose a Planner? And He might be put out, to say the least, if one of his smaller creations attempted to meddle with His design. Such an idea, of course, was as antithetical to Jan's modern rationalism as all the other crazy notions she had been considering.

She wanted to reach Jonathan, and not only for selfish reasons. He was so unhappy and so confused, and he was heading deeper into danger. If she could reach him she could tell him—what? That his dreams were boyish folly, his hopes doomed to failure? That the only sane life was one of withdrawal from a world too corrupt to accept positive change?

Jan threw herself flat and pummeled the pillow. Never mind what she wanted to tell him. She wanted to reach him, never mind why, and there was only one hope of doing it that she could see.

She was wise enough to know that most people who claim to have a pipeline into the next world are either charlatans or self-deluded fools. But she would have to try the commercial mediums and psychics and hope to find one that had a glimmer of genuine talent. There was no time to seek out the serious investigators of the subject. The next few days might bring the denouement of the story she had been following.

She was not sure how she knew this, but she was convinced of it. For one thing, the last time interval was shorter than those between earlier dreams. The meeting between Charles and Jonathan at the Raleigh had taken place in early 1781, less than a year after the dream that had preceded it. She no longer needed to research her history, she knew it. Charles was back in Williamsburg after the battle of Cowpens. That had taken place in January of 1781, and the hero of the battle, General Morgan, had followed Greene for several weeks before the latter finally sent the crippled warrior home. The date of the last night's dream, then, was sometime in February, 1781.

The most important battles of the war in the South were to follow. If Charles returned to duty soon he would arrive in time for the battle of Guilford Courthouse in the middle of March. That had been a frustrating encounter, for we had come close to winning it. But it was a Pyrrhic victory for the British; General Cornwallis had lost a fourth of his men, most of them when he ordered his gunners to fire through his own troops in order to stop the American advance. After that, Greene, the ex-Quaker whom Washington considered his ablest subordinate, had continued his skillful campaign of retreat and withdrawal, pulling the British farther and farther from their supply lines and gathering men and supplies as he moved. South Carolina, which Cornwallis had thought conquered, rose in flaming rebellion, and Cornwallis was forced to try elsewhere. He tried Virginia.

Tarleton's dragoons, now accompanied by Charles's and Jonathan's old enemy, had a well-deserved reputation for ferocity. They were the terror of the South Carolina campaign, and they came with Cornwallis when he faced Lafayette in Virginia. The young Frenchman never had enough men to fight a battle, but he was almost as good as Greene at keeping the British on the move.

Charles would survive the next months of deadly fighting, Jan knew that. But what about Jonathan? She still didn't understand the game he was playing, and she couldn't blame Charles for thinking the worst. She had knowledge Charles did not have, knowledge of the meeting between Jonathan and Walforth, in which Jonathan agreed to commit treason against his home state. What role would Jonathan play when Cornwallis came to Virginia accompanied by the feared and hated troops commanded by "Bloody" Tarleton?

I've got to warn Jonathan, Jan thought. He's on the losing side after all. In the morning, as soon as it's light. . . . I'll try the phone book. And on that last farcical note she fell asleep; and did not dream.

II

The medium's habitat did not create much confidence in her powers. Jan stood on the sidewalk in front of the shabby apartment building and looked at it doubtfully. It was the right place, unquestionably. There was a sign in a window of one of the first-floor apartments: Madame Renoir, and a drawing of an outspread hand.

Aunt Camilla would have said the building was on the wrong side of town. It was certainly on the other side of one of the major interstate highways that bounded the old town, and it was a long walk from the Duke of Gloucester Street. Jan had walked. There was no other way of reaching the place. She was hot and sticky and disgruntled when she finally arrived. The sky was overcast, and as she stood wavering, it began to rain. The rain helped her decide. She might not have gone in but for that.

The inside of the building was even more dispiriting than the exterior. The hall runner was tattered. Jan caught her toe in a hole. Everything was tired and worn, like the woman who answered the door when Jan rang the bell.

She was dressed for the part, in a long, sweeping robe with tarnished gold trim. With a broad smile that released a distinctive smell of bourbon she waved her client in.

At first Madame Renoir seemed to be as bored by the procedure as her skeptical client. With a cigarette dangling from her mouth, she spread the cards out and recited a patter that must have been so familiar she could have done it in her sleep. "A tall dark man . . . the Queen of Spades, that's another woman, an enemy . . . water . . . money. . . ."

But long years in the profession had given her the instinctive insight practitioners of the psychic arts depend on for much of their apparent success. The medium was aware of Jan's restlessness, and the tension that held her rigid. Possibly she was also aware that her client might be good for more than the usual fee. Breaking off abruptly in the middle of her spiel, Madame looked up, fixing Jan with surprisingly intelligent brown eyes.

"This isn't what you came for."

"I don't know exactly what I came for," Jan said.

The woman grinned suddenly. It was a warm, cheerful grin, and Jan couldn't help responding.

"Okay, so if I was really good I could read your mind and tell you what you came for. It doesn't work that way, though."

"How does it work?" Jan asked.

"Look, honey, I can read your mind about some things. Most of my clients fall into two types. One wants reassurance, attention, somebody to talk to. That kind believes any damn thing I tell her. (They aren't always women, though, honey.) The other kind is younger. They come for a gag, or maybe a dare, then they go back and tell the girls at the office all the dumb things I said, and everybody gets a big laugh out of it. Only they wouldn't come if they didn't partway believe. But they usually come in bunches, two at least. That's half the fun, coming together. So—what is it you really want?"

"That's rather clever of you," Jan said, a little dazed by the sudden burst of loquacity.

Madame shrugged. "You gotta be a kind of amateur psychologist in my business. I do good for people, you know. I got clients that come once a week, like a doctor. They can't afford a fancy shrink, but they're lonesome and scared of the world just like the rich folks. So for five bucks they get a nice soothing spiel, somebody telling them things are going to work out all right. Anything wrong with that?"

"I never thought of it that way," Jan admitted.

"So most of it is crap—see, I'm reading your mind again!" Then Madame's grin faded. "You know what's the really ironic thing, though? It isn't all crap. There are times when all of a sudden, in the middle of a spiel—*I know*. It just comes to me. When I was young, just getting started in this business, it used to come pretty often. And I thought, geez, what the hell—I can learn to make it come. Only it doesn't work that way. The more you try, the less you get. And maybe . . . other things dull it too. I guess you think I'm giving you a line of bull, don't you?"

"No," Jan said. "I believe you. I'm sorry. For both of us; I was hoping . . ."

"Might as well ask." The medium lit another cigarette.

"I'm interested in—in reincarnation," Jan began.

"Aren't we all? I get a lot of people like that; want me to tell them they were Cleopatra or Marie Antoinette—though why anybody would want her head chopped off I don't know."

"Cleopatra came to a sticky end, too," Jan said, laughing. She had given up hope of getting anything useful from this raddled old witch, but she was enjoying the conversation.

"Did she? I saw a movie once, something about a snake, but that didn't make much sense. I figured it was some writer's idea of a sexy scene. Well, you know that's a bunch of—"

"Yes, I know. But couldn't there be something to the idea, even if everybody wasn't Marie Antoinette, or a queen?"

"Who am I to say?" Madame inquired elegantly. "If you want my personal opinion, I think yeah, there's something to it. If I'd been the smart business lady I thought I was I'd have worked that angle. It pays off, especially if you can write books about it. Only—see, honey, I'm honest with you—I never got a clue about it myself. You know what you want? A hypnotist. That's how they do it, they hypnotize you and take you back, through your own childhood and farther back. I don't fool with that stuff. Hypnotism can be dangerous, and not just for the client. Some clunk gets the idea you put a post-hypnotic spell on him, he comes around and beats you up. Or calls the cops. If you want to go in for that, make sure you pick a pro."

"Thanks for the advice." Jan reached for her purse. "How much . . . ?"

"Tell you what." Madame was eyeing her speculatively. "Want I should go into a trance? I charge extra for that, it takes a lot outta me. Or maybe I could give the Tarot a try. I don't bother with most people, they're just as happy with the regular cards, they don't know any better. But I get good results with the Tarot. Only cost you three more bucks," she added enticingly.

"Okay," Jan said. "Why not?"

Thanks to her mother's interest in fortune-telling she had heard of the Tarot—the ancestor of the modern deck of playing cards. The use of cards in divination had the sanction of antiquity; they were probably used for magic originally, before card games developed. The Tarot has never lost this function. But although Jan knew about it she had never seen the cards themselves. She leaned forward, watching with interest, as Madame spread out the big cardboard shapes on the worn red plush table cover.

There were suits, as in a modern deck, but the symbols were not the familiar diamonds, clubs, and so on.

"Cups, wands, swords, coins," Madame said in a low crooning voice. "The lesser tarot. And the greater tarot, the major arcana . . ." Her fat hands dealt out a series of cards bearing grotesque figures. "The Empress. The Female Pope. The Lovers. The Tower. . . . The lesser cards indicate. The greater control."

Jan's fascination did not last long. The cards were unusual, but the fortune was not; it was the same old meaningless mumble about dark men and blond women, enemies, friends, success, danger. Then Madame turned up the last card, and Jan caught her breath.

The Hanged Man.

The name was more frightening than the picture, for the victim was not hanging by his neck but dangling upside down from a cord around one ankle. Arms crossed, smiling, he looked quite debonair for a man in his position. But Jan knew why the silly design induced a thrill of horror. She was thinking of Jonathan and the fate meted out to spies.

Madame's plump dirty hands swept the cards together in a jumble. She looked at Jan, and the latter saw that she was pale.

"That's all. I can't tell you any more."

"What does it mean? The last card?" In her excitement Jan reached out, meaning to grasp the other woman's shoulder. Madame shrank back.

"Sacrifice. An ordeal. God, I need a drink."

The bottle was conveniently located in the drawer of a massive sideboard immediately behind the table, so that Madame did not even have to leave her chair. She drank straight from the bottle, and at length. Then she wiped her mouth on the back of her hand and shuddered pleasurably.

"I haven't lost it," she said. The liquor had slurred her voice and quieted her alarm. She looked fuzzily pleased. "Boy, did I get a jab just then."

"What did you see?" Jan demanded.

"You don't *see,*" Madame said irritably. "You don't *hear.* It's sort of. . . . Ah, hell, I never could describe it. It's an idea, that's all. Like—well, like sugar. Once I got sugar. The guy had diabetes and didn't know it. I might of saved his life, telling him." She drank again. "Yep. I saved that guy's life. . . . What was I talking about?"

"Sugar," Jan said shortly.

"Oh, yeah. Well, like I got the impression of sugar. Not a picture, not a five-pound bag or anything, just—"

"I get the idea," Jan said.

"Yeah. Well, what I got just now wasn't clear either, not a word or a picture. There's something *wrong* with you. Not sickness, something out of focus—like gears scraping. You're off the track somehow. You better go see a doctor."

"What kind of doctor?"

"Damned if I know," Madame said gloomily.

She would say no more. She kept refreshing herself from the bottle; before long she was asleep. Jan put a ten-dollar bill on the table and let herself out.

It had stopped raining and the sun was struggling to break through. Jan walked down the street, avoiding the muddy puddles on the broken sidewalk.

The interview had been frustrating but more useful than she had expected. The suggestion of hypnotism was a good one. When Madame mentioned the technique Jan remembered reading about the process for sending the mind back into past time. Time . . . again, the frustration of too little time. Where could she find a reliable person who would be willing to put her through the process—and keep quiet about it?

The woman's final comments had been interesting too. Something wrong. . . . Of course you could interpret that in several ways, Jan thought wryly. A lot of people would think her mind had slipped the track if they knew what she was thinking.

In order to cross the busy highway she had to go several blocks out of her way. There was a park or playground along the route she followed, with a high wire fence around it. Some boys were playing baseball and Jan paused to watch. Alan had spoken of working with a team of boys; was this the place? It wasn't far from his apartment. The building nearby looked like a school, possibly a junior high.

The boys seemed to be about twelve or thirteen years old. They were both black and white, and uniformly shabby— which indicated nothing about their parents' social and financial standing. It was the fashion for the young to look as wretched as they could; the shabbiness of the child was often in inverse ratio to the income of the parents.

Jan leaned against the fence and watched the game with a critical eye. She had enjoyed baseball, not just the game but the vigorous competition and the carefree years when

she had been playing. Her father had been alive then. He had
come to all the games and yelled louder than anybody else.

Her mood was so gently reminiscent that she was neither
surprised nor annoyed to see Alan approaching.

"You *are* following me," she said.

He neither admitted nor denied the allegation. He didn't
even look at her after the first glance.

"What a bunch of duds," he said, scanning the field.

"They aren't your team?"

"Yes, they are. Not a ballplayer in the lot."

"Then why do you spend time with them?"

"Keeps me off the street," Alan said. "Did you think I was
trying to teach them noble ideals about playing the game and
good sportsmanship?"

"At least they are learning something about friendly rela-
tions between the races," Jan said. The catcher was a white
boy and the batter was black.

"Friendly? One of the reasons why I try to drop by from
time to time is that they fly at each other's throat whenever
the slightest thing goes wrong. If two kids of the same race
mix it up, everybody chuckles about the volatility of youth.
If they happen to be black and white, the papers pick it up
and build it into racial tension."

"You mean the kids don't care?"

"Sure they care. They're the most godawful bigots you
ever saw. What do you expect, seeing they get their ideas
from subnormal adults?"

As he spoke one of the incidents he had mentioned occurred. The batter connected, awkwardly, with a ball he
should never have struck at. Spinning halfway around, he
took off for first base, flinging the bat behind him. It described one of those parabolas that only occur by pure
chance, and landed on top of the catcher's head.

The boy was wearing one of the plastic caps that have
replaced softer headgear in the American sport, but the im-
pact was hard enough to make his knees buckle. Gathering
himself together he started after the runner, and although he

was some distance away, Jan could almost see the blood in his eye.

Alan's voice boomed out like a bullhorn.

"Fraser! Get yourself over here. On the double!"

Fraser stopped. He hesitated for a moment, looking from Alan to the runner, who was now safe on first. Then he shrugged and headed for Alan, although his pace could not be described as rapid.

"You have to yell at 'em," Alan said calmly. "They don't hear anything less than a roar. That's why you soft-headed liberals in the ed business have lost your grip on the kids. You walk in twisting your hands and bleating, 'Can I teach you something, please, dear boy, if it won't interfere with your finding yourself?' No wonder they despise you."

"You're the most inconsistent man I ever met," Jan snapped. "One minute you talk about bigotry in a lofty voice, and then you come on like a little fascist."

"As I said on a previous occasion, who wants consistency? Fraser! Move it!"

Fraser actually broke into a jog trot. When he reached them, Alan told him to take off his cap.

"Got a lump?" he inquired.

"You're damn right," Fraser said bitterly. He had big gray eyes and a head of damp, red-gold curls.

"You'll never notice another one," Alan said unsympathetically. "Stay here and take a breather."

Another boy had already stepped into the vacated catcher's spot; Alan had the team better disciplined than he claimed. Fraser looked sulky, but obeyed.

"Bill Fraser," said Alan. "This is Miss Wilde."

"Hello," Jan said.

"Hi," said Fraser.

"How's your old man?" Alan asked.

"The same. The old bas—" Fraser glanced at Jan and, somewhat to her surprise, altered the noun. ". . . louse is always at me. 'Cut your hair, wash your feet, why don't you talk nice to your momma? Get a job, stay at home nights. . . .'

Who'd want to stick around that place? Him in front of the TV drinking beer like it was about to disappear, with his belly falling on his knees. . . ."

"Tough," Alan said. There was no sympathy in his voice, and Fraser obviously hadn't expected any. He glanced uncertainly at Jan, and then decided that since she was with Alan she must be harmless. He went on in a whining voice.

"Sure, it's easy for you to say. Why can't he lay off me? I'm not all that bad. I mean, compared to some of the guys. . . . But no, he can't see anything good I do, he just bitches about the times when I don't do so good. What's the use of trying? It's like he has this picture in his mind, see, what I oughta be like. He don't get mad 'cause I do things wrong, he gets mad when I do anything different from what he wants. Is he always right?"

The whining voice went on, but Jan didn't listen. She was trying to remember when she had heard similar thoughts expressed. They were a familiar-enough gripe among the adolescents she had known, but somewhere, more recently, she had heard the same sentiments spoken with more eloquence than this grubby child could command. When she did pin down the memory it came to her with a certain shock. Charles had said the same thing about his father. Coming from Charles, the sentiment had aroused her sympathetic agreement. This boy and many of his peers felt the same way, but she had not recognized before that they might have a valid point. They were so generally repulsive it was hard to give them credit for any sense.

She roused herself, realizing that Fraser had stuttered to a stop and Alan was watching her.

"I think I'm inhibiting you," she said. "You can both express yourself more freely when I'm gone. Glad to have met you, Fraser."

Fraser emitted a grunting noise that sounded fairly affable. As Jan walked away she heard Alan's voice and knew by the tone that he was administering a strong tongue-lashing. He *is* a bully, she thought. The kid only wants someone to listen to him and sympathize. . . . And then she forgot the unfortunate Fraser.

III

Candle flames and gold coins. Gold coins were in short supply and candles might be dangerous. An open flame, if she did fall asleep. . . . But she had a gold locket whose back side was as smooth and flat as any hypnotist could desire.

Jan sat before her dressing-table mirror and dangled the locket. She kept her eyes away from it because she wasn't quite ready to begin.

She had found a book about hypnotism in the bookstore on Merchants' Square and had stood reading it for some time. It had not occurred to her to buy it and bring it home; already her habits resembled those of the drug addict, who must conceal the evidence of his addiction.

The book hadn't been very helpful. It contained some dire warnings as to the dangers of hypnotism, and Jan wondered sourly why the author had bothered to describe the process if it was that deadly. She didn't really mean to hypnotize herself. She didn't know whether she could if she wanted to, and the fear of being found in a helpless, blank-eyed condition by her aunt or uncle was almost enough to keep her from attempting the experiment. But desire was stronger than fear. Surely, she told herself, I can stop if I feel I'm losing control.

Since Camilla and Henry both napped in the afternoon Jan was able to spend a few hours in her room without arousing comment. She had drawn the shades and draperies, and the single lamp allowed her to see only a shadowy image of her face in the mirror. She didn't look at it. With fingers that shook slightly she lifted the locket and set it swaying.

Ten minutes later she dropped the locket and admitted defeat. She was more relieved than disappointed; in fact, she felt relaxed and a little drowsy. She decided to lie down for a few minutes—not to sleep, just to rest her eyes. They ached from staring so fixedly. The room seemed to be getting darker. Perhaps it was going to rain again. Jan closed her eyes. Yes, it was raining. She could hear the soft rush of water striking the window panes, drumming gently on the roof—soporific, hypnotic, opening paths the waking mind could not follow. . . .

The rain was a wavering gray curtain, blurring the outlines of trees and houses, turning the Duke of Gloucester Street into a river of red mud. . . .

Chapter
15

March 1781

JONATHAN HAD PLUNGED STRAIGHT THROUGH THE MUD; his boots were red and his cloak was splashed to the shoulders. He was a pitiable figure as he stood streaming on the threshold, his lank hair dripping and his face a mask of distress. The old butler, who had opened the door for him, protested as the dissolute figure headed blindly across the hall toward the closed door of the parlor.

"Mr. Jonathan, you can't go in there, not like that. Just lemme wipe you off, suh, you track mud on the parlor rug—"

Jonathan stopped obediently. He had left rusty tracks across the floor.

"Is Colonel Tucker here?"

"Yes, suh, he inside. Back from that big battle. He got hurt, but he fine now."

"I must see him."

"Yes, suh, you sure can; but first take off the boots. I get you some slippers."

The old man dropped to his knees and began tugging at the stiff, slippery boots. Jonathan stood like a statue, his eyes fixed glassily on nothing; then, starting, he woke up to what was happening. His big wet hands closed on the old man's shoulders and raised him effortlessly to his feet.

"Not on your knees," he said. "Not to me."

The old man winced, and Jonathan, stricken, released his grasp.

"Forgive me, Bob. It seems I can do nothing without causing pain. . . . I'll remove the boots, I promise."

Standing on one foot, he tugged at the recalcitrant footgear while the old man, mumbling discontentedly, carried off his dripping cloak. One boot came off, with a sucking sound and a flood of water; the other was loosening when the parlor door opened. Startled, Jonathan gave the boot one last jerk and stood holding it.

Mr. Wilde had aged twenty years. There was something pathetic about his attempt at neatness, for the fine coat hung loosely on his shrunken frame and the brave curls of his wig framed a face where every muscle sagged, as if the underlying bones had come unhinged. His eyes, sunken in circles of liverish flesh, looked without emotion at the dripping figure.

"I—" Jonathan began. He cleared his throat and tried again. "May I extend, sir, my deepest sympathy on the loss of Mrs. Wilde?" The old man's dead face did not change. Jonathan's throat had closed up again. He added, with difficulty, "She was like my mother, sir."

Wilde's face quivered. "She was spared this last," he said. "I thank God for that."

"What do you mean?"

Wilde held out his hand. "Come in. I am glad you have come. You of all people will want to hear . . ."

Jonathan gestured wordlessly with his muddy boot and a pitiful travesty of a smile touched Wilde's face.

"She does not care, now, for her carpets and furniture," he said. "Come in, Jonathan."

His shoulders hunched as if in anticipation of a blow, Jonathan went, on squelching stocking feet. He had just enough presence of mind to drop the boot outside the parlor door, but it was apparent that he knew what he was about to hear, and that it took every ounce of his courage to face it.

Mary Beth sat on the sofa near the fire, her handkerchief

pressed to her face. The only other person in the room was a tall man in Continental uniform, wearing a colonel's insignia. The years of war had changed St. George Tucker. He had risen from private to colonel, and his cheeky grin was no longer in evidence.

He greeted Jonathan courteously but with reserve. Then he glanced at the sobbing girl and drained the glass of wine he was holding.

"I dislike asking you to repeat your story, Colonel," Mr. Wilde said. "But Jonathan will wish to hear—"

"I had barely begun," Tucker said. "But if the details distress you, Mr. Wilde. . . . And perhaps the lady may wish to retire."

Mary Beth lowered her handkerchief. Her face looked dreadful, splotched unbecomingly and shining with tears.

"I thank you, sir, but I would rather remain," she said, not without dignity. "If my tears disturb you I will endeavor to restrain them."

Her distress was genuine, but she was unable to keep her eyes away from Jonathan. He did not even glance at her.

"Charles," he said. "Is he—"

"I am sorry." Tucker looked at his host. "If you wish me, sir, to give you the details—"

"Please. Everything."

"Guilford Courthouse lies along the main south-north road through North Carolina," Tucker began. "General Greene had established his position astride the road. We were to the east, in the second line, with North Carolina militia in front of us. I assure you, sir," he added seriously, "that the position was no dishonor. The North Carolinians are notoriously unreliable and one of our purposes was to strengthen their courage. What we feared transpired, in fact. The Carolinians broke at the first attack."

Tucker's eyes were fixed on the floor. Soldier that he was, he was finding this task difficult, and the deliberate, detailed narrative made the job a little easier. He could not simply blurt out the bare fact to this audience.

"The British regulars are no longer the awe-inspiring sight they once were, though they are terrifying enough to raw militia. The red coats, and the green and the blue, were faded, ragged, strained. They were tired and hungry as well, having followed us for two days. But their crossbelts and gaiters had been freshly pipe-clayed, and their polished buttons and buckles and breastplates shone dazzlingly. It was a cool but sunny day and we could see them clearly as they came on through the trees, marching in step to the beat of the drums, their bayonets sparkling in the sunlight. The Carolinians had the courage to fire a volley before they ran, but it was not enough, and suddenly we found ourselves facing the bayonets. Had it not been for our Virginia riflemen, on the flanks, who kept up a steady fire, we should have been swept away at once.

"As you know, sir, in a battle one loses sight of what is going on immediately outside one's own narrow section. It was not until later that we learned the entire center had broken at that first assault. Our men managed to hold at first. But we soon found ourselves surrounded. Holcomb's regiment and ours instantly broke off and dispersed like a flock of frightened sheep. Beverley, Charles, and I tried to rally them. It was then . . ."

"I was sorry, Colonel, to hear of your own wound," Mr. Wilde said, as the even voice stopped speaking.

Tucker shrugged. "It was a humiliating accident. A flesh wound, in the small of my leg, from a soldier who either from design or accident held his bayonet in such a direction that I could not possibly avoid it as I ran up to stop him from running away. It is healing nicely. But it prevented me, when it occurred, from going to Charles's aid. I hope it will comfort you to know that he was not subjected to the humiliation I endured, in being struck by one of his own men. It was a British bayonet that . . ." He paused, glancing at Mary Beth, and did not finish the sentence. "He received the wound in defending another young officer, who had fallen. It was a gallant action, sir."

Silence fell, broken only by the beat of rain against the windows and the more imminent drip from Jonathan's sodden clothes. It was he who broke the silence.

"Are you sure?"

"That he was not merely wounded?" Tucker's cool gray eyes turned to Jonathan. "He was not among those brought back next day. I went to the battlefield—"

"It was good of you, sir," Wilde said. "With your wound—"

"I could hobble about with a stick," Tucker said brusquely. "Your son was my friend, sir. I would have gone if I had had to be carried. I knew the spot, you see, and found it without difficulty. I had hoped to send his body home, at least. But the burial parties had been there before me. I regret infinitely that I cannot tell you where he lies."

"Are you sure?" Jonathan repeated, as if he had not heard a word of the speech.

Tucker's finely arched brows drew together.

"I would not be the one to remove the last spark of hope from a parent and an affianced wife—and a friend. But . . ."

"I see." Jonathan squared his shoulders. "I ask your pardon, sir, I am selfish in my grief not to consider yours. I . . . forgive me. I will return, Mr. Wilde; but I must now . . . I must . . . forgive me."

He turned abruptly and made for the door. Mary Beth rose, but he blundered past without appearing to see her and she sank back onto the sofa, fresh tears flowing down her cheeks.

Jonathan closed the parlor doors and leaned against them for a moment, his hands over his face. When he lowered them he saw the girl who was standing under the stairs. The hall was very dark, the overcast skies turning afternoon into twilight, and no one had thought to light the candles. The house lay in darkness as if in mourning, and Leah's face was a pale blurred oval. The soft gray of her gown blended with the shadows.

She and Jonathan stared at one another.

"You have heard?" he said at last.

"I listened at the door," she answered. After a moment, when he did not speak, she went on in a flat, calm voice, "Come upstairs, Mr. Jonathan. You are wet. You will take cold."

Jonathan followed her. It was clear that in his present state of mind he would have followed any familiar voice, like a dog. But when she closed the door of his old room after them he said vaguely,

"Should you be here, Leah? It is not fitting—"

"Do you think I worry about what is fitting now?" she interrupted, in the same flat voice. "Take off your wet coat."

He stood staring at her, and with a wordless sound whose tone betrayed the emotions boiling under her calm, she began undoing the buttons of his waistcoat. The dampness of the heavy material made this process difficult; her hands faltered and suddenly she said softly,

"He isn't dead. He can't be. I would know."

Shaken out of his misery by this first expression of hers, Jonathan gently detached her fingers.

"I know how you feel," he said. "But it is not true, Leah. On the day she died I was in a tavern in Winchester, playing the fiddle for friends who wanted to dance. The news did not reach me for three weeks, and when I realized. . . . There are no words. But never once—no, Leah. I did not know."

"She? Mr. Jonathan, I didn't know. You never said—"

"Charles knew. No one else. I met her in Philadelphia, when I was engaged in . . . that business you know of. Her father was a friend of Benezet, and the family is deeply committed. I am still in communication with him. He never realized. . . . We only knew each other for a short time."

"I am sorry, Mr. Jonathan; so very sorry. But I still can't feel—"

"Stop," Jonathan said harshly. "Must you add to my guilt? If I had not done what I did, during that year—"

"It would have made no difference. Why do you torture yourself?"

"Who knows what difference it might have made? I could have forgotten my stupid, childish scruples; gone with him, been at his side at Guilford. How many men died as a result of my actions in seventy-eight? I was like Pilate, washing my hands; but surely it is more honorable to fight openly, to defend a friend, than to bring about the deaths of men I never knew, who committed no crime against me?"

Leah put warm hands on his breast where the shirt clung damply to his body.

"Stop blaming yourself," she said. "If anyone is guilty of Charles's death, it is his father." And as Jonathan stared at her she nodded vehemently. "He sent him away. You know why. I shouldn't have come to Williamsburg with you. I knew better, but when you told me how sick Charles was, I couldn't stay away. Oh, don't think I blame you! At least we had those few days. . . . And then his father told him to go. Charles was not fully recovered, he still had the fever; he was sick and shaking with it when he rode away, and that day at Guilford . . ."

The last words were lost in sobs. Jonathan took her in his arms and held her while she wept.

When he came down the stairs a little later, Mr. Wilde and Mary Beth were in the hall.

"Colonel Tucker has just left," Mr. Wilde said. "I am sorry, Jonathan, that you did not stay. His words were comforting, very comforting; he spoke of Charles's gallantry."

Jonathan's mouth twisted uncontrollably, but he answered in a gentle voice.

"I am sorry too, sir. It was inexcusable of me to leave so abruptly. And now I must repeat my rudeness. I have— business down the street."

"But will you not stay here?" Mary Beth asked.

Jonathan shook his head.

"I will not try to persuade you," the older man said wearily. "But you know you are always welcome, Jonathan. All the more so now, since. . . . If you will excuse me, I believe I will rest for a while."

The two young people watched him slowly ascend the stairs, his head bowed, his steps dragging. When they heard the sound of a door closing, Mary Beth turned to Jonathan.

"You must not be so cruel, Jonathan. He is all alone now. He needs you."

"Me? I'm the last person he needs, Mary Beth. It's a wonder the Sons of Liberty haven't paid me a visit long before this, with their buckets of hot tar and bags of feathers. I wouldn't like to be here when they—"

"Don't say such things!" She caught at him with both hands. Jonathan's eyes widened.

"Why, child, you are becoming very fiery. But it's no wonder; you are overwrought. Don't worry about me, I was only joking about the tar and feathers."

"It is not a joking matter. If you are in danger you must come here, where your friends can protect you."

"I'm in no danger," Jonathan said patiently. "Truly. Thanks to men like Mr. Wythe and Mr. Jefferson, there has been no violence here. People seem to accept the fact that Mennonites, like Quakers, will not bear arms; we have been treated fairly, on the whole. And the town bullies only bother women and old men, they won't attack a great hulk like me."

He tried to smile, but the effort was too much for him. Detaching her clinging hands, he started backing toward the door.

"Mary Beth, I must go. Should you need me, I am staying at the tavern near the landing."

"Jonathan, if that is the King's Mare, it is most unsuitable. I have heard people speak of the rude crowds that gather there. Why not the Raleigh or Mrs. Vobe's?"

"I am not popular at such Patriot centers," Jonathan said shortly. "The 'rude crowds' don't care what I think so long as I buy a round of ale occasionally."

"Will you come this evening? Or for dinner tomorrow—"

"I will not come again. Unless you need me—"

"I need you," she said, and a wave of crimson washed over her mottled face.

Jonathan stared as if he had not heard correctly.

"I need you," she repeated more firmly, although she was still flushed. "Jonathan, I never thought I would speak to you like this; but I have lost so much. . . . The whole world seems to be crumbling, all the old values lost. I grieve for Charles, truly I do; I would have married him, although he never loved me, and I. . . . It was always you, Jonathan. Always."

She concealed her blushes behind the slim white hands that were her chief beauty.

It was as well she did not see Jonathan's face. It had the look of a man who has just received the last of a series of staggering blows, and who has reached the end of his endurance. His forehead wrinkled.

"No," he said. "Please. Don't do this. . . ."

"Why not? What have I to lose?" She lowered her hands, facing him defiantly; but at the sight of his face the color faded from hers. "I see," she whispered. "I did not know. . . . Who is she?"

"You don't understand." Jonathan shook himself like a wet dog. "I cannot think what to say. You know I am fond of you, very fond. . . . Mary Beth, I will speak with you later. Now I am too. . . . I have business."

"What sort of business?" Her eyes widened and again she caught at his sleeve. "Jonathan, promise you will do nothing rash."

"I will speak with you later," Jonathan repeated.

He pulled himself away and plunged out the door. He forgot to close it. The rain was still heavy, and the evening had darkened. In a moment he had vanished, like a ghost, into the dusk.

Chapter
16

Summer 1976

JAN HAD FORGOTTEN SHE HAD AGREED TO JOIN CAMILLA
in a visit to a dear old friend that afternoon. When Camilla
reminded her of it, she was still dazzled and drowsy from her
nap, and her first reaction was violently negative. She was
in no mood to be charming to two dear old Southern ladies.
One was bad enough.

But she could think of no reasonable excuse—a plea of
illness would only start Camilla fussing—so she went.

She was becoming an expert at living with less than half
her mind on the job. As she and Camilla strolled along the
shady sidewalk she was able to engage in idle chatter while
her thoughts were elsewhere.

This was the first time she had dreamed during the day. It
was definitely a bonus, and she wondered what had brought
it on. Apparently Richard was not the catalyst after all—or
else she was now so adept that she no longer needed outside
help.

All this was more than satisfactory. However, there was
one disturbing thing about the afternoon's episode. Charles
couldn't have been killed at the battle of Guilford Courthouse. He had died in the 1830s, a plump and prosperous
patriarch.

Yet it was difficult to doubt Colonel Tucker's description of his death. Jan knew about Tucker; he was a real historical personage. There were only two possibilities: either Tucker was mistaken, or her dreams were merely fantasies of the sleeping mind, with no basis in historic fact.

And that she was unable to accept.

When they reached their destination she had to stop brooding about the problem and concentrate on her manners. A plump, silver-haired lady with snapping dark eyes, Mrs. Cox had sold her Historic House outright and had moved to an apartment, but she still retained her aristocratic weakness for Family.

She was related to everybody. Jefferson, Madison, George Washington—all were distant connections, and when Jan mentioned St. George Tucker, Mrs. Cox promptly claimed him as an ancestor too.

But the twinkle in her eye made Jan suspect that some of her boasting was in jest. She rather liked the peppery little old lady. Mrs. Cox seemed to like her too, and when Camilla announced proudly, "My niece is writing a book," Mrs. Cox was quick to offer assistance.

"I know everything about the Revolution," she explained cheerfully.

"I should think you would," Jan said, unable to repress a smile. "With all those ancestors. . . . Maybe you could help me, Mrs. Cox. I've become interested in some of the other, non-English groups who helped found Virginia."

Camilla sniffed, but Mrs. Cox nodded, with a sidelong smile at her old friend.

"Ask Cam and she'll tell you nobody but the English matter. That's not true, though. The western parts of the state were settled by Germans and Scotch-Irish. And, although we all hate to admit it, most of the English settlers weren't gentry. . . . Now don't you sniff at me, Camilla Wilde. Our very own ancestress was an indentured servant, or worse. I've always suspected the worst of that redheaded woman."

"Many aristocrats," said Camilla coldly, "were reduced to

poverty after giving their entire fortunes to serve the ill-fated King."

Mrs. Cox guffawed unkindly. Jan tried to turn the subject back to the one that interested her.

"Germans and Scotch-Irish? Do we have any of them in our background?"

"Oh, yes," Mrs. Cox said. "There was that Lutheran connection of the Wildes, Cam. What was the name of the family?"

"It was not in the direct line of descent." Camilla obviously didn't care for this topic. "One of the younger sisters. . . . I never pursued that particular line."

"Naturally," her friend said. "Have more tea, Cam. Your ancestors aren't as interesting as mine, anyway. Jan, let me tell you about Washington and that minx Sally Fairfax. There was a lot in that affair that didn't ever see the light of day, let me tell you!"

It was impossible to change the subject without rudeness. Jan heard a lot more than she wanted to know about the gallivanting of the Father of his Country. It sounded pretty harmless to her, but Mrs. Cox enjoyed every innuendo.

When they took their departure, Mrs. Cox invited Jan to come back anytime.

"Especially if you want to hear some gossip," she said, with a wicked grin. "I can tell you things the history books don't print."

Camilla waited till they were out on the street before she expressed herself.

"Poor Marian, she has altered, and not for the best. I hope you will disregard her remarks, Jan. General Washington carried on a casual flirtation with Mrs. Fairfax, no more. He was a handsome man, and most attractive to the ladies."

"I'm sure. . . . About that German family, Aunt Cam—"

"As I told you, I never traced that line. It was a collateral branch, and quite undistinguished."

Jan could have shrieked with frustration. Here was a hint at what she most wanted to know, and Camilla didn't even remember the name of the family. She continued to question her aunt until Camilla agreed to show her some of her genealogical records.

Camilla continued to talk about the noble family and exalted social standing of the Wildes all the way home. Jan tried to shut out the sound of her voice, but was only partially successful. Nor was she pleased to learn, from Uncle Henry, that Richard had called and announced his intention of dropping by for a few minutes on his way to rehearsal.

"I told him to come for dessert and coffee," Henry explained and added, looking pleased with himself, "I'd have asked him to dinner, but I know how you girls are about unexpected guests. I can see how you feel. If there are only three chops—"

"There *are* only three chops," Jan said grimly. "And there is no dessert. I was going to make instant pudding. I can't offer Richard—"

"He said he'd bring some ice cream. Peach. He asked me, so I told him, peach—"

Jan fled into the kitchen. She adored Uncle Henry, she really did, but. . . . And damn Richard. What business had he dropping in whenever he pleased? He would want to know the answer to the rather important question he had asked her. . . . Was it only yesterday?

Richard arrived while they were still at the table. He had brought not only peach ice cream but chocolate ripple, which was Camilla's favorite. Everyone had a nice time except Jan who said little. Nor was she particularly gracious when Richard asked her to walk to the car with him.

"Don't worry, honey, I'm not going to heckle you," he said, as soon as they were out of the house. "I'm not going to say another word until you're ready to talk about it. I don't suppose. . . ."

"No," Jan said. "I mean, I'm still thinking."

"Sure, you take your time. I'm sorry I've been so busy. How about Saturday? We could spend the afternoon. Have lunch, go swimming."

"All right. Thank you."

"What are you mad about?" Richard asked, with the smile that could be so charming.

"Aunt Cam, I guess. Honestly, Richard, I get so tired of the ancestors! They couldn't all have been cavaliers fleeing from Cromwell; there must have been a bank robber or a pickpocket somewhere on the family tree."

"Sure there was," Richard said. "More pickpockets than barons, after all. You and I enjoy them, but your aunt. . . . Let her revel in her aristocratic ancestors. It doesn't hurt."

"I guess you're right."

"And I know you wouldn't say anything to hurt the old lady. Come and yell at me when you get mad." He stopped and turned to face Jan. "Damn this daylight saving," he said, with a glance at the crowded street. "You're safe, Jan, I won't try a passionate embrace in broad daylight in front of fifty gaping tourists. Good night, honey."

He is a dear, Jan thought, as she went back up the steps. Sweet, thoughtful. . . . Why can't I love him?

But she knew the answer.

Chapter

17

May 1781

THE TAVERN WAS THE ONE JONATHAN HAD MENTIONED to Mary Beth the day they learned of Charles's death in battle. It deserved every opprobrious epithet she had given it.

The taproom was not the handsome paneled chamber one found in such hostelries as the Raleigh, but a small room with walls of rough planking and a crude brick fireplace. The corner bar had a wooden grill that could be lowered when the bartender left the room in order to prevent patrons from helping themselves. The fireplace was drawing badly and the room was thick with smoke. Ale and rum spilled by hundreds of drinkers had left the splintery tables sticky to the touch, and the stains on the bare planking of the floor were evilly provocative.

Jonathan sat on one of the settles before the smoking fire. The contents of the mug he held had not been touched, and the ale had gone flat. The man next to him snored in a drunken stupor, his flabby body sprawled over most of the seat. Jonathan ignored him. From time to time he slipped his watch surreptitiously from his pocket. His clothing did not match the handsome gold timepiece. He had never been noted for the elegance of his attire, but his present costume had slipped far down the social scale; it was the rough homespun shirt and breeches of a laborer.

Finally the watch's lagging hands indicated the hour he had been awaiting. He gave a small, quickly stifled sigh and went out.

The night was dark, and so was the man who slipped noiselessly out of the concealment of the empty stall in the stable. Sensing rather than seeing the movement, Jonathan spun around, and the dark shadow let out a breath that would have been a laugh if it had had any sound behind it.

"You sure nervous tonight."

"James," Jonathan whispered.

"You expectin' Gen'ral Cornwallis?"

"Or one of his associates. I walk in that expectation hourly," Jonathan admitted.

A blur of white teeth showed briefly. The other man's voice held sympathy as well as amusement when he said softly,

"Cain't blame you for that. You worse off than me, an' I startle easy myself. . . . What you got this time?"

Paper crackled—thin, much-folded paper—and two hands met briefly in the darkness.

"Cornwallis is on his way to Petersburg to join Arnold," Jonathan whispered. "He is expecting reinforcements from New York shortly; the details are written here. That will bring British strength to about seven thousand men."

James made a soft clicking sound with tongue and teeth.

"I dunno what the Gen'ral can do. He say he ain't even got enough men to get beat."

"Where is Lafayette now?"

"Somewhere's around Richmond."

The reply had been slow in coming. Jonathan sensed the other man's hesitation; his voice, though soft, held a note of bitterness when he replied.

"I don't blame you for not trusting me, James. I've turned my coat too often."

"One thing you never change your mind about," James said slowly. "Don't mistake me, Mr. Jonathan. The less you know—"

"The less I'll be tempted to tell to save my neck from a noose," Jonathan finished. "All right. I understand. Has there been any word from Saul?"

"They don' catch him yet, if that's what you mean," was the grim reply. "We all dream 'bout ropes, Mr. Jonathan."

An involuntary shiver passed through the black man's body, and Jonathan said impulsively, "Why do you do it, James? Why do you risk your neck for a cause that makes you another man's slave?"

"I druther be a slave here than in the West Indies," James answered. "That's where the British sell the folks they catch. They don' free 'em, that's for sure. Besides . . ."

"Well?"

"It's a fine word—freedom," the other man said hesitantly. "There's gotta be more to it than a word."

"God grant that it be so," Jonathan whispered. "If the ringing phrases are no more than words, then you and I and hundreds of others are victims of the bitterest jest in history."

"I get my freedom, though," James said confidently.

"Did your master say so?"

"Mist' Armitage? He let me come, but. . . . The Gen'ral done promise me."

"I hear that Lafayette is a fine man."

A soft chuckle relieved that taut atmosphere.

"He not a man, jes' a boy that ain't outgrowed his baby fat. But he gettin' bald already."

"Marie Joseph Paul Yves Roch Gilbert du Motier, Marquis de Lafayette," Jonathan murmured. "Nineteen years old when he ran away from France to join us, against King Louis' express command. . . . They say Washington loves him like a son."

"Cain't help likin' him," James admitted. "An' you can trust his word; that counts more. . . . Why don' you come meet him, Mr. Jonathan? He ask about you."

"No. You promised, James."

"An' I keep my word too. But I dunno why you do this. Seems like this way everybody out to hang you, Mr. Jonathan."

It was Jonathan's turn to chuckle, but his laugh held little humor.

"You have summed up the situation admirably, James. But it's an uncommonly productive arrangement, while it lasts. I had a hunch last time I saw my . . . friend in Tarleton's brigade that he was getting suspicious of my zeal."

"Then you better stop," James said, concern deepening his voice. "Your fren' be waitin' for you with a pistol one o' these days."

"I can't stop quite yet. There is something afoot. I suspect they are planning a raid on Charlottesville. It was a good idea to move the capital, after what Arnold did to Richmond last year; but I fear they did not move it far enough. And if the British can capture the governor, or the members of the legislature. . . ."

"I tell the Gen'ral."

"There's nothing to tell yet. If such a move is planned, I'll have to find out the date and the movements of the troops. I'll try to inform you."

"Mmm." James managed to convey agreement, apprehension, and admiration in the single sound. "All right, I see what I kin find out too. I gotta go now, the Gen'ral, he waitin' for me."

"I know. I appreciate your staying to talk to me, James. It was selfish of me to delay you."

"It's a lonesome thing, what you do," James said gently. "You take care, Mr. Jonathan. You hear?"

"You too. Next week, the other place."

There was no answer, no visible movement, only the slightest shift of the darkness. Jonathan was alone.

Instead of returning directly to the inn he took a roundabout path, following the creek for part of the distance, and stopping every few minutes to listen. It was uneasy weather, with a brisk erratic wind that created strange sounds among the leafed branches. Tattered clouds, driven across the half-moon's face, shaped shadows in places where none should be. The eeriness of the night did not help Jonathan's taut nerves.

He hesitated for some time before entering the grove of firs that separated the inn path from the main road; and when the dark figure moved out from behind a massive tree trunk, his hands encircled its throat before it could utter a sound.

Almost as quickly he released the strangling hold and caught the swaying figure by the shoulders. The hood of the cloak that enveloped it had fallen back, but he did not need the evidence of sight to identify her.

"Leah! What are you doing here? You shouldn't have come. If you were seen—"

"I had to see you. Should I have gone to your room?"

"It wouldn't have damaged my reputation," Jonathan said shortly. "Come; put up your hood and I'll walk you home."

"I have to talk to you."

"We'll talk as we go. This is the worst possible place for a private conversation. A regiment could creep up unseen."

He did not wait for her to answer, but arranged the folds of the cloak so that it concealed her face and figure. Then he took her arm. Neither spoke until they reached the open area of the road. It was a narrow track, barely wide enough for a wagon. They walked along the weedy verge, next to a field that lay open under the fitful moonlight, and finally Jonathan relaxed.

"How did you know I would be . . . out tonight?" he demanded.

"The slave knows what the master does before he does it," she answered. Her face was hidden in the shadow of the hood, but the irony in her quiet voice told Jonathan how much she had changed since Charles's death. "Don't worry," she added. "None of the ones who know would betray you. But it's a dangerous game."

"I didn't mean you to know," Jonathan said, ignoring the implicit warning. "What you did tonight was dangerous too. Why didn't you speak to me today when I visited Mr. Wilde? I didn't even know you were in Williamsburg."

"Why shouldn't I be? There is no danger now to his precious honor. He doesn't know or care where I am."

"He's a broken old man," Jonathan said, disturbed by the cold hate in her voice. "You mustn't blame him—"

"I do blame him. If I could do him an injury, I would."

"Hating will only hurt you, Leah, not him."

"You sound like a preacher," she said savagely. "Why don't you go and live with him then? He dotes on you. 'Mr. Jonathan, Mr. Jonathan,' all day long. It's very funny. If he had the faintest idea what you have done—"

"You wouldn't tell him?"

"I wouldn't hurt you," she said, after a moment. "I don't want to talk about him anymore. Do you think I like feeling this way? I don't want to hate. Especially now. . . . Please stop here. We're almost in town and I have something to say to you. You must tell me what to do."

Trudging along, a worried frown on his face, Jonathan seemed to have forgotten his fears of being seen. They had not met anyone on the road. Now, as her hand tugged at his sleeve, he stopped obediently.

"I wish you could find it in your heart. . . . Oh, very well," he said as she let out a muffled sound of exasperation. "I'll be happy to advise you if I can. You might have chosen a wiser mentor; God knows I haven't done well with my own life. What is the problem?"

The answer was short and simple. Three words expressed it.

Jonathan literally staggered. His face, whitened by the moonlight, went even paler.

She waited, her hands clenched, while he struggled to assimilate the news, but her own nerves were strained to the breaking point, and soon she burst out,

"Turn your back and walk away if you want to. I thought you would understand. You're horrified, I can see you are. Why don't you ask me who the father is?"

"Why—I know that," Jonathan said, in a gasp. "When did—Oh. Of course. In March, before he went back. How can you—are you sure?"

"I'm sure."

"Poor child."

She shook her head. There were tears on her cheeks, tears of relief that he wasn't angry, but she held her head high.

"You don't have to be sorry for me. I'm proud. Can you understand that?"

"Yes," Jonathan said.

"Only . . . it's so hard to know what to do."

"You don't want to tell his father? He has so little to live for now—"

"And you think this would bring him joy? How can you be so innocent? You don't understand people at all, you never see evil in them. Do you know what he would do if he found out? He'd sell me. As soon as he could, as far away as possible. He couldn't stand to see me, or the child; we would remind him of too many things he can't face. I wouldn't mind going away. But I won't belong to another man, not now. And I won't let Charles's son, the only thing that's left of him, be a slave. I know what I have to do, that wasn't hard to figure out. But I need your help."

"You want to run away," Jonathan said slowly.

"I want to be free. I want Charles's child to be free. You can help me. You have to! That's what you did all those years, help people get away—"

"But they were men," Jonathan said. "Able-bodied men who could earn a living. Or women who had men to take care of them. What could you do, alone—worse than alone, with an infant to support and tend. . . ."

His voice trailed off helplessly. Leah took a step back, her eyes narrowing.

"You must help me," she said. "If you don't, I'll tell them about you. I'll tell Walforth that you're tricking him. I can, you know. Men still go to the British, they go every day. We have our secret ways. . . ."

Jonathan stood like a man turned to stone. Leah's voice broke in a sob.

"I'm sorry," she gasped. "I didn't mean it, I wouldn't do that; you know I wouldn't. But I'm so afraid. . . ."

Jonathan put his arm around her and pulled her against his shoulder. She clung to him while he stroked her hair.

"I know," he said gently. "It was my fault, I should have made myself plain at once and not driven you to desperation. I was just trying to think of the best way to proceed. How could you suppose for a moment that I would abandon you? I promised Charles—and for old friendship's sake, Leah, for that alone I would do my best. As it is. . . . Why, child, don't you realize what a great gift you've given me? You've given me a chance to do something for Charles. Now calm down and let's think."

She drew back from him, wiping her eyes with her fingers.

"I'm so ashamed. You mustn't help me because I said those terrible things."

"Look at me," Jonathan said. "Do I look frightened?"

"You really aren't angry," she said, hardly daring to believe.

"Of course not. And I think I know what must be done. Here, your feet are getting soaked standing in this wet grass. You mustn't take chances with your health, not now. I'll tell you my plan as we walk. But you must promise you won't scream, or faint, or—or slap my face."

"As if I would ever do that." She fell into step beside him, her hand in his, her head barely reaching his shoulder.

"You may want to," Jonathan said. He looked down at her with the oddest expression, half amused, half shy. "I want you to marry me. No . . . keep walking. Remember you promised not to scream. Is the idea so repugnant?"

Only the grip of his hand kept her moving.

"Not repugnant," she said faintly. "Only mad. Are you insane?"

"Oh, yes," Jonathan said calmly. "Everyone knows that. But this is the only sensible idea I've had in years. It will solve everything. And it will give me . . . great happiness. Do you believe that, Leah?"

"You don't love me," she said, still dazed. "I know about your lady."

"There are different kinds of love. You don't care for me as you care for Charles. You never will. I don't expect that. I don't even want it, Leah; I'll be honest with you, as I hope you will be with me. But you know I am very fond of you. And is there any man alive who would cherish Charles's child as I would?"

"But you talk—you talk as if such a thing were possible," she exclaimed. "I'm sorry, I can't . . . I feel dizzy. Like the time I fell out of the apple tree and hit my head."

She was speaking the literal truth; her feet stumbled as she tried to obey Jonathan's command to keep walking. He put a brotherly arm around her shoulders and steadied her.

"It is possible," he said. "Not here, no. In Philadelphia. I have friends there, you know. They are Friends, indeed; and we have worked together for several years on the project dearest to our hearts. I don't know that I shall tell even them the truth. There is no need. Thanks to your quick ear and mind, your speech is indistinguishable from that of a white woman, and your appearance presents no difficulty. We'll have to invent a background for you, but that should be no problem. You can be an orphan from a western county, your parents killed in an Indian raid. . . . You see how easy it is? You might even change your appearance. Women know how to do these things, don't they?"

His anxious voice made her laugh, although the sound was strained.

"Yes, we know. But . . . Jonathan—"

"Good," he interrupted, squeezing her shoulders. "That's right. You couldn't call your husband 'Mister,' could you?"

"Stop," she said breathlessly. "Stop a minute, I can't walk and think at the same time. This scheme is so . . ."

Jonathan obeyed. His hands turned her to face him, his eyes searched hers.

"It's the only thing to do," he hesitated. "The best thing. You will, won't you, Leah?"

She stood passive in his grasp, her head tipped back so that she could look up into his face. She was lovelier than ever; grief and worry had only given her face a new maturity. Though she was as small as a child next to his great height, there was a tender, almost maternal smile on her lips when she spoke.

"The best thing? Would it be best for you? I know how you feel, that you'll never love another woman as you did her. But someday you might meet someone else. It's different for me, I'll have his child. I'll never be able to give any man the kind of love I had for Charles. And you deserve that kind of love, you deserve a fine lady, not a—"

Jonathan's hand closed gently over her mouth.

"Never say that." His fingers moved, to stroke her hair back from her face; the gesture was tender but completely without passion. "That word will never be spoken again between us. As for the rest—why, we're perfectly suited, my dear. We understand one another. The marriage will be whatever you wish, Leah. I would not insist on . . . anything you don't want."

"But I would want that," she said. "It's only fair. Unless you feel . . ."

He understood her meaning and answered her in the most direct way. She responded with a kind of desperate generosity, her lips parting under the pressure of his. When they stood apart there were tears in her eyes, but Jonathan was smiling.

"You see?" he said. "It's going to be all right, Leah."

She shook her head dumbly, and Jonathan's smile was replaced by a look of keen anxiety.

"Please, Leah. Don't you understand? If this succeeds— and it will, it must—it will be the only thing I've ever done in my entire life that wasn't flawed, the only thing that didn't turn in my hands and hurt someone. Don't deprive me of this chance. Please say yes. Please."

The appeal was too strong to resist. She nodded. Jonathan kissed her again, gently, and then took her hand.

"Come. We must think of the practical arrangements. Can you—that is to say, is there any urgency about leaving?"

"No. Not for several months. Two or three."

"Oh, that's splendid," Jonathan said, relieved. "Another month should finish my present work here. It will take that long to make the arrangements in any case."

"What do you want me to do?"

"Nothing. Just be ready. I'll try to give you ample notice, but one never knows; the military situation is precarious and we might have to leave suddenly."

"What if he sends me to Patriot's Dream?"

"Then I'll come for you there. I'll handle everything. Don't worry, and take care of your health."

"You must do the same," Leah said. "I had forgotten, I was so upset. . . . But I meant to warn you, and tell you to be careful. We have our own means of getting information, you know; you ought, you have used it often enough. So you must believe me when I say there are rumors that make me uneasy for you. The man Walforth. . . . Jonathan, couldn't we go now?"

"But, my dear, it will take time to make the arrangements for our journey," Jonathan said reasonably. "Don't worry, I won't take chances. I'm not too happy about Walforth either, it will be a relief to put an end to my dealings with him. You see? You're doing me good already, giving me a reason to quit my unsavory trade—"

The word ended in a catch of breath as Jonathan whirled, putting out his arm as if to shield Leah.

"What is it?" she gasped. "What is wrong?"

Jonathan relaxed.

"My brain, I think," he said wryly. "Or a shadow, shifted by the wind. . . . For a moment I thought there was someone else walking with us."

"There is no one."

"I know. It's nothing, only a projection from my frightened mind. I am not a hero, Leah, I'm terrified most of the time. I see shadows frequently. Most of them wear red or green uniforms, and carry ropes. . . . I shouldn't admit my cowardice, should I? Especially not to you."

"Courage is facing something you're afraid of," she said, with her gentle, maternal smile.

"Thank you. At any rate, you understand how you are helping me, don't you? My trade becomes even more dangerous if I lose my courage. You may be saving my life by making me give it up now."

"Stop here, Jonathan. I can go the rest of the way alone. We shouldn't be seen together."

"All right. Before you go, Leah, I want you to have this." He fumbled in his pockets and brought out a bundle of paper which he pressed into her reluctant hand.

"Money?" she said doubtfully. "I don't want to take—"

"It's good money, not our local paper; heaven knows that hasn't much value these days. These are notes on the Bank of Philadelphia, the only sound currency in the country. I'll send you more from time to time, and you must hide them— sew them into your corsets, or whatever ladies wear, ready to be taken away with us."

"I don't understand. Why don't you keep it?"

"Because for once in my life I am trying to anticipate. If anything should happen to me. . . . No, child, don't start; I have no reason to suppose that it will. But if it should, you must go alone. Whatever happens, you—and Charles's child," he added, seeing the stormy rebellion on her face, "you two must find safety. I shall give you the name of my friends in Philadelphia. Should you hear—and you have ways of hearing—that I have been caught, then go. It will be a difficult and dangerous journey alone, but you have keen wits, and with money and the thought of friends waiting, I know you can accomplish it."

She clutched at his sleeve with anxious hands, her upturned face rigid with fear.

"You know something you haven't told me. Or have you—have you had a vision?"

Jonathan laughed heartily.

"Good heavens, no. I'm only trying to be sensible. I have made such a mess of everything I have tried to do; I don't know why, I tried so hard, but I suppose I haven't much common sense. Well, this time I am trying to think ahead. Of all the things I have ever wanted to do, this means most to me. It must succeed! I intend to take every possible precaution, however farfetched. If I knew a spell against witches and night demons, I'd say it."

"I'll say it for you." Leah's smile was forced, but she tried to take heart from his utter conviction. "Thank you, Jonathan, thank you. Good night."

He watched her until she had reached the back of the Wilde property in safety and slipped through the gate.

Chapter
18

Summer 1976

"ALAN'S COMING TONIGHT FOR SOME CHESS," UNCLE
Henry announced at breakfast, with a guilty look at his wife.

"Great," Jan muttered.

"These are fine muffins, just fine," her uncle said, taking
his third. "How come you aren't eating, honey?"

"You spoiled her appetite," Camilla said.

"Now, Aunt Cam," Jan said. "Really, Uncle Henry, I'm
glad he's coming. I have a—a headache, that's why I'm
in such a grumpy mood. Would you like to ask him for
dinner?"

"No, no, that's too much trouble."

But her uncle was easily persuaded. Jan didn't have the
heart to refuse a gesture that pleased him so much. However, she was not looking forward to an encounter with Alan.
He could be nice when he wanted to, but that wasn't very
often.

She had turned down Richard's invitation to have lunch
with him. She couldn't face him. She didn't want to see anyone; she could hardly wait until it was possible to go back
to bed.

The dream had come in the afternoon yesterday. It
might—it had to!—come again this afternoon.

As soon as she could Jan escaped from the house, pleading that she needed fresh air. She would have to come back in time to get lunch, but then it would be only an hour or so until naptime.

She walked east along the Duke of Gloucester Street toward the Capitol, where the British flag flapped in the breeze. It was as if she were suffering from double vision, seeing the eighteenth-century houses superimposed on their modern shapes. In front of the Raleigh a long line of tourists waited for admission. Their shorts and sports shirts looked bizarre to Jan. They should not have been there. Her inner eye saw horses tied to the hitching rail, backwoods militiamen in their fringed hunting shirts, prosperous burgesses wearing satin coats and powdered wigs. Across the street the King's Arms had its own shadowy clientele. Mrs. Jane Vobe had served Washington and William Byrd, as well as Charles and Jonathan. . . .

Jan passed the Capitol without stopping. It was a handsome building, but it didn't look right to her, not after seeing the revolutionary capitol in its original state. She wandered past the small brick building that had been the Public Records Office, and followed a path toward Nicholson Street.

In the yard in front of the gaol a line of giggling tourists were waiting their turn to try the stocks. Fathers would take pictures of grinning children with their neck and limbs enclosed by the wooden boards. Husbands would photograph their wives; and when the slides were shown, on a winter evening, the viewers would make funny remarks about the good old days when nagging wives got what was coming to them.

The stocks weren't really very funny, though. Helplessly exposed to the regard of his fellow townsmen, an unpopular prisoner might suffer serious injury if they chose to pelt him with rocks and sharp objects in addition to rotten vegetables. Now, the stocks and the ducking stools and the other implements of punishment were humorous—because they were no longer used. Like the tar and feathers that sounded so grotesquely comical, until you stopped to think that the tar had to be heated to boiling point before it liquefied, and that a dipperful of hot tar in the face, or in an equally vulnerable area, could cripple a man for life. The eighteenth century was not a gentle era. The law that condemned a traitor to be hanged, drawn, and quartered was still on the statute books, and the last two processes were not performed on a dead body. The prisoner was cut down while still alive and disemboweled: the body was beheaded and divided into four parts which were displayed in prominent places for the edification of the disaffected. If the Revolution had failed, American heads might have adorned Temple Bar in London.

Jan shivered. They wouldn't do that to Jonathan, but they would hang him, and they wouldn't worry about dispatching him with merciful quickness. They? As James had said, everybody was out to get him.

The revelations of the latest dream were startling; but she should have anticipated some of them. Evidently Jonathan had gone to Patriot's Dream that bitter night after Charles's collapse and brought Leah to Williamsburg to nurse him— another of his impetuous, warm-hearted acts that did not consider the possible consequences. The consequences had been more or less inevitable. Charles had looked like death walking that night, but part of his illness was due to exhaustion and nervous strain. Malaria couldn't be cured; but they had quinine and other remedies that would control it. Charles might be fit for duty—and other things—within a few days.

Jonathan would have taken steps to protect Leah even if she had not been carrying his friend's child. His overactive conscience, still tormented by Charles's death, made the solution he had suggested to Leah understandable. To Jan it seemed a logical and sensible solution, though rather sad; but perhaps he and Leah could find affection, if not love, in second best. She knew, though, that to a man of Jonathan's era the idea of marrying a slave would be little short of heretical. As a radical Jonathan made modern rebels look like amateurs. Yet he was a pacifist; it would never have occurred to him to threaten violence in order to gain his ends, much less carry out such threats.

She was surprised at the intensity of her relief at learning that Jonathan was not a traitor to the American cause. She thought she had no particular emotional bias on the subject; after all, there was not that much difference in ideology between the colonists and their so-called oppressors. The oppression had been essentially financial. And yet she was both pleased and proud to learn that Jonathan had seen the light and was on the "right" side.

The latest development sounded like a historical James Bond novel, but Jan knew that espionage is not a modern pursuit. Jonathan's fellow spy, James, was no figment of her imagination. The slave of a man named Armitage, James had really gathered information for Lafayette, traveling back and forth between Williamsburg and the British base at Portsmouth with his life in his hands. James did win his freedom, in 1786; it took the Virginia legislature another thirty-five years to vote him a pension for his services. He had been one of several slave spies. The Saul whom Jonathan had mentioned was probably Saul Matthews, who was also active in the Portsmouth area. It was reasonable that Jonathan should work with men like these, since he was known and trusted by the slaves of the area.

However, she couldn't blame Charles for misinterpreting the facts. Jonathan had dealt with Walforth, not to serve the British cause, but to help the oppressed people who were his chief concern. Now he was using that earlier contact to act as an eighteenth-century double agent, pretending to work for the British and making use of the information to serve his country. The role of a spy is never comfortable, but Jonathan's part was doubly perilous. Walforth was the greatest danger; if he so much as suspected that Jonathan was playing him false. . . .

And the fighting was coming closer. Virginia had experienced sporadic raids before, but in 1781 it was to become the main battleground of the war. One of the generals in command of the British forces was Benedict Arnold, whose name had by then become anathema to the country he had betrayed. In January of 1781 his troops raided Richmond, burning and looting. In April another British force landed at the mouth of the James, and Lafayette, in command of the ill-equipped American troops, could only try to wear the British out by getting them to chase him around the colony. He was in no shape to risk a battle.

It was around the middle of May when Cornwallis and Arnold joined forces. That date suited the details of the latest dream—the mild weather, the newly leafed branches, the muddy roads. And Jonathan was right to suspect that another raid was planned. The apprehensive Virginians had shifted capitals again, after Richmond had proved to be so vulnerable. But Charlottesville, near the home of Governor Thomas Jefferson, was no easier to defend with the inadequate forces Lafayette had at his disposal. The raid, at the very end of May, had almost succeeded in its aim—to capture Jefferson and the members of the legislature. It had been led by the man who had earned his nickname at Waxhaws and a dozen other skirmishes—"Bloody" Tarleton.

The episode had been one of the most romantic in a war that had its full share of romantic legends. A young aristocrat, John Jouett, enjoying a quiet drink at Cuckoo's Tavern, overheard Tarleton himself discussing his plans. Jouett got out of the tavern without being noticed and started out on a ride as daring as Paul Revere's, and more successful. He rode straight across country, through the tangled Virginia woods; for the rest of his life he carried the scars where branches had slashed his face. He reached Monticello at sunrise and woke Jefferson, who sent his family off to safety; and then—a typical Jefferson gesture—got out his telescope and ate a hearty breakfast on the terrace while he watched for the hated green uniforms. When they appeared at the foot of the "little mountain," Jefferson mounted his waiting horse and trotted away through the woods, making good his escape.

It had been a near thing, one of Tarleton's few failures,

and worse was to come. Williamsburg itself was in danger. Lafayette had not enough men to defend it or any other town. Cornwallis would march in, quite unopposed, on June 24.

Jonathan didn't know that, of course. He didn't know that the next six months would bring about an almost miraculous reversal of fortune for the bedeviled American forces under Lafayette, who would stand at Washington's side on the October afternoon when Cornwallis surrendered at Yorktown. The war would drag on for two more years, but it was effectively won at Yorktown.

Where would Jonathan be in October?

Walking along Nicholson Street, Jan passed Richard's shop without a second glance, but as she approached the Palace Green she stopped to look at the rambling white house across the street. It had been the home of St. George Tucker, who had brought the news of Charles's death to his family. The house hadn't been built then; Tucker had bought the property after the Revolution, and settled in Williamsburg, where he became a distinguished jurist and proponent of emancipation. His wartime letters to his wife were charming—gay, witty, devoted. The house was not open to the public. Too bad, Jan thought. I'd like to see it. He was a nice man. . . .

Was, will be, is. . . . She still had not come to grips with the problem of time. Indeed, her infatuated mind refused to face any of the problems, including the vital question of Charles's death. Jonathan's fate was the only one that concerned her now. She felt she was making some progress. For a moment, on the moonlit, muddy road, he had seemed to sense her presence. But she still could not break through the barrier, and there was so little time.

Time again—always time. Too much of it in one sense—too many years between her life and his—too little in another sense, for she knew the dreams must end sooner or later.

It's wrong, though, Jan thought—the way we conceive of time. The past behind, the future ahead, as if we were walking along a road—walking backward, because we can only see what was. Scientists don't think of it that way. The fourth dimension—whatever that is. It's all around us. There are no words to describe it because our reference points are those of the three dimensions our limited senses can grasp. Past, present and future. . . . Coexisting, eternal.

Her wanderings had brought her back to Market Square. In the distance she could hear the shrill tootling of fifes, the roll of drums; the junior members of the militia were parading. That meant it was noon. Time to go home. Cook lunch. And Alan was coming for dinner. More cooking.

If I could just get my hands on that anonymous caveman who first insisted that his mate broil the mammoth haunch, Jan thought viciously. He started the whole thing. . . .

And then she thought, it's got to work this afternoon. It's got to.

Chapter
19

June 1781

THE WAGON JOLTED ALONG THE RUTTED ROAD. ITS SPLIN-
tered sides looked worn in the gray moonlight, but it was a
stoutly built vehicle, and the horse that drew it was sleek and
strong. The seat was only a plank laid across the sides of the
wagon. The man who sat there was hunched as if against
the cold. The night was not cold, however; it was a typical
June night, heavy with moisture and sweet with the smell of
honeysuckle.

The driver seemed to choose the narrowest and roughest
tracks he could find. But when he came to the outskirts of
town he had to follow the main street for a short distance. He
slumped even farther down on the seat and pulled his broad-
brimmed hat over his eyes. He was dressed like a farmer
from the frontier, in worn, heavy clothing. For once, he had
remembered his hat.

Even a casual observer would have realized that something was wrong in Williamsburg that night. The Duke of
Gloucester Street was neither the busy, bustling place it was
during Publick Times, nor the somnolent thoroughfare of a
normal summer night. Many of the houses along the way
were dark, their shutters closed. There were few people on
the street. Only the taverns showed signs of life. Jonathan

reined in the horse as three men came tumbling out of the Raleigh, voices raised in unharmonious song. One fell and was solicitously raised by his equally unsteady friends; they went reeling off down the street, still singing.

Jonathan drove on. When he was able to turn off the Duke of Gloucester Street he drew a long sigh of relief. He was about to proceed into the courtyard behind the Wilde house when a man stepped out of the shadow and caught the horse's nose. Jonathan's hand went down into the wagon and came up with a heavy cudgel.

"Let go," he said in a low voice. "I don't want to hurt you, but no one interferes with me tonight."

"I shore hope not." The man stayed in the shadows, except for his black hand, but Jonathan recognized his voice.

"James! I thought you were with Lafayette. What has happened?"

"I been with Gen'ral Cornwallis," James said, with wry humor. "'Course he don't know why I was there; an' I hope it stay that way. He know 'bout you, though."

"What?"

"This bad news, Mr. Jonathan, an' you gotta hear it. That why I come here, 'stead of goin' straight to the Gen'ral. He be at Bird's Tavern, with the rest o' our army tomorrow or the day after; but Cornwallis, he be *here* tomorrow. Simcoe and Tarleton they with him, and there someone with Tarleton, you an' I know who, who may not wait till tomorrow to come lookin' for you. They know 'bout you warnin' Mr. Jefferson."

"How? I had a story prepared—"

"I know, that story already goin' around, and Mr. Jack Jouett a big hero for ridin' forty miles to warn the governor. But Tarleton, he know Mr. Jouett didn't see him and Walforth tell Tarleton you the only one who know where they headin' that night. It ain't hard to figure out you was the one who got the word to Mr. Jouett. So Walforth, he after you. They only a few miles away, Mr. Jonathan, and they ain't nobody or nothin' stop them from ridin' into this town whenever they please. Do they know where you stayin'?"

"I don't know." Jonathan seemed dazed by the news.

"If they don't, they find out easy enough. You get outta town, fast."

"Yes." Jonathan took a deep breath. "I was leaving, James. As you seem to know."

"I dunno where you goin'," said James. "Or who you goin' with. None of my business. Jes' you go. Good luck to you . . . an' anybody that go with you."

Before Jonathan could thank him, he was gone.

For a short time Jonathan sat quite still. Then he gave himself a shake and climbed down from the wagon. Leading the horse, he went on a few paces toward the back gate. It was closed, but when he shoved at it, the leaves swung back without even the traditional creak of rusty hinges. Jonathan let out a mutter of satisfaction.

He closed the gate after him and led the horse and wagon behind one of the outbuildings—the smokehouse, to judge from the enticing smell that clung to its walls.

The Wildes were in the habit of keeping a skeleton staff in the Williamsburg house even when they were at Patriot's Dream; but tonight there was no glow of fire or candlelight from the windows of the rooms occupied by servants over the stables, the kitchen, and other outbuildings. The house was dark, too, except for a single light in an upper window.

Seeing this, Jonathan made another soft, wordless sound of satisfaction. The approach of the British was proving to be an asset to his plan. The Wilde servants must have fled, as many other townspeople had done. Tomorrow the town would be wide open, for burning and looting; and slaves, especially "rebel" slaves, were considered part of the loot. Although it was unlikely that any of Leah's fellow servants would betray them, Jonathan was pleased to have no witnesses. Leah would simply disappear. She would be one of many, and there would be nothing to connect a runaway or stolen slave girl with Miss Mary Blythe, orphaned by war, who would come to Philadelphia as his affianced wife.

He and Leah had prepared their story. It was detailed, and

full of pathetic incidents. Leah had proved herself adept at subterfuge; she had even collected a suitable wardrobe. Her clothing and other necessities were already packed in the wagon. When Leah joined him she would have to bring only a small bundle containing last-minute needs.

His eyes fixed on the single lighted window, Jonathan waited. As the time passed, he began to show signs of restlessness. Suddenly he spun around, his eyes probing the darkness near the corner of the smokehouse. There was nothing visible to ordinary eyesight that should not have been there, but Jonathan was unable to relax. He kept turning his head to glance uneasily in that direction.

What was keeping Leah? There was no reason for delay; the sooner they left, the better. Perhaps one of the other servants had remained faithful to his post and Leah was unable to elude him. Jonathan was reluctant to enter the house; but as the slow minutes slid by, he became more and more worried.

Something might have happened. If she was ill, or injured. . . . Finally he could wait no longer. Keeping in the concealment of the buildings as much as possible, he made his way to the back of the house.

The door was not only unlocked, it stood ajar. Jonathan slipped noiselessly in. He went as rapidly as possible toward the front stairs. It was lucky he knew the house as well as he did, for he had to feel his way. The stairs received some light from the window on the landing. Now thoroughly alarmed, Jonathan was about to plunge up them when he heard a door open up above.

"Leah?" he called. "Leah, is it you?"

There was no answer in words, but footsteps came pattering rapidly along the uncarpeted upper hall and a flickering light strengthened. It came from a five-branched candelabrum, and Leah was carrying it. The candle flames blew wildly as she ran down the stairs, straight at Jonathan. He caught the candlestick from her hand and set it on a table, and then put his arm around her waist.

"Child,. what has happened?" And as she gasped, seemingly unable to speak, he went on, "Never mind. Whatever the danger, we'll soon be away from it. Hurry, you are late—"

She resisted the pull of his arm.

"I'm not going with you."

"What?"

"I'm not going. I had forgotten. I should have come to tell you sooner, but I. . . . Jonathan. . . ."

She stood shaking in the circle of his arm, her breast rising and falling rapidly. As Jonathan studied her face he saw that her agitation was not that of fear. An incredulous exultation brightened her eyes and softened her lips.

Jonathan's own breath caught in his throat. There was only one thing that could make Leah look like that.

"What a touching sight."

Half prepared as he was, the sound of the voice he had never expected to hear again made Jonathan stagger. He looked up. Charles was standing on the landing.

He was wearing his uniform breeches and scarred, spurred boots. His hands were busy with the buckle of his swordbelt, and as Jonathan gaped, openmouthed, Charles gave it the neat automatic twist that brought the weapon into position. The upper part of his body was bare except for bandages, which looked startlingly white and clean in comparison to his filthy clothing and his bearded, haggard face.

As he came slowly down the stairs, holding the rail, Jonathan turned to the wall, his hands pressed tightly over his face.

But there was no time for shock, or prayer, or anything but action, and Jonathan recovered himself before Charles reached the foot of the stairs. Leah ran to the swaying, scarecrow figure, but Charles put her off.

"No, Leah. It seems I have inadvertently interrupted a previous appointment. Tactless of me. A ghost has no right to interfere with the living. Do go on with whatever you were about to do."

"We must all go," Jonathan said. His voice was shaking,

but the hands he extended were steady as rock. "Charles, we thought you dead. I cannot express. . . . Nor is there time. The British will be here by morning; some advance troops may come in tonight. If they learn you are here—"

Leah cried out in alarm and flung her arms around Charles. He staggered, even under that gentle embrace, and Jonathan went on quickly.

"There is no time for any of the things we would say. Not even to correct your misapprehensions, Charles. I tell you, Tarleton is probably on his way here—"

"I know where the British are," Charles said. "I've been one jump ahead of them for days. I lay too long abed in that farmhouse in Carolina. Not the wound so much as the damn malaria; there were times I didn't know my own name. But I should have left sooner. Something told me you'd be up to your old tricks, Jon—or rather, new tricks, this is a variation. Where were you planning to take Leah? No doubt you have a comfortable little house in New York, where your British friends can protect you. What a pity I arrived when I did. Because of course I shan't let you take her."

Jonathan made a clumsy gesture of despair.

"There is no time for this, Charles! Leah—the wagon is in the courtyard. Help him to get there, I don't suppose he will accept my arm. . . . The Americans are at Bird's Tavern, six miles away; we can't leave Charles with the surgeons there."

"I won't leave him," Leah said. "I'm sorry, Jonathan."

In spite of the need for haste, Jonathan could not disregard this.

"You know this changes nothing," he said. "The plan we made is still the only one that solves your need."

"I don't care. You can leave us both at Bird's Tavern and go on."

"But, Leah—"

"No."

Charles's eyes, bright with fever, moved from one speaker to the other.

"Something's going on," he said with an effort. "Something I don't know. . . . Never mind. Get out, Jon. Take your damn wagon and go."

"Almighty God," Jonathan exclaimed, beside himself. "You can't stay here. I tell you, there is probably a troop of British dragoons on their way here right now. Walforth would like nothing better than to see you—"

"Walforth," Charles said softly. "I had forgotten your fondness for Cousin Henry. Yes, you would know his plans, wouldn't you? Thank you for the warning, Leàh. Go out and get in Jon's convenient wagon. Open the gate and wait for me."

"Come with me," she begged, tugging at him.

"Something I must do first." Charles pulled away. His sudden burst of strength caught the girl off balance. She stumbled and fell. Charles unsheathed his sword and started walking toward Jonathan.

"You're mad," Jonathan said, retreating. "You haven't strength enough to split a loaf of bread. Go with Leah, Charles. If you won't endure my company, I'll go elsewhere."

He glanced at Leah, who had scrambled to her feet, and shook his head. She stopped, obeying the implicit command; but her eyes were wide with horror.

"Leave you here, to tell Walforth where we've gone?" Charles laughed. "Stop backing away, Jon. It's not such an unfair fight. As you say, I'm not at my best. . . ."

The lifted blade gleamed in the candlelight, and then fell clattering to the floor as Jonathan's left arm swept it out of Charles's hand. His other arm moved in a narrower, controlled arc that ended at Charles's chin. Jonathan caught him as he fell and lifted him in his arms. He was not much of a weight.

"Open the door," Jonathan said. Leah ran ahead of him toward the back of the house.

They got Charles into the wagon and covered him with a blanket. Leah was scrambling onto the seat when a sound from the street reached them. They both knew what it

signified—the jingling of harness, the pounding hooves of
horses.

"They'll follow us," Leah gasped. "Charles's room—I
changed the bandages, they'll know he was here—"

There was no time for directions, and no need for them.
When Jonathan snatched the reins and thrust them at her she
took them and sent the horse on its way with a sharp command. The wagon rattled through the gateway, and Jonathan
ran back to the house.

Someone was pounding on the front door when he entered the hall. The candles burned clear in the still air. Jonathan stood for a moment trying to control his breathing and
force his shaken mind to thought. His eyes fell on Charles's
sword, lying where it had fallen; with a queer, twisted smile
he bent and picked it up. Then he opened the door.

Walforth had brought a dozen men. It was a testimonial,
of sorts; Jonathan's strange smile broadened as his eyes went
from the mounted dragoons at the gate to the three officers
who stood on the doorstep.

They looked so elegant, compared to the tatterdemalion
figure that had just left the house. The polished helmets with
their sweeping black feather cockades made them look taller
than life. The tight-fitting white breeches and black boots set
off Walforth's well-shaped legs, and the green jacket fit like
a glove. The sword slung at his side had a gold hilt.

Jonathan stepped back.

"Come in, gentlemen. Are you looking for someone? I'm
afraid I'm the only one here."

Walforth entered, ducking his head.

"You're all I would ever want, Jon. I'm so glad we
happened to find you in. No doubt we would have failed
in that hope if we had waited to march in with the others
tomorrow."

"How did you know I was here?" Jonathan asked. The
question sounded casual, but it was not. If an informer had
followed him tonight, Walforth might know about Leah—
and the wagon.

The answer relieved this anxiety.

"We stopped at your old hideaway first. Finding you absent, I followed a hunch. Gloating over your future inheritance, Jon? I fear you are premature. I'd like to hang you now; it would be so symbolic, to dangle you from a limb outside this very house. But that would be too quick. I want you to have time to reflect on your mistakes. Besides, General Tarleton must be convinced of your treachery."

"You mean he isn't convinced yet?" Jonathan asked with interest. "Ah, I believe I understand. Your friends and fellow officers out there—why don't you invite them in, Henry?—might report that you had acted prematurely if you hanged me out of hand. I may have useful information for the General. Why don't you ask me, Henry? Bring your friends in; we'll all have a glass of Mr. Wilde's excellent Madeira and discuss the situation."

"Do you have any idea how ridiculous you look waving that sword?" Walforth demanded. "Put it down—you don't know how to use it anyway—and come along. You can discuss the situation with Tarleton—although I doubt that he will offer you a glass of Madeira. I don't blame you for stalling, Jon. No man is in a hurry to meet death. But I haven't time to indulge you. My men are anxious to see the sights of Williamsburg."

As he spoke, Jonathan was listening with every nerve in his body. Apparently the fugitives had gotten away undiscovered; there would have been sounds of alarm if any of the soldiers had seen the wagon. So far so good. With his quarry in sight, and no knowledge of any other quarry, Walforth had not sent his men to search the grounds. But if they went out into the town in search of loot and casual pleasure, one of them might stop the fugitives. He had to keep Walforth occupied as long as possible. Every extra minute put Leah and Charles farther along the road to Bird's Tavern.

In any case there was no profit for him in tamely giving himself up. The evidence of his double-dealing was there, if anyone looked hard enough, and Tarleton was notoriously disinterested in legal evidence anyway. If he went with Walforth now, he went to his death—a nasty, ignoble death by hanging.

He had been standing in a slouched, wary position, the naked blade dangling awkwardly from his hand. Now, as the inevitable conclusion took shape in his mind, leaving no room for doubt or indecision, he straightened up. It was as if he flung off a burden that had bowed his shoulders for months. His smile was the old carefree grin, and his brown eyes sparkled.

"I don't want to talk to General Tarleton," he said cheerfully. "He's a very tiresome man. I never liked him. I don't like you either, Henry. If you want me to come with you, you'll have to fight me."

He raised the sword into the position of guard he remembered from lessons long ago.

Walforth's stupefaction made him look almost human. He sputtered.

"You—you're insane! You don't know how to use that thing. I'll cut you to pieces."

"I took lessons," Jonathan said indignantly. "With Charles, when we were boys."

"And then you decided that fighting was naughty," Walforth said, grinning wolfishly. "Well, by God, why not? If you think those lessons, years ago, will now stand you in good stead . . ." His eyes narrowed. "Wait, there must be some trick to this. What are you planning? If you think you can get under my guard and grapple with me. . . ."

"I did it once before," Jonathan reminded him. "What a splash you made in that punchbowl, Henry!"

The taunt had the effect he anticipated. Walforth turned scarlet and glanced at the other two officers, who had come into the house wondering what was prolonging the arrest. One of them wiped off the grin that had spread over his face, but not soon enough. Walforth's flush deepened and his always hasty temper got the better of him. He ripped his sword from its scabbard.

"Better remove your coat and hat," Jonathan said. "That bunch of feathers might get in your way."

Foaming with rage as he was, Walforth was too careful of his skin to neglect the possible handicap. He began to struggle out of his jacket.

"Just a moment." The older of the two officers, dignified in his powdered wig, spoke in a cold voice. "Am I to understand, Captain Walforth, that you are honoring this spy by crossing swords with him?"

"We have a personal quarrel," Jonathan explained, since Walforth was too angry to speak coherently. "It is of long standing. I assure you, sir, my family is as good as Captain Walforth's."

"I see. But if I understand correctly, you are not accustomed—"

"Oh, let them fight," said the younger officer, a stout, cheerful-looking man of about twenty-five. "If Walforth can let a little blood, we may find the chap easier to handle; personally, I'd rather not attack anything that size without an ax."

The older officer looked doubtful, but said no more. It would have been useless in any case; Walforth was already advancing, his sword weaving complex patterns.

The blades clashed. It was immediately apparent that Jonathan didn't have a chance. At first his strength and his memory of a few basic moves kept him from being seriously hurt, but Walforth pinked him twice, glancing cuts on the cheek and forearm. Then a change in the pace of the duel took place, and the older of the two officers sucked in his breath as his experienced eye told him what was happening.

Secure in the knowledge that he had his opponent at his mercy, Walforth was deliberately prolonging the fight. Several times he passed up openings in Jonathan's clumsy guard, contenting himself with feints that made his opponent stumble back. When he had Jonathan backed up against the wall, he began playing with him, until he was streaming with blood from half a dozen cuts, and his shirt was a gory mess. The watching officers pressed forward. The younger of the two was no longer smiling. As Walforth's blade ripped Jonathan's right sleeve from shoulder to elbow, leaving a bloody trail, he shouted suddenly,

"Damn it, Walforth, make an end, if you must!"

Walforth jumped back, lowering his reddened sword. He kept a wry eye on Jonathan, although he must have known there was no danger from that quarter. His chest pumping like a bellows, Jonathan was barely able to stand. His left hand, pressed against the wall, had left scarlet prints against the pale-buff paneling.

"Did you speak, sir?" Walforth said politely to his fellow officer.

"You sicken me," said that honest young man. "Like a damned cat, by God. . . . Kill him and be done with it."

"There is no need for that," said the older officer curtly. He turned to Jonathan. "Sir, I will be honored to accept your surrender."

"I thank you," Jonathan wheezed. "But I don't—surrender."

"You see?" Walforth raised his eyebrows and smiled mockingly at the other two. "It's a stubborn creature. I had hoped to deal with it gently; but since you insist, gentlemen—"

Raising his blade, he stepped back a pace.

"*En garde,* Jon," he said; and lunging at full length, he ran Jonathan through the left breast.

For a long moment Jonathan stood upright, pinned like a beetle by the blade. Then Walforth withdrew; and the tattered figure, still holding the useless sword, fell forward on its face.

Frowning as if in thought, Walforth bent over and wiped his sword on the back of Jonathan's shirt, which was unstained except for the spreading patch where the last thrust had gone through.

"He was up to something," he muttered. "Now what . . . ?" And with a sudden exclamation he turned and bounded up the stairs.

The younger officer knelt by the fallen man and turned him over.

"We didn't bring a surgeon," he muttered.

"It would do no good." The older man, standing, studied the still body knowledgeably. "That thrust probably pierced a lung. He's a man of strong physique, but he won't live an hour."

"We might at least stop the bleeding," the younger man said. "Or would it be more merciful to put the poor devil out of his misery?"

"He'll bleed to death; that's an easy way to go. Let's leave him. I don't think you could call me squeamish, Jackson, but damn! I've a nasty taste in my mouth."

"Then we'll wash it out with some ale. But I'd rather not drink with Walforth. . . ."

Walforth came running down the stairs, his sword still in his hand, his eyes wild.

"The treacherous swine! I might have known he would trick me at the last!" His booted foot swung and struck Jonathan in the side. The older officer shoved him back as he raised his foot for another kick.

"That will do, Captain. Cursed if I'll watch any more of your tricks tonight."

"But you don't understand," Walforth snarled. "He's back—Charles Wilde—one of Washington and Morgan's aides—back from the dead, damn his eyes. He must have gotten away just before we arrived; he left his coat. . . . It had to be Charles, it's the Virginia facings, captain's insignia; hurry, perhaps we can catch him. He can't have gone far, on foot and wounded—there were old bandages and a basin of bloody water as well. That's why this one kept us here, so Charles could get away. Send the man out to look for him. He may be on horseback. Jon's horse. If I could get him—both of them, in one night. . . ."

He flung himself out the door, shouting orders.

The other two exchanged eloquent glances before they followed. But neither of them spoke; they were soldiers, and they had seen far worse than this night's business.

II

Jan stood where she had been standing during the duel, in the doorway of the parlor. In her horror at what was happening she had tried to interfere early in the proceedings; her hands had passed through what felt like thin air, although her eyes told her that the space was occupied by Walforth's sword arm. It had been a futile and idiot act; she knew better; but she had hoped that her efforts to reach into the past were beginning to bear fruit. Surely Jonathan had been dimly aware of her presence earlier that night. He had looked straight at her, but had apparently seen nothing.

Now she felt only a merciful numbness, the emotional anesthesia of shock. Jonathan was dead; or, if he still lived, it would not be for long. There was nothing she could do to save him. A modern hospital, equipped with antibiotics and surgical instruments, might have done so. But she could not even stop the bleeding with her hands that could not reach through time.

She crossed the room and knelt down. He was still breathing. There was so much blood she couldn't see the wound through which his life was ebbing away. She put out her hand. It felt nothing. Not the stickiness of blood or the warmth of human flesh; nothing.

She wondered vaguely why the dream was continuing. Nothing more would happen—unless Walforth came back with prisoners. Was that why she was still trapped in the past, to learn the fate of Charles and Leah? She was too benumbed to care what happened now, but it would be good to know that Jonathan's last gesture had been successful. Everything else he had done had backfired, somehow; he had even failed in his attempt to save Leah from the fate to which she had been born. She would become Charles's mistress now, if Charles lived—her children born to slavery. But perhaps Walforth would catch them. Such a denouement would fit the pattern of the story, reducing even Jonathan's death to futility.

Jonathan's breathing changed. As Jan bent over him, he opened his eyes.

He saw her.

She couldn't believe it at first; but there was no doubt, she had seen his eyes move past and through her too often, unfocused and unaware of her near presence. Now they fixed on her face, blurred and dim as they were, and his lips curved in a faint smile.

"Patience."

"No," she said stupidly, knowing he wouldn't hear.

"No," he agreed. His forehead creased. "No, you aren't Patience. I thought. . . . You looked. . . . Who are you?"

The room whirled around, a blur of color and light. Jan thought the dream was fading; she threw out mental hands, clung. Never had she exerted her will so strongly. And then, as his face came back into focus, she forgot the strangeness, the impossibility of what was happening, and was aware of only one thing.

"Never mind," she said gently. "Don't talk. You're hurt. Save your strength."

"No, I feel . . . fine. No pain." He smiled at her. "Did they get away?"

"Yes." Jan didn't hesitate.

"Good."

"Jonathan . . ."

"You know my name," he said wonderingly. "But I don't know you. I feel I ought to know you, though. Your face isn't familiar, but there is something. . . ."

"Please don't talk. You are badly wounded. I could go for help. . . ."

But she knew it would be useless. He could see her; in the borderland between life and death all barriers were down, all definitions meaningless. But it was unlikely that anyone else would be aware of her presence. And even if they were— where in the panic-stricken town could she find help? There was none for Jonathan now, except in a future he could not reach.

"Am I hurt?" he asked, in the same tone of childish bewilderment. "I remember Walforth slashing at me. . . . But I don't feel bad. I don't feel anything. It's like floating. How peculiar. I can't even feel the floor under me. I must be lying on my back, I can see the ceiling. . . . I can't understand it. Unless . . . unless I am dying. That must be it. And you are. . . ."

The wide, ingenuous eyes traveled over her, from her tumbled hair, down her bare arms, over the flimsy gown. A muted sound came from the parted lips; and Jan realized that he was trying to laugh.

"Don't," she gasped.

"I'm sorry. I was just thinking—you don't look like an angel. I don't mean to be rude, you are a very pretty young lady—it is very obvious that you *are* a young lady—but I thought angels had longer hair and more—er—modest dress. Not that I mind. . . ."

"How can you make jokes at a time like this?" Jan asked.

"What better time? I remember thinking, once, that all our ideas about life after death might be wrong. I never envisioned anyone quite like you, though. . . . I must be dying or I wouldn't be able to accept this so easily," he went on. "It is really a very unusual situation, isn't it?"

"Yes," Jan said, choking.

"You mustn't cry," he said dreamily. "There's no reason to cry. I don't know who, or what, you are. It doesn't matter. I'm glad to have . . . someone here. I'm sure that whatever happens afterward, it will be all right; but the dying itself. . . . That's a lonely business. I'm grateful to you—or whoever sent you. . . ."

His eyes closed and his lips tightened in a sudden spasm. Jan wrung her hands together. She would have given anything to be able to touch him—not for her own comfort, but for his. The only thing she could give him was the sound of her voice.

"Close your eyes, then," she said softly. "I'll be here. I'll stay with you."

And she hoped and prayed that was true.

Jonathan's eyes opened.

"It hurts," he said, sounding surprised. "Why does it hurt?"

"It won't last long," Jan said. "It will soon be over."

"Not that." Jonathan tried to shake his head. "Not what you think. Suddenly I'm afraid. This isn't what I thought. . . . Was I wrong? Have I been wrong about everything? My life has been such a succession of blunders. I hoped that after life. . . . Can't you tell me that, to ease my dying? *What is going to happen to me?*"

"I can't tell you," Jan said. "I don't know."

"You're crying again. I can't see so well now, but I can tell you're crying. And you wouldn't cry, would you, if you knew. . . . I'm sorry. I didn't mean to distress you, you have been so kind. Don't feel bad. I don't mind. Only I wish. . . ."

"What?" Jan tried to steady her voice.

"I wish I knew it hadn't all been futile." Jonathan's voice was weaker, and the rigidity of his face showed the effort he had to make to keep from showing the increasing pain. "Charles and Leah. . . . If he escapes, my death won't be completely without meaning, but I will have failed with her. Failed with all those others I tried to help. Are they doomed to live in servitude forever? Was this dream of freedom a chimera, all that blood spilled for nothing? Including mine?"

"No."

Jan didn't stop to think. The words came out as if she had prepared them for days, pondered and edited them for maximum effect. She had very little time now. His eyes were glazing; horror and pain and despair were in their brown depths. As his grasp on life lessened, her foothold in the world was fading with it. Before she left it forever, there was one thing she could do for him—to ease his dying.

"No, it isn't a chimera, or a bad joke. It will be a long fight, the fight for freedom and equality, but you made the beginning, you and others like you, and the fight will go on. It was your friend Jefferson who said that the tree of liberty must be manured with the blood of patriots. He also said, 'Nothing is more surely written in the book of fate than that these people shall be free.' They will be free, Jonathan. One day this country will see black legislators and judges, doctors, lawyers, teachers. Leah's children's children will be able to go to college, marry whom they please, vote and serve in the army. And that's only part of your dream. All the other things you hoped for will come true. Religious freedom, equal franchise, advances in medicine and surgery—even the roads you thought about, remember? Great highways, a network of them from one ocean to the other. . . ."

And, her rebellious mind added—pollution, crime, corruption, bigotry. The great highways arenas of slaughter, the virgin forests and clear streams laid waste; race riots in school halls, the dream of democracy shattered by demagogues and thieves. . . .

But those words went unspoken, and the words she had said aloud had the desired effect. Jonathan's fading eyes brightened. He tried to smile.

"It's true?" he whispered.

"True. I know this. I wouldn't lie to you, Jonathan. Not now."

"Thank you. . . ."

"And Charles." She leaned closer, seeing his face through a thickening veil, feeling her grasp on his world loosening. "Charles will live to be old, Jonathan. He got away, he'll inherit Patriot's Dream and live, rich and happy. Your side is going to win. There will be a big battle, at Yorktown, a few months from now—"

At the very end she thought she felt his hand touch hers. Then the gray veil blinded her and the silence between the worlds closed her ears so that she could hear nothing except her own strangled sobs.

For a few seconds after she woke she thought the miracle had happened. Surely she could still feel Jonathan's hand clasping hers—a big hand, strong and hard and warm. But when she opened her eyes she saw her own room and a circle of familiar faces. She was still crying. Her nose was running and the tears were streaming down her cheeks and soaking her hair. It was horrible. She didn't want to make an exhibition of herself in front of Alan. . . . What was he doing in her bedroom anyway? It was late. The windows were dark and the light was artificial. Anyway, she was well chaperoned. Her aunt, shaken and trembling, her white hair on end; Uncle Henry, Richard. . . . Was it Richard's hand that held hers, like a lifeline, pulling her back into her own world? What business did they have in her room, staring down at her as if she were a specimen under a microscope? She tried to stop crying, and couldn't.

Then another face came into view through her blurred vision. Frank Jordan—Doctor Jordan. He said something to Alan, and Alan nodded, tight-lipped.

"I am not hysterical," Jan shouted. "I'm not. . . . Oh, God, he's dead. He's dead and I couldn't help him. . . ."

She didn't feel the prick of the needle, but she saw the hypodermic when Dr. Jordan stepped back from the bed, and she tried to tell them they didn't have to hold her; she wasn't fighting it, there was nothing she desired more than oblivion. Then the drug took hold and she fell toppling into a bottomless blackness, and peace.

Chapter
20

Summer 1976

WHEN SHE WOKE THE SECOND TIME IT WAS MORNING. Her mind was working slowly but rationally; she remembered what had happened, but without emotion, as if it had happened to someone else. Her arm was sore; it felt as if she'd had several shots, not just one. Something to put her to sleep and then, perhaps, a tranquilizer? That was why she felt so calm, so remote.

She heard a creak of wood. Turning her head languidly, she saw Alan sitting by the bed and accepted his presence as unemotionally as she had accepted the other facets of reality. He looked terrible. The stubble of beard was a quarter of an inch long and his eyes were sunken. His coat and tie hung over the back of the chair where he had obviously spent the night.

"Silly," Jan said drowsily.

"How do you feel?"

"Fine."

"Want some coffee? I've got the dregs of a thermos. It's lukewarm, but it'll wake you up a little."

He helped her sit up and held the cup while she drank. The coffee was lukewarm.

"I'll get you some fresh in a minute," Alan said, seeing

her grimace. "But I don't want to wake the others till we've had a chance to talk."

"What is there to talk about?"

"First and foremost, what is to become of you. You're going to have to shape up and get with it, Jan, or you will find yourself in a psychiatric ward. If I hadn't threatened Jordan with a lawsuit, he'd have committed you last night."

Jan thought about this remarkable statement.

"Why did you do that?" she asked curiously.

"He gave you too much of that damn dope," Alan muttered. "That question is irrelevant and immaterial, Jan, and anyhow, I don't know the answer myself. I just had a feeling. . . . Wake up and think, will you? Jordan can still stick you in the booby hatch, and he'll do it, if you can't prove that you've recovered from whatever hit you yesterday."

As he bent over her his dark face looked threatening, and Jan's numbed brain began to function, in response to the urgency in his voice.

"What happened?" she asked. "I woke up and saw you all—"

"What's the last thing you remember?"

The question almost broke Jan's drugged calm. If she told him what she really remembered. . . .

"I took a nap," she said. "It must have been about two o'clock when I went to sleep."

"It was six when I arrived and found your aunt and uncle trying to wake you up," Alan said. "They had let you sleep late because they thought you looked tired. By the time I got here, they were convinced you were dead; and for a while, I. . . . I had to hold a mirror to your lips before I was sure you were breathing.

"We called the doctor, and Camilla sneaked off and called Richard—visions of deathbed scenes, I suppose. Anyhow, we had quite a party. I don't know what ailed you. Coma, trance—I've never seen anything like it, and I don't think our medical friend had either. He didn't admit it, though. After he tried everything in his little black bag, he wanted to put you in the hospital. Maybe I should have let him. I don't know; I just had a crazy feeling that you should stay where you were. . . .

"I was on very shaky ground, though, and I might not have been able to fight them all off if you hadn't started show- ing signs of life. You were kicking and screaming when you woke up. It was a good old-fashioned case of hysterics, so I let Jordan put you out. He has an operation this morning, but he'll be around later; and I advise you to think up a convinc- ing story. You scared hell out of everybody last night. He'll want you in his office for every test known to man, including those funny little inkblots psychiatrists play with."

"I don't know what to tell him," Jan said. The tranquilizer must be wearing off. She felt panicky. If Frank started asking questions, jabbing and prying, she might break down.

"You could say you don't remember a damn thing," Alan said thoughtfully. "Amnesia. Nobody knows how it works, so he can't prove you're lying. You might invent a story about a tragic love affair and admit it has been preying on your mind. . . ."

"You've thought it all out, haven't you?"

"I had all night."

"Why did you say that—about the tragic love affair?"

"Maybe you do have amnesia. Don't you remember what you were screaming about?"

"What did I say?"

"'He's dead,'" Alan repeated flatly. "'I couldn't help him.' There was more, before that, but it was less coherent. You babbled about blood quite a lot. Hey, there's a thought. You told me about seeing a knife fight between two of your students. Jordan would like that one, it's a nice simple neu- rosis, and should be easily curable."

"You're incredible," Jan said angrily. "Making up sto- ries, inventing things. . . . Don't you care what really happened?"

"Jan is herself again," Alan said, smiling. "Mad and mean . . ." The smile vanished. "Yes. I care. If you ever want to tell me I'll listen. But until you do, it's none of my business—and it's nobody else's business either. You ran up against something you couldn't handle. I've seen it building for days. Maybe you still can't handle it. But I think you can. And I think you're the only one who can. Jordan is fine with chicken pox and sprained ankles, but he's too conceited to admit your problem may be out of his province, and I don't want him messing around with your mind."

Jan couldn't think what to say. She was spared the effort; Alan, whose ears had been alert for them, heard the sound of footsteps and moved back from the bed.

"Here comes the first wave," he said. "Good luck."

II

Thanks to Alan's warning, Jan was able to put on a convincing show of normalcy; and if her girlish laughter was a little forced and her mind not quite on the job, the people who were close to her were anxious to see only positive signs. She managed to talk her aunt and uncle out of telephoning her mother. Since they shared her opinion of that lady's usefulness in a crisis, they were easily persuaded. Besides, Jan said gaily, she was fine now, wasn't she?

She had decided that the safest course to take with Frank Jordan was one of wide-eyed ignorance. No, she couldn't remember a single thing. Wasn't it queer? No, nothing like that had ever happened to her before—and she certainly hoped it never would again. Yes, she had been feeling a little tired; could it be hormones or something?

As she flirted shamelessly with him, displaying an undeniably healthy body, Frank was only too glad to dismiss the incident in glib, meaningless terms. There was certainly nothing wrong with her physically; the tests he administered had all produced normal results. He didn't think she ought to take any more sleeping pills, but a mild tranquilizer, just for the time being, couldn't do any harm. Tension was certainly a factor. It always was in these cases. . . . And would she have dinner with him one evening next week?

She knew, of course, that the peculiarity of her attack couldn't be dismissed that casually. Frank meant to watch her unobtrusively, and she was aware of her aunt and uncle's surveillance. Since she was anxious to keep busy, and everyone else had the same idea in mind, her social life expanded considerably. Camilla used all her connections and introduced a succession of "nice young girls"—granddaughters of old friends, students, summer employees. Jan found most of them agreeable bores, but she dutifully played tennis and went swimming and made dates for sewing classes and lectures and concerts. Richard was also assiduous in his attentions.

Jan never asked him why it had been Alan, not he, who sat with her that night. Richard never referred directly to the incident. In fact, Richard wouldn't talk about the incident at all. Her stumbling attempts to refer to it were deftly turned aside. Nor did he mention his proposal of marriage. In all other ways he was the pleasant, devoted companion of the first week.

Alan was neither pleasant nor devoted but he was ubiquitous. He came to play chess with Uncle Henry almost every night, and she met him so often on the street that she accused him of neglecting his business.

After a week had passed without a repetition of the attack, everyone began to relax, including Jan. The first night was the worst. She was afraid she would dream—and afraid she would not. Fear overruled hope, however; she would not willingly experience that last dream again. But nothing came, not even fragments, and when night followed dreamless night, she knew nothing more would ever come. It was over, and she still did not understand why it had ever begun.

The meaninglessness of it all still rankled. It was the major factor in the rebellion that seethed under her smiling facade during the days that followed. Frank's tranquilizers dulled the other pain. It was nothing less, an agony of loss;

and it was part of the other problem, for although she would have been willing to dismiss the dreams as fantasy, her rational mind would not allow her to do so. The more history she read, the more she found to confirm the incredible accuracy of the dreams.

Yet she knew a skeptic wouldn't accept this as proof. She herself could no longer remember when she had learned certain vital facts, before or after the dream in which they had appeared. Not that she had any desire to prove anything to an outsider; the thought of discussing Jonathan made her wince, like the idea of describing the intimate physical details of a dead love affair. No, it was herself she needed to convince. Even evidence that proved the unreality of the dreams would be better than uncertainty.

She had done only one thing during that week that was a tacit admission of weakness. She had taken Jonathan's portrait down from the wall and put it in the closet.

It was almost ten days after the last dream when Jan found herself one afternoon with nothing to do. Even Camilla's invention had failed; she had exhausted all the "nice young girls" and was apparently beginning to feel she could now safely leave Jan to her own devices for a few hours. She and Henry were both worn out, not only with worry, but with unaccustomed activity; they had thrown themselves heroically into the breach when all other assets failed, and had walked and gone to horrid movies they didn't want to see. Today Jan had been able to persuade them to stay at home while she went out for some exercise.

It was a glorious day. A storm the preceding night had swept out the low-pressure system that had been hanging over the area for weeks, bringing heat and smog and humidity. It was warm, but not too warm, and every object in town, from the green leaves of the trees to the houses themselves, looked newly washed and polished.

Jan eventually found herself in front of the school where she had watched Alan's protégés play baseball. The playground was deserted this afternoon. A few butterflies, their scalloped wings brilliant orange and black and gold, clung to the purple spikes of the butterfly bushes along the fence. Jan looked at them indifferently. She had not always been so unresponsive to beautiful things, and she wondered whether this lethargy would accompany her through the rest of her life. Maybe it was the medication she was taking. She couldn't do without it, not yet. Everyone thought she was making excellent progress; she was the only one who knew there was something buried, festering under the healing surface.

She looked up and saw Alan walking toward her.

He was his usual disheveled self, his tie loosened and his hands jammed into the pockets of his jacket, dragging it out of shape.

"Following me again," Jan said. "Don't you get bored?"

"I do. Come on, I'll buy you a drink."

"It's too early for a drink. Anyhow, I shouldn't take alcohol with those pills Frank gave me."

"Coffee, then. Or a double butterscotch-pecan sundae."

Jan shrugged and fell into step with him. They strolled on without speaking for half a block. Then Alan said, "You're still taking those tranquilizers?"

"I suppose you don't approve."

"I don't believe in retreating from reality."

"What a pompous speech."

Alan muttered something. She had a feeling he was trying not to blurt out what was on his mind, but it was no use.

"Can't you find anybody in this town to talk to?" he demanded. "God knows I don't approve of this self-pitying verbal diarrhea known as catharsis; but there are times when people have to spit out what's bugging them, get it out of their system."

"I'm doing fine," Jan said. "What makes you think I'm in need of catharsis?"

Alan waved this question away with a contemptuous toss of his head.

"How about Richard? If you can't tell him about it, your prospects for matrimony don't impress me as good."

"I couldn't tell Richard!" Jan exclaimed. "I—I mean, I don't have anything to tell."

"Too late," Alan said, sneering. "Trapped you, didn't I?"

"I'm not going to whine to Richard," Jan said sullenly.

"What you mean is you don't dare tell Richard anything that might rip the neat little plastic cocoon he's hiding in. He has chosen to ignore unpleasantness—"

"And you despise him for it."

"No," Alan said. "He had reasons for retreating from life. Understandable reasons."

Jan looked at him in surprise. His dark, homely face broke into one of its more saturnine smiles.

"You don't expect me to be kind to the downtrodden, do you? I don't despise Richard Blake. I don't agree with him, but I don't despise him. As I said, he has his reasons."

"What reasons?"

"Think, if your brain isn't fogged by dope," Alan said rudely. "Richard is about thirty. What was going on when he was in his twenties?"

Jan didn't know why it came to her as such a shock. She had never thought of Richard. . . .

"Viet Nam?"

"The works." Alan nodded. "Combat, prison camp, brainwashing. . . . If he has now decided to cop out from the rest of life he has my sympathy, if not my wholehearted support."

They walked on in silence while Jan struggled to assimilate this new information with the image she had formed of Richard. Stupid of her not to have realized. . . . Of course it increased her sympathy and admiration for him enormously.

"Why did you tell me?" she asked, looking up at Alan.

"Why?" He stopped, in the middle of the sidewalk, and slapped his shirt front. "Because underneath I am still a Southern gentleman, in spite of the signs of vice and corruption you see written on my face, like that of Dorian Gray. Although the man is my bitter rival, I am too noble to take advantage of his equally noble reticence. Your happiness means so much to me—"

"Oh, shut up," Jan said amiably. They walked on.

"How long has it been since you took one of those pills?" Alan asked.

"After lunch." Jan glanced at he watch. "It's almost four. I can take another one."

She reached into her purse. Alan snatched the bottle from her and examined the label.

"At least it's a fairly mild dosage," he muttered. "You could have a drink, the last one has worn off by now. Just don't take any more."

"Why are you so anxious to ply me with alcohol?" Jan asked. "It's just as bad as tranquilizers."

"It can be, yes. But I don't think you have the makings of an alcoholic."

"Whereas I do have the makings of—a dope fiend?"

"Actually," Alan said, putting his hands—and the bottle— into his pockets, "I am trying to lure you into my lair. Hadn't you figured that out? I don't have any etchings, so. . . . Well! Look where we are!"

Jan had been so absorbed in his revelations about Richard that she had not noticed where he was leading her. She recognized his apartment building just ahead. If there had been any doubt in her mind, the sight of a distinctive little shape advancing toward them would have settled the matter. The peke had already recognized Alan; it was barking shrilly and tugging at the leash. Mabel had gone from bad to worse—from culottes to shorts. The shorts were magenta, and the halter top was green.

Apparently she had forgiven Alan for mistreating the dog, who certainly bore no malice; dog and woman figuratively cast themselves on his bosom. The dog would have done it literally if he could have jumped that high; he had to settle for damaging attacks on Alan's knees.

"It's almost happy time," Mabel said, beaming. "Come in and have a dinky-poo with me."

"I am drinking with this lady," Alan said. "I have to spread my favors around, Mabel, it's only fair. And although I am well known for my prowess, I can only handle one of you at a time."

They left Mabel in convulsions of laughter.

"Why do you have to go around playing comedian?" Jan asked. "You make yourself look silly."

"That's a good question." Alan appeared to ponder it. "You know, I never thought about it; but I expect there is some deep-seated neurosis there. Probably goes back to my childhood. I was ugly, unpopular, painfully shy. . . ."

The apartment looked as if it hadn't been cleaned for a week. There were crumbs on the coffee table, stacks of records everywhere, and a pile of cat dung in the middle of the living-room rug.

Alan pounced on this with a piece of newspaper, mumbling angrily.

"Damn that animal! I told her last time she did this I'd throw her out."

"What did she say?" Jan asked, laughing.

"Couldn't repeat it. Very rude. Ghetto-type cat; found her in my garbage can last week."

"Where is she?" Jan asked, glancing around the room.

"On my bed, probably," Alan said gloomily. "On the pillow. She's shedding like crazy. I think I got rid of the fleas, though."

"I never would have thought of you as a cat lover."

"I'm not. What'll you have? Bourbon, vodka, Scotch—"

He went into the kitchen to mix the drinks and Jan cleared a space on the couch. It was typical of Alan that he had not even mentioned the mess, much less apologized for it. Jan was conscious of a faint urge to find a broom and get to work; but the urge was easily overridden. The clutter was comfortable. It was the sort of room where a person could take off her shoes, or eat crackers, or put glasses on the table without coasters under them. If it were hers, she would probably try for a slightly higher level of cleanliness, but . . .

But it wasn't hers. Good Lord, she thought, amused; I'm

developing housewifely instincts. It must be all those TV commercials.

Alan came back with their drinks and a bowl of potato chips. Following him, its green eyes fixed on the bowl, was the offending cat. She would have been a handsome creature if she had not been so thin. Even the long gray-and-white fur could not disguise the leanness of her ribs.

"No, you can't have any potato chips," Alan growled, as the cat made hypocritical passes at his ankles. "Your food is in the kitchen. Go get it. . . . Oh, hell."

The cat ate the potato chip, not too neatly. Jan didn't blame it for looking smug.

"She's so thin," Jan said.

"You should have seen her a week ago."

"She doesn't look like an alley cat, even now."

"No, she was somebody's pet. They dumped her when they got tired of her. Probably when she went in heat the first time."

"How awful," Jan said indignantly.

"They used to do it to unwanted babies," Alan said.

"You don't have to convince me it's a rotten world."

"There are laws, now," Alan said. "Even laws forbidding the abandonment of animals. Hard to enforce them, but they are on the books. The very idea of laws like that would have been inconceivable two hundred years ago."

The drink wasn't very strong. There was no sensible reason why Jan should have started to cry.

She didn't sob or get hysterical as she had before. She simply sat staring dumbly at Alan—and the cat, comfortably and inconveniently ensconced on his lap—and wept.

"Go on. Talk," Alan said.

Jan talked. She told him the whole thing. It took quite a long time. The sunlight deepened from gold to bronze, and the shadows lengthened across the floor. Alan didn't interrupt or ask questions. He sat stroking the cat till it fell asleep and its rumbling purr died away. Then he just sat. When Jan had finished he continued to sit, without speaking, for some time.

"Fascinating," he said, at last.

"You sound like Sherlock Holmes," Jan said, wiping her wet cheeks with her fingers. "Or is it Mr. Spock?"

"Feel better?"

"Yes," Jan said in surprise. "I need to blow my nose."

"Paper towels in the kitchen. Put on the kettle, will you, and we'll have some coffee."

The kitchen was cleaner than she expected. There were a few dishes in the sink, but they had been rinsed, and the stove had been cleaned in the recent past. The jar of instant coffee was conveniently located on a shelf above the stove.

When Jan came back Alan hadn't moved. He accepted the cup she handed him. She sat down, her eyes fixed expectantly on his face.

"No wonder you've been in a state," he said.

"Do you think I'm crazy?"

"Probably. Almost everybody is. At least you've got an interesting and unusual neurosis. Most of them are so damn dull. Oedipus complexes all over the place."

Jan's eyes fell.

"I've told you what happened," she said. "But I didn't tell you—I couldn't—how real it was."

"Yes, you did. That came through quite clearly. I could almost imagine I knew those people myself. And I can understand why the death of—Jonathan?—hit you so hard. He sounds like quite a guy."

"Alan, I couldn't have invented anyone like that."

"Sure you could. Shakespeare invented Hamlet, didn't he?"

"Not exactly. The play is based on—"

"What astounds me is the extent of your knowledge. Where did you hear about James—James Lafayette, as he called himself later in his life?"

"He's in a book," Jan muttered. "I suppose he's in several books, actually, but I only read one. Alan, don't you see, that's the trouble; I don't remember anymore what I knew beforehand. I could swear I never read the book before the dream in which James first appeared. It never would have occurred to me that a slave would risk his life for the Patriot cause; it seemed so unlikely I had to look it up. How could I have invented it?"

"You can't prove you didn't read the book, or hear someone mention the story, beforehand."

"How can you prove that something didn't happen?" Jan's shoulders slumped. "I don't expect you to believe me," she muttered.

"I believe in your honesty," Alan said coolly. "I don't trust your memory any more than I would my own."

"But why would a story like that one come to my mind? I mean, dreams are supposed to indicate a person's subconscious problems, and all that; but I can't make any sense of my dreams, in terms of my hang-ups."

"You can't?"

"I suppose you can!"

"Easily. You're fed up with the world, right? You don't like it. People are no damn good, this country is going straight to hell, virtue is dead—if it ever existed—and nothing is worth fighting for. You come here in that frame of mind, and what do you find? A never-never land that enshrines a glamorized past which is no more real than your dreams. The eighteenth century with all the dirt and dung and stink left out. The Raleigh Tavern, where the heroes met to talk about freedom— but the fact that the slave auctions were also held there is gently glossed over. You are fascinated by this unreal world, you prefer it to your own. So you invent a hero and a set of dramatic incidents; they are well constructed and based on fact, because you are an intelligent woman and your subconscious wouldn't stand for a sloppy plot. Only you are essentially too sane to permit yourself this indulgence on a permanent basis. So your dream world develops problems, and your hero dies. The shock you felt was grief at the death of a dream—the fantasy world no adult can really accept because he knows he has to cope with reality."

"Do you really believe that nonsense?" Jan demanded.

"No."

"Then why—"

"Look, Jan, I can sit here inventing theories till dawn. What I *believe* is irrelevant. I don't *know* what caused your dreams. There is no evidence. I don't know whether you need a psychiatrist, or a psychic investigator. Or a minister of the gospel, or a good swift kick in the pants. Does it really matter? Can't you accept it as something . . ."

His voice died away, and Jan looked at him curiously.

"Something . . . ?"

"Extraordinary," Alan said. "A source of wonder. Must you pin a label on it? It was rather wonderful, wasn't it?"

"Yes," Jan said slowly. "Until the end."

"Even that. Your Jonathan sounds like a man who requires reasons. Reasons for living, reasons for dying. Not many people are privileged to give their lives to save a friend. And you were there to comfort him—"

"But I lied to him."

"What did you tell him that was a lie?"

"Oh—that the slaves would be free, that they would be able to vote, go to school—"

"That's a lie?"

"It's only part of the truth," Jan said despairingly. "I lied by omission. I didn't tell him any of the bad things. I let him think this country was going to be paradise."

"Truth that hurts needlessly isn't a virtue, it's a bloody sin. But even if he had known the whole truth, don't you think he would have considered the game worth the candle? Wouldn't he feel that there had been progress?"

"You talk about him as if he were real," Jan said.

"He is real, to you."

"But he isn't!" Jan banged the coffee table with her fist. The cat woke up and gave her an indignant look. "If I just knew one way or the other! I wouldn't mind admitting he was a figment of my imagination—you're right, he was wonderful and I'd be proud to have invented him—if I could just be sure."

"You mean that?"

"Yes."

"Then let's go find out." Alan scooped up the cat, stood up, and deposited the animal on the chair. It curled up on the warm spot where he had been sitting.

"How?" Jan asked.

"I don't know yet. But I'll think of something. Did you tell me there was a portrait of him? I'd like to see that first."

"You mean right now?"

"Why not?"

They stopped on the way home to pick up some prepared food for supper, after calling the Wildes to reassure them as to Jan's whereabouts. Uncle Henry, who had a plebeian fondness for mass-produced fried chicken, was delighted to see them; and the meal turned out to be the most relaxed Jan had ever eaten in that house. Alan bullied Camilla mercilessly. He wouldn't let her set the table; they ate with their fingers and drank beer and Coke from the cans so they wouldn't dirty any glasses. When they had finished Alan swept the residue into a paper bag, dumped it into the trash, and insisted that Camilla admit this was the only sensible way to live.

Although Camilla sputtered indignantly during the entire transaction, Jan suspected she rather enjoyed it. She looked livelier than she had for days, with her cheeks flushed and her eyes snapping. She answered Alan's last question with an unladylike snort and finished her can of Coke.

"How about some chess?" Henry asked, winking at Jan.

"Later. I'm going to help Jan with her book now."

"But you can't go to her bedroom—" Camilla began.

Alan produced a magnificent leer.

He was serious enough when they entered the room and Jan took the portrait out of the closet. It was the first time she had looked at it since The Night. She handed it to Alan and went to stand by the window.

"Chicken," Alan said. "Come here and tell me about it."

"What is there to tell?"

"How closely it resembles the—let's say the original. It is a lousy portrait, isn't it? I wouldn't give it a second look myself."

Unreasonably annoyed at the criticism, Jan turned. The portrait still made her feel uncomfortable. She forced herself to look at it critically.

"It's like seeing someone after he's laid out," she mumbled morbidly. "All flat and dead. . . . Yes, it is a rotten portrait, but the details are accurate. Hair color, eye color, even the shape of his ears."

"I'm beginning to see why it got to you. It is a poor work of art, but there's something about it. . . . I feel as if I've seen that face somewhere before."

"Really? I looked every place trying to find out who he was. Camilla didn't know—"

"Shut up and let me think." Alan frowned. "Where the hell was it? Hey. Wait a minute. . . ."

He picked up the portrait and ran out of the room.

Jan followed him down the stairs and into the parlor. Camilla and Henry looked up from their television program. Alan paid no attention to them. He headed straight for the fireplace. Picking up a table lamp, he held it as close to the portrait as the cord would permit. Charles Wilde smiled down at his descendants.

"Look at it," Alan said. He placed the other portrait on the mantelpiece, next to the one of Charles.

"I don't see," Jan began. But she was beginning to see. A funny sinking feeling invaded her stomach.

"The shape of the ears," Alan said impatiently. "It's almost as distinctive as fingerprints, something that doesn't change with age or girth. Look at the line of the jaw under those sagging muscles. Look at the setting of the eyes, the shape of the eyebrows."

"They were probably cousins," Jan said, forgetting the audience; Camilla and Henry had abandoned their program and were watching with interest. "Closely related. . . ."

"Only identical twins would share features like that," Alan said. "Face it, Jan. These are portraits of the same man. One done in youth, one forty or fifty years later. And we know who that man was, don't we? Your ancestor, Charles Wilde."

Chapter

21

Summer 1976

CAMILLA WAS SO PLEASED SHE WAS ALMOST GRACIOUS to Alan. "Fancy your seeing that," she exclaimed. "All these years, and no one else has ever noticed it! But I suppose a fresh viewpoint was needed; we were too familiar with the portraits. What a nice addition to the family records!"

They left her gloating over the portraits and went back upstairs. As soon as Alan had closed the door, Jan said,

"That does it. He was my own invention after all."

"You have a logical mind," Alan said.

"Oh, don't try to sweet-talk me. Of course I can see the obvious conclusion, who couldn't. If the portrait isn't Jonathan, then my Jonathan wasn't real. Neither was my Charles. He didn't look anything like either of those pictures. And if I had seen a replay of real events, I would have seen the people who took part in them, not my own creations. And that means—that means the whole thing was made up."

Alan smiled faintly at the word.

"A brilliant reconstruction," he said soothingly. "Like Williamsburg itself."

Jan sat down on the bed and stared at her folded hands.

"I feel as if you had killed him again," she muttered.

"Hey, now—"

"I'm sorry. I shouldn't have said that. You've been nice. You didn't laugh at me or tell me I was crazy. You have been very—"

"Nice," Alan said in an indescribable voice.

"Kind, then. When I first met you, I certainly didn't think of you that way. And I don't know why you've taken so much trouble with me, I was nasty enough to you. Not that you didn't ask for it—"

"Kind," Alan said. "Nice. . . . Oh, damn it, that's more than I can stand. I wasn't being nice. I was trying to get some honest responses out of you. I had a suspicion that under those layers of premature ennui there might be a woman worth knowing. I still think so, but I'm beginning to wonder whether you're worth it. I never thought I would fall in love with a girl who is such a pain in the neck."

He wasn't actually gritting his teeth, but the tone of his voice gave that impression. His heavy brows had never looked more Neanderthaloid.

"Well!" Jan said, getting her breath back. "If that is a declaration—"

"What did you expect me to do, get down on my knees? I suppose Richard did. . . . I've had a job offer from Washington. Justice Department. I'll be a very small cog in that big rusty machine, and I probably won't last long, since I've never learned to keep quiet about things that annoy me. But I'm going to take the job. I'm sick of stagnating in this petrified backwater. You can go with me if you want to. I'll have a run-down apartment in a first-rate urban crime area, and when I get home at night—if I get home, through the muggers and the addicts—I'll be in a rotten mood because of all the crap I've taken all day."

Jan didn't answer immediately. She knew his face well enough by now to see the signs of emotion he concealed from casual friends. His sallow cheeks were slightly flushed, and his mouth was set against the refusal he fully expected. It was not a handsome face; even the eyes of love could not have considered those misshapen features aesthetically pleasing. But even if she did not love him, she would never again think him ugly.

"Alan," she said gently. "Why do you always try to make everything seem as—as negative as you can? You can't fool me with tricks like that, not anymore. But you never indicated you cared anything about me. You never touched me—"

"There were reasons for that," Alan said. "You would probably find all of them equally ludicrous. . . . Okay, Jan, no hard feelings. You don't have to let me down lightly. I only mentioned it because. . . . Damned if I know why I mentioned it. I'm going down and give Henry his chess game. See you around."

"When are you leaving town?"

"Next month."

"What are you going to do with the cat?" Jan asked.

She didn't know what had prompted her to ask that inane question, but it served one useful purpose. Alan's glowering eyebrows went back into position, and he smiled.

"Dump her back in the alley where she came from, of course," he said.

"Of course," Jan said.

After he had gone she remained seated on the bed, thinking. His unexpected proposal—if it was a proposal—had shaken her so thoroughly that for a time she had forgotten the shock of the disclosure about the portraits. Was that why he had done it, to take her mind off. . . . Oh, no. Not even Alan would do anything so absurd.

Honest wasn't a strong enough word for him. He had been fully aware of the contrast between the picture he had drawn, in a few brief words, and the life she would have as Richard's wife. The days would follow one another in peaceful succession, with music and books and good conversation. . . . The country club, the conventional dances, golf and tennis, quiet people with soft, well-modulated voices, saying courteous things. . . . Richard's lovemaking. Nothing quiet or boring about that. . . . And the tiny gracious house, with its exquisite furnishings. Richard had no pets. Naturally not;

you couldn't let a puppy chew on the legs of a Chippendale table, or piddle on a Persian rug. And the things a cat could do to the brocade chairs. . . . Children were pretty messy, too. She wondered how Richard felt about children.

Not that she was limited to those two choices. There were others. She could go back to teaching, or to some other kind of work. Whatever happened, she had no intention of living with her mother again.

Jan contemplated this new knowledge openmouthed. She hadn't given the question serious thought, but suddenly she was certain of the answer. Ellen would have to find a cheaper apartment if she couldn't manage on what Jan was able to spare. And Jan would live in a room, a closet, rather than share the jumble of Ellen's emotional life ever again. She couldn't imagine why she had put up with it as long as she had.

She was still sitting on the bed trying to sort out her confused thoughts when she heard Alan leave, an hour later.

II

Jan went to sleep that night in an excellent frame of mind, feeling that she was finally beginning to get a grip on things. But the next day turned out to be one of the kind that try men and women's souls—a series of petty mishaps much harder to endure than absolute tragedy.

In the first place it rained—steadily, drearily, ceaselessly. Uncle Henry had been planning to have someone come and spray the roses. The black spot was particularly bad that summer. Of course no one could spray in a pouring rain, and Henry wandered around the house muttering discontentedly and disarranging every room as soon as Jan had straightened it up. The damp brought on Camilla's rheumatism; but instead of lying down with heating pads and hot-water bottles, she decided to make a martyr of herself and helped Jan clean house, groaning out loud every time she bent her elbow. Jan finally persuaded her to sit down and work on the family records. She insisted on doing it in the parlor, where Henry was irritably watching a game show. He hated game shows. His comments were rude and, Camilla said, very annoying to someone who was trying to concentrate.

Jan fled into the kitchen and put the kettle on. While she waited for it to boil she reached for a touch of the optimism she had felt, and encountered only an empty void. It was all very well to say that she had made a decision, but even if she was able to carry out her plan to move away from her mother, that still left the greater part of her life hanging in limbo. What was she going to do this fall? Perhaps she had been optimistic to suppose there were three choices open to her. Richard might have changed his mind about wanting to marry her. She couldn't blame him if he had. No man who loved peace and quiet would take a wife who might go into screaming fits without warning.

She made tea and arranged a tray, and carried it into the parlor, from which she could hear her aunt's and uncle's bickering voices.

Tea and cinnamon toast soothed them a little. Food always had a calming effect on Uncle Henry, and after eating three pieces of toast he switched off the television set, announcing that he intended to go to the library and work on a chess problem.

"That's a relief," Camilla said shrewishly. "Now perhaps I can get some work done. Jan, if you aren't busy, I would appreciate some help. Ordinarily I wouldn't ask you, but my fingers are so stiff today. . . ."

Jan had no excuse for refusing, although the last thing she wanted to think about was her ancestors. The ending of her fantasy had left her filled with sick disappointment. She had not been truthful when she told Alan she wanted to know one way or the other. What she had really wanted was confirmation, not contradiction.

She looked through the pile of letters Camilla handed her. They had been written by one of her great-aunt's great-uncles, who had made the Grand Tour. The young man wrote an incredibly bad hand. His spelling was nothing to brag about either.

"Aunt Cam, I think we ought to rent a typewriter," she said. "I can copy these ten times as fast, and they'll be much more legible."

Camilla considered the suggestion.

"I suppose that would be sensible, wouldn't it? I don't know how to typewrite, so it never occurred to me."

"Well, I do know how to type. Why don't you sort through this and decide what you want copied? I'll go downtown later and see about renting a machine."

Camilla was delighted at the idea. She started going through the untidy piles of papers. There was very little Jan could do to help with the sorting, so she leaned back in her chair and contemplated the two portraits.

The smaller of the two was still propped against the wall where Alan had left it. As Jan looked from one face to the other, she wondered how she could have missed the resemblance. There was no doubt about it. But the unanswered question still remained. Why had she invented an imaginary personage to go with that face? It would have been more natural to assume that the subject of the portrait was a member of the Wilde family.

With a sigh Camilla sat back and rubbed her fingers. Seeing the direction of Jan's gaze, she too looked at the portraits.

"I think we should have the smaller one cleaned," she said. "So far as I know it has never been removed from the frame."

"Is that the original frame?" Jan asked.

"I suppose so. Perhaps we ought to get a new one. That one's rather tacky, isn't it?"

"Old things often are tacky," Jan said with a smile. "No, I'd keep the frame, Aunt Cam."

"But the picture does need cleaning. It would be interesting to have it out of the frame. Who knows, there might even be an old bit of newspaper or other document backing it up."

"Yes," Jan said slowly. "Yes, there might be."

Stirred by sudden excitement she ran to the mantel and brought the portrait back to the table.

It was approximately eighteen inches square. The frame was about two inches wide, a simple border of stained wood, with a narrow incised line as its only ornamental feature. There had never been glass in the frame, which was natural, since the portrait was an oil painting. Exposure to the air had darkened the varnish, and minute cracks had developed.

Jan turned the picture over.

The frame might be original, but the backing had been renewed more recently. The coarse brown paper was brittle, but not as fragile as two centuries would have left it. Jan began to tear it away.

"It will have to come off anyway," she said, in response to Camilla's squeal of protest. "The paper isn't worth preserving—see, it's blank."

There was nothing underneath except the canvas itself. Jan continued to scrape off the scraps that clung to the edge of the frame, where the paper had been glued. Camilla came to watch. They both saw the writing at the same time. It was in the lower left-hand corner—only a few symbols, sketched in by a brush holding blue paint, the same blue that had been used for the sitter's coat.

"It must be the painter's monogram," Camilla exclaimed. "How fascinating! We may be able to identify him. And a date, or part of one. Seventeen something. The rest is lost."

Jan stared speechlessly. She knew the initials were not those of the painter, and the numbers were not a date. They gave the age of the man who had been portrayed, and the initials were his: J.M.

III

Jan fed her aunt and uncle lunch and bundled them off upstairs for their naps with a speed that left them gasping. Then

she went back to the parlor and sat down at the table where
Camilla's genealogical materials were spread out.

Her first impulse after she saw the initials was to call
Alan. The second impulse canceled the first. She knew what
Alan would say: that the initials were those of the painter,
and it was only a coincidence that the first letter was a *J*. He
would point out that many masculine names began with that
letter—James and John, just for starters. No, she was not
going to tell Alan. He had been much more fair-minded and
receptive than most people would have been, but he wasn't
interested in proving that her dreams were real. He had already dealt them one stunning blow.

What she had found that morning didn't resolve the difficulty. The subject of the second portrait was unquestionably
Charles Wilde; not only family tradition but the prominence
of the painting in the house made it virtually impossible for
her to question the identification. There was no way out of
the dilemma, except to deny that the earlier portrait was of
the same man.

Camilla had mentioned that one of the Wilde daughters
had married into a western Virginia family of German origin.
If she could only locate the family, and if the name began
with an M. . . . It wouldn't prove anything, but it would give
her something to work on.

There were several Wilde genealogies, drawn up at different times by members of the family. The earliest one was
the longest. It carried the family tree clear back to William
the Conqueror. Jan smiled sourly, and tossed it to one side.
Why not King Arthur, or Adam, while you were at the job of
inventing ancestors?

The other genealogies were more plausible, but most of
them traced only the direct line of descent—father, grandfather, and so on, in the masculine line. Frustrating as this
was for Jan's purposes, she could understand the reason for
the limitation. To give a complete family history you would
need the wall of a banquet room, for, of course, the line
branched and burgeoned the farther back you went. Four

grandparents, eight great-grandparents—and the brothers and sisters, aunts and uncles, each with his or her own
branching line.

Camilla's was the latest effort to coordinate previous work
on the family tree, and she had done a fairly complete job,
listing all the children and, when applicable, the names of
the persons they had married. She then chose one child—the
eldest son—and followed out his line, but at least the names
of siblings were mentioned. Jan's search was simplified by
the time factor. The marriage she was looking for had occurred between the early sixteen hundreds, when the Wildes
had arrived in Virginia, and seventeen sixty or thereabouts.
Even so, it took some time to find the right name.

Miller. Charles Wilde's aunt Martha had married a man
named Karl Miller.

So Charles and Jonathan were first cousins. Jonathan was
Mr. Wilde's nephew. No wonder they had seemed so close.

It was strange how at this period the fertility of the Wildes
had faltered. Before and afterward the nurseries had been
full—for a time, at least—but during those two generations
the line had come close to extinction. Charles had been the
only living child of his parents, and his father had only one
sister who lived long enough to reach marriageable age. It
was not surprising that old Mr. Wilde had been so obsessed
with Charles's marrying.

Jan stacked the papers neatly and wrote a note which she
left on the table. It was still raining. Methodically equipping
herself with raincoat, hat, and umbrella, she slipped out of
the house and walked to Merchants' Square, where she was
able to get a taxi.

As she slopped through the puddles on the broken sidewalk, she wondered if there was some omen in the fact that it
had been raining both times she came to this place. She had
not telephoned for an appointment and was taking a chance
on finding the fortune-teller in.

Madame was at home, but the face that peered through
a crack in the doorway did not seem pleased to see her. Jan

reached into the brown paper bag she was carrying and held up the bottle.

"So what do you want now?" Madame asked, two drinks later. "I told you everything last time. You're a crazy kid, you know that? What's a pretty girl like you want with all this stuff?"

Jan filled the woman's empty glass. Ordinarily she would have despised herself for pandering to such a pathetic weakness, but she would not neglect any means to the end she desired.

"I have to find out something," she said. "I promise, I won't bother you again. Can you—you said something last time about going into a trance. . . ."

"Cost you ten bucks," said Madame.

"That's all right. But do you really—I mean, is it just an act?"

"Depends. Sometimes yes, sometimes no. Damn it, honey, you can't just turn on the power."

"Can't you do something to help? Is there any particular technique?"

She moved the bottle out of the way as Madame's fingers groped for it. The old woman scowled at her.

"A little drink helps," she said.

"A little more will just put you to sleep," Jan said coolly. "I'll leave the bottle, but you can't have any more till you tell me."

"Well, I wasn't kidding. You need something to relax you, see? Then you have to learn how to concentrate your mind. It helps to have some object you can look at. Now if the object is something that belongs to the person you want to find out about—"

"What makes you think it's a person?" Jan asked, flushing.

"It's always a person, honey. Point is, the object has to have some connection with your problem. It's an old method, a lot of mediums use it. There's a fancy name for it, but I forget what it is. I had some woman give me a glove once—so help me, I didn't know a thing about it, or her—and I felt death in it, death and water. It was her sister's glove. The sister had died, drowned, the year before. Got a cramp while she was swimming."

"Uh-huh," Jan said.

"So don't believe me. What'd you ask me for?"

"I didn't mean to sound skeptical. Go on."

"Want me to try a trance?"

"Why not?" Jan said.

If she had been a believer, the process that followed might have disillusioned her. With a last longing look at the bottle of bourbon, Madame flung herself back in her chair and closed her eyes. She began to breathe heavily through her nose.

This went on for several minutes, and Jan was frankly fidgeting. Then, rather horribly, the quality of the woman's breathing changed. Her respiration became very long and slow and deep. As Jan watched, in mingled hope and doubt, Madame's eyes opened. The pupils had rolled back into her head so that only the whites showed.

"I am waiting," she droned. "Ask."

Jan was taken aback. She had not expected any results. Even now she was skeptical. But she might as well try. . . .

"Miller," she said. "Jonathan Miller. Who is he?"

"He is and he is not," the droning voice answered. "A man like other men—and unlike any other man. . . ."

"Oh, stop it," Jan shouted suddenly. "You old fraud! Aren't you ashamed of yourself?"

Madame's eyes rolled back into normal position. She sat up, flexing her arms.

"Had to do something for ten bucks," she said, unabashed. "Hey—you are gonna pay me, aren't you? I tried—I told you you can't always turn on—"

"The power." Jan laughed in spite of herself. "Sure, I'll pay you. Here. If I don't see you again, it's been nice knowing you."

"You're a good kid," the medium said, folding the bill and

pushing it down the front of her robe. "Sorry I couldn't get anything. Listen, honey, I wasn't kidding. You don't need this sort of thing. Get yourself a man and a few kids and live."

"Don't worry about me." Jan rose and picked up her purse. She was almost at the door when the medium said suddenly,

"I did get one flash of something. Doesn't mean anything, but you've been square with me; who knows, maybe it means something to you."

"What?" Jan turned eagerly.

"Sounds silly," Madame grumbled. "Just a flash, came and went. Bunch of kids, singing. Like in a school auditorium. There was a flag hanging up, and they were all standing up and singing."

"I was a teacher," Jan said. "I've led school assemblies and classes in the national anthem. Was it like that?"

"I guess so. I couldn't hear what they were singing. Stupid, isn't it? But it was the only thing that didn't fit with what I was thinking."

Jan knew what she had been thinking about. Her hand was already stretched out for the bottle. Jan was no longer amused. She felt depressed and thoroughly disgusted with herself.

"Good-bye," she muttered.

Madame didn't answer.

It had stopped raining when she left the building, and she sloshed through the puddles, not caring whether she got her feet wet. What a rat she was. It was no use telling herself that Madame was drinking herself into an early grave and that a single bottle would make no difference one way or the other. She was a rat, a despicable rat. Madame was a likable old cuss; once she had been a little girl with pigtails, singing "The Star-Spangled Banner" in a school class, while the flag rippled in an artificial breeze. Jan knew that they used a fan, in the old days, to make it ripple.

It hit her then like a dazzle of light, so bright it blinded her. The national anthem wasn't the only song they sang in school assemblies. Because it was so difficult to sing, the school often substituted another patriotic number that was easier for young voices. "My Country Tizza Thee," as the kids called it, or "America the Beautiful." "O beautiful for patriot dream. . . ."

Why hadn't she thought of it before? The dreams had stopped because the part of the drama that centered in Williamsburg was over. When Charles came home after the war, he would have settled at Patriot's Dream. If there was an answer to the impossible dilemma of the dreams and the two portraits, it might lie at the plantation house. Somehow the very incongruity of the hint made it seem more plausible—a bunch of kids singing a patriotic song. . . .

She didn't stop to think, because she didn't want to think, that the essence of fortune-telling is that the listener can make anything he likes out of the deliberately ambiguous clues.

IV

Jan arrived at the house with the rented typewriter ostentatiously displayed.

"You shouldn't have gone out in the rain for that," Camilla scolded. "And carrying it all this way. . . . But I must admit it's done you good to get out. You look better."

"I feel marvelous," Jan said truthfully.

Richard had called; he called again soon after she got back to ask her to have lunch the following day. He noted the difference in her voice.

"What happened to you?" he asked. "A letter telling you you have inherited half a million from a forgotten relative?"

Jan laughed. "I just feel good, that's all; and I'd love to have lunch. I need your advice, Richard. . . ."

Richard was happy to recommend a craftsman who could clean the portrait, and Jan was happy to learn that the shop was not within walking distance, but on the outskirts of town. It was all working out, just as if it were meant to happen.

"Do you suppose I could borrow your car tomorrow afternoon?" she asked casually.

Richard's hesitation was barely perceptible.

"Why . . . sure. I could drive you there, though, after lunch."

"I have a couple of other errands," Jan said glibly. "It's hard to do things here without a car. I'm a good driver, Richard, you needn't worry."

"Honey, I wasn't worried a bit. Sure you can have the car. I'd say keep it overnight, but I have to go to Richmond after supper. . . ."

"I'll return it by six," Jan promised.

She did a little dance of triumph down the hall after she had hung up; and Uncle Henry, passing through, beamed at her, glad to see her spirits so improved.

Alan dropped by after supper—again. He too observed her exuberance, but unlike the others he did not find it reassuring. Cornering her in the kitchen before the game began, he demanded bluntly, "What's up?"

"Me," Jan said. "Do I have to have a reason for feeling good again? I've been down long enough, haven't I?"

"I don't trust you when you're being cute and cheery."

"It's just as well I didn't take you up on your offer, then. I would hate to have to repress my normally happy nature to avoid arousing your suspicions."

Alan flushed darkly and turned away.

"You fight dirty, don't you?"

"I'm sorry," Jan began. But he had left the room.

V

All next morning her impatience mounted. The omens continued to be propitious. Camilla was delighted to have her take the portrait in for cleaning, and nodded amiably when

Jan said she would probably be gone all afternoon, taking advantage of the car. It had stopped raining. The ground would be damp, though. Jan found an old blanket, which she used to swathe the portrait.

Richard hadn't gone quite as far as champagne this time, but as soon as Jan saw the beautifully arranged table she knew he was back on the old track—if, indeed, he had ever left it. Naturally he would refrain from pressing her while she was disturbed. Now—apparently he had decided she was no longer disturbed.

She responded to his first tentative embrace with a warmth that obviously surprised and pleased him. He couldn't know that part of her ardor was calculated and cold-blooded. She meant to omit nothing that might bring the success she hoped for that afternoon.

"Richard," she murmured, as the mantel clock chimed sweetly. "I hate to mention it, but aren't you late?"

"Damn." Richard sat up and pushed his hair back from his forehead. "Why don't I call in sick?"

"Better not. What kind of wife would I be if I led you from the path of duty?"

"Jan!" His eyes shone. "Do you mean it?"

"I'm almost sure, Richard. Not quite but—"

"Darling." He reached out for her; then he glanced at the clock and stood up. "I promised I wouldn't pressure you, but you sure as hell don't make it easy. Honey, how about this weekend? Saturday, for dinner? Here?"

"Lovely," Jan said.

She knew what he had in mind, and she had no objection to the idea or any conclusion that might come out of it. She would have agreed to anything in order to get on with her plans for the day. Beyond that she was unable to think or plan.

Richard stood watching as she drove away, and Jan turned the corner with a precision that would have given her one hundred percent on a driving test.

She continued to drive carefully; she didn't want anything

to interfere, now that she was nearing her goal. It was hard to keep from speeding on the four-lane highways near town, but when she turned off onto the narrower county road that led to the James River plantations, she found herself often slowed to a frustrating crawl because of farm vehicles ahead. Though she had only come this way once before, she remembered every landmark.

Finally she found herself on the rutted track that led to Patriot's Dream. The closer she got, the more impatient she became, but it was impossible to go fast on this stretch. The trees dripped moisture, the potholes were filled with water, and the red clay surface was very slippery.

She left the car near the gatepost. When she got out, the blanket-wrapped portrait cradled in her arms, she was struck by the utter silence. For a moment common sense overruled her eagerness and she looked around uneasily. It was certainly an isolated spot. Of course Alan had been exaggerating when he warned her about tramps and drunken hunters. Compared to the city streets she habitually walked, this place was as safe as a convent. All the same, it might be sensible to lock the car. Children roaming in the woods might be tempted to do the damage if they could get into the vehicle.

Wrapped as it was, the portrait was an awkward thing, just a little too large to fit comfortably into her arms. The weeds were scratchy and waist high in some places. The lower stalks were still wet, and before long her jeans were damp to the knees. Shorts would have been more comfortable, but they would not have protected her against the brambles and poison ivy.

Panting and dripping with sweat, she reached the top of the rise and saw the river beyond, sparkling in the sunlight. The weedy slope looked like a hayfield, with the yellowed stalks rippling in the breeze. She looked around, trying to decide where she should settle.

She was standing near one of the fallen walls of the office. She moved left, toward the ruins of the main house, picking her way with care to avoid the sunken cellars. The foundations were so overgrown that she tripped over a section before she saw it. She tramped down a patch of weeds; then, unwrapping the portrait, she spread the blanket on the ground and sat down.

She was going to be uncomfortable. The blanket was too thin to protect her skin from the stiff weed stalks, but it was better than nothing. Jan propped the portrait up against a stone and stretched out on her side. From her purse she took the bottle of tranquilizers and swallowed two. They were small and went down easily, even without water.

There was no shade. The sun beat down on her. As soon as she stopped moving, every insect in the vicinity headed her way. Flies swarmed and crawling bugs plodded across her body. At first she swatted irritably at them. Then she set her teeth and ignored them. She stared fixedly at the portrait.

Despite the flies and the discomfort of her position she might have dropped off to sleep eventually. But she didn't sleep. What happened was entirely different.

As she continued to stare at the portrait, the outer periphery of her vision darkened and the painted face stood out as if a spotlight had been focused on it. The soft sounds of summer blended into a low hum. She could no longer feel the flies, or the stalks that pressed into her side. And then as she floated into a state of half-consciousness, the ruined walls began to rise.

Chapter
22

Winter 18—

THEY WERE TRANSPARENT AT FIRST, WAVERING AND TWO-dimensional, like cellophane cutouts swayed by the wind. As they took shape and grew solid, the interior details began to form. Paneling and floors, furniture, stairs—still transparent as glass, disturbingly superimposed; through the shadow shapes the yellowing grass and cloud-strewn sky could be dimly seen. Jan was free of her body, floating; and the walls closed in. She caught glimpses of a paneled hall with a superb sweeping staircase, its brackets carved with flower shapes. A corridor, uncarpeted, with sunlight pouring in through a tall window at the end. A door . . . and then a room, a bedroom, with a brick fireplace and a huge bed with heavy dark curtains. A polished highboy had brass handles on its drawers; they shone in the sunlight.

Sunlight . . . but it was winter. The branches seen through the window were leafless; a thin sparkle of snow frosted the distant fields. A fire roared up the chimney. The man in the bed was wrapped in a heavy velvet robe; his head was swathed in a turbanlike covering. He was an old man now, but a big man still; his brown eyes were sunken in wrinkles, but they were alert and kindly in expression.

The years had been less kind to the woman who stood by

the bed. She had kept her figure. The thin body under her elaborate blue plush gown was so stiffly boned she could hardly bend over. Her aging skin, with no superfluous fat to round it out, had sagged into a thousand wrinkles, and her mouth had a sour, discontented droop. Her hair was piled high and powdered; drifts of the white stuff sprinkled her shoulder.

"No, I will not drink any more of that foul stuff," the man said irritably, pushing away the glass she held under his nose.

"Dr. Jones said you were to take it."

"Dr. Jones can go—elsewhere," said the man. "All the fool can think of is bleeding. I've been bled enough."

"But, Jon—" The woman clasped her hand over her mouth.

Jonathan smiled.

"My dear, why do you fight it? Call me that if you like; it is my name, after all."

"Not any longer. I don't know why, after all these years—"

"You were always self-conscious about it. It was no secret, Mary Beth; why pretend?"

She turned away and put the glass down on a table. Jonathan watched her. He looked tired.

"When is Fletcher coming?" he asked.

"This evening, if he sets out as soon as he receives your message. Why are you so determined to see a lawyer now? You aren't dying; this is only your old winter catarrh. And you have a will—"

"I want to add to it."

Mary Beth turned.

"You wouldn't change it? You couldn't be so unfair as to deprive James of his proper inheritance."

"He has Fairhill," Jonathan reminded her. "I made it over to him when he married. Not to mention the loans I have made him almost every year since. . . ."

"You were always unfair to him."

"And you were always too partial. Perhaps that is why he turned out. . . . Well," he added quickly, as she started to speak, "we won't quarrel, my dear. I have no intention of changing my will. I simply want to add a few statements."

Mary Beth's eyes narrowed.

"That crazy scheme of yours of emancipating the slaves? You can't do it. You wouldn't be so unfair as to burden your son with a scheme that would ruin him!"

"It is an expense, certainly, if it is done properly and the poor creatures are not simply cast out into the world with no means of support," Jonathan admitted. "I had hoped to do it myself, without leaving it to James, but I simply have not had the means. Yet the families I settled on those acres near Winchester are doing well. I could have expanded the scheme if I had not had to support James in his various financial misadventures. And if you, my dear, had not done such a splendid job of presenting me with progeny."

Mary Beth's face, which had hardened at the reference to her son's improvidence, softened a little in response to the unregenerate gleam in Jonathan's eye.

"God was good to us," she said sincerely. "Only three dead. . . . But you must see that this makes your ideas impractical. You must consider your grandchildren as well as your children. It is such a—a radical scheme! You will make us a laughing-stock if you insist."

"General Washington did it," Jonathan said mildly.

"And left Mrs. Washington in an intolerable position! They were to be freed on her death; but how could she feel that her life was safe in their hands when it was to their interest to get rid of her? So she freed them immediately, and what was the result? Being a good Christian woman, she felt herself responsible for them, and their food and clothing cost her a pretty penny. The aged she would not cast adrift, so she had to support them till they died. The General's heirs are still making pension payments to some. Do you consider this a kindness? It is cruel to slave and master alike."

Jonathan's face lengthened as this tirade went on.

"I know," he mumbled. "I know it is not easy—"

"It is impossible!" Sensing her advantage, Mary Beth rose to new heights of eloquence. "You speak of poor James's improvidence . . . What of yours? Schools and doctors for our own slaves, contributions to every harebrained enthusiast who calls on you—and your private charities, let us not forget those! How much have you taken from your children and sent to that—to Philadelphia?"

"He would never accept a penny," Jonathan said quietly. "Except as a loan, which was promptly repaid. You know that, Mary Beth."

Mary Beth's mouth twisted. Her voice took on a whining note.

"But since he died she has not scrupled to rob us! She and her dozen mixed-breed brats—"

"Be still!" Jonathan's voice rose to a roar. Mary Beth shrank back, her hands pressed to her mouth. There was life in the old man yet; but he was as tenderhearted as ever. When he saw his wife's show of terror he immediately repented.

"Forgive me, my dear, I should not have shouted at you. But I would have thought you could spare her some kindness. Does my life mean so little to you?"

"That is unreasonable—"

"If she had not come back, that night, to see what had happened to me, I would have died," Jonathan said. "She risked not only her own safety but that of the one she cherished more than her life."

Mary Beth was silent, but the stubborn set of her thin mouth spoke volumes, and Jonathan went on,

"At any rate, you have no reason to complain. From that night and its sequel you gained what you wanted—or so you made me believe. And in a manner so strange, so unexpected. . . . Indeed, my dear, if I did not know you so well I might have suspected you of casting a spell."

There was no answering smile on Mary Beth's face.

"Perhaps there was witchcraft in the business. It is hard to account for it otherwise. But I suppose, men being what they are, it was not surprising that she should prevail, with her whorish tricks—"

Jonathan heaved himself up in bed, his hands hard against the covers. He did not speak, but his expression silenced his wife; and for a moment the two eyed one another warily.

"I begin to understand," Jonathan said at last. "After all these years you still believe I. . . . We are both too near the Final Judgment, Mary Beth, to indulge in hatred. Try to cultivate charity."

"She bewitched you," Mary Beth said stubbornly. "You would have gone away with her."

"But I did not." Pity replaced the anger that had darkened Jonathan's face. "Mary Beth, we never spoke of that time. Strange, isn't it, that now, after all these years. . . . But perhaps it is a good thing; I had no idea how your thoughts had festered. Have you never wondered why I agreed to the arrangement?"

"It was the only thing to do. You were the nearest heir, there was no other closer. . . ."

"But there was."

"Not in law. It was his father's right to cast him off."

"The old man was ill," Jonathan said quietly. "Mad, I think. But it was not his decision. Charles was the one who refused to come back."

"Then he was mad." Mary Beth's sallow cheeks were an ugly red. "Mr. Wilde would have taken him back, but he refused to give up his concubine—harlot—"

"No, you are wrong. He refused to abandon his wife." He seemed not to see the expression of disgust that distorted her face; his own grew gently reminiscent, and he chuckled. "Who would have thought it would end as it did? I was the radical, the fire-eater—and I became the prosperous country gentleman, while Charles. . . . Life is a strange thing, my dear. What was I saying?"

"He refused to abandon his. . . ." She couldn't say the word. "It was no marriage, Jonathan, not in the eyes of the law."

"In the eyes of God it was doubly sacred. Love of that degree does not happen often. When it does, it sweeps all else before it. But that was not what I meant to say. I must be getting old, my memory is failing me. . . . Oh, yes. We were speaking of my reasons for consenting to such an unjust settlement. I would not have seen Charles disinherited, declared dead, if there had been any alternative. Since both parties to the quarrel refused to give way, there was none; and Mr. Wilde—God rest his troubled soul—presented me with a threat I could not ignore."

A spark of interest broke through the sullen anger on the woman's face.

"I never knew that. What threat?"

"Well, you see Leah still belonged to him. He could have traced her and brought her back to slavery. He would have done it, too, out of pure vindictiveness, if I had not agreed to give him the heir he wanted. I had, at least, the family blood. Such nonsense, as if blood could carry invisible family crests. . . ."

"So you gave in," Mary Beth said, "because of the nobility of your nature, to save your friends. And I thought. . . ."

"What, my dear?"

"I thought perhaps you cared for me, just a little."

"I did care for you," Jonathan said gently. "I always have. There are many different kinds of love, my dear."

"Yes," Mary Beth said. "Many different kinds. . . . Jonathan, will you still insist on putting it in your will—that the slaves are to be free?"

Jonathan spread his hands wide in a gesture of appeal. They were still big hands, although the veins stood out harshly across their backs.

"Mary Beth, I must. I have struggled all my life in this cause, and life has had a strange habit of turning most of my efforts to naught. I exchanged lives with someone else—I did it gladly, I have no regrets—but in doing so I was forced to abandon my dearest hope. My duty to you, to Mr. Wilde, to our children, superseded other duties. Indeed, there were times when I wondered if there was any purpose to it all. The only thing that kept me going. . . ." His eyes took on a strange gleam, and he laughed softly. "You would never believe me if I told you about that; and I have often wondered whether it was only a dream, the kind of dream that comes when one is near death. . . . At any rate, this last thing I must do. It won't be so hard, my dear; if James can't manage, the other boys will help you out, young Charles would never let you want. . . ."

"Will you do it?"

"Yes."

The sun was gone. Winter clouds covered the sky, and a few flakes of snow fluttered against the window, like small white creatures trying to get into the warmth. Mary Beth's face was gray too, and as old as time.

"Yes," she repeated. "You were right, Jonathan, when you said there are many kinds of love. . . . I will go and fetch you a bowl of hot soup. Will you take it?"

"Yes, of course." Jonathan's old bright smile warmed his face. "How thoughtful you are, my dear."

And as she bent over him, to touch his forehead with her lips, he said in surprise,

"There's nothing to cry about, my dear. It's only my old winter catarrh, you said it yourself. Do you know, I have seldom seen you weep. You used to quite a lot when you were a girl, but after we were married I don't remember. . . ."

She straightened and stood looking down at him. The tears sparkled in the myriad creases of her old, gray face.

"There was nothing to weep for then," she said. "I will make the soup myself, Jonathan."

Chapter
23

Summer 1976

JAN OPENED HER EYES. THERE WAS NO TRANSITION between sleep and waking. She had not really been asleep; she had closed her eyes, at the end, because the look on the woman's face had frightened her so.

For a long moment, as she lay, she saw the walls of Patriot's Dream still standing, shining with an inner light against the night sky. Gleaming panels, painted walls, mellow red-pink brick. . . . Then they crumbled and fell, shattering into shards of bright shadow, and she was alone in the dark.

Jan struggled to her knees. Her mouth was dry and her body ached in every muscle. At first she thought she had gone blind. The sky was overcast, there was no moon, no stars—no sound, except for the melancholy moaning of frogs in the marshes near the river.

She knew all the answers now, and she wished she did not. Stiffly she got to her feet, and as she stood straining her eyes to see something—anything, some landmark—through the muffling darkness, the full enormity of what she had done swept over her.

She had meddled with matters a human mind is not meant to experience—clumsily, in childish haste and arrogance. What if, in trying to find a path between two worlds, she had lost her way in the maze of time? She had been here for at least six hours, much longer than she had expected; night had fallen, and the family back in Williamsburg would be frantic about her absence. But she had no way of knowing how much time had really passed. It might be days, or years, instead of hours. There was nothing in the hot, still night to tell her *when* she was. It might be a hundred years before 1976, or a century later. When she reached the place where she had left the car would she find only a heap of rusty wreckage, obscured by weeds and creeping vines?

She was still unsteady from the shock of what she had seen, and this thought sent her over the edge into panic. Without stopping to pick up the portrait, or the blanket, or her purse, she started blindly across the ground, pushing through the weeds like a swimmer.

It was the weeds that saved her. They kept her from running, and they presented some slight resistance, just enough, when her right foot found nothing under it, to let her throw herself to the side instead of toppling forward. She fell heavily and painfully; for a while she lay still, gasping and seeing stars. Then she realized that the tiny lights were not stars. They were fireflies.

They had been there all along, but she had been too frantic to see them. Somehow the homely reminder of the real world brought her back to her senses—or the near tumble, into the slimy cellars, shocked her into sanity. She had learned at least one thing from her curious encounter with the past. That other world had had as many problems and sorrows as her own; but unsatisfactory as life could be at times, it was preferable to being dead. Or lying with a broken leg at the bottom of a deep, dank hole.

When she tried to stand up, a stab of pain from a twisted ankle flattened her out again. Setting her teeth, she began to crawl. It was an unbelievably inconvenient means of locomotion. Her ankle ached and the weeds scratched her face and got into her open mouth. There were mosquitoes as well as fireflies abroad in the night. She had completely lost her sense of direction. How was she to find the car with her eyes practically flat on the ground?

When she heard the voice she thought she must be imagining things. She had been thinking about Jonathan and visualizing his face, not with the abnormal clarity of the visions, but as one remembered the face of a friend, for comfort. At first the voice was unidentifiable, being distorted by volume and distance. . . .

Jan scrambled up and stood swaying on one leg. Then she saw the light.

"Alan!" she screamed. "Alan, I'm here. Over here!"

The bobbing light swung in her direction.

"Here," she yelled, hopping up and down on one foot. "Over this way."

"Okay, I hear you. Stay where you are."

"I have to, I hurt my foot. Oh, Alan, watch out for the cellar, you could fall and—"

"I know, I know. What are you screaming for?"

With the light to orient her, the dreadful dark landscape came into focus. She could see the shapes of the trees near the road and the shimmer of water off to the left. The light came steadily closer and finally she saw Alan, as a dark shape behind the flashlight. Then his arms went around her, lifting her clear up off the ground and squeezing the breath out of her.

"Damn you," Alan said. "Of all the stupid, inconsiderate, dangerous, dumb things to do—"

The tirade might have continued for some time if he had not found something better to do with his mouth.

As a first kiss it was quite successful, although Jan was horribly thirsty, her ankle hurt, and she couldn't breathe. The ferocity of Alan's embrace gave her some idea of the fear that had driven him and the passionate relief he was feeling now. He of all of them had known how far into danger her mind had wandered. He had every reason to fear he might find her—if he found her at all—in a frozen huddle of catatonia. But when he finally freed her lips and her powers of speech, the words she gasped out had no reference to her danger, or his reaction.

"You are Leah's descendant. Leah and Charles's. No wonder Aunt Cam doesn't like you!"

II

Alan swung her up into his arms.

"This is no time to discuss genealogy."

"You don't have to carry me."

"I thought you said you hurt your ankle."

"I can hop. How did you know I was here?"

"I knew," Alan said briefly. "I'd have been here sooner if those idiots hadn't waited so long to call me. By that time they had tried all the obvious things—police, hospitals, the picture restorer. . . . Where's the portrait?"

"Over there," Jan gestured. "I have to get my purse too."

Alan found the spot—she had not gone far from it in all her wanderings—and collected her possessions. With the aid of his arm Jan made it back to Richard's car. By then Alan had gotten over his outburst of sentiment and was being as disagreeable as only he knew how to be.

"You'll have to drive that damn thing out. If we leave it here, it may be stripped by morning, and Richard will never let you hear the end of it."

"I don't know whether I can." Reaction had set in; Jan's hands were unsteady as she tried to fit the car key into the lock.

"Which ankle did you hurt?"

"The left."

"It's an automatic shift. You only need the right foot. I'll lead. Follow me and for God's sake don't run into me."

Without waiting for an answer he got into his own car and started the engine.

As she followed the taillights along the dark tunnel of the road, she thought what a typical action it had been. She would never get any coddling from Alan; his big hand would always be flat in the middle of her back shoving her into things she didn't want to tackle. But it would be behind her to catch her if she fell.

She had braced herself for the interminable drive back to town, hoping her shaking muscles would hold out and that she wouldn't expire of thirst before she got there; but Alan only drove for a few miles before turning off into a parking lot. There was a small cluster of buildings at a crossroads. Jan had noticed them earlier, and she was surprised to see that the lights in the little diner-tavern were still on. It must not be as late as she had thought.

It was nine twenty-five. The shabby room was empty except for a waiter and a couple at a corner table. Alan sat her down in the opposite corner. When the waiter had brought them two glasses of beer, Jan snatched at hers with both hands. Nothing had ever tasted so good.

She had finished the glass by the time Alan got back from the telephone. He ordered sandwiches and a refill, and then sat back on the seat and looked at her.

"Go on," Jan said. "Get it over with. You were saying: dumb, stupid, thoughtless—"

"I told them you had decided to take a joyride out to the ol' plantation; while wandering around you fell, twisted your ankle, and banged your head. I found you crawling around trying to locate your purse and the key to the car, which you had stupidly mislaid in the dark."

"Are you sure you haven't omitted anything that could make me look like more of a fool?"

"I could have told them the truth," Alan said.

Silenced, Jan bit into her sandwich. Thirst had preoccupied her, but she was also extremely hungry. She had not done justice to Richard's lunch, nine hours earlier.

"Now," Alan said, when she had finished the first half of the sandwich, "how about telling *me* the truth? This joint closes in half an hour, so you'll have to be concise."

"I don't know where to begin."

"You might start with that astounding remark about my ancestors."

"Camilla didn't tell me—"

"She couldn't. She doesn't know. I don't know myself, it's just one of those vague family legends."

"So," Jan said, "you came back to the old home town and shot your mouth off all over the place about how your great-great, however many greats—grandmother was a slave. Tact is not your strong point, is it?"

"I wasn't ashamed," Alan said.

"Of course not. But of all the ways to endear yourself and build up a business among Southern aristocrats. . . . Did you know about the Wilde connection?"

"That's part of the legend, that there was such a connection; but no one ever knew precisely what it was. I still don't see. . . . You'd better start at the beginning."

Jan took a deep breath.

"They exchanged lives, just as Jonathan said," she finished, some time later. "Charles and his father were already estranged, and I guess war had taught Charles that all his old values were hollow. All of them except love and honor. . . . If he had gone back home, his father would have sold Leah and her child. Unless Charles abandoned them, he could only follow the path Jonathan had already chosen. The groundwork was laid; all he had to do was step into Jonathan's shoes. The people in Philadelphia knew he wasn't Jonathan, of course. He probably said he was a cousin or something. Called himself Müller, for fear his father would track him down if he used his own name. Somebody anglicized it, later, from Müller to Miller.

"Leah would have told him the truth about Jonathan, how he not only risked his life to help them escape, but that he had been an American spy for months. So Charles could accept help from Jonathan in getting himself established in Philadelphia—references, a loan. What kind of business did he get into?"

"He was a printer and later a publisher," Alan said

dazedly. "That is, if you are referring to Karl Müller, my great-great—however many greats—grandfather. The truth about his origin was never written down; it was passed on, so to speak, and after a century or more had gone by it became one of those meaningless traditions. . . . Nobody in my family has ever been hot on genealogy."

"As for Jonathan," Jan continued, "I told you what happened to him and why he agreed to the exchange. To me he is the really tragic character in the story. Everything he did went wrong, and he tried so hard. . . ."

"Tragic, maybe, but not pitiable," Alan said. "That's the truest form of courage, to settle into a life of quiet desperation instead of the desperate deeds youth burns to accomplish—and never let anyone know how desperate you are. He lost his sweetheart, his best friend, his hopes, but from what you tell me he never lost his kindness or his dreams."

"She killed him," Jan said suddenly. "I didn't tell you that. His own wife."

"How do you know that?" Alan was startled. "Did you see her do it?"

"No. I don't know how I know, but I'm sure. The way she looked at him—she practically threatened him when she asked him not to make the change in his will. It was obvious from the way they talked about their oldest son that he was a rotten bum, and his mother's darling."

"It makes a certain amount of sense," Alan admitted. "I get quite a good picture of her from your description. That kind of weak, rather stupid character often has one solid stubborn streak. Initially hers was her infatuation with Jonathan. When she had what she wanted, she found, as people so often do, that she didn't really want it. She could never have all his heart and all his mind. So she turned onto her son the abject devotion she had not been able to shower on him.

"As for the poison angle—I hate to resort to clichés, but truth really is stranger than fiction. You know Mr. Wythe of Williamsburg—the signer of the Declaration of Independence, the teacher of Jefferson. But do you know how he died?"

"No. I was only interested in his earlier life."

"He was poisoned," Alan said. "By his own grand-nephew, a man named Sweney. Wythe had made a will leaving his house and a good deal of his property to his freed mulatto housekeeper, Lydia Broadnax, and an additional sum of money to her son, a boy named Michael. Sweney poisoned the lot. Lydia survived, but young Michael died and so did Wythe, although he lived long enough to realize that he had been murdered. At least he was able to cut Sweney out of his will. But Sweney was acquitted when the case came to trial, although arsenic had been found in his room."

"Acquitted! How could that happen?"

"Virginia law. No black could testify against a white person. Wythe was already dead. But the point was that the trial had to be quashed because of the scandal. Why would a Virginia gentleman leave his property to a freed female slave and her son? Wythe had asked Jefferson to be executor in charge of young Michael's maintenance and education. It was pretty obvious, at least to the prurient-minded aristo-crats of Virginia, that Michael was Wythe's son. The sooner the story could be forgotten, the better. It was a scandal at the time, though; Jonathan and his wife must have known about it. Those were happy days for the poisoner. No tests, no limi-tations on the purchase of poison. . . . One of the minor ad-vantages of the present era, Jan. It's a lot harder to bump off rich relatives these days and get away with it."

"I hate people who point out morals," Jan said. "Alan, you're talking as if—almost as if you believed it. What do you really think?"

"What do you think?"

"I also hate people who answer one question with another. I think it really happened. I can't prove it, though."

"It is basically unprovable," Alan said. "If you find inde-pendent substantiating evidence, people will claim you knew about it beforehand. If the evidence is missing, it can't sub-stantiate anything."

"But the fact that I knew about your ancestry—"

"No proof," Alan insisted. "I mean, we can't prove that Karl Miller and his wife Mary were really Charles and Leah. Perhaps Jonathan corresponded with Charles and later with his widow; but none of the documents have survived. If they were not destroyed deliberately, they went up in smoke with the plantation house, as did the documentary evidence of Jonathan's adoption by Mr. Wilde. The family wouldn't pass on that tradition. And my family doesn't give a damn about its ancestors. The only thing we have is the unsubstantiated rumor that Karl's wife was a runaway slave. We're inclined to brag about that, I guess. The Millers were active in the Underground Railroad in the eighteen forties and fifties."

"Radicals all down the line," Jan said, smiling.

"Radicals and rebels," Alan agreed. His face was thoughtful. "Including Charles. . . ."

"You believe it," Jan said. "Don't you?"

"It hangs together too well. I don't think you're smart enough to make it up." He grinned at her, and then sobered. "I believe it because you believe it. How you could learn so much about a different world—"

"It wasn't so different. That's what surprised me the most. People were just about the same."

"I don't know what is so surprising about that. The trouble with your generation—" Jan laughed, and Alan raised his voice and continued, "The trouble with your generation is that you expect instant nirvana. When you find the world isn't to your taste, you start to kick and scream and throw bombs. The perfect world won't come in your lifetime; maybe it will never come. But that's no excuse to give up. The only defeat is to stop fighting."

"Charles said something like that. The fight *is* the victory."

"Then he must have been a pompous, pontifical idiot like me," Alan said. "If he was my ancestor, that probably accounts for it."

"He was not an idiot. He wasn't a hero, either. There weren't any heroes. All those big, stately figures we read about— Jefferson and his slaves, Morgan and his rheumatism—"

"That's what a hero is, you ignoramus. A man with rheumatism who gets on his horse and rides off to battle."

"Oh, shut up," Jan said.

"I think I will write a book. It's a pity to waste my magnificent aphorisms on you. So—have you decided to stick it out in this rotten world?"

"I don't have much choice. There never was any place for me in that one; and it did have disadvantages."

"Smallpox, outdoor privies, muddy roads, no central heating. . . ."

"There's only one thing," Jan said, ignoring this deplorable list. "I don't understand why I should have felt the way I did about Jonathan. Unless—"

"Well?"

"Unless there is a pattern of some kind. Why did you come back to Williamsburg? Why did I come here at the same time?"

"Heart called to heart," Alan said, watching her intently. "The silver cord bound us to one another. I am the reincarnation of your long-lost love—"

"Don't joke about it."

"I don't dare take it seriously. Of all the insane, seductive notions—"

"But you are like him," Jan said, her eyes widening as she finally saw the truth. "Much more like him than Richard ever could be. The way you plunge into things without stopping to think of the consequences. . . . You care about people—and animals, even—more than you care about your convenience, or your safety—or your furniture. . . . I do think we ought to get a new couch, though. That one of yours is pretty awful."

For the first—and last—time in their acquaintance Alan was speechless. He stared at her with his jaw hanging as she continued.

"I'll have to help support Mother, she's rather useless. But I don't think I'll have much trouble getting a teaching job in D.C., even at this late date. Inner-city schools aren't too popular. If I have any problems, I'll call you and you can rush over with a baseball bat."

"Carry your own baseball bat," Alan said, recovering himself. "Do you mean you—"

"Why didn't you ever kiss me before?"

"Because your mind was on other things. And because— oh, hell, Jan, must I expose all my feelings of inferiority? Because I'm graceless and rude and homely, and Richard—"

"It's your ears, mostly," Jan said. She leaned toward him and flattened the offending features against his head with her hands. "Maybe we could use some of that tape, the kind that sticks on both sides. . . ."

"They're turning the lights out," Alan said. "I think they're trying to tell us something."

"Let's go, then."

"Richard offered to get a lift out here and pick up his car."

"Quite unnecessary. I can manage perfectly well."

"That's what I told him," Alan said.

> *O beautiful for patriot dream*
> *That sees beyond the years;*
> *Thine alabaster cities gleam*
> *Undimmed by human tears!*
> *America! America!*
> *May God thy gold refine*
> *Till all success be nobleness!*
> *And every gain divine.*

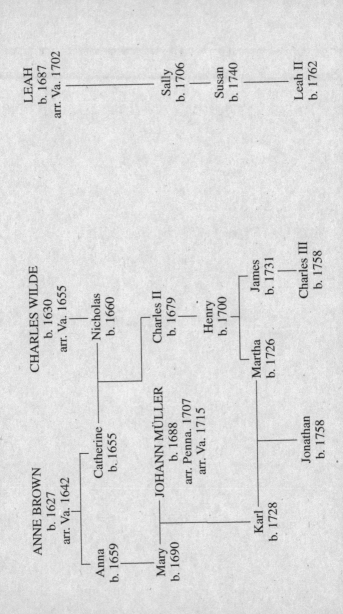